When Love Gives You Lemons

Also by Steven Salvatore

Can't Take That Away

And They Lived . . .

No Perfect Places

When Love Gives You Lemons

STEVEN SALVATORE

BLOOMSBURY
NEW YORK LONDON OXFORD NEW DELHI SYDNEY

BLOOMSBURY YA
Bloomsbury Publishing Inc., part of Bloomsbury Publishing Plc
1359 Broadway, New York, NY 10018
50 Bedford Square, London, WC1B 3DP, UK
Bloomsbury Publishing Ireland Limited, 29 Earlsfort Terrace, Dublin 2, D02 AY28, Ireland

First published in the United States of America in May 2025 by Bloomsbury YA

Bloomsbury books may be purchased for business or promotional use. For information on bulk purchases please contact Macmillan Corporate and Premium Sales Department at specialmarkets@macmillan.com

Library of Congress Cataloging-in-Publication Data
available upon request
ISBN 978-1-5476-1527-8 (hardcover) • ISBN 978-1-5476-1528-5 (e-book)

Book design by John Candell
Typeset by Westchester Publishing Services
Printed in the United States by Lakeside Book Company, Harrisonburg, VA
2 4 6 8 10 9 7 5 3 1

To find out more about our authors and books visit www.bloomsbury.com and sign up for our newsletters.
For product safety–related questions contact productsafety@bloomsbury.com.

This is a book about telling people you love them, so if you haven't yet done so today, tell someone you love them. "Don't let the moment pass you by."

FOR CHRIS,
for being my family and protecting my heart
forever and one single day.
I love you.

and FOR JULIA ROBERTS, *obviously*

When Love Gives You Lemons

ACT I

@LemonAtFirstSight ✓ 1d ago

Views: 1.9M

❤ 275.1K

AUDIO TRANSCRIPT: Fielder Lemon coming at you from popular hot spot the Sinking Venetian in Astoria, Queens! I went all out, bringing my ma, *the* Queen Giuseppina, to celebrate her birthday. We couldn't resist dancing to this balls-to-the-wall menu, that raises necessary awareness about Venice, Italy, disappearing into the sea due to climate change and rising sea levels. What doesn't disappear is the flavor! Every dish is themed, so we were *not* disappointed. Our outrageous six-course meal started with an aperitivo—bite-sized crispy polenta piled high with whipped ricotta topped with generous drizzles of hot honey and flaky sea salt—perfetto! That crunch! And the ricotta explodes with flavor. Served in a tiny gondola, it's peak camp! Next was the antipasto: Creamy risotto with peas and *strawberries*! Ma wasn't expecting to like this, but she licked the bowl clean. The primo course was a black squid ink gnocchi topped with crispy fried sardines, and Ma was pawing at it like a raccoon in a dumpster! The sauce was wicked with garlic, and I *had* to soak my bread in it! For the secondo course, the most perfect, juicy filet mignon topped with a seafood ravioli that, once broken open, runs like an egg yolk down the meat, drenching it in a briny goodness. It wouldn't be Venetian without a platter of imported cheeses and seasonal fruits, a palate cleanser before topping off with the dolce course: dark chocolate gelato that sinks into oblivion when creamy, warm espresso is poured over and topped with more flaky sea salt to bring out the warm nuttiness of the caffè!

Verdict? Inventive, confident, bellissima! Molto bene! Don't wait! And, as always, when life gives you Lemons, take a bite!

CHAPTER 1

I Can Do It with a Broken Heart!

The houses of Blossom Avenue are lost to time, ripped straight from an old sepia-filtered photo from the 1970s, which is precisely how long Nonna has lived here. Most are built of faded red brick, wooden doors with small stained-glass windows, and two-tone seafoam-green porch overhangs. Weather-worn American flags hang over rusted wrought iron railings that lead up from cracked cement walkways. Two houses smack-dab in the center of Blossom Avenue have matching washed-out Italian Pride and Pride flags. Which, dear reader, are two entirely separate flags.

One of those houses is the Lemon house.

The other belongs to the DeLucas.

I make it a point not to look at *that* house as I pull into the driveway, instead channeling my attention to the thousands of notifications from my latest video on (the popular app that could very well be banned by the United States government by the time you read this, and, if not, *oh well* because henceforth it shall be known as) the Clock App.

External validation is not only delicious; it's nutritious, too. Tastes a lot like Nonna's Sunday sauce—a garlicky ragù with fresh mint that zings on the palate, the smell of which wafts out from a rickety open window in our modest brick house, lead paint chips peeling off its frame.

Immediately, my phone is out and recording as I burst inside—my followers love home-cooked family dinner content, especially Nonna's famous meatballs.

"Fielder's home!" Ma shouts to Nonna, who is streaming old episodes of *The Price Is Right* at such a loud volume I'm surprised there hasn't been a noise ordinance.

"You get me for the whole day." I stop recording and swipe open the remote app on my phone, lowering the TV volume. Right on cue Nonna cries out as if an axe murderer broke into the living room.

Ma snickers. "It's like a special occasion or something!" Italian guilt, her specialty. She acts like I don't live here.

"I saw you *all day* yesterday, remember?" I kiss her cheek and hand her a potted flower. It's been our tradition since I was small to help her plant new flowers in Nonna's garden every year on her birthday. "I have the rest of the flowers in the trunk of my car. Went out early for a run and then Home Depot for plants and soil."

"Such a good boy I raised!" She pinches my cheeks, then slaps them for good measure. "Go get Nonna out of that damn chair. I keep telling her to move around; she's gonna get sores on her ass."

"All right." I wave her away and stop at the window over the kitchen sink. From here, I can see straight into the DeLucas' house. Nobody is home. No cars in the driveway. A For Sale sign in the front yard. Mr. and Mrs. DeLuca have been down in South Carolina on and off since *he* graduated last year. Sienna, *his* older sister, hasn't lived here in Westchester since I was in middle school, and—

"Oh!" Ma exclaims, stirring the pot of Nonna's tangy sauce bubbling on the stovetop. "Guess who I saw this morning at church!"

My chest tightens and I stop breathing. Every time she says this, I think she's going to say *his* name.

"Zia Gabriella. She says you don't call her."

"Ma, I *just* had lunch with Zia Gab two Saturdays ago." Or was it three? "You see your sister all the time."

"Be nice to me today. It's my birthday. I'm twenty-two times two today."

"You don't look a day over eighteen times two," I say, checking notifications, swiping through and responding to comments and DMs.

She says nothing, and I don't know how long she's standing in front of me waiting for me to look up, but when I do, she plucks my phone from between my fingers so swiftly I don't register it. Ma's got expert spy skills. If you've ever met a scorned Italian woman, you've basically met a trained assassin.

"Hey!"

"You're on this thing too much. You're missing life, Field." She shakes her head in disappointment the way only an Italian mom could.

"No, I'm not. I hate when people say that." Anxiety bubbles inside me. I reach for my phone, but she swivels out of reach.

"I hate phones. Life was better before cell phones. In my day . . ."

Dear reader, I roll my eyes so hard my entire body follows and I crash to the floor in dramatic fashion.

"All right, stugots! Get up! Zia Gab, Zia Rosa, and Matty are coming over for sauce. Go wash up. You smell."

I sniff under my arms. She's not wrong.

Then, randomly, she asks, "Have you heard from Topher?"

I haven't spoken to Topher in a couple months, at least. "No, why?"

She clicks her blush-pink manicured nails together. "There's some wonderful family news. But first—" She mimes a zipper closing across her lips.

Curiosity: piqued. "Why so cryptic?"

She shrugs. "What happened with that boy?" She's trying to throw me off the scent of something much larger than a boy.

My head whips around. "Huh? What boy?"

"The one who was over the other day." Ma's nostrils flare. "Good thing it was me who saw him, and not Nonna. She'd give him a lecture about the proper way to court her grandson, and then scream at you for being disrespectful and not introducing him. Was he the neighbor's kid from down the street, Rye? He's a nice boy, but he's no R—"

"*Ma!*" I cut her off before she can say the name. My cheeks heat faster than Nonna's Bialetti espresso pot. "First of all, Ma, I'm sorry—I'd never disrespect you or Nonna like that. Rye's just a friend."

Ma's eyes narrow. She's too smart for that. "It's nice to see you moving on, finally."

"Mm-hmm." I don't have the heart—or balls—to tell her that Rye's also a friend I occasionally hook up with. After my heart was crushed by the boy next door in what I call "the Great Commencement Massacre," I needed to have fun. Kiss lots of boys. And nobody ever got hurt kissing a boy, right?

Stares directly at camera. *Anyway.*

I've discovered over the last year since *he*, the big fat *R* in the room, broke up with me, I can pretend I'm completely fine day-to-day: film online content, go to school, do homework, hook up with guys on the football team while saving my heart for the guy who ruined me yet not be able to say his name out loud, *and* do it all with a broken heart!

Some call that delusional; I call it containing multitudes!

"But, yeah, the guy—erm, yeah, he isn't gonna work out."

"You're young." She avoids eye contact. "But while you live under my roof—"

"Nonna's," I correct.

She clears her throat in an interrupt-me-again-and-I'll-whoop-your-ass way. "As long as you live here, you live by *my* rules. Once you're old enough to get your own place, you can have any Kevin, Joe, or Nick you want over."

Dread creeps into my chest.

"Did you just name Jonas Brothers? Ma—"

It's not like I haven't thought about moving out. All my high school friends are about to move on to their various campuses, into run-down dorms, and I don't *want* to be stuck in my same bedroom wallpapered with posters of Pedro Pascal, Orville Peck, Billie Eilish, Chappell Roan, a Ryan Reynolds–autographed *Deadpool* poster—who doesn't love a fourth wall break?—and

Polaroids of high school friends, family—and *him*—a time capsule for who I once was. But where would I go? I like being home.

Part of Ma's "No College? Fine, but You're Learning a Thing or Two from Me" agreement included paying rent and contributing to household bills and expenses, which I've had to do all through high school anyway to help make ends meet. But the part Ma really goes hard on is wanting me to focus on a career beyond social media.

Ma's rule—I have *one* year of living at home (not rent-free, to clarify!) to sustain an Italian mom–approved career outside of the Clock App. Even though my only marketable skill is the million-plus user following I've built *using* the Clock App. Right now, I'm laser-focused on being a Clock influencer and riding that to whatever comes next. At the very least, it's a bullet train to gaining more followers and building more "fame." Expand my platform. As it stands now, I've done a stellar job doing that on my own. My Clock account is a success by any metrics or standards.

That's all I need, right? At least, that's what I've told myself—and Ma.

Stares directly into camera, blinks twice.

Anyway.

"I can move out soon. Ish. If you want," I offer, though I know she'd never go for that. Italian moms would keep their kids until they died if they could, Norma Bates–style.

"Nonsense!" She waves away the thought. She moves in closer and grabs the side of my face. Her hands are soft and smell like marinara, onions, and garlic. "Remember what I told you when your father died? Sometimes the plans we thought we had for ourselves don't always work out. They change. Life changes. I mean, look at me. I never thought I'd be living with my mother at this age. I wanted to see the world, do something important, you know? Now I'm forty-four, and what do I have to show for it? Besides you, I haven't done much with my life. And you're not a kid anymore." She plants a wet kiss on my cheek and sings, "But you'll always be my baby. I want better for you, than *this*." She gestures around Nonna's small house, the one she could never make it out of due to her and Dad's money struggles, then Dad's cancer diagnosis and eventual death. Ma wants more for us. For me.

I want more for *her*. "Ma, you're super young. You *can* see the world. Do whatever you want. You act like you're in the final stages of life."

She shrugs. "I'm stuck with Nonna."

If there's one thing I want you to know about Italian women, it's this: They're soldiers. They take care of everyone at their own expense—feed the family at dinner, loading everyone's plates twice over before even taking a slice of bread, break their backs until they bleed and never so much as complain. And don't you dare feel sorry for them. Just do better.

"Zia Gab and Zia Rosa can help with Nonna."

The door swings open and slams into the Formica counter, chipping the corner. Ma curses.

"What can I do? I heard my name. You shit-talking, nephew?" Zia Rosa sets down a platter of pignoli and rainbow cookies, and stomps her boots on the welcome mat before beckoning me for a hug.

On her tail, Zia Gabriella peeks her head inside, a bouquet of flowers with one of those miniature helium balloons-on-a-stick that says, "Best Sister Ever," and a stuffed bear with a silk heart in its hand clutched to her chest.

"Why do you keep getting me that shit?" Ma asks her sister.

"Shut up, it's a present," Zia Gabriella exclaims.

"*You* shut up! It's *my* birthday, and you don't have to live with all these tchotchkes!" Ma says. "I told youse guys, no presents for my birthday."

As I look around, she's not wrong. Nonna's house is severely outdated, not having had a facelift since the 1990s when apparently pastel pinks and soft grays, off-white cabinets, and cheap countertops were all the rage in home décor. It makes it worse that Nonna likes to buy a lot of garbage from Walmart and Five Below that she'll never use, and Ma has to work smart to collect these "treasures" and donate them without Nonna knowing. Zia Gabriella's penchant for giving everyone useless trinkets doesn't exactly help.

"Come on, Gab," Rosa says. "I'd kill you if you brought this trash to my house."

"Well, luckily for you all, this is *Ma's* house," Zia Gabriella snips.

"Why you gotta come here and be a bitch, Gab?" Ma quips back.

"It's Queen G's birthday," I say. "Can we all relax?"

"Yeah, Zia G." I hadn't noticed my cousin Matty standing in the doorway. "Take it down a couple thousand notches." He kisses Zia Gabriella hello, slips past his mom, Zia Rosa, to kiss my ma. "Happy birthday, Zia Guisy!"

"Thank you, handsome nephew!" Ma says, squeezing him. "You don't come visit your aging zia anymore."

Matty's eyes widen in shock. "I was here last weekend!"

"Can you believe our kids are all graduated now, Rosa?" Ma says, ignoring him.

Zia Rosa holds up her hands. "No, don't get me started."

As if summoned by some unknown force, the Coven as they're known—Ma, Zia Rosa, and Zia Gab—huddle together in prayer for their collective sons' loss of innocence, do the sign of the cross, look to the heavens, and mutter a Hail Mary.

Rosa Lemon is the baby of the three sisters. A bit flighty, yet shrewdly perceptive, Rosa is the fun, carefree, perpetually unbothered sister. She lives for designer brands, and somehow always convinces the men she's dating to buy her the finest jewelry and tags. Everything about her is vibrant and sassy with hips for days and an hourglass body that the Kardashians wish they had (naturally). She's always singing and dancing to the latest Top 40 hits, much to Matty's chagrin. I think it's hilarious. Quintessential "cool mom" vibes. Rosa is definitely my favorite—just don't mention that to Gabriella; she'll rip my head right off.

Queen Guisippina Lemon (also known as G, Guisy, or just Ma) is the middle sister. I have stories for years and still wouldn't crack the surface. She wears long, flowy shirts, mostly muted colors because she's insecure about her body, which is something I inherited, and she'd rather hide her curves than show them off. She likes a good sparkle or sequin. Despite being the middle sister, she actually gives major eldest sister energy, always the one to steer the ship and offer the sagest advice. The realist of the Coven,

Queen G will tell you exactly what you don't want to hear, but make you believe it's what you needed. Respect.

Gabriella Lemon is the oldest, but gives middle sister vibes, constantly wanting to be the center of attention. She insists on letting the natural gray in her jet-black hair grow out like Michelle Visage. Except she doesn't keep it up, so it's slightly unsettling. Everything she wears is vintage but has just aged out of trendy and into "Should Be Donated but Won't." Everything is slightly too big for her thin frame, and she has a Third-Grade Art Teacher but Make It Italian aesthetic. Her son Topher is the oldest cousin by a good six years. Topher Lemon is a tech whiz kid who dropped out of Cornell before the end of his freshman year and now, at twenty-five, is already a multimillionaire because he invented and sold software that can crack "uncrackable" social media algorithms, including the Clock App's. Having grown up impoverished, living in a paycheck-to-paycheck household like every Lemon, he now has houses in Malibu and the Hamptons, and a ski chalet in Colorado. We're like brothers—growing up in a small suburban town in Westchester, New York, in an Italian family means we're all suffocatingly close to one another—but I don't see much of him these days. He's too busy chartering private jets to the Maldives and meeting investors in Dubai.

Matty, Topher, and I call our moms the Coven because they look like a trio of witches. The Sanderson Sisters, but make it Italian. All of them have long, curly black hair, olive skin (though Ma is the fairest by far), and aside from some extra wrinkles on Zia Gabriella, and Zia Rosa's breast implants, they all have similar facial features and body types. Outsiders have trouble telling them apart, which they all hate with a venomous passion because all three of them think they're nothing alike. Each member of the Coven is unmarried, and thus all retained the Lemon family name and passed it down to their three respective sons, and the six of us plus Nonna have been one medium-sized dysfunctional family unit for as long as I can remember. I'm the only one who knew my dad. Topher's dad is rumored to be some famous rock star from the 2000s, and Ma's dropped hints that Matty's dad has been on a reality TV show, but won't say which one, and after some serious reconnaissance, I narrowed it down to one appearance on a game show and gave up because it became far less interesting. In short, the dads don't matter. Slap that on a T-shirt, huh?

A lot of people have asked how we have such an unusual name, and, as the story goes, my great-great-nonno, who immigrated here from Fascist Italy through Ellis Island, didn't want to give his real last name. He didn't know a lick of English, except one word: Lemon. It's become a sense of pride for our family. Lemons and lemonade and all that. Maybe more like limoncello in this family.

Matty shakes his head at the Coven's usual chaos, the familiar cackling of their voices filling every nook and cranny in the house, before pulling me into a bro hug. "What up, brother?"

"Long time no see." I choke beneath his grip. I may be built like a linebacker thanks to Dad's Swedish genes, but Matty is a short king brick house. In a lot of ways, we're very similar. Two gay himbo cousins trying to make it in the world.

"We got bagels this morning," he says. He's not too quick with the wit, despite how hard I try. Matty and I are the same age, but we've grown so much closer this last year after he came out to me and asked me to help him come out to the rest of the family since I'd done it at such a young age (I was ten—when you know, you know, you know?). Ever since, we've been inseparable, sort of a gay Jedi master and Padawan type thing, hanging out most weekends, talking about guys and life. He's my best friend.

"Can you believe Topher?" he says.

The room goes quiet, save for the bubble-popping pot of sauce.

"What about Topher?" I ask. "Seriously, what's going on?"

Matty's eyes go wide.

"Why don't we go sit with Nonna?" Zia Gabriella suggests.

We pile into the small, dimly lit living room. Zia Rosa takes the remote control and mutes the television, and Ma lets out an involuntary sigh of relief.

"What the hell is this?" Nonna tries to stand. "A funeral march?"

"Ma, sit!" Zia Rosa commands, bending down to hug her mother tightly.

"My beautiful daughters." Nonna claws at Zia Rosa's back before shoving her aside and pawing for Zia Gabriella. "Where are my handsome grandsons? Get the hell over here! I love you both so much!" She grabs us both and pulls us in one at a time, cheek by cheek until we're wet from her lips. "How are the boys treating you, Matty? Beating them away with a bat, I bet."

Matty blushes. "I wish." Kid's so awkward, despite being a smokeshow.

"When you get to college, don't— Well, I guess you can't get 'em pregnant, but wrap up your dingaling. You gotta be safe out there, you hear me?" Nonna looks directly at me, *into my soul*, and I wish I could disappear. She knows more than she lets on. I avoid Ma's glares. "Where's Topher?"

"He's in LA, Ma, remember?" Zia Gabriella says. "He's gonna call any second."

Zia Gabriella jumps. "I'm so excited. Where's your phone, Fielder?"

"*My* phone?" I feel my pockets, and panic sets in because it's not there.

Ma holds it in the palm of her hand, and right on cue, it vibrates. Topher's face flashes across the frame.

"How'd you know—"

Zia Gab's brows furrow, angry I don't immediately answer her son's call. "Pick up!" She grabs it from Ma's hand faster than I can and swipes across the screen, and Topher's smiling face bursts into full frame.

"What up, fam!" he shouts, grinning ear to ear. He looks so much like the Coven—all Italian features, dark and defined, with lines around his eyes and a face full of scruffy brown facial hair. I'm the outlier in the family with blond hair, blue eyes, and pasty-ass skin that can't grow facial or chest hair to save my life.

The Coven and Nonna, our Supreme, take turns fawning over the firstborn boy in the family, and they're all scream-talking so loudly over one another that my temples ache just a little. If you didn't know us, you'd think all we do is yell at one another. Nonna asks him what he's been up to with his business ventures, and every member of the Coven chimes in before Topher can even finish a sentence. Typical.

"Matty! Fielder! I'm so glad you guys are here." Topher's voice cuts through the noise, and Matty elbows me. "Matty, we talked last night, and Fielder, man, I've been meaning to call you; I just didn't know . . ." His voice trails off.

What the hell is going on?

"I'm sure you know by now, but I wanted you to hear it from me," Topher says.

Sweat trickles down my back. I wrestle the phone away from Zia Gab. "I don't know anything."

Topher cheeses into the camera. "I'm getting married! In a couple weeks."

I nearly drop the phone. "In a what now?"

Zia Rosa whispers something like, "It's too soon," to Ma, who purses her lips and nods in agreement, then mouths a standard, "Whatareyagonnado?"

"Yeah, man, it all happened so quick," Topher says. "I wanted to tell you, and ask you and Matty to be my best men. You're the closest thing I have to brothers! But I didn't know how you'd handle it."

"That makes no sense, Toph." I fight back tears. Why would he think that? "I'm so happy for you I could cry. Congratulations!" I wipe tears from my cheek. "Why would you *not* tell me? Who's the girl? I didn't even know you were dating anyone."

The room once again goes silent.

"It's, um, a destination wedding." He ignores my question. "I got a private jet hooked up for the whole family to fly you all to Amalfi, Italy, in three weeks."

Reader, have you ever heard a room full of Italian women gasp? They're not so much gasps as they are nasal shrieks and hollers in harmony with some epic hand-flapping like wings. It's enough to cause my temples to throb.

I break through the chatter with the one question he still hasn't answered. "Dude, who are you engaged to? Why haven't we met her?"

Topher clears his throat. "Well, that's the thing. You *have* met her. You all have."

My brows furrow. I twirl the ring on my thumb anxiously.

He rotates the camera so it's front-facing, and the last person I expected to see is smiling and waving at me, and my heart literally stops. Like, *911, world-stopping GIVE ME THE PADDLES, I'm having an actual heart attack here! level* stop.

Topher's disembodied voice, all low and in distorted slo-mo, says, "You remember Sienna DeLuca." Then, as if I would have forgotten, he reminds me, "Ricky's sister."

Oh, I *remember* Ricky DeLuca.

The love of my life—

—who broke my heart, shattered it into a bajillion pieces and left without a trace.

How could I forget?

CHAPTER 1.5

Fielder Lemon and Ricky DeLuca's Great Commencement Massacre, Precisely One Year, Two Weeks, and Three Days Earlier (But Who's Counting . . . ?)

Dear reader, did you know "commencement"—as in a commencement ceremony at a high school graduation—means "a beginning"?

It's supposed to be poetic.

The end of the most vital eighteen years of a person's life (to date, anyway) is the beginning of a new chapter. I learned that at Ricky DeLuca's graduation. He was a year older than me. As I sat in the crowd watching my boyfriend (and best friend/next door neighbor of the last nearly twelve years) clad in his emerald-green and gold cap and gown, all I could think about was how this was a new beginning for *us*. After an epic all-night party, Topher surprised Ricky and me with a free, all-expenses-paid week in the Hamptons at his beach house to celebrate, to give us privacy away from the Coven.

Glittery waves crashed on the Long Island shoreline from a dark obsidian ocean lit by a bright white moon. Millions of stars dotted the sky, but Ricky and I were the only two on the beach. A warm breeze wrapped around us, lulling us into a trance. Nestled against a dune, our legs entangled, we stargazed together. Our tradition.

We spent so many nights wrapped up in the stars.

Something about that night felt delicate, a shaky breath before a plunge.

There were too many strange silences, like we were suspended midair, and nothing moved except the Atlantic tide. I told myself it was because tomorrow we would head home to face the real world, whatever that looked like for us, Fielder and Ricky. But mostly for Ricky, who didn't have high school in the fall to look forward to, unlike me.

On the blanket next to Ricky a battery-operated lantern cast a soft glow on the sand, illuminating a well-worn leather-bound journal I bought him two Christmases earlier. We'd been best friends since his family moved in next door when I was five and he was six. We became instantly inseparable. But the summer before I entered high school, a strange tension bubbled its way to the surface; I went from carefree to breathless when I saw him, my sweaty skin prickling with electricity. Every time we were together, which was every damn day, it felt like we hovered around each other but couldn't quite connect the way we used to, like someone holding two magnets and pointing their, like, poles at each other, ensuring they never meet.

Our immediate families spent Christmas Eve together—you

know, the whole Italian seven fishes shebang that brings everyone together, even non-blood neighbors. When it came time for us to do our usual best friend gift exchange, and he opened the journal and read the inscription I wrote in the front flap that he was an incredible poet, working words the way he would wood, and how I couldn't wait to be by his side when he won his first Pulitzer Prize. His cheeks went beet red, and he dashed outside and into the snow, fluffy piles of the stuff billowing inside as he slammed the door behind him. I ran after him with a jacket, yelling his name so that he'd stop and at least not freeze to death. When I caught up to him and yanked on his shoulders so that he would face me, he spun around, and his eyes were red and glassy. I asked him what was wrong, what I did, and when I grabbed his hand, it was like the magnet poles flipped, and he leaned forward and—

—kissed me.

Middle of the street. Golden glow from the streetlamps, massive snowflakes fluttering around our heads like we were in a damn snow globe. It was sloppy and messy as he mashed his teeth against mine in a way that reverberated through my skull. Horrible. Borderline painful. Wet. Yet *perfect.*

"I've never done this before . . . kissed a *dude.*" He shuddered. "Or anyone."

"Neither have I." My words trembled, from the cold or nerves I couldn't tell.

"But you've been out for, like, years already!" he said.

"I've kissed lots of dudes in my head."

"Have you ever kissed me?" He looked down, dragged his foot in concentric circles in the snow. "You know. In your head?"

My cheeks got so hot I no longer cared about the snow. I swallowed hard. "I—"

"Sorry—that was weird. Did I make it weird?"

"Dude, you actually kissed me. *That* was weird."

"Was it? I-I—"

"Shut up, I was kidding. Of course I want to kiss you. I've always wanted to kiss you." As much as I wanted it to be a movie moment where I grabbed him and pulled him in quickly, I was too nervous.

I gently placed my hand at the side of his face; my thumb brushed his lips. Before I could lean in, he gingerly grabbed ahold of me and placed his soft lips on mine. It was delicate, light, innocent, beautiful. His lips were pillows I wanted to rest on forever.

"I've wanted to kiss you, too."

Two and a half years later, we never stopped kissing.

"Fielder?"

I looked over at Ricky, moonlight in his eyes. Or was that irritation?

"Sorry. Got lost in the moment." I could feel his tension, and it pooled in my chest. I pulled out my phone instinctively. Scrolling made me feel less anxious. I had a few new notifications from my growing Clock channel. I'd posted a review of a cool new local food truck earlier, the most amazing Indian-French fusion dosas/crepes, and it was doing great numbers. "Y-you okay?"

He scoffed. "Why wouldn't I be? Got the sand. Waves. Moon in my eyes." Ricky's shoulders and upper body were tense, like he was holding his breath. "Or maybe it's just the reflection of your phone screen. As always."

"Ouch. Sorry. My bad." *One last look, sleep mode.* "It's our last night in Topher's Hamptons paradise bubble. And we haven't talked about what's next for you. Not in a while—I feel like you've been avoiding talking about it with me?"

Like me, Ricky never aspired to attend college. Though Ricky could be an incredible poet one day, he came from a long line of Capital M Men who worked with their hands. Woodworkers. Ricky idolized his nonno, and that became his dream: to be a woodworker. He dreamed of one day building his own artisan tiny home, having his own line of wood pieces—furniture and such—and living in the middle of the woods, completely off the grid. Live off the land. Write poetry in a journal of his own handmade paper. Ricky was impossibly cool.

College wasn't for me, either. Unlike Ricky, though, I'd never really known exactly what I wanted to do with my life. As a rising senior, all I wanted to do was spend time with my boyfriend, but I had a lot of pressure from Ma; we had no expendable cash. Not since Dad died. Well, not before that either, but it only got worse. Like a good Italian son who had no choice but to become the head of his household, I had a duty to help Ma.

I started @LemonAtFirstSight, a food-slash-restaurant review account on Clock last year because I loved to eat (shocking for an Italian, I know) and try new places and cuisines. Ma and I had been driving up and down the entirety of New York State looking for hole-in-the-wall restaurants with banger food. The account was steadily growing, and I'd had a few viral moments, even a sound that made the rounds. My follower count grew when Ricky and I posted boyfriend content, especially when we reviewed together. Nonna, my biggest fan, was convinced I could have my own show on Food Network. When the account started to pick up, I figured maybe I could grow it enough to monetize. Become an influencer (in addition to working as a busboy on the weekends and after school) to help Ma make ends meet.

"I have something for you." Ricky reached around the other side of his body, grabbing at his backpack.

"For me?" My birthday wasn't until August, but as any good Leo would, I gladly took the present. "I thought I was supposed to get you a commencement gift. I figured my presence would be present enough, but—"

He rolled his eyes.

"You love me."

He closed his eyes. "More than you know, Fielder." His words, the same ones he always said to me, hung in the air between us, and I wanted so badly to kiss him, draw whatever was on his mind out like venom from a bite.

"I don't want this to end." I stared up at the night sky, the endless pattern of stars I could never reach. "I wish we could get in a rowboat and sail out into the middle of the ocean and be surrounded by stars."

"Where the horizon meets the sky," he said.

"Like dancing among them. Just you and me. I'd stay there forever."

Then he whispered, "If only," and handed me an unwrapped wooden box, the finish natural, almost raw. He had hand-carved the top with an intricate lemon on a vine. There was an iron hitch and hook on one side, and small hinges that allowed it to open on the other.

"It's a dream box," he explained. "It's kind of like a time capsule. But not. Instead of a box of the past, it's a box for your future. The idea is to put what you want for yourself in there, places you want to go, things you want to accomplish, whatever! And it manifests!"

"If Nonna heard you right now—"

"She'd call me a hippie-dippie, I know." He smirked like a kid who'd gotten into the cookie jar.

My fingers ran along the crushed velvet interior. "It's empty."

"Only for now." He closed the lid and tapped it. I studied his face, his moonlit eyes flickering over the surface of the wood like flames. Following his line of sight, I realized the lemon notched into the oak had the map of Earth etched into its bulbous body. "The world is yours, Fielder Lemon."

I leaned over the box and into him, kissing him. "Ours."

Through our interlocked lips, he hummed, "Ours." His stubble scratched my upper lip. His hands found mine. He played with the ring on my thumb.

"I love you," I told him.

He didn't say it back that time.

What happens now?

CHAPTER 1.75

Spoiler Alert: The Act One Breakup!

My question lingered on the warm Atlantic breeze.

What happens now?

The hem of my shirt billowed open.

What happens now?

His hands found their way to my exposed skin.

What happens now?

"Fielder," he whispered, his fingers sending shock waves through my system.

I shuddered.

His ocean eyes were millions of miles of endless dark waters.

Normally our lips moved in syncopated rhythm, and I would get lost in him, but something tugged at me. At him, too.

His fingertips were cold. His touch distracted. His eyes full, wet.

I moved back beside him, elbows digging into cool sand, and stared up at the stars, my new dream box in my lap.

He stood up, brushed the sand off his legs, grabbed his hoodie, and threaded it over his upper body. “Let’s do something wild.”

“Like?”

“I don’t know,” Ricky said, bouncing on his heels. His nervous energy over the last week had grown in intensity every day. I usually knew how to read him. But there was something strange in the way he avoided looking directly into my eyes. “Skinny-dipping!”

“With the sharks? Lord.”

Though it elicited a small laugh, it ended quickly.

It wasn’t unlike Ricky to suggest being naked—he liked being one with nature and all that—but this felt forced. Like he was trying to be spontaneous as a distraction for something else.

Suddenly, as if he was unable to achieve the desired outcome, he groaned.

His head tipped back as he vibrated like he was trying to expel his demons; the whites of his eyes glowed in the moonlight. When we were kids, Nonna would watch us while our parents worked, and her favorite pastime was making us fried meatball sandwiches and sitting us down to watch those ridiculous “documentary” shows about “real people” who experienced hauntings and demonic possessions. While we watched poorly acted reenactments of children getting possessed by the devil or a lesser demon, she would say, “This is why you need to be good.” Ricky and I used to take turns pretending to be possessed, and Nonna would call upon Jesus and grab her crucifix. Ricky’s sister, Sienna, would laugh at us from the corner of the living room, where she lived on her phone, and tell us we were going to hell. At night, Ricky and I would sneak out onto the roof to stargaze.

We talked about ghosts and demons, god or the gods, love, and whether or not we thought any of it was real. How, together, we would find answers.

The thing about ghosts was that they lingered; even if you couldn't see them, you felt them.

On the beach, Ricky shouted the sign of the cross in Italian: "Nel nome del Padre, e del Figlio, e dello Spirito Santo. Amen!" Dropping to his knees, he clasped his hands together in prayer above his head. A hungry look came over him, the one he got right before he speared his opponents during wrestling matches in school, and he darted toward me, launching into my midsection, and tackling me into the sand.

Nonna called me "Pasta Dolce," sweet dough, because of my blond surfer hair and soft linebacker body—but I didn't date the captain of the varsity wrestling team for all those years without learning a move or five.

Using my weight against him, I pinned him to the ground.

"I win," I panted. I knew he let me, but it still felt good.

His face twisted like an evil Disney villain right before the sneak tickle attack. Shooting up between my pits, his fingers wriggled until they found my switch, and my entire body convulsed, folding into the sand. Writhing, scream-laughing, begging him to stop, I eventually got him to concede, and he pulled me into a hug on top of his chest. His lips pressed against my forehead.

I caught my breath and kissed the fabric of his shirt.

My head tried to find comfort nestled into his neck, but his body writhed out from under me, and I fell off him.

My phone screen lit up in a small, dark pocket of sand. It

must have fallen out of my shorts when he tackled me. There were hundreds of new notifications from that latest video. I muted my notifications and looked back to where Ricky had been lying. But all that was left was an impression of his body in the sand.

Ricky was at the water's edge.

The smooth sand was cool against my bare feet, and it grew chillier the closer I got to him. The moon hung overhead like an ethereal night-light, illuminating the peaks of small waves. The salt water rushed toward us and splashed our legs as we teetered between land and sea. Ricky felt miles away.

"You ready to talk to me?" I borderline begged. Okay, maybe I whined. But there was a knot in my chest that moved up into my throat the longer the night waned.

He looked away.

"Dude, really?"

"Did you just *dude* me, bro?" he asked.

"Did you just *bro* me, homeslice?" I mimicked. This was our routine; usually it happened in the middle of our epic make-out session where we pretended we were straight bros using ancient slang.

"Did you just *homeslice* me, buddy?"

"Nah, pal." I pushed him, and he puffed out his chest.

His temporary smile flickered and I was over it.

"Okay, Riccardo Guiseppe DeLuca, spill."

"Not the full name!" His voice shook.

With my Spidey-sense tingling, my heart started to race, faster and faster and faster until it throbbed in my ears. Since I was a kid, I suffered from panic attacks, which my therapist thought started when Ma and Dad would scream at each other, fighting all night. They continued after Dad left, and got worse when he moved back in years later because it all felt so fragile, and they fully kicked into high gear when Dad passed. It was like playing a never-ending game of midnight manhunt without flashlights, always on edge waiting for someone to dash out from a bush and grab you. Ricky was supposed to be a safe zone, my home base.

"Look at me."

He refused.

"What's going on with you?" The words burst through my chest like a parasite, latching on to him. The therapist I started seeing after Dad died said I had a tendency to say what was on my mind, unfiltered, especially in moments of intense emotion because I wanted people around me to show up authentically. So I pushed for a reaction. It wasn't intentional, but subconscious.

Ricky braced for a Fielder blowup, but all I could say was, "You're so far away. Talk to me?"

"It's hard." He picked his head up, but the way he did it, slow and pained, his head looked like it weighed a million pounds. "To look at you." His lip quivered.

"Why?" My eyes stung.

His body tensed, but he didn't look away. "Because you've been my everything. For as long as I can remember, Fielder."

"And you're mine—"

"That's the point. I don't know who I am outside of you. *Us*." He paused, licked his dry lips. "Do you ever think we moved too fast?"

His words retreated into the ocean, lost in the undertow.

"Too fast?" I repeated, unable to grasp his question.

"Yeah, like, we did everything backwards. Fell in love at freaking five years old, and planned out our entire lives before taking the SATs. This is, like, the time when everybody is supposed to grow up and move away and find themselves. I need to find myself." He was breathless, his voice soaked and shaky.

Nonna used to say I was born with sneakers on my feet, that once I came out of the womb, I was unstoppable, rolling, crawling, running, bouncing off the walls. Sometimes, when she would watch me and put me to sleep, she let me keep my shoes on because she knew once I woke up, I'd tear off down the halls and she wanted me to be ready. This resulted in me habitually putting my shoes on before pants, and it became a theme in my life that everything happens backward.

I was constantly skipping important life steps and having to backtrack. I blamed my parents, who got pregnant with me when they were barely old enough to buy cigarettes, never got married, and then broke up when I was five, only to get back together when I was thirteen. They had a single year of engagement bliss before Dad got sick and I had to start working as a busboy at a local gastropub when Dad lost his job and we couldn't make ends meet, effectively ending my "Age of Innocence," as Ma put it.

Maybe that was why I grew up deconstructing food, parsing the ingredients out on my plate just to put it back together and critique it. Or why I preferred reading spoilers to books and movies before reading or watching because I *had* to know the endings before I began.

I often wondered if Ma had known that Dad would eventually

get sick if they would have gotten back together at all. Or maybe sooner, instead of wasting all those years because that wasn't how life was supposed to happen.

Life always felt backward.

Until Ricky. In a world that never made sense, Ricky DeLuca did. He understood *me*. We were in this together.

"You're the only thing I've ever been certain of," I told him, but the world around me felt fuzzy. Fog rolled over the ocean, but the sky was still clear. Panic set into my chest. It didn't make sense when he said he needed to find himself. If anybody knew who they were, it was Ricky DeLuca. "You're the only person I know who is certain of who they are. And you make sense of me when I don't make any sense." I wanted to reach for my phone, google the answers, find a way to tell him *not* to do what he was about to do.

"You're not listening, Fielder." He was pacing the beach now. "I need to be on my own. We skipped too many steps, and I feel like I don't have any control now because all I think about is you. Us. I need to think about me." He was talking with his hands, gesturing widely in front of him, crashing like a wave, a tsunami on the shore. "I can't do long distance. You know me; I work in measurements. No matter how many times I look at it, it just doesn't square . . ."

He continued talking, but I snagged on two words.

Long distance.

What was he talking about?

"I feel like I'm always having to take care of you, Fielder. I'm the responsible one. And I know I'm older and it looks like I have everything figured out, like what I want to do with my life, but sometimes I just want some room to figure it out like you." He stopped moving, his arms falling to his sides. The moon reflected the wetness in his eyes.

"What do you mean, 'long distance'?"

He exhaled through his nose, then took out his phone. "I got this a few days ago." He flashed his screen to me, an email from some man named Christian Richards.

Catching his gaze, he nodded toward the screen in a "read it" motion. He waited for me to start before repeating it word for word.

> "It's my pleasure to offer you a coveted apprenticeship at Sawdust Woodworkers, working directly under myself—"

I heard the words and saw them on the screen, but my brain couldn't absorb them.

"This is amazing, Ricky, but—" My eyes skipped down to the bottom of the email:

> Seattle, Washington.

My throat closed.

"I leave in three days."

Three days?

Breathe, Fielder, breathe.

"Yes, breathe," he instructed.

"We can make it work. You there, me here. I can move to Seattle next year after graduation. I can build my audience more, monetize my channel, and—"

"Fielder—" Ricky said, and I immediately knew.

Tightness pulled at his jaw, and he squeezed his eyes shut the way he did when he was trying to prevent himself from crying.

"Don't do this, Ricky."

Silence—it built in my ears, my chest, every cavity in my body until I was a balloon so full of air that my elasticity was at its breaking point. "If you're doing what I think you're doing, you need to say it. Full voice."

He moved in for a hug. My body went rigid.

"We can make it work," I pleaded.

"You still have another year of high school. I think time apart will help you find direction, what you want out of life—"

"I know what I want!" I cut him off.

"Clock doesn't count. You do that for fun, you're always about having fun, but you have to get serious." Like *him*—I knew what he meant. "You have, like, two thousand followers, Field. You have to want more than to define yourself in followers and views," he said, and just as I was about to add that he was the biggest part of me, he beat me to the punch, adding, "And me."

"What if I don't want to." The words barely audible.

"*I* need to know who *I* am without you," Ricky said, avoiding eye contact, as if he didn't believe his own words. "I think doing everything backwards put us at a disadvantage." He was so matter of fact. So practical about this. Like I was a spreadsheet or a piece of wood that wasn't fitting a mold or molding.

"How?"

"Maybe we met too soon."

"Please, Ricky, don't—" I couldn't finish.

"The world is *yours*, Fielder Lemon."

"But not *ours*," I barely got out.

He shook his head. "No, not now." He squeezed me so tightly, and the certainty in his voice crushed me more than anything. "Maybe one day."

"Is this the part where you vow to marry me one day if neither one of us is married by twenty-eight because I'm the love of your life but we just don't work *now*?" No filter.

"You don't have to do that thing, Fielder," he said softly. "Hide behind humor."

I wanted to argue, but nothing would have changed our trajectory.

"I'm so sorry, Fielder," he whispered. "I really loved you."

Loved. That *D* did the most.

I thought "Ricky and Fielder" were endgame. But the future I had mapped out for myself, with Ricky at its center, washed away with the tide.

He left before I woke up the next morning.

As I packed, I found his leather-bound journal beneath the bed. The well-worn pages opened to a fresh poem where an exploded pen fell out. The ink on the page was still wet, bleeding like a dark blue bullet wound to the chest.

I kept it as a reminder of what I had and lost.

That day, I vowed to prove to Ricky DeLuca that he was *so* wrong about me lacking direction and definition, and that he just made the biggest mistake of his life.

FROM THE JOURNAL OF RICCARDO DELUCA

CLARITY

—is the breath
before the phrase
"I love you,"
and the exhale
after the admission.

—is the silence
that comes after
the earth shifts
and ground settles
before the aftershock.

—is the calm,
after the rain,
the quiet erosion;
the promise of a future
is what grows after.

—isn't second-guessing,
it's knowing
to measure twice
and cut once
is "I love you" enough to sustain?

CHAPTER 2 *(Present Day, Again!)*

Wishin' and Hopin' and Thinkin' and Prayin' and Doin' My Best to Avoid a Panic Attack!

And that's the end of the sad, shitty part of my life, folks!

Kidding.

If that were true, I wouldn't be here, one year, two weeks, and three days later—not that I'm counting—still on the edge of my bed.

The mere mention of Ricky is enough to send me into a tailspin. Mostly because I think about him daily, dreaming about all the ways I could get him back.

Pathetic, I know.

Breathe, Fielder, breathe.

Topher keeps calling.

Ignore. Send to voicemail.

I can't believe Topher never told me he was dating Sienna DeLuca.

My older cous-brother is not only dating, but also *engaged* to the older sister of the love of my life-*slash*-guy who dumped me. I know it shouldn't, but it feels like a betrayal that he didn't tell me, warn me. Attending this wedding will put me face-to-face with Ricky before I'm ready. Topher knew what Ricky did, how much I loved Ricky, how he dumped me without warning, left without a goodbye.

I'm brought back to that morning, so vividly. The warmth of the sunlight contrasting how cold and desolate I felt. I didn't know what to do. How to move without him. I wandered around Topher's mansion alone, from room to room without purpose, searching for something to help make sense of what happened, how everything went so wrong. I was numb. I blocked Ricky's number and all his social media accounts: Snap, Insta, Clock App, *everything*. It wasn't until Topher arrived that night that I fully fell apart, and he held me as I sobbed nonsense. After a few days of getting blasted with Topher on the beach and feeling sorry for myself, he told me I needed to pull myself together because I needed to show Ricky I was better than "this."

I reread Ricky's poem "Clarity" until the words blended together. Nothing made sense. Ricky's excuses didn't make sense. It felt like he was running away from me. He was scared. It didn't excuse his behavior, but maybe it meant that deep down, he still loved me.

I held on to that thought tightly. It eventually evolved into a vision board with a six-step plan to prove Ricky wrong and win him back. Complete with magazine cut-outs (like a serial killer) and old pictures of us, I hung it above my desk, adding to it as new ideas come to me:

1. *Grow my Clock channel to monetize it to prove content creation is a career, not just a "fun" hobby*

2. *Save money to be independent after graduation*
3. *Get a super-hot revenge bod!*

That last one was Matty's idea. After watching every romantic comedy on Netflix, he convinced me that weight training with him would help me to feel more confident in my body. Not to mention I'd feel stronger both physically and emotionally. He's not wrong, though I did momentarily question how changing my body would make me more desirable to Ricky when Ricky himself used to worship me for being thick.

4. *Work on being independent!*
5. *Graduate high school with decent grades*

To show I'm more than online content! I'm (kind of) smart, too.

6. *Casually run into Ricky again, show him what he's missing, thus leading to us reconnecting*
7. *Grand romantic gesture to win him back!*

Still workshopping that last one.

If I could be independent, self-sufficient, and not defined by being "Ricky DeLuca's himbo boyfriend," but instead by being Fielder Lemon, successful food critic with a high-profile TV internship on his résumé on top of a successful, monetized Clock channel, then Ricky would have to see me differently. Right?

Don't answer that, reader.

I've barely seen his parents because even though they technically have residence next door, they bought a house in South Carolina in September and spent the winter there. Now that their family house next door is for sale, I was worried I might never see him again. But now, this?

This is inevitable.

I'm not ready. The plan isn't fully realized. I'm not at my peak yet.

Clutching my phone, I slide off the edge of the mattress and to my knees until I'm digging beneath the bed frame using the flashlight on my phone to illuminate the dark, cobwebbed, cavernous hoard I don't want found: the empty bottles of cheap vodka Ricky and I stole from his parents' liquor cabinet that I never threw out, a near-empty box of condoms, an oversized Tupperware bin full of the Barbies and *Toy Story* dolls I played with as a kid, and an overstuffed shoebox.

I yank it out, and the disturbance elicits a strong succession of sneezes. Just as I'm about to open it, there's a loud knock at the door.

"Go away, Ma. I'll call Topher back in a minute!" I shout, but I don't mean to get angry at Ma. It's not her fault I'm emotionally unwell.

"Field, it's me." Matty's voice triggers a sense of calm.

"*Just* you?" I ask.

Silence. "Thought so."

Whispers. Matty is hissing. Three separate sets of feet shuffle down the hallway.

Then he answers. "Yeah. Just me now. Can I come in?"

Stretching, I reach up and unlock the door, and he slips in

and quickly closes the door behind him. He knows the Coven well.

"Dude," he says. "You okay?" I glare at him, which prompts him to tip his head and roll his eyes. "Dumb question."

"Did you know about Toph and Sienna?"

"I found out last night when he called me to ask if I wanted to be in the wedding. He asked me not to say anything to you because, well, you know. He wanted to tell you himself."

"In front of the whole family?"

"In hindsight, not the best idea, but Toph loves you." Matty rocks back and forth on his heels. "I bet he thought it'd be easier having everyone around."

"Why didn't he tell me sooner? Clearly, they've been together a while."

Matty hops onto my bed and lies back. "I don't know, man. Topher exists in Topherland. You know that. Maybe he thought you'd freak out."

"I have so many questions."

"Talk to him," Matty urges. "He loves you."

My heart races, thinking he means Ricky.

"Topher," Matty clarifies. Sitting up, he eyes the shoebox. "What's that?"

Popping the lid off prompts a familiar anxious bubbling in my chest. Inside is the dream box Ricky gave me with the lemon carved onto its face, surrounded by other mementos of our relationship: Playbills from Broadway shows we saw together after winning cheap lottery tickets, handwritten Christmas and birthday cards with poems he wrote for me scribbled in ink next to hand-drawn hearts, a thin, hardcover photo book Ma made of us for his graduation that she never got to give him, and the customized Funko Pop! of Ricky he made for me when Topher flew us out to LA for New Year's Eve—we went to the Funko Pop! store and made a Pop! of ourselves for each other, so he has the one that looks like me, and I have him, immortalized in cute plastic.

I wonder if he kept me, too.

"What's that wooden box?" Matty asks, and I tell him its origin while trying not to cry. "Damn. You kept it?" He shakes his head. "Bad vibes. Did you put anything in it? Like a voodoo doll?" His fingers absentmindedly fondle the golden cornicello around his neck—a thin, twisted horn-shaped pendant that looks like a chili pepper meant to ward off evil.

"Relax, Matty, it's not cursed."

"You don't know that. Maybe Ricky put the malocchio on you." Matty makes the sign of the horn with his hand and points it at the box.

"You're really making me feel better about all this, you know."

"Sorry." He swallows. "What's inside?"

Upon opening the creaky lid, I pull out Ricky's leather journal of poems. "I never gave this back to him." The binding is worn, but still supple, and the texture brings me right back to the morning I found it, left behind. I toss it to Matty, who bats it away and onto my bed like a hot potato.

"I would've burned it," Matty says.

He grabs the journal and flips through it with one hand, while the other clutches his cornicello. "Ricky wrote these?"

"He wrote poems all the time."

"That's romantic as fuck. Like, if a guy wrote me shit like this, I dunno what I'd do. Be on my knees."

"I was. Often."

"Ricky had it bad for you." He attempts to show me a page, but I turn away.

"*Had* being the operative word."

"Feelings like this, they don't just vanish."

I look down. "What if they did for Ricky?"

Matty clears his throat, and slams Ricky's journal shut. "Maybe this"—he jiggles the book—"is a sign. The wedding. Italy, the most romantic country in the world. Our ancestral birthplace. It's the perfect opportunity to win him back."

Though I've spent a year thinking about nothing but winning Ricky back, now that I'm faced with an actual opportunity, I'm terrified. Over the past year, I've monetized my Clock channel, but I'm still living at home with no clear life plan. How am I supposed to convince Ricky that I'm independent and won't hold him back? How am I supposed to prove that he needs me when for the past year he's probably been doing just fine without me?

"I don't know. What if he doesn't want me back?"

"I bet he's hotter now."

I stare at him blankly. "Not helpful."

He shrugs. "Look, you're ready now. Six months ago, I would've said you'd crumble. But, hey, if you don't try to win back the love of your life, you'll regret it." Matty taps his fingertips together, hatching a devious plan, and my cheeks heat. "You don't just love someone your whole life and then stop loving them, right? Even if you got shit to work on." He clears his throat. "You two are gonna see each other, and it's gonna be love at first sight. Or one millionth sight. Bet."

I play with the ring on my thumb. I hope he's right.

"If not, we're gonna be in Italy! The motherland. Surrounded by hot, hot Italian guys. We can be each other's wingman. Not that you have any trouble getting guys. But you can help *me* out for once." Matty usually isn't jealous, he's too jovial for that, but his pent-up sexual frustration is getting the better of him. He's a hopeless romantic, not exactly waiting for love to get laid, but for the perfect feeling and ideal scenario. He wants to feel a connection like the one I had with Ricky. Which is sweet. He wants to be swept off his feet, like the main character of a romantic comedy. Meanwhile I've spent the better part of the last year "getting over" Ricky by getting under pretty much everyone with a pulse. It's been a stellar distraction.

We high-five, and I'm momentarily disgusted by my own show of machismo. "I hate being a guy."

Matty punches my arm. "Topher keeps calling." He stares at my phone's lock screen. "Pick up, tell him you're gonna be his best man with me. Do it for Topher. But also for you because you're a fucking Lemon."

Fist bump. He's right.

I pick up the FaceTime call. "Sorry, Toph, I didn't mean—"

"Fielder! Please don't hate me!" Topher shouts quickly. I don't see any sign of Sienna. "You know I love you, man, so much."

"I know, I know, I'm not—"

"I wanted to tell you about Sienna so badly; you have no idea! I didn't know how because, well, the Ricky part. I'm sorry."

"Don't apologize! I'm happy for you guys. I *am*." I may be trying to convince myself here a little bit, pushing away the twinge of anger about why he didn't tell me if he's my brother, but despite everything, Sienna's like a sister.

He exhales in relief. "I can't tell you how happy that makes me to hear. You're my brother. I love you. *And* there's no pressure for the wedding—I'll take care of everything, all the expenses. I only want my two brothers next to me."

"If I didn't make it clear," I say, "I can't wait to celebrate you." As the words tumble out, I realize I'm tearing up because I really do love him, and I want him to have the best wedding ever, and if his version of that includes me standing right next to him, probably staring at Ricky, I'll do it. For Topher. "As one of your best men."

Topher cheeses into the camera as he howls, "Let's gooooooooooooo!"

Fielder—

Hi. Hope you're well.

Neither of us want to talk to each other, but for the sake of our soon-to-be shared family, let's be cool in Italy.

olive branch extended.

Ricky

Fielder Lemon
104 Blossom Ave
Hudson Valley, NY

CHAPTER 3

When Life Hands You Sour Lemons . . .

. . . you spiral out of control!

It's two weeks before we depart for Italy when a handwritten postcard from Ricky shows up. *In the mail.* Like, from the mailman. With a stamp!

I shriek, and Nonna thinks the Russians are bombing us.

Turning over the card in my hands like it could catch fire, I study the picture on the front and actively avoid reading his message: it's a cheesy postcard of the Space Needle in Seattle, one you can get at any souvenir shop or corner bodega. The art is very 1950s "space race" with bold colors and a cheesy "Reach for the Stars!" slogan splashed across the front.

Nonna waddles into the kitchen behind me and peers over my shoulder. She sucks in a deep breath. "From *Ricky*?! Madonna mia. What's it say?"

Without a word, I quickly run out of the house.

My hands tremble, the postcard flapping.

Do I?

I have to.

Right?

Okay, Fielder. Deep breaths. You got this.

Maybe it's a love letter and everything I've wanted to happen is about to happen and the way to win Ricky back literally landed in my hands, and and and—

And the actual words he writes? "Hi. Hope you're well." With periods! He might as well just come out and say, "We're complete strangers"! A shiver runs down my spine as I realize Ricky's voice, that of a poet, is gone here, his words so cold, yet measured. To end it with, "Olive branch extended" and saying neither of us want to talk to each other? I mean, if anybody would not want to talk to anybody, it'd be me not wanting to talk to him. I was the dumped party, after all.

Where is this coming from?

Maybe we are strangers now.

Winning Ricky back is going to be a lot harder than I thought. Impossible with a cold-ass postcard like this.

My head is spinning.

Sweat trickles down my temple and pools at my chin.

I can't think about this and how it might be a wrench in my plan to win him back.

The worst part of this postcard is that—

—I just want to feel wanted.

By Ricky.

The need to not feel alone is overwhelming, like I'm suffocating, unable to breathe, and, wow, I sound dramatic, but as sweat beads my forehead and trickles down the small of my back, I reach for my phone. I want so desperately to text a friend, a reliable make-out buddy from the football team, or hit up Rye on Snapchat, my hot semi-straight neighbor friend who is only "gay" after homecoming, prom afterparties, and summer Thursdays.

No. I can't. Ricky swims through my mind, so I do this trick Ma taught me when she feels like she's drowning: I pause and feel the ground beneath my feet. I touch the side of the house, feel the rough brick beneath my fingertips. Take a deep breath. *In. Out.*

I sulk into the shed behind Nonna's house, which I've converted into my Clock "studio" (hold your laughter, please). It's precisely the size of a small pantry, but it allows me privacy when editing content or hanging with friends.

The air in here is hot and thick, made worse by the intense early July heat wave outside and lack of AC. It's enough to make me woozy and heady, yet Ricky and his passive-aggressive (or was it just passive-passive, as if he never cared about me at all) postcard keep me hyper-fixated.

Whispers of Ricky whirl around my head like too many goldfish in a fishbowl.

"We did everything backwards."

"I feel like I don't have any control."

"Time apart will help you find direction, what you want out of life."

"You have to want more than to define yourself in followers and views."

"I *need to know who* I *am without you."*

"The world is yours, *Fielder Lemon."*

"But not *ours*," I whisper.

I nibble my cuticles.

Check my Snap, texts, Clock notifications. Swipe up, switch apps, wait for anything, anyone, to distract me.

Notifications, views, comments, sex, restaurant reviews, food truck reviews, reviews, reviews, reviews, DMs, taps, taps, taps, hook-ups, Ricky, Ricky, Ricky, from two thousand to over a million followers, somewhere, somehow, everything blurred together, and now I don't know what's real.

My followers define me based on what I curate, and I crave their validation, the instant gratification that comes with, well, how I've curated my life in Ricky's wake.

An unsettling thought percolates in my brain:

Am I good enough for him now? Have I done enough? Or have I just avoided—

Nope. Not going there.

This is fine, everything is fine.

My forehead *plonks* down on my desk, and my chair wobbles as I wallow.

An email alert buzzes through my phone. I pause my spiraling thoughts to read.

SUBJECT: **Congratulations, You've Been Selected As a "FOOD FOR CAUSE" Finalist!**
July 1

Greetings, Fielder!

We're writing with wonderful News! Your channel @LemonAtFirstSight and your compelling content featuring the Sinking Venetian and the awareness you raised about the impacts of climate change on Venice, Italy, has been voted by viewers as a finalist in Food for Change's sustainability awareness contest. Here, influencers across the Clock App will be using their platforms to share content aimed at raising awareness about sustainability, green-eating, and conservation. As a finalist, your job is to post up to three long-form videos relating to food sustainability, green-eating, and conservation by August 1st. Please tag @FoodForChange and hashtag #FoodForChange in your captions. One winner will be chosen to intern on the set of the new TV competition cooking series *Out of This World* hosted by world-renowned Michelin-star chef and online sensation Mars Lyon in London, England. The winning content will not only spotlight efforts of sustainability, but will highlight the importance of the hard work of conservation efforts, something Chef Lyon and *Out of This World* is passionate about highlighting, all while showcasing the viral, yum-worthy, drool-inducing food content that @FoodForChange is known for!

Along with your content, please submit a 500-word personal essay outlining your personal goals, how the mentorship would benefit you, and about your efforts toward sustainability as a content creator.

We can't wait to see what you've "cooked" up!

Sophia Brookes @FoodForChange

I suck in a breath and hold it. This is a sign. It *has* to be.

This contest from @FoodForChange is *exactly* what I need to change my life. There is a link to more information about the coveted internship and how it's an opportunity to work behind the scenes in promotion and marketing, making content for a real show and their social media accounts *and* guest on the actual show as a special mini-challenge judge. This is the type of real-world experience that is sure to appease Ma, and, who knows, maybe I'll learn something, too.

Except. I don't know anything about sustainability, but I know food, so I can fake it until I make it. Hell, it's a better bet than bankrupting myself with school loans and taking classes for a major that would be useless in practicality, right? If I can win this thing, I might actually have a chance to show Ricky that I'm more than my Clock account.

Nonna always says, "Pasta Dolce, when life hands you lemons, make lemonade. La Famiglia Limone è forte!" But I've never been a glass of lemonade. I'm not watered down or overly sweet. I'm a Lemon. Sour, bright, electric. A versatile ingredient.

I can make my family—and Ricky—proud.

Content. Contest. Internship. Wedding. Italy.

Ricky. Two weeks to prepare myself for Ricky.

Another great commencement, hold the massacre.

Four until the contest content has to be posted.

Stay focused. *Figure out my shit*.

I may not have always done things the "right way," in the "correct" order, and I may not know how to cook or have much direction beyond @LemonAtFirstSight, but I *know* I need this.

Here's hoping I can make something better than lemonade.

Wedding Week

SUNDAY

CHAPTER 4

Good Luck, Babe!

"A private jet is a baller move." Matty's eyes widen as we reach the tarmac and he sees the PJ in the distance set against a hazy July sky.

"See—you should go work for Topher, Fielder," Ma says. "Make real money instead of relying on that ridiculous Clock App."

Lay off, Ma.

I must've said that out loud because she smacks me upside the back of my head. *Lightly*—relax, readers. It's not child abuse; it's a love language for Italian moms.

"I'm just saying, you gotta figure out how to make a sustainable career for yourself, baby. That was the deal. No college, but make something of yourself; don't just let time pass you by like the hands on a clock. Ticktock, ticktock."

In other words, *Good luck, babe!*

"I'm trying. Not everyone can be a college dropout multimillionaire at twenty-one." I remind myself to make sure the content

I've filmed over the last two weeks reviewing restaurants and devouring food is set to post at certain times to keep the algorithm in my favor. I don't have anything yet for the @FoodForChange contest. I haven't told Ma about it yet to manage her (and my, frankly) expectations. It's hard enough being on a trip where I'll be constantly reminded of how successful Topher is and that I should follow in his footsteps or learn from him. *Deep breath.* "Don't worry, Ma."

"That's my job," she says. *That and good old-fashioned Italian guilt!*

The runway of Westchester County Airport is clear just for us, something I've never seen (because it's far too expensive to fly out of Westchester versus JFK or LaGuardia or even Newark, so this is my first time here, period). I'm *deeply* uncomfortable because I feel like a rich douchebag walking toward a private jet, which could not be further from the truth, but if I saw our family traipsing across the tarmac, I'd be hardcore judging us for our extravagant spending and enormous carbon footprint.

But, alas, here I am, craving a cappuccino and knowing I can probably get one aboard the flight. Being human is weird like that.

Lush green trees and flat plots of perfectly trimmed grass present a kind of serenity that major New York metropolitan airports don't. It's free of city noise.

The air is slightly dewy.

Zia Gabriella scoffs. "I cannot believe Topher did this." Her suitcase has one wheel that pulls maddeningly to the right, and she keeps having to yank it with every five steps she takes. "He spent too much money on us."

"That's not what she said when Topher flew her out to LA for Mother's Day," Zia Rosa whispers. Except nobody in the Coven ever whispers, so it's more like a dull scream.

"I'm just saying," Zia Gabriella continues. "We could have flown coach on a regular plane. It's not like any of us are strangers to that." She eyes Ma up and down. The shade is real. "There are better ways for Topher to spend his money."

"Than on his family?" Ma scoffs.

"Meanwhile, he's constantly flying all over the world," Zia Rosa adds. "Didn't he post on Instagram last week that he was in Paris *just* to eat at a Michelin-star restaurant for dinner?"

"He loves luxury, my son." Zia Gabriella waves Rosa's comments away like a gnat.

"Really, Gab?" Ma says. "Topher's generous enough to charter a plane for his family, the little people who can't afford to up and go to *Jersey* on a whim, let alone Italy, and you're complaining? Shut up."

"*You* shut up!" Zia Gabriella quips.

Matty and I exchange knowing glances. Gabriella and Ma are oil and water. They can't exist in each other's orbits for longer than a couple hours without going off on each other. It's been like this for as long as I can remember. According to Lemon legend, the genesis of their feud was when Ma convinced Gabriella, always the weaker willed of the two, to let Ma cut her hair when they were eight and ten, respectively, right before school picture day. The most prized picture in our family is Zia Gabriella with a scrunched-up face and red, teary eyes, balding with angry, wispy hairs tied into a heinous bow at the top of her head, looking like an onion freshly plucked from the ground. Zia Gabriella claims she forgave Ma, but I've noticed whenever they fight hard, she grabs at her long black hair in an act of protection. Still, don't ever get in the middle because they'll go after you—they fight hard, but love *each other* harder.

"Can you both shut up?" Zia Rosa shouts.

Matty links his arm with mine and forces us to walk at a gayer speed in hopes of outrunning the Coven.

He's trembling, his body brimming with excitement, electricity firing in his veins.

"You all right there, Flash?" I ask, tugging at our hooked limbs.

"What do you think *Italia* will be like?" He emphasizes "Italia" like every other Guido in our neighborhood might. All-American with a Westchester twist. "More importantly, what do you think the guys will be like?"

"One-track mind," I say.

He cranes his neck and looks behind us, making sure the Coven are far enough away that they can't hear our conversation—though I'm convinced they all have bionic ears and no private chat is safe. "I'm determined to lose my virginity, bro."

"What happened to romance?"

"Always romance, dude!" Matty says. "But, ya know. Both is optimal."

At that exact moment, a golf cart carrying Nonna whizzes by, and she cackles, lifting her purse in the air like she just scored a touchdown. "Suckers!"

Matty's ears go bright red. His breathing gets shallow.

"Nonna can barely hear the TV when it's on max volume, relax." I knock into him. "My little Matty, all grown up. I'm so proud. Why now, though?"

"No place more romantic than Italy to meet the man of my dreams." Matty's face beams with excitement, but the way he swings his arms as he walks, flexing and stretching like he's prepping for a track meet, betrays his nerves. "When it's right, it'll be right. Right?"

"Right," I say confidently, hoping he eases up. He overthinks sex and wants perfection, but if anybody deserves a rom-com moment, it's big, beautiful Matty.

Just up ahead, at the top of the aircraft stairway into the PJ, a flight attendant descends toward the tarmac to greet Nonna.

"What do you think the guys in Amalfi are like? Think they're cool?" Matty grimaces, a blend of excitement and nerves on his face. Though he talks a big game around other people, he's a puppy. He won't have any problem once he's ready to have sex. He may be my cousin, but he's objectively hot. He's got auburn hair and hazel eyes with flecks of green—the Sicilian jumped out. He's paler than Topher and the Coven, like me, but unlike me, he tans instantly in the sun, so he's got a nice pre-glow from the summer already. A total himbo, hence the inspiration, he works out like a maniac, having played nearly every sport in high school, so again, objectively great body. He's never dated anybody, partially because he claims that high school guys are too immature and he wants someone more "worldly," less concerned about getting head and more focused on getting ahead. "I don't want just anyone. I want a big ole Italian romance, like in the movies. You know, a guy who's a little rough around the edges, maybe works with his hands so he's strong and—" He shifts his junk in his shorts. "I want someone who isn't afraid of emotions. Every guy who's asked me out is so quick to just, like, ditch once it gets real. I don't want that."

Sounds like Ricky. "So when you go off to Stony Brook at the end of August, you'll be long distance with some dude who lives in Campania?"

He makes a lovesick face. "You think that could happen?"

"You're hopeless."

"Speaking of hopeless," he starts, "how're you? You know, seeing Ricky tomorrow."

"Concocting an evil plan to make him love me. The usual."

He pops his tongue and glares at me. "For real though, you ready? Because we haven't really had the chance to plan our attack the last few weeks. You've been MIA since you got that postcard from Ricky, filming content and *avoiding* feelings."

"I'm going to see him, and he's obviously going to drool because I look damn good." I wait for Matty to validate, but all he does is roll his eyes. "And like one of those movies you always watch, I'll give this big speech about how I've changed and grown, which will make him realize he made a huge mistake, and then I'll use the powers of Amalfi and the romance of it all to make him love me."

Matty squints. "Cool. But, like, how? That postcard . . ."

I blink, then shrug. "That was a fluke. I have a ten-hour plane ride to think about the *how* because, according to Topher, Ricky is flying to Italy directly from Seattle, so at least I have time. But in my head, the way I've been picturing it, dreaming of him and our reunion, Ricky's face will soften and the cold words of his postcard will be erased, and he'll be excited to see me, drawn to me like a magnet, and our bodies will press together beneath the orange Italian sunset, and just as a slight breeze brushes his hair across his face, he'll apologize for letting me go and grab me like he used to, and our lips will meet, and music will play for us and—

Matty smacks my chest in approval. "Be honest. Raw. Not rehearsed, real. Bareback it."

I squeeze my eyes tight. "Never again."

Matty laughs. "Speaking of. Think Topher's friends are hot?"

I roll my eyes and laugh.

Now Zias Rosa and Gabriella are bickering so loudly with Ma that their voices carry over the quiet tarmac. Not even the sound of nearby airplane engines revving can drown them out.

"Tea?" Matty leans in and whispers so low not even the Coven's collective bionic ears can hear. "Topher told me Sienna's parents flew to Italy a few days early to spend extra time with them. Zia Gab doesn't know."

I bet Ricky did, too.

Matty eyes me because of course I said that out loud.

"Zia Gab is gonna spiral," I say. Zia Gabriella is—how do I put this delicately?—mildly obsessed with Topher. Like Ma and Zia Rosa, she's a single Italian mother who lives and breathes for her kid, often telling people Topher is her best friend. She's got serious FOMO. It killed her when he moved out of New York, so she's been trying to find a way to take her custom jewelry-making business on the road to follow him to LA, or wherever he ends up next. She'd never say this out loud, but I don't think Zia Gab likes the idea of sharing Topher with Sienna. Which, for anyone who didn't grow up in an Italian family, probably seems weird, but for us, it's standard.

"I think she already is." Matty elbows me, clueing me into the Coven arguing over Topher paying for everyone to fly to his wedding on a PJ.

Zia Gab hates how generous Topher is with his money.

As someone who grew up poor and on SNAP benefits, surrounded by poor extended family, if my wildly successful and rich-ass cousin wants to pamper us, why shouldn't he? I would do the same if I had the means, in a heartbeat.

Zia Rosa throws her hands in the air and storms past us. "You two are unbelievable." Then she mutters something in Italian—"Va funculo!"

Nonna hisses from inside the now-parked golf cart at the foot of the jet.

"Sorry, Ma." Zia Rosa grabs hold of Nonna's underarm with one hand to steady her as she hobbles out of the golf cart.

"I feel like royalty," Nonna says, waving a cupped hand like the queen mother. "What the hell does my hair look like? I told the driver to slow down!" Firmly on the tarmac, she primps her coifed chestnut-brown pixie cut, voluminous and freshly dyed.

"You look gorgeous, Nonna." I bend down to kiss her cheek.

She grabs my cheeks and squeezes. "Love you, kid."

Matty, not to be outdone, does the same to Nonna's opposite cheek, and, in an effort not to seem biased, Nonna grabs Matty's face next. Rinse and repeat.

I grab my phone and start recording for @LemonAtFirstSight; a private jet is the exact opposite of "sustainability," so it surely won't win me the prize, but I won't tag @FoodForChange. I also doubt I'll find much in a tourist destination about conservation, so the real contest-worthy content will most likely happen once I'm back in the States, post-wedding chaos. Hopefully.

I don't have a plan for that yet. So . . .

Fingers crossed.

The lens starts on Nonna, then pans to Matty who sticks out his tongue and flexes his biceps before ascending the stairs up into the bowels of the private jet.

Which, *ohmygod*.

Flying private is a completely different world than flying with the unwashed masses of a regular airliner, and honestly if I sound like a privileged bitch, it's because in this moment, after nearly eighteen years of being so poor it hurts, this feels like a small victory.

Large white leather couches facing inward line the walls of the jet, with a few rows of regular seats—and by regular, I mean massive La-Z-Boy recliner-looking monsters. There are pillows and built-in champagne buckets and a massive TV in the center of the plane with state-of-the-art surround sound. I could cartwheel down the center with how much space is here. There's a freaking bed, which I'm sure Nonna will claim. I make sure to film every square inch; with a well-timed song, a spontaneous video that's slightly (okay, majorly) off brand can do relatively decent numbers. I also plan to find hidden-gem restaurants and eateries in Amalfi for the channel. Right before I stop recording, everyone already seated waves right on cue.

I recognize virtually none of these people. Except Sienna

and Ricky's older cousin, Benny Gorga, and his mom-slash-their-maternal-aunt, Francesca, who I know from countless Christmas Eves with the DeLucas. Me and Ricky used to idolize Benny because he was so brazenly out he called himself a walking stereotype. Everyone made fun of him because of his flamboyance, but I loved growing up seeing him live his truth. Growing up, he was our gay sherpa, but after Ricky dumped me—*breathe*—I haven't so much as liked a picture on Benny's Instagram.

I wasn't ready for the knot in my stomach from being *this* close to Ricky's bloodline.

"Ohmygod, shut the cockpit!" Benny jumps up and rushes at me, wrapping his long-ass arms around me. "You've grown up, my little gayling! I'm sorry about you and my dumbass cousin."

"Thanks, but I'm—I'm over it." I quickly add, "*Him*. I barely think about him anymore."

Benny narrows his eyes. "To quote Jinkx Monsoon: 'Delusion, convince yourself,'" he says, and Matty chokes out an incredulous laugh from behind us. "If you ask me, he's still not over you. Definitely wasn't at Christmas, or at—"

"You saw him at Christmas?"

Right as I'm about to probe Benny for more, Zia Gabriella bursts through the doors like Kuzco in *The Emperor's New Groove*, shimmying, doing a cringy dance, and screaming, "Benvenuti al mio matrimonio Italiano!"

"It's not your wedding, Gab," Ma says.

Zia Gabriella ignores her and instead makes her way down the aisle to hug and greet everybody.

"Ma, relax," I say. "It's her big day."

"You're bad," Zia Rosa chimes in.

"I just can't deal with her." Ma leans in. "Who are all these people? Besides you, Benny!" Ma and Benny hug. "You've grown up!" Then she moves on to Francesca.

Zia Gabriella claps, demanding attention. "Does everybody know everybody?" She doesn't wait. "You all know me, Gabriella Limone." My entire body crumples from secondhand embarrassment when she turns our last name into a showpiece. "Topher's mom! Mother of the groom!" She whoops, or raises the roof, or some other old-person move. "If you don't know my beautiful mother, Topher's nonna."

"No name, just Nonna. Like Beyoncé," I add.

Topher and Sienna's friends laugh.

It's clear nobody quite knows what to do—do they stand up and greet the matriarch of the Lemon family, or wave awkwardly from their cushy seats? The deer-in-headlights of it all makes me chuckle.

"I'm crying," Benny says. "This is—"

"*So* much," Matty adds.

"An epic start to a wildly unnecessary destination wedding!" Benny says.

After introducing the Lemon clan, Zia Gab goes around the rest of the jet. "The whole guest list is here. Well, almost!" She starts with the two other groomsmen on Topher's side, grabbing the broad shoulders of a blond-haired white guy so hot my nonexistent ovaries burst. "This is Tyler Dell, Topher's freshman-year roommate at Cornell, and"—she moves on to the guy across the aisle, yet another smokeshow, tall, dark, and douchey with a buzzcut—"Trav Ridgewell the Third, who went to Cornell but didn't room with you boys, right? But they were in the same circle. Topher may not have lasted at an Ivy, but the friendships he built did!"

"I should play a triumphant instrumental as she does this," Benny quips.

"I'd like to play any music with Tyler," I say.

"Or Trav," Matty adds.

"They're devastatingly straight, boys, and far too old for you both," Benny says.

Zia Gabriella then introduces Sienna's second cousin Jenni Lee, a two-names-at-all-time law student who looks like an airbrushed model.

"What the hell is *she* doing here?" I whisper to Matty.

Jenni Lee DeLuca and her dad, a local conservative politician who is Sienna and Ricky's father's first cousin (I hope you're keeping up because this is confusing!), moved to the neighborhood when Ricky and I were really young. Her mom, an author of "inspirational romance" (aka super religious), left her dad for a younger man, and it was the scandal of the century in our small Hudson Valley town. And Jenni Lee, who became her father's protégé, leveraged the sympathy vote to win student body president as a high school senior touting a "No Labels" message to bring "all students" together. She claimed to be the "A" in LGBTQIA+, but after Jenni Lee swept the election, she wrote an op-ed in the school newspaper about how "A" meant "abstinent ally" and ended up campaigning the school board to cut funding to the Sexuality and Gender Alliance, get books with any queer or "nonreligious" themes in the school library pulled from circulation, and went so far as to support a nearby school district's decision to kick a genderqueer student out of their high school musical. That was big news around the Hudson River towns. It seemed she had a lot of support from parents who thought exposure to "mature content" was harmful to teens. I knew she was bad news. She always gave me the ick, and I never understood how Sienna and Ricky were related to her. I do a sweep to make sure her father isn't on board, but Ma whispers, "Don't worry, the bigot isn't coming. He's on the campaign trail. *Governor.*"

A shiver runs down my spine. *Good god, save us.*

Ma elbows me to be quiet.

Zia Gab then announces, "Jenni Lee and Trav started dating last year after meeting through Topher. Isn't that just wonderful?" Zia Gab makes a kissing motion with her hands that's borderline gross.

Jenni Lee wastes no time rushing to my side and telling me she follows me on Clock. "Last time I saw you, you were a kid! Now you're spicy on Clock." She releases a honk laugh, referring to content I filmed with Matty, both of us shirtless but wearing aprons, and cooking with Nonna. It was a joke video, but it blew up.

I don't smile or give her anything.

She clears her throat. "Dumb food pun. I don't mean it in a bad way; lots of gay guys get spicy online."

"Wholesome family content," I say casually. "Right?"

Her smile tightens as she hums. "Not exactly the word I would use. It's a shame. You could use your platform for *good*. Appeal to . . ." She chooses her words carefully. "More people."

My chest rises and falls rapidly, in anger, but I won't make a scene with one of Sienna's bridesmaids, so I bury it, decide not to engage further. I'm enlightened or whatever. What she's saying is that I should appeal to *straight* viewers. Growing up in a more conservative old-school Italian suburb, even in blue New York, which isn't so blue outside the city, I've had to contend with that mentality of having to curb my gayness for others. But my art is *mine. My* space. If you don't get it, it's *not for* you, Jenni Lee.

She must register my irritation, because her eyes calculate a way out. Then she smiles sweetly, mechanically, like a politician. It's unnerving. "How excited are you for Sienna's big day?"

"Very. I'm going to, uh . . ." I hitch my thumb and swerve away from her.

Moving on.

"She still gives me the ick," Matty says under his breath, and I nod in agreement.

The final girl is the last of Sienna's bridesmaids, with a fabulous hot-pink blowout, the fiercest fifties-style cat eye mint-green eyeglasses, clad in a ratty old band tee she obviously thrifted. Her makeup is beyond flawless, and while she definitely stands out among Topher and Sienna's bridal party, she's also by far the coolest. Monroe Cooper, Sienna's college roommate at FIT while Sienna studied fashion merchandizing.

An expectant flight attendant materializes. "If we can all get seated and buckle up, the pilot is almost ready." The flight attendant is tall with dark hair pulled back in a tight bun. In a navy-blue blazer and tailored slacks, she walks around the cabin handing out hot towels before taking drink orders.

"When do we take off?" Matty asks after ordering a rum and coke and getting turned down because the manifest revealed his age.

"We're waiting on two more passengers," the attendant responds.

"Two more? Who else are we—"

My words dissolve like foam when I see *him* round the corner—

Ricky DeLuca.

Reader, when I tell you I nearly pass out . . . *Woof.* Though I'm not sure if it's from the surprise of seeing him, or from how he takes my breath away.

Cliché, I know, I get it. Relax, I'm a red-blooded himbo with an increasing rush of blood to my dick and heart all at once. But if you saw what I'm seeing, you'd get it!

Effortless charisma; he's the most confident guy on the planet in loose blue jeans that hug his waist and a V-cut tank top that reveals how muscular he's gotten as a woodworker's apprentice. His biceps could act as flotation devices should the plane go down. His face—gone is the smooth, clean-shaven boy I knew a year ago, replaced by scruff. He's grown out his dark hair so long he looks like a heartthrob in those old magazines from the 1990s Ma keeps stored in the garage. It's effortless and cool in front of his eyes, and ridiculously hot, especially when he tucks it behind his ears.

The earth stops rotating.

He turns and catches my gaze, his mouth parting slightly.

I've bulked up a lot over the last year thanks to spending time at the gym with Matty. My pasta body has some musculature to it now. Add the blond scruff to the mix, and I'm no longer the soft, unshaped doughy kid he left on the beach. If that's true, then why do I suddenly feel like that kid again, fragile and alone, needing his affection?

Ricky stops dead in the entry; his nostrils flare, and a stony gaze falls over his face.

He looks right through me.

I'm frozen in place as he steps aside and, in slow motion, another guy comes up behind him and drapes his arms around Ricky's neck, kissing his cheek.

Ricky proceeds to introduce everyone to Cam Wallace.

His *boyfriend.*

CHAPTER 5

It's Amazing the Clarity That Comes with Psychotic Jealousy

"You okay?" Matty asks.

I clear my throat. "What kind of name is Cam Wallace? What is he, an analog camera? Also, it's July, and this guy is wearing a beanie."

He does have supercute eyeglasses, though. Very Professor Moriarty chic.

But that's it.

Okay, fine. He's also tall. And nerdy in a way that's super adorable, and the more I stare the more I'm convinced he's one of those guys who is completely unassuming, but once his shirt comes off, he's ridiculously ripped. Sleeper bod.

I hate him.

Matty laughs. "Quiet!"

Benny hands me the mimosa the flight attendant serves him. "You need this more than I do."

I down it in one gulp. My thoughts rapidly fill the airspace in the cabin. Ricky looked right through me. Like I didn't exist.

I yank the ring on my thumb off and quickly slip it into the pocket of my short shorts. "I can't be here."

"Where ya going, Sparky?" Matty asks. "We're on a plane."

"I can't do this."

Benny looks to Matty. "Take him to the back row; I'll run interference. Ohmygod, did I just make a sports reference?" After quickly rushing to Ricky, Benny hugs him and screams, "Cousin!" far too loudly. Zero chill.

Matty ushers me down the aisle.

I look back.

Ricky's eyes follow me, but he doesn't move past Benny.

My mouth is dry.

Ricky's line of sight never leaves me.

Matty plops me down in a cushy row that's one long couch, between Monroe and Tyler, who, until we raided their territory, looked on the verge of respective naps.

"Not a good flyer?" Monroe adjusts the eye mask on her forehead. "Me neither."

Matty intercepts. "He's good, just dramatic. But I'll take one."

"I like you two," Monroe says. "I'm not really the best flyer—this is my first time flying out of the country, and I don't really know anyone here, so I'm kind of freaking myself out. Do you guys know Sienna well? I went to college with her, and she's the best. I've spent a lot of time with your cousin, and I love him so much. He's good people, and I get good vibes from you even though I don't know you at all. Does that make sense? I can kind of read auras."

I don't think this girl took a single breath while talking.

"Read auras?" I ask, almost distracted enough to look away

from Ricky and Cam who are entwined in each other's arms, nuzzling necks, giggling. My stomach cramps, and bile rises in my throat.

"I'm kind of an aura and energy reader. My grandma is one, too. She's also a pretty famous tarot card reader. I can totally read your cards if you want."

Matty and I look at each other. Nonna would scream if she heard Monroe right now. I can hear her now: *She'll put the malocchio on you!*

"Maybe later."

"I'd be down," Tyler, Topher's hot Cornell roommate, says.

Matty is giving him serious "kiss me" googly eyes. I elbow him.

"Ouch, dude," he says.

Tyler laughs. "Did I miss something?"

"He thinks you're hot," Monroe says.

I unleash a cackle so loud nearly every head in the cabin turns toward us.

"What?" she says. "He does."

Matty's face turns crimson.

"Energy reader," I repeat.

Tyler doesn't miss a beat. "You're a good-looking guy yourself, buddy." The compliment plus the friend zoning with "buddy" sends me. "I'm straight, but flattered."

"All the good ones are!" Matty cries.

"Tell me." Monroe leans in, eyes narrowed. She wants us to spill the scalding, piping-hot tea on the tension in the PJ. "What's the drama here?"

Without hesitation, Matty fillets me open: "Fielder is Ricky's ex. Love-of-each-other's-lives-level exes. Fielder thought that when they saw each other at a romantic wedding in Italy, they'd immediately run back into each other's arms. Except Ricky is here unexpectedly with a *boyfriend*."

I grind my teeth. "Thanks for that."

"Oh, I sense a plot," Monroe says.

"To destroy the Jedi?" Tyler asks.

"No." Monroe shakes her head playfully. "So are we planning to win Ricky back and dump the new boyfriend into the Mediterranean? Because honestly that would be *such* a movie moment."

"We?" I ask.

"We're obviously in on this now," Monroe says, grabbing Tyler's hand. He blushes. "I need something to distract me and calm my nerves. How long were you guys together?"

"Officially, two and a half years," Matty responds for me. "Unofficially, for twelve years, since they were five and six. We all knew. The tension was ridiculous. We all thought they would get married once Fielder graduated high school."

"Marriage at eighteen feels a bit sus," Monroe says. "But I get the sentiment."

"So Ricky has a new boyfriend? That guy?" Tyler points so brazenly at Cam that I reach for his arm and slam it down.

"Dude, you have no chill," I say.

Monroe snort-laughs.

"I ask 'cause Ricky has been hardcore staring at you," Tyler says.

I want to look for myself, but my head weighs a billion pounds and I won't turn.

A bubbling anxiety in my chest makes me nauseous, and I can't tell if it's nerves, anger, or something more, something I wasn't expecting. Ricky's impersonal postcard plays in the back of my mind like subtitles in a movie. In so few words, he said so much. He hates me. Maybe he's mad I blocked him and went zero communication, but he dumped me. Still, there was never anything passive-aggressive about our friendship-turned-relationship. We were each other's everything, best friend, family, past, present, future. What happened? Did he do that thing that some people do post-breakup to heal and mentally turn their ex into a monster in their mind?

Am I Ricky's monster?

I sit back as Matty continues to talk about me and Ricky's relationship to Monroe and Tyler as if it's some storybook romance, a canon fairy tale with a whole fandom complete with cosplayers and fanfic.

Seeing Ricky now, unexpectedly in such close quarters with a boyfriend on his arms, is jarring, and because even though he hasn't been my boyfriend for over thirteen months, I guess I just assumed Ricky still loved me the way I still loved him because it was embedded in our DNA. It was our history, our future. The poem he wrote in his journal I found the morning he left, hell, everything in that journal, all the love letters to me I was never meant to read but have read over and over again the last thirteen months told me a story that we would find our way back to each another.

Yet here he is, with a boyfriend. While I was cycling through boys like parts on a factory belt in an attempt to avoid dealing with his absence and fill the hole—insert obvious joke here—he left, actually moved on. Maybe that's why he said that in his postcard; he thinks I would cause some sort of scene at Topher and

Sienna's wedding, that I would see Cam and act like a complete psychopath and push him into their tiered wedding cake and light the whole villa on fire or something. Which, fair point.

But no. Ricky is wrong.

My fingers tap the pocket of my shorts where my phone rests.

Tap-tap-tap on the screen.

I go to pull it out, hide behind it, scroll endlessly, get lost in DMs and comments and tweak drafts of whatever content I have set to go live later today, tomorrow, three, four, five, six days from now, anything to distract me from *Ricky, Ricky, Ricky.*

Benny crashes next to Tyler. "What's the game plan?"

"There isn't one now," I deadpan into my screen, responding to a new comment. "He's got a boyfriend. There's nothing to p—" The word gets lodged in my throat.

At once, in an uproarious fashion, Matty and Benny yell at me to fight, and the rest of the plane looks in our direction.

"Incognito mode, guys, really," Monroe says in exasperation, shaking her head. Then she turns to me. "You're giving up? That easy?"

Not looking up, I shrug. "Nothing to give up." I heart a few more comments.

"This defeatist attitude will not win you any heart," Benny says. "You have to be doggedly persistent for the guy you love. My aunt and uncle are selling their house because Sienna is gone and Ricky lives in Seattle now. What if this is your last chance?" His eyes widen. "Ohmygod, the rom-com basically writes itself. Picture it: Italy. Last-chance romance. Star-crossed lovers. Very *My Best Friend's Wedding*. You're Julia Roberts. It's divine intervention! Cosmic design!"

"I don't know that reference, but I'll take your word for it." I'm razor focused on the comment section, particularly drinking in the thirsty comments from guys who post "woof" with heart-eyed emojis. A piss-poor substitute for actual affection, but alas, here we are, trapped in a steel box of emotion with our ex and his new boyfriend over an ocean, so this will do.

"It's a classic," Matty says.

"Of course you know that movie," I say.

"We have a long flight to Naples," Benny says. "We can stream it. Consider it a study session. Win back what's yours."

Monroe waves him away. "Pin in that. Back to reality. You do love him, right?"

Matty plucks my phone from my hands. "Pay attention, dude."

Tyler's eyes widen, shell-shocked.

"Ricky isn't a prize to be won." My hands are shaking. "I love him. Even after he . . . broke me." An echo of the howling ocean breeze from our last night together fills my ears. Everything we were, and could be.

Matty puts his hand on my shoulders. "If you don't want to do this—"

"I do, though." Heady and out of breath, I say, "I have to try." Loving Ricky is all I've ever wanted, and I'm not about to let some temporary boyfriend get in the way of a lifetime of history and the only future I've ever wanted.

Benny is right.

This could be my last chance, and if it is, I can't regret a single moment.

"He's my home. I *have* to get him back."

FROM THE JOURNAL OF RICCARDO DELUCA

"HOME"

When I leave your house, you say,
"Don't be sad, I'll see you tomorrow."
But tomorrow isn't now,
Now is the stretch in between,
the silent waiting,
unbearable weight of having you
and being apart again,
when all I want is to be home
because my home is you.

Every time you leave my house,
though you're right next door,
a piece of you stays here.
I care for it like I do for my own body,
the way I watch your Nonna tend to her garden,
tenderly, from the roots,
clearing out debris so it has room to grow,
so when you return, what you left behind is not just safe
but thriving.

Sometimes I worry,
what will happen to the home
you built for us when I leave.
Tomorrows aren't promises I can keep.
What then? Will you keep it for me?

Is that too much to ask?
Will you live here and find yourself
and wait for me to come home?
That's too much to ask.

You ask me where I go when I'm far away.
I say, "Home, with you."

CHAPTER 6

He Adored Me for Twelve Goddamn Years! Me!

Benny has Matty, Monroe, Tyler, and me hunched around one of the flat screens watching and taking notes on *My Best Friend's Wedding*. I quickly learn that the movie is about Jules, a famous food critic (which Benny swears is divine coincidence given my viral content and further cements the need to watch this as a blueprint for "our" plans), who gets a phone call from her best friend (a very hot dude named Dermot, apparently?) that he's getting married. There's only one problem: she's in love with him. So she flies out to Chicago intent on stopping the wedding and proclaiming her love for her best friend. When her best friend's fiancée asks her to be her maid of honor, she resorts to a whole lot of evil scheming and backstabbing, and eventually at the final brunch the day before the wedding, Jules kisses her bestie and tells him to "pick me, choose me, love me, marry me," but then! Spoiler alert! Dermot sees his fiancée and leaves Jules to chase after her and basically does not choose Jules in the end, which, like, weird choice, right?

Benny even has his iPad out, propped up on a table, with a whiteboard app open. At the top in red digital ink, he scrawls the following:

Operation: Ricky @ Second Glance

"Very funny." My restless leg is acting up. Matty puts his hand on my thigh to calm it, but nothing helps.

"I thought so," Benny says. "Okay, so as we learned from the incomparable rom-com queen herself, Ms. Roberts, we might need to resort to some trickery here."

"But here's the thing, I don't want to scheme. And she doesn't even end up with the guy in the end. So, this doesn't bode well for me." My head knocks against the wall of the plane, feeling the effects of the mimosa.

· Lite Sabotage, Benny suggests as bullet number one.

"Maybe let's look at where Jules went wrong," Monroe adds. "Instead of backstabbing, trying to manipulate Ricky into thinking the worst about Cam, you have to get him to remember what he loved about *you*."

"Which shouldn't be too hard," Matty says with a smile.

"Sure, that sounds super easy and not at all vague," I say.

Benny scribbles:

- *Win over Ricky's family*
- *Get Ricky alone to see if he still has feelings for me*
- *Remind Ricky what he's missing*
- *Show him how much I've grown and changed*

- *Compare/Contrast: Pros of Fielder vs. Cons of Cam*
- *Figure out if Ricky actually loves Cam*
- *Isolate (then eliminate) Cam!*

"How's that?"

"Great. Now all we need is a movie script to follow. Should be easy," I say, completely checked out as everyone else is fully invested and I'm unconvinced that this can work in real life.

Matty looks up and sees the Coven making their way toward us. "Maybe we should table this until we land." He looks to me. Neither of us needs the family to know about this plan, so Matty motions for everyone to be quiet. "I think Fielder is overwhelmed."

Ding-ding-ding.

The rest of the flight is a blur of talking about Ricky, thinking about Ricky, trying not to look at Ricky (and Cam), and wistfully daydreaming about all the ways in which I can flush Cam down the airplane toilet or push him out of the emergency hatch door midflight.

Just kidding.

Though not really.

Monroe and Benny are great distractions, though.

At the airport baggage claim, after spending an hour in a hot line going through customs, Matty, Monroe, Benny, and Tyler create a protective barrier around me, making me the center of attention, laughing loudly, all to make Ricky jealous.

Except he doesn't seem to care. In fact, he looks away!

As the Lemon wedding party makes its way to the Sprinter vans Topher booked for us—the Lemon clan plus Tyler in one, and the other seven, including Monroe and Benny, in the other—Ma makes small talk with Ricky and I want to die. Granted, he was like her second son, but I'm her actual son! I do my best to eavesdrop without getting too close, but I think I catch him saying, "I've missed you, too."

My head throbs, and I'm unsure how to process all this. I need to get to the villa, take a nap, and uncoil to prepare and think—

—about strategy: how to get Ricky alone to see if there's anything still between us, free of any onlookers and airplane pining. If there is, *how* to woo him back in one week surrounded by family and friends amid the backdrop of an Amalfi Coast wedding? See above plan, as concocted by Benny, courtesy of *My Best Friend's Wedding.*

—about what to do *if* Ricky still loves me, but also loves Cam. How do I surgically remove the boyfriend without coming off as the villain in my own book? This whole thing is bound to cause newbie Cam some complicated emotions. (Insert: world's smallest violin here.) At least he's in Italy, right? No need to feel *totally* sorry for the guy.

—about how to survive this next week because (a) I'm about to be in paradise, and want to enjoy it as best I can *and* be there for my cousin, and (b) because there's a good chance Ricky will reject me, again, especially if I don't go about this the right way, which is quite possibly the worst feeling in the world, and I know what you're thinking—why don't I let this go, ignore Ricky altogether, and enjoy the wedding? And to that, I say absolutely not. I have no chill. I'm a mess, I realize this.

So, no. It's not as easy as "just talk to him and solve all my problems" because the fact of the matter is that I haven't seen or spoken to Ricky in over thirteen months, and as much as I've changed, I bet he's changed, too. Though I've known him practically my entire life, I probably don't know him at all anymore.

The words to Ricky's poem "Home" rattle in my brain, and I can't help but think it was a plea for me to wait for him. In the months after he left, as I read through his journal over and over again, I guessed by the placement of that poem before "Clarity" that he must have written it after he learned he got the mentorship and would be leaving New York for Seattle, but before he decided to end our relationship.

Call me delusional, but it was something I held on to, a little bit of hope. A clue that let me know he would come back to me one day.

Because despite Cam, Ricky adored me for twelve goddamn years!

Not Cam. *Me!*

Cam's known Ricky for, like, five seconds.

And this might be the jetlag or Benny's insistence that I'm Julia Roberts talking, but I don't feel sorry for anything that's about to happen.

MONDAY

CHAPTER 7

I've Got Exactly One Week to Use This Wedding to Win Back the Bride's Man of Honor and I Haven't One Clue How to Do It

The drive from Naples to Amalfi is among the most harrowing experiences of my life. Strada Statale Amalfitana, the two-way single-lane "highway" carved into lush green mountains lining the Amalfi Coast connecting Sorrento to Salerno is about as wide as an American sidewalk. The road is cut into steep cliffs a few hundred feet over the Tyrrhenian Sea. Its turquoise waters lap against a cloudless cerulean sky in a stunning, breathtaking panoramic view. I take out my phone and film some segments for the "Destination: Amalfi" video I started filming when I got on the PJ in New York.

Endless expanse of blue waters dotted with white sailboats and yachts. Mountainside gardens with flowers of pink and white and yellow nestled into the rock as if they've always been there, like altars to the nature gods. It's as if we found a majestic road to the heavens with towering bluffs and pastel villages built into the hillsides. Roadside fruit stands with the brightest oranges, biggest lemons, garlands of dried red chili peppers, plump vine clusters of grapes, baskets of ripened pomegranates, and the most mouthwatering cherry tomatoes that look like fake berries because they're so red and juicy. When the van stops from a traffic standstill, I dash out quickly for the tomatoes, recording the entire interaction.

"Oh, hell," Matty groans.

"What the hell is this crazy sonovabitch doing?" Nonna yells after me.

Matty shouts, "He's living his European girl vacation fantasy."

Drool escapes the corners of my lips as I reach for a vine of tomatoes. I spent the past few weeks brushing up on my Italian—thank you, Duolingo and Nonna, so it comes quickly: "Quanto costa?"

An older woman who looks a lot like Nonna, graying hair pulled back into a tight bun and wearing a deeply beige sundress, says, "Tre euro."

The horn honks, and the fruit stand worker points behind me. The whole family is screaming at me as I reach into my pocket and pull out three one-euro coins that I got from the airport in Naples and turn on my heels to dash back to the van.

The driver is cursing in Italian, throwing his hands in the air, but I don't care. I hand my phone to Matty to keep recording as I rip the first tomato off the vine with my teeth.

Bright and sweet and beautifully acidic, the tomato pops in my mouth, seeds bursting on my tongue. "Madonna Mia!"

"Dammi," Nonna demands, and I hand the vine to her. After partaking, she passes it on until everyone in the van has tasted the fruit.

It doesn't take long before the winding, perilous drive brings acid to my throat and burns. It's easily the most anxiety-inducing ride of my life. Cars zip around hairpin turns at alarming speeds as our driver hugs the very edge of the bluffs. But it's not just the cars—it's the buses, massive tourist caravans maneuvering the turns like they're race cars that legit take my breath away. Like, sucking my soul straight out of my body. The road bends, zigging and zagging so often I have to shut my eyes or I'll throw up. Nonna shouts for the driver to "watch out," and Ma keeps yelling for her to shut her eyes until we get to the villa, but apparently we have to weave through the highly dense Positano to get to Praiano, where the traffic won't be as harrowing, and then head through Conca dei Marini until we reach the town of Amalfi.

With how this driver bobs and weaves and nearly sideswipes every jalopy on the road, I'm certain none of us are making it out alive.

"Dude, you look green," Matty says.

I press my finger hard to his lips. "Shut up." I swallow acid.

"Close your eyes, go to sleep," Ma commands.

I do as told partially because I fear Ma's wrath, but it's also the only way I won't succumb to carsickness. I can't fall out of the van and straight into Ricky and Cam covered in my own puke, right?

Right. My resolve to look as cute and unbothered as possible is stronger than any of the ancient stone buildings we pass as we carve through Positano, the car braking and accelerating, braking and accelerating, braking and accelerating, without warning until the car stops near piers in Amalfi that stretch out like arms into the Tyrrhenian Sea and I burst out of the car and puke up my lunch.

Right in front of Ricky and Cam.

Kill me now.

For a moment, Ricky looks like he might feign concern, but Cam lurches and turns away from the gross scene and Ricky turns to comfort him. *Not* me.

Once my green skin turns back to normal and everyone stops fussing over me and force-feeding me water, we have to drag our luggage into the thick of the town, across the cobblestones of Via Lorenzo D'Amalfi to the Piazza del Duomo, right in front of a cathedral wedged in between shops and cafés. The steps lead up to the striking sanctuary of black-and-white alternating marble, adorned with golden cross-work tiles that make the building itself look like a three-dimensional mosaic, setting it apart from the soft pinks and peaches of the stone buildings surrounding it.

Topher's explicit instructions: wait for a man named Vincenze, a hairy ape of a middle-aged man with thick dark sunglasses and a beard leading a troop of golf carts to pick us up a few at a time and take us through the city and up into the mountains, past endless lemon groves toward the villa. The carts bounce and zip up the winding streets, which narrow the farther we get from the bustling Piazza. I record more content for my channel, making sure to capture the carts behind and in front of mine and Matty's. The air smells of crisp citrus, fresh salt water, and, oddly enough, old library books. As the road turns from cobblestone to cement to dirt and rubble, I feel like I'm in a horse-drawn carriage.

It makes me want to put my phone away and just *be*. To not worry and *breathe*.

But I don't because this is great content for the channel and I have to capture it.

The road winds farther from civilization up a mountain through dense trees; it seems we left the town entirely until the shaky-ass carts seemingly weave us back toward the sea and down the mountainside again. The constant change in elevation is messing with my head.

We reach a plateau in the dirt road. Sun bursts through the canopy, and the sound of crashing waves in the distance is carried on the breeze. It's like we've entered Narnia, or the Shire, or a travel influencer's Clock channel. Except no amount of editing and tropical filters or CGI enhancements could do this place justice.

Nestled in the rolling hills, atop vertical rock cliffs that cascade down to the sea, sits the private villa. Lemons the size of small cantaloupes drip like dewdrops from low-hanging trees lining the river rock and painted terracotta paver entryway. Large black iron gates with swirling lemons dipped in gold swing open to Villa Limone Regale (appropriately named, huh? Well done, Topher!). It's, well, exactly as its namesake suggests: fit for a king, queen, or nonbinary royal.

Its expansive white stone exterior is enrobed in ivy, giving it the appearance of being part of the mountains it's built into, and the driver of our golf cart explains to us how the villa is multi-floored, but what we see on the ground is the top level—every other floor descends into the cliffs closer toward the sea. The guide suggests we spend time exploring the property once we settle in, to meander through the orange and lemon tree groves and to get lost on the private passage down to the shoreline and wade in the cerulean waters. Find the expansive infinity pool carved into the rocks that appears to spill directly into the Tyrrhenian, but instead has a waterfall that cascades over a cavern below into a smaller pool designed to look like one of the famous Amalfi Coast grottos. My mind wanders to Ricky, shirtless, next to me in the cave, hidden from view as the sound of crashing water drowns out everything. A picturesque sunset in the distance as his hands wander across my thigh—

The golf cart stops short, and we jerk forward.

"Thank god we're here," Matty says, voice shaky. I look over, and his skin is a pale green. "I need a nap. You okay?"

Before I can answer, the oversized white arch doors push open and white curtains billow in the wind in slow motion like a freaking movie, revealing Topher and Sienna dressed head to toe in chic white linen, both wearing tortoise sunglasses, a lit cigar dangling between Topher's lips as the wind blows back the curls on the top of his head.

Topher always did like an entrance.

He's unshaven, but it's not sloppy, it's meticulous. Planned chaos. Beauty in mess. In the days since he announced his engagement, he's been taking to his own social media for a hard debut of his impending nuptials with Sienna, who always looks airbrushed to within an inch of her life, which she's not and I'm here to attest—she's model-hot. Long honey-blond hair in blown-out waves, pore-free skin with makeup meant to look natural. Like she just got out of bed. If her bed was a red carpet. I haven't seen her since Ricky's graduation party before we went off to the Hamptons and he annihilated my soul, and though she hasn't fundamentally changed, she's always been stunning; she's discovered the power of Topher's money in labels and traveling glam squads.

It's unfair how attractive they are together, the perfect image of curated hotness.

Yet all I can do is look at Ricky, who beams when he sees his sister, cherub cheeked and waving with a champagne flute in her perfectly manicured hand.

In a split second, Ricky turns, and I try to look away, but it's too late. He's caught me staring.

In a bout of perfect timing, Topher descends upon me, scooping both me and Matty into a brotherly hug. "My guys, let's goooooo!" I'd forgotten how strong he was, his grip nearly choking me. But it's enough to ground me after nearly an entire twenty-four hours of constant-turned-perilous travel.

"My own son doesn't even hug me first!" Zia Gab growls. Legit. Then she pouts, crossing her arms and huffing. If there's one thing the women in this family know how to do, it's cast their witchy guilt magic. Within seconds, it spreads over all the lands, covering us in a dark cloud of glares.

Topher laughs, rich and hearty. "Love you, Ma!"

She eyes him, but immediately breaks her spell and practically leaps into his arms.

Topher signals for me to come close. "Listen, dude, I swear I didn't know until yesterday Ricky was bringing someone." He prattles on about how Sienna wanted to save Ricky the money by him flying back to New York for the free PJ, but I'm not really listening.

"A boyfriend," I correct, and he winces. "Dude, it's fine. I'm chill."

"Since when do you say 'dude'? You've been hanging around Matty too much?" Topher asks, pulling me in for another hug.

"Hello?" Zia Rosa yells. "Are we chopped liver or something?"

"Yeah, get out of the way," Ma commands. "I need to hug my nephew!"

"Eh!" Nonna yells, and the crowds part like she's Moses and we're the Red Sea. She waddles over, and he instinctively bends down to meet her five-foot-two frame. He may be over six feet, but her demeanor towers over all of us. She grabs and holds his chin steady with both hands. "Let me get a good look at you, mio regazzo! So big." She kisses each of his cheeks. "That flight nearly killed me. You're lucky I love you." Then, without warning, she shoves his face to the side, and peers around him for Sienna, who is flanked by Ricky, Cam, Monroe, Benny, and Jenni Lee. She coughs and everyone stops talking.

"Mi amore." Topher reaches out to Sienna, who gracefully moves toward us.

Sienna kisses the ring of the Lemon Coven Supreme. "Hi, Nonna! It's so nice to see you; it's been so long!"

"You've grown up too! I feel so old," Nonna says, right before grabbing Sienna's face and pulling her forward for an invasively wet kiss on either cheek. In one swift move, Nonna wedges herself between her and Topher. "Show me around; I've been cooped up with all these chickens for too long. I need to stretch my legs."

I don't bother to stifle my yawns. Matty elbows me.

Topher laughs. "Rough travel on the PJ? Why don't you guys

get settled in your suite—you two are sharing. I figured you guys don't want to be with the Coven." Topher tries to whisper, but Zia Rosa and Ma both hiss. "I got *them* in a three-room suite on the other side of the villa."

"They're gonna kill each other," I say.

"Welcome to the circus. You guys are down a level, with your own hot tub and hammock." Topher motions Vincenze, who moves to grab our luggage. "Per favore, portali nella loro stanza?" He turns his attention back to us. "Sienna's parents are hosting dinner tonight in the main dining room in, like, two hours."

It makes me slightly uncomfortable that ~~Ricky's~~ Sienna's parents are hosting. I also feel awkward seeing them—I shouldn't, they were practically my second mom and dad growing up, but it felt like I lost them when I lost Ricky. I just hope I'm not stuck sitting across from Ricky and Cam looking all perfect and in love.

"You guys are ripe. Go shower and relax," Topher finishes. "After dinner, we'll have all the time in the world to catch up. I've missed you guys."

"It's nice to see you again, little brother," Sienna says to me. Growing up, since Ricky and I spent nearly all our time together, Sienna was the big sister I never had, and though we lost touch, seeing her does feel like seeing family. "Topher told me you were *still* having a hard time with the breakup."

Still? Though it's a good reminder that she's Ricky's sister. Her loyalty is to him, despite the empathy in her tone. She grabs my arm gingerly, like I'm a porcelain doll that might break.

I plaster a fake smile on my face. I'm not about to ruin her wedding by telling her how I feel about seeing Ricky with Cam, or divulge my evil plan to break them up.

"Me, I'm great! Honestly thriving. Never been better." Okay, Field, you're laying it on thick. Reel it in. "Best year of my life."

Her pupils expand as she narrows her eyes. "It *has* been great seeing you thrive on Clock. Your content is so fun and funny. You're so good. You could totally host a TV show, I tell Topher all the time!"

Cam and Ricky are watching, so I hook my arm into Sienna's. "Thanks so much, sis. I've missed you. It's been so long; we have *so* much to catch up on!"

"Yes, please!" she squeals, and we start filling each other in like no time had passed at all. I watch as Cam tries not to look fazed, hooking his arm on to Ricky and talking with Ricky's mom, which, won't lie, makes my side pang with jealousy. "Oh! I have a big favor to ask of you for tomorrow."

I can't help but smirk because she says it so loud Cam turns.

Operation: Ricky @ Second Glance commences *now.*

First stop—winning over the family. Check!

Your move, Cam.

🍋

The courtyard in the center of the main villa is full of lush, manicured grass and cobblestones dotted with hammocks and lounge chairs. Grand staircases wind down stone walls to new levels, and the pool.

Matty and I follow Vincenze away from the pool and around a bend toward a private entrance. Outside is a hot tub beneath a lemon tree and, inside, our room. I exhale the second we step into our bright white, airy room. It's nothing special—standard room with two double beds and a standing shower, very minimal. There's a large double picture window that's currently open on both sides, letting the warm breeze in. I move to close it, hoping to cool down the space. The sun beams directly inside.

"Sorry, but there's no air-conditioning in this room," Vincenze says, carefully choosing his words. His accent is thick, but his pronunciation is impeccable. "If you leave it open, it will cool down at night. There's acqua and Coca-Cola in the fridge. Formaggio. Vino from a local vigneto in Ravello. If you desire, I can make espresso or cappuccino."

"Oh god, yes, I would love a cappuccino," I say. "Get rid of this headache. Do you have soy milk?"

Matty laughs.

"Sì. Soia."

"Wow," Matty says. "This ain't half bad. I'll take one, too. No soy for me; I'm not difficult like my cousin here. Thanks, Vincenze."

Vincenze nods and backs out of the room.

I immediately swan dive onto one of the beds and shimmy my phone out of my pocket. Given the time difference, it's been too long since I've posted anything to my Clock feed, and though I have filmed content scheduled over the next week, I want to pepper my channel with documentations of my trip, starting with everything I got on the journey here. I did my best to edit in the Sprinter van, but I got sick. All I need is a hot sound and *boom*.

Post.

Done.

"How you feeling?" Matty's voice is froggy from airplane exhaustion.

"Great. This post is fire."

"Nope, about Ricky."

I bury my face into the comforter. "Ask me in three to five business days."

"You're pulling it off well," Matty says. "If it's any consolation. Wanna talk about the Cam of it all, now that we're alone?"

"What's there to talk about? That the love of my life is here in the most romantic place in the entire world with another guy?! I—" I stop because I might break down. My emotions are a tangle of bedsheets, and I'm trapped inside. "Is it ridiculous? Naïve? To think I can win him back with some evil plot?"

"Probably." I appreciate the honesty as Matty laughs. "But you two belong together. If what you really want is another chance with Ricky, I'll help you get him back."

"I'm not wildly unhinged?"

"Never said *that*. But as your best friend, I'll run interference with Cam, help you get alone time with Ricky. Run reconnaissance. I got your back. Just . . . have a plan."

A grin stretches over my lips as he closes the door to our suite, and I clasp my hands together like a villain, remembering some of what Sienna told me quickly about the details of the next few days before Matty and I came down to our room. If I learned anything from *My Best Friend's Wedding*, it's that it's crucial to take any opportunity to isolate the object of my affection—Ricky—from his love interest—Cam—while also doing everything in my power to come off as the best version of myself to Ricky's family.

Glancing at my phone, I see my latest Clock is 99 percent loaded. "I have an idea."

@LemonAtFirstSight ✔ 53 min ago

Views: 7889k

❤ 462

CAPTION: In the most romantic place on earth. What could go wrong?

AUDIO TRANSCRIPT: Amalfi is lit, and so am I! Can't wait to show you some local spots, so stay tuned; I have a lot of great Italia content coming, and as always, when life hands you Lemons, take a bite!

109 COMMENTS

Grouchy.1505

Is that Ricky in the background on the plane? Omg are you guys back together?

VIEW 7 REPLIES

Lemonstan007

that's absolutely ricky. we missed you ricky!

Joey_Italiano

omg how could I miss that? damn, ricky glowed up. zaddy!

Grouchy.1505

RIGHT? And that caption about being in the most romantic place? With Ricky? Seems like life handed Ricky a Lemon . . .

amithedrama

Word on the street is Ricky and Lemon hate each other.

Grouchy.1505

@amithedrama Lol you don't know them troll

amithedrama

K lol. My friend went to school with Ricky and Lemon and he said they don't speak. Ricky moved cross the country and Lemon sleeps with anything that moves. I have receipts.

Joey_Italiano

@amithedrama u don't know shit. i hope they got back together. they were goals.

CHAPTER 8

I Should Have Stopped in All My Evil Plotting to Have That Manicure, But It's Too Late Now!

The neon-orange sun is disappearing behind the cliffs, casting the Amalfi mountains in gold. The fading blue sky is streaked with purples and pinks, like a magical moving watercolor painting splashed across the walls of the villa, a perfect backdrop as Matty douses me in cologne until I can't breathe. He flicks the top three buttons open on my shirt, exposing my collarbone and my few chest hairs.

"How do I look?"

"Like you're about to bottom." Matty cheeses.

"If all goes to plan!"

"You—" He narrows his eyes devilishly, pinches his fingers, and gestures at me.

We mull over the plan for tonight and cross-reference with Operation: Ricky @ Second Glance. Part one consists of a casual family run-in in the villa's luxurious kitchen. Ricky's mom, Bianca, can't resist being in the fray, so I'll bet anything she'll be in the kitchen, noseying around the executive chef. Perfect opportunity to apply the charm.

Then, standard family gatherings with the Lemon Coven tend to stretch into the wee hours of the morning, especially factoring in wine, limoncello, a couple decks of playing cards Nonna the gambler stashes in her purse. We'll use this and the time difference to our advantage. To not rope in Topher or Sienna and keep them drama free, Matty will enlist Monroe and Benny, both of whom have the uncanny ability to talk nonstop about anything, to separate Ricky and Cam. If they can loop Cam into a conversation and lure him away from the party, Matty will swoop down on Ricky and ask if they can have a best man to man of honor one-on-one using a "surprise" for Topher and Sienna as a ruse. As all this is going on, I'll casually excuse myself and make my way down to the pool area, which will already be lit with fairy lights thanks to the impeccable décor choices of our villa hosts. Matty and Ricky will stumble upon me, and Matty will act all surprised that I'm there, but that'll be the moment I finally get to talk to Ricky. Everything else will melt away, except for us.

A happenchance rendezvous beneath the stars? What could be more romantic, right? *Fuhgettaboutit.* I can see the stitched reaction videos now . . .

He'll get all flustered because he knows deep, deep, deep down he loves me, not Cam, and then we'll laugh about how silly the emotional distance between us is, and Italy will imbue us with all the magic we need to have a super-charged moment that is sure to reignite his feelings for me, leaving Cam in the dust.

"Are we bad people?" I plop down on the bed.

"Nah. Just horny and in love." He palms his chest and pointedly says, "Horny," then moves the same palm to my chest. "In love. And love conquers all. Especially doe-eyed nerdy new boyfriends who can't hold a candle to history."

"You gotta stop watching old Disney movies and listening to Benny." I pick at my cuticles, ripping off a rogue slice of skin. Blood pools in the crevices of my nail bed. I really should have gotten a manicure before the trip.

"And *you* gotta stop giving off bottom energy. Channel top energy tonight. Ricky is going to take notice of just how much you've changed, and what he's missing."

Have I really *changed?*

"(A) that is heterosexist and slightly homophobic," I start, which Matty appreciates because he's working on his internalized homophobia and likes being called out when he uses stereotypes. "(B) Ricky and I were both vers, but that's beside the point. (C) Ricky does give off dom energy, huh?" A slow realization pushes me to the edge of the bed. "He said the night of the Great Commencement Massacre that he felt like he needed to take care of me. Maybe I need to show him that I can take care of him, too." I hold out a shaky hand. Now the blood drips onto the floor. Matty bolts to the bathroom to grab me a washcloth to blot and wrap my finger. Then he shoves Ricky's journal in my face and turns to a page he'd dutifully earmarked for me. Written on opposing pages are two poems close enough in proximity that they *obviously* mean something when read together:

FROM THE JOURNAL OF RICCARDO DELUCA

"THE WOODWORKER AND THE DREAMER"

Holding him is like carving wood,
raw beauty untapped
as I shape our present with precision,
callused pads and chisels,
hand saws and carving knives,
he dreams of a future
wild and untethered, a digital fairy tale
from a single childhood promise
where creation is limited by edges,
infinite for a woodworker, and his dreamer

Adorable, right? Swoon-worthy, even. But this untitled poem is on the next page:

If love is a tree
who planted its seed?
Each branch an extension of us,
wild and twisting, fortified by years,
each leaf a memory,
verdant, thick, and full.
What happens when the last one falls?
are we still rooted?
Were our seedings too young—
two seeds planted to split,
in nutrient-rich soil.

Trees don't survive deforestation—
buds bloom again?

The question mark at the end is erased, but I can still see it.

"Remember what Nonna used to tell us every spring when she would plant her garden?" Matty says as he grabs my still-shaky, mummified hand, and I remember how Nonna would sit Topher, Matty, and me down and try to get us to help and listen as she methodically taught us about the resiliency of seeds. "She would say, 'Seeds may seem fragile and small, delicate, but they have a hard shell that protects them. They are built to survive. And when they're in the right conditions, that hard shell breaks open, and something beautiful grows.' You're a seed, Fielder. You just gotta bloom. Make yourself undeniable."

How do I do that?

I pull the washcloth off, and the ring slides with it. Dark red liquid coats the exterior now. I curse and furiously polish the ring.

"Field, it's fine. Just run it under water—"

"No!" I hop to my feet and dash to the bathroom, dab a clean end of the washcloth under the faucet, and wipe the ring clean. When I'm sure it's free of blood, a sigh of relief escapes my lungs so strong I nearly collapse into the vanity.

"What's the big deal? It's just a ring," Matty asks from the doorway.

"It's not just a ring. Do you remember after Ricky and I got together, and we spent New Year's with Topher in LA?"

"How could I forget that wild house party? I got so wasted," Matty says. "Our moms would kill Topher if they knew. We were way too young."

I laugh. "That was my first time with Ricky. *Our* first time."

His eyes bug. "Oh. You never told me *that*!"

"You weren't out yet, and it felt weird telling you that part, and anyway, that's not the point. After, he looked at me and said, 'Promise me we'll always be together?' He pulled a ring off his finger and slipped it onto my thumb." He had thick fingers, so it only fit my thumb.

"Zaddy." Matty's line of sight goes straight to the ring. "A little piece of Ricky and Fielder canon."

"Ricky made it, carved it in his nonno's workshop the summer before freshman year, before we got together." It's exquisite, too—not only did he make a ring out of freaking oak, but he also fit it into a mold with tiny tigereye gemstones and used resin to bond the materials, and then buffed it so it's super shiny. It's gotten a bit dull over the last three and a half years, because I rarely take it off. Except on the plane.

"Naïve, huh? *Always* didn't even last high school." I lower my voice. "What am I doing?"

"Finally confronting the reality of your breakup?"

"Which is?"

"That you've spent the last year doing everything you could to prove to Ricky that you're good enough for him. Everything has been for him. Built up your Clock channel to prove him wrong. Went to the gym to make him drool when you finally saw him." He pauses. "What about *you*? What's been *for you*?"

"When you put it like that, I sound pathetic." Have I been stunting my own growth this entire year, molding myself into the kind of person Ricky wanted rather than the kind of person I want to be, for myself?

"No, I didn't mean it like that."

I put the ring back on my thumb. "I don't want to move backward."

All the thoughts swirling inside my brain get tangled. I wish, for once, something in my life would make sense. Out of everything I've endured—Dad's death, having to work away my high school years in restaurants and not getting to be a regular kid because I was worried about Ma's bills, breaking the news to Ma, Nonna, and the rest of the very judgmental Coven that college wasn't for me, living in Topher's very successful shadow—Ricky abandoning me has proven the most impossible season to weather.

Maybe it's because I'm a seed that can't bloom without the right conditions—and the right conditions are Ricky DeLuca.

I owe it to myself to see if there's anything left of *us*, the dreamer and the woodworker. He said it himself in his poem: *our* "buds bloom again." No question mark.

Once my hand is cleaned up and we're ready to go, notifications start to roll in on my latest Clock video, and my heart drops.

All the comments are about Ricky.

How much they love him, and speculating about *us* in some way.

My followers are *eating.* It. Up.

Likes roll in faster than I can keep up with. One user in particular, @AmITheDrama, has been a constant commenter for months now, but has gotten more and more negative and gossip hungry over time as they've gone back and watched old content. I constantly get notifications from Clock videos I posted years ago. I often wonder who's behind accounts like that.

Ignoring Matty, I scroll through at double speed for answers. And there he is. Ricky. On the PJ in the background. In the airport. Behind me as I shot selfie footage in front of the Piazza del Duomo in Amalfi. Staring *at* me. How did I *not* notice? A burst of hope warms my chest. Maybe I do have a shot.

"Earth to Fielder. Topher's welcome dinner."

I grip tight to Ricky's ring. The universe is telling me I'm moving in the right direction. Toward Ricky. Seeds planted. All that's left is to follow through.

If I can be patient and confident (two things I've never been), Cam will be toast. *Should be* ~~the hardest thing I've ever done, holy shit I'm sweating through my shirt, is it too late to bail?~~ *easy*!

CHAPTER 9

Say a Little Prayer: Nel nome del Padre, e del Figlio, e dello Spirito Santo, Amen!

I'm easily distracted by shiny objects.

So when I stumble upon a glittery box outside the kitchen with stacks of rose-gold-ribboned scrolls addressed to everyone at the villa, I'm *obviously* going to snoop.

For research purposes only.

Finding my name, I unfurl it, and a stack of thick embossed tickets and euros fall out and onto the floor. Matty scrambles to scoop them up quickly before we're caught, mumbling curses in Italian at my feet.

FIELDER LEMON ITINERARY

Monday –

Arrival to Villa Limone Regale

Welcome Dinner

Tuesday –
Appointment at Massimo Andreozzi (Tailor for Wedding)
Amalfi Lemon Groves Tour + Lunch

Wednesday –
Free Day!

Thursday –
Yacht Excursion around the Amalfi Coast

Friday –
Rehearsal
Rehearsal Dinner at La Sponda in Positano

Saturday –
Lemon-DeLuca Wedding!
Pictures Start at 10:30 AM
Ceremony at 1 PM
Cocktail Hour 2 PM –3 PM
Dinner at 4 PM
Party All Night!

Sunday –
Relax at the Villa

Monday –
Fly back to the States!

Sienna always was extremely detail-oriented. Each one is a list of activities for the next four days leading up to the wedding, including what looks like important tickets.

I cross-reference. Because Ricky and me are man of honor

and best man, respectively, we're scheduled to do a lot of the same activities. Which would be the perfect opportunity to get him to fall back in love with me, except Cam is scheduled for all the same activities, too.

Matty hands me the stack of tickets and euros, and I sift through them like Pokémon cards: lemon farm tour, yacht excursion, a bunch of vouchers for meals, snacks, and drinks at local vendors and restaurants between Amalfi and Positano that Topher and Sienna prepaid. I'm getting the idea that most of the places around here are more old school than back home in the States, which could actually work in my favor.

What if something were to happen to something *on Cam's itinerary?*

"Fielder, no," Matty says with a wily grin.

"I can't, right?"

"Nobody would know," Matty argues.

"Dude, you're supposed to talk me out of this."

"Who said that?" Matty scratches the top of his head. "I won't say anything. See no evil, hear no evil, speak no evil." He turns his back toward me, but, with his elbow, pushes the glittery box toward me.

Leaving mine undone in a pile to the side, I rummage through until I find Cam's.

Unraveling Cam's scroll, I fumble with the stack of Cam's tickets and euros, trying to decide what to do. My heart beats so loud and fast it drowns out every other noise in the villa, and I barely register Matty telling me someone is coming.

I grab the ticket to the lemon grove tour because quite frankly that sounds the most romantic, and Ricky is more a farm guy than a boat guy. It wouldn't be the worst thing in the world if Cam's ticket just so happens to be lost, right?

"Field, hurry," Matty whispers frantically as I shove Cam's stolen ticket into my pants and quickly roll everything else back up into the correct order, tie up the rose-gold ribbon, and get it back in the box.

A woman in a chef's coat with jet-black hair tied back into a tight bun slides beside me. "Che cosa?! Scusi, the others are in the main dining room." Her accent is thick, on the edge of business and pleasure. Her expression is stony, her glance making my back straighten. With one swift word, she could probably have me executed on the spot.

"Hi, sorry—" I take my scroll and quickly place it back into the box. "I'm—"

"Fielder!" Bianca, Ricky's mom, shouts from behind the chef. "Chef Vittoria, these boys are Topher's cousins, Fielder and Matty."

Matty cheeses hard, which usually works on anyone of any gender. But for Chef Vittoria, no dice. She's glaring. Hard.

I don't know if it's from the gentle crime I just committed, the ticket burning a hole in my pocket, or seeing Ricky's mom properly for the first time in over a year, but my nerves are shot and it takes all of me not to cry.

Bianca maneuvers past Chef Vittoria with ease, gives Matty a quick hug, then turns toward me, her eyes wet. "Fielder." She nods, acknowledging everything that can't possibly be said. "We've missed you, son."

I want to tell her I've missed her too, and I even open my mouth to say the words, but nothing squeaks out. It's like I've lost the power of speech.

She pulls me into a hug. "I know, but we're so happy you're here."

I nod because I can't say anything else. I close my eyes and allow myself to give in to the hug because it feels like Ricky is hugging me.

Don't cry, damnit.

When she pulls back, a little mascara is trickling down her cheeks. "I just did my makeup." She lets out a boisterous laugh that fills the room. "So much for waterproof."

"Is all bad," Chef Vittoria chimes in before tossing Bianca a makeup bag. "In my line of work, you find the good stuff."

Matty and I follow them back into the kitchen, and I'm hit with the incredible smells wafting from the oven and stovetop.

"So tell me," Bianca says as she tends to her face. "What have you been up to? Your mom told me you've been making some really good money from Clock."

She did? I clear my throat. "I'm a food blogger with over a million followers. And I'm verified." As if this matters to her. "I like to think I have a good palate. I love food. I'm a foodie!" *Cringe.* "Only thing I'm good at, is critiquing food." I *need* to stop rambling. I nod toward the massive, covered pot on the stovetop. "Zuppa di pesce?"

"Zuppa di moscardini." Chef Vittoria grabs the lid, and my cheeks heat in embarrassment.

Matty starts filming, though I'm not sure that's a good move.

Bianca looks on, intrigued.

Before opening the pot, the chef says, "Tell me, food blogger, what do you smell?"

"Garlic, for sure. Roasted tomatoes. The tang in the air—red wine."

Her expression doesn't soften, exactly, but she removes the lid. "Dai!" She motions for me to move in closer before snapping her fingers for her sous chef, who instinctively hands her a bowl and a ladle. With one swift stir, she scoops a small amount of the liquid into the bowl. "Mangia."

The liquid in the bowl is deep red—it's not watery, but it's not thick, either. One baby octopus tentacle, almost purple from the wine, peeks out from the surface. She hands me a spoon.

I go straight for the tentacle; it's so tender it cuts like butter.

"Va bene, eh?" she asks, kissing the air.

"Molto bene!" I say into the camera on Matty's phone. "The key to a perfect zuppa di moscardini is to do a quick sear on the octopus, then simmer until it's tender, like this, so it soaks up all that flavor from the broth." I sip from the mouth of the spoon, making sure to get the velvety broth with the meat. "So many layers! The vegetables are so fresh, the octopus so velvety. That rich umami. The garlic, the warmth of . . . chili?"

"Sì, you do have quite a palate." A smirk twitches at the corner of her mouth.

"This is beyond." My eyes roll in the back of my head. "This dinner is going to be bananas, Chef Vittoria." Matty zooms in on her embroidered jacket.

"Grazie," she says.

"Prego," I say. "Do you mind if I come back one night this week and film you cooking, try your food on camera? I could give you some really great exposure. Blow you up. You could become huge!"

You ever regret something *as* the words are coming out of your mouth?

"*You* could give *me*?" Chef Vittoria slams the lid down on the pot. "Disgraziato." Her hands fly up into the air in my direction. "I don't need your followers. Not every chef is looking to make a fool of themselves online for likes. I don't cook for billions of people; I cook with *love*. For art. This is my life. I'm not some kid looking to have fun on vacation. You come into my kitchen and make a mockery of me?"

Matty's hands fall to his side.

My balls shoot so far up inside my body I might as well cease to exist.

"I'm sorry, I didn't mean—" I start.

"Delete that video," Chef Vittoria says. "Leave my kitchen, per favore?"

I nod, grab Matty, and we exit quickly, me keeping my head down.

The last thing I hear is Bianca's voice saying, "Sorry about that. He means well, but he's a bit much sometimes—"

Chef Vittoria cuts her off and mutters something in Italian, and I yank Matty harder so that we can get away faster. I don't want to hear any more.

So much for winning over Ricky's family.

Lanterns drip from the ceiling of the main dining room overlooking the Tyrrhenian Sea. Stone arches frame the room on nearly all sides, ivy lining the walls and ceiling, making it look like an undiscovered paradise embedded with magic. One long wooden dining table sits in the center of the room, adorned with exquisite white china with delicate rose-gold trim, amber glass vases with pale pink flowers, and terracotta bowls of lemons and grapes. Long glass bottles of bright yellow limoncello and carafes of burgundy-red wine are scattered throughout. It smells of citrus and salt water and freshly cut grass, with a tang of blistered tomatoes and my flesh after Chef Vittoria charred me alive.

Matty and I are last to arrive because I had to lick my wounds in the bathroom and delete the footage. Matty asks how I'm doing, and between me seeing Bianca and getting eviscerated by a talented chef in front of her, my nerves are frazzled.

All sixteen people including Topher and Sienna are deep in conversation, and between the Lemons and the DeLucas, two loud-ass Italian families, the voices carry like sirens over the quiet night air.

Topher, at the head of the massive table next to Sienna, jumps to his feet and booms, "My boys! Now it's a party!"

Normally I don't mind being the center of attention—in my family, it's eat or be eaten—but all I can see is Ricky's face staring directly at mine like he's the only one at the table. Or in the room. Or in the entire damn country. I wonder if Bianca told him what happened in the kitchen already. My cheeks heat.

Ricky's eyes are soft? Maybe it's the reflection of the lanterns over him, but a flash of memories take hold. Us at a local carnival last spring. Recorded footage of us taste-testing crispy, sugary funnel cakes and fried Oreos, juicy sweet-and-hot sausage and pepper wedges dripping with tomato sauce, and root beer floats. Ricky playfully smashing my nose into the whipped cream, laughing hysterically as the lens zooms in on my shocked face. The way he licked it off my nose and kissed me, grabbed a handful of napkins and wiped it off for me while apologizing. I remember looking into the camera of my phone and saying, "This is true love." I went to dump a tray of Mexican street corn on him, but stopped, which caught him off guard because he fully expected retaliation. Instead, I kissed his cheek, and the way his face softened still takes my breath away.

Not that I rewatch that video. Because I super don't.

But I still get comments on it, and it has sixteen million views!

Ricky's face now reminds me of him being surprised by his own surprise.

Riccardo Sr., Ricky's father, stands and offers me a head nod. It might not seem like much, but he was always a man of few words, like Ricky, so the acknowledgment and respect—big in any Italian family—is all I could have asked for.

I spot my name on a placard. Two of the villa staff pull out chairs for me and Matty, far enough away from Ricky that I don't have to interact with him, but close enough to where I can't help but glance over at him.

I stifle a laugh when I notice Zia Gab managed a seat next to Topher. I bet any amount of money she moved around the name cards since it seems like their college friends are seated closest to them, while family is on the other end. Matty notices too, and we share a wide-eyed gaze. Typical Zia Gab move.

Sienna stands with her champagne flute and a rose-gold knife. She delicately taps the glass. "I want to thank everyone for being here. We're so lucky we get to have our families here to celebrate our love. We're all family now." It's amazing how much she looks like Ricky with her facial expressions.

Then Topher launches to his tiptoes. "I'm sure a lot of you were a little taken aback when you found out we were together." He grabs Sienna's hand. "But we wanted to be sure this was right. Our families basically all grew up together, and when we reconnected, we wanted to protect what we felt for a while. Just in case. I never thought I could love somebody the way I love you, Tinkerbell." He kisses the tip of her nose, and her face softens, eyes flutter, and she nuzzles into him. My bottom lip quivers. Matty grabs my leg under the table to hold me steady. "And for us to have time to really be together and build on us before the families came together because, well, you know how you all are."

"Hey!" Zia Gab shouts. "What does that mean?"

Matty boom-laughs.

"I just did my makeup, damn it," Ma says, dabbing herself with a napkin. Black mascara smears under her eyes.

"Join the club," Bianca adds.

"I love heterosexual love," Benny says. "There's not nearly enough of it."

Matty and I burst out laughing, and Jenni Lee hisses at us.

"I love you too, Pooh-Bear," Sienna says before rapidly waving her hand in front of her face to stop herself from crying. With one heavy breath, she says, "Before we eat this incredible dinner, we also wanted to acknowledge that there's a lot going on over the next few days. So we made personal itineraries for everyone."

Matty and I look at each other out of the corners of our eyes.

"We figure everyone is going to get drunk tonight, so we won't bother distributing them now, but they will be by the front door tomorrow, each one labeled by name, with paper tickets for the major group events, and some euros so you all can enjoy yourself without breaking the bank since we know it was a big ask to be here. Make sure you grab yours first thing in the morning," Sienna says. "The girls are going to an exclusive shop in Positano for couture dresses bright and early, so be ready to go by eight a.m., while the boys will be going to a tailor here in Amalfi. Then, we'll meet at the Piazza Del Duomo around one thirty for a big group tour of Amalfi's biggest lemon farm, where we'll have an exclusive lunch and get to make handmade pasta and limoncello!" Topher winks at me. "It'll be a great bonding experience for all of us!"

Zia Gab claps. "My son is so generous! You know we'd all be happy just hanging out here in this beautiful villa; you don't have to do all this for us."

"Shut up, Gab!" Ma and Rosa scream at the same time.

Nonna interrupts. "Can we all say a little prayer?" She does the sign of the cross. "Nel nome del padre, e del figlio, e dello spirito santo, amen!" she continues, urging the lord to watch over Topher and Sienna and to bless their union, yadda yadda yadda. She takes her time, and we all start to nod off until Ma tells her to hurry up.

"Amen to that." Topher raises his glass. "I say, saluti!"

As predicted, by the time dessert—a rich, layered lemon tiramisu—is done, the Coven is wine-drunk and Nonna has whipped out a deck of cards.

It's time to execute the next part of the plan.

Matty texts Benny, who looks up and over at us.

Benny slyly leans into Monroe, showing her his screen.

"What did you text them?" I ask.

"Don't worry 'bout it." Matty sounds like a cross between an Italian mobster and a Jersey Shore goon. "It's handled."

Within seconds, Monroe and Benny descend on Cam, trapping him in conversation.

Matty must sense me getting anxious because he says, "Relax, there's nothing to worry about here. They got this. Also, is it just me, or is Cam kinda cute?"

"Annoyingly so," I admit. "Look at him chatting with everyone, little miss perfect over there with his glasses and cheekbones. I hate him." I lean into Matty. "What are you gonna say to Ricky to get him alone?"

"No idea." He shrugs. But then Ricky makes a move toward the bathroom, and Matty stands up so quickly the chair skids. "I'm gonna take a leak." His fingers dance as he does some sort of spy sign language, and I get the hint that he wants me to make the move and head toward the pool for the rendezvous.

I wait a few minutes to ensure that everyone is deep enough in conversation around me before standing up.

Ma catches me. "Baby, where're you going? You okay? Have *you two* talked yet?"

"Not yet, but all's good." I catch Bianca's gaze and kiss Nonna's forehead, and before anyone else can call me over, I slip out.

The infinity pool is dimly lit with fairy lights, an extension of the endless night sky. It's like a scene from a Disney movie. All I need are talking fireflies and singing rabbits urging me to "kiss the boy."

To make time pass as I wait, I contemplate posting the footage from dinner service and critiquing the food. I decide it's not the best idea, given Chef Vittoria's reaction, so instead, I make a quick montage of the food and splice it with some footage I shot of the sea and villa at large—that's when I notice Ricky in the background. I toy with the idea of clipping him out, but I know my viewers will be looking for him, for context clues as to whether we're back together. I've already gained more followers in the last few hours, so it certainly can't hurt to just have him there, right? Pull a Taylor Swift and plant hidden messages and sit back and collect on views? Especially given the upcoming @FoodForChange contest, I'm going to need all the likes and viewer power I can muster to vote for my content once I figure out what the hell I'm doing for that.

It's fine—*this is fine.*

Except. It doesn't feel fine, or right, but neither does cutting Ricky out.

Then again, it's not like I'm zooming in on Ricky or anything. He's just . . . *there.*

When I hear footsteps, I don't bother editing the sound levels and audio because my adrenaline is pumping, so I press the upload button and shove my phone into the pocket of my jeans.

Matty and Ricky turn the corner.

Ricky freezes.

God, he fills out a button-down shirt so well these days. And those pants. The thighs. His face in the low light is hauntingly beautiful, and I can't help myself; I have to stare, to study him, take him in the way I used to.

"Sorry!" Matty waves his hands in the air overdramatically. An actor, he is not. "I did not know you would be down here, bro. I'm gonna jet." Matty turns on his heels.

"Wait, Ricky," I call after Ricky, but he hasn't moved. "Can we—"

"Talk?" Ricky finishes for me.

@LemonAtFirstSight ✔ 3 min ago

Views: 10

♥ 10

CAPTION: Amalfi FTW!! Bellissima!

HOT MIC AUDIO:

FIELDER: . . . this lemon tiramisu is the best thing I've had in my mouth since—

MATTY (WHISPERS): Let me guess, does his name rhyme with Mickey?

1 COMMENT

amithedrama

How gauche. This is who you want representing you @FoodForChange?

CHAPTER 10

I've Got Moves You've Never Seen

There's nowhere for either of us to hide.

Like the sun, I avoid staring directly at him. If I do, I risk being blinded.

"You've been avoiding me," I say.

He scoffs. "You're one to talk." His voice isn't exactly warm as he snakes around the far edge of the pool area and leans over the stone wall.

"Uh . . ." Approximately one million questions zip through my mind, anger I've suppressed for the last year bubbling to the surface. Still, I love him and want us to be who we were before the Great Commencement Massacre. The urge to grab hold of him and kiss him is there. It's confusing as hell, especially because it makes me want to cry remembering what his lips feel like against mine, and—

"Your wheels are spinning." Ricky turns toward me. "Your eyes are doing that fluttery thing."

Is he being flirty? He doesn't sound like he is, but there's only one way to find out: “You don’t know me.” A hint of a smile grows on my lips.

He doesn’t smile back. “Guess not.” His tone is stony.

Ouch.

“It’s been a while.” I straighten my back, puff out my chest, hoping the last few weeks pulling double duty at the gym did something for my chest. “I’ve got moves you’ve never seen.” Pop my ass, and—*augh!*—too far, still not properly stretched out from the plane! Now I’m hopping like I pinched a nerve trying to steady my breathing!

I expect Ricky to laugh like he would every time I made a fool of myself in front of strangers because I have zero chill, but he doesn’t.

His face grows cold; his body goes rigid. “You’re right, I don’t know you.”

“I—what?” I wasn’t expecting that.

“Don’t worry about it, Field.” His voice is ice and I have frostbite.

I move beside him and do the same, resting my arms on the cold, gritty surface.

“No, what do you mean by that?”

He clenches his jaw, the way he does when he’s looking for ways to swallow his anger. He doesn’t bother to look at me. “You really want to do this now?”

“Do what, Ricky?”

“Talk, Fielder. Actually talk to me.” His bottom lip is quivering and he bites it back.

“I don’t understand what *you’re* talking about—you broke up with me, and *you’re* mad at me?”

He lets out a howl-laugh like an evil villain before shooting his hands through his long hair in frustration. "You're so freaking dense, Fielder, ergh!" He paces back and forth, back and forth before landing in the same spot.

I don't know this version of Ricky. The one from the postcard he sent me, where apparently I am the monster in his story.

We both study the warm, bright lights of the stacked buildings and houses of Amalfi glowing against the dark mountain like strands of Christmas lights. Haunting how beautiful that can be while we continue to find ways to fall apart.

"Beautiful, huh?" The words are so frail they nearly break on the shores of his lips.

"What happened, Ricky?"

"It doesn't matter now," he says.

"Doesn't it?" I ask, the air between us so fragile.

He used to tell me that I couldn't hide around him. Now he's the one hiding.

Our eyes meet.

I'm right here.

He hums in recognition, and every bone in my body turns to mush. "You look"—his lips flap—"really good, Fielder." He glances to where the dining room is, and I wonder if he's feeling guilt for complimenting me.

As much as he looks the same, up close, I see the last year on him. A bit fuller, weight and muscle from working with his hands day in and day out. I can see new calluses on his fingers. They were in the process of hardening his fingers, and now they're more pronounced, his fingers thicker, wider. His shoulders are broader, and he fills out his shirts more. Ricky was one of those guys who had a five-o'clock shadow by the middle of freshman year, but now he's got an actual beard. His brown eyes with flecks of green sparkle in the moonlight. His larger nose now fits his face. Nonna used to say Ricky looks like a younger version of some Italian actor, Giulio Berruti. I Googled him and thought, *Someday.* Now, I see it. Ricky does look older, but he always did.

I open my mouth, but clamp it shut.

"What?"

I want to ask why he ended things, ended us, why I wasn't enough, why he didn't try harder, why he never reached out, how I became his monster.

I want to fill him in on my entire last year, pull him down to the ground and talk to him for hours, filling in the blanks, the missing pages of our stories.

I want to ask what I missed of his life, see what he's made with his strong hands, hear what he's learned.

I want to nuzzle into his shoulder until my eyes flutter and the sun comes up over the mountains and bathes us in light.

"You're still wearing the ring." He points down.

I hadn't realized I was fiddling with it, twirling it around my finger.

He moves closer, and I search his fingers for the ring I made him. And by "made," I mean I watched Ricky make it after I picked out the materials. We'd been dating for about six months when one day he mentioned how much he missed wearing a ring after giving me his. I told him I wished I could make him a ring, and he got the wild idea to bring me into his nonno's workshop. He showed me a piece his nonno was working on, an oak family tree that Sienna loved. After telling me about every tool, machine, and wood type, he asked me to pick out the wood to carve (oak leftover from his nonno's project), and moonstone fragments he later infused into the oak ring with resin. I watched him work methodically for hours, unable to take my eyes off him.

The precision, the execution, was magic. At points, when I was in such awe I couldn't believe he was able to possess such power of creation, I recorded him to capture that magic, even posted it to Clock, which my followers ate up, but he hated. When the ring was almost ready, resin dried, and it was time to polish and smooth it out, he sat me down and moved in behind me, placing his hands on mine, and guided me to completion.

When the ring was ready, Ricky wore it every day until our last.

Now, his fingers are bare. He rubs the center of his chest and looks away.

"Of course I am. I've never taken it off," I say.

His eyebrows arch. "Really?" His surprise takes me back and fills me with a sadness I didn't expect.

"Really." There's so much more I want to say, but nothing seems right anymore. I don't know why I thought it would be easy to just get him alone and we'd see each other and, what, fall immediately back in love?

This is the moment I've been waiting for, the one I've spent all year hoping to get, yet I'm realizing how wholly unprepared I am. Where he once was my sun giving me strength, now he's my kryptonite, crippling me.

Though we're finally alone, I can't break through either of our walls.

I don't know how to not love Ricky, but in this moment, I don't know how to stand here and love this version of us, either.

"You look like you have more to say." Ricky folds his arms across his chest.

I do, but don't know how. So I take the cowardly route and say, "Cam seems nice." Again, my words come out twisted and mangled, and it sounds like I'm being sarcastic, but I'm not—*Oof.* What am I doing?! This is too damn awkward!

He shakes his head, a show of disappointment, and turns to walk away in silence.

"Ricky, wait—"

He stops beside me.

Cedar and sweat, Ricky's signature scent, envelop me. His warm breath prickles my skin and smells like a full-bodied red wine. Shivers shimmy up my spine.

"What?" He's impatient.

Say something, Fielder!

We were always each other's kryptonite—uninhibited and raw, our bodies magnets. I fight the overwhelming urge to grab and kiss him.

Every fiber, muscle, tendon, bone in my body pulls me closer until—

"There you guys are!" Topher's voice is a crack of thunder that splits us apart. "What's, uh, happening here?"

I'm breathing so hard I might throw up.

Think fast. "I was going for a swim maybe?"

The water ripples and jiggles like neon-blue Jell-O.

At the edge of the pool, I dip my foot in, and water soaks through my shoe.

Ricky storms off angrily, leaving me behind. Again.

Topher moves beside me, his arm wrapping around my

shoulder as I shake water off my shoe. "Everything okay?" He looks down at my sopping wet foot, then in the direction where Ricky disappeared.

One sock squishes as I push down more brand-new emotions that threaten to completely derail me. Again. "Totally. All good. Never better."

Topher sighs. "This must be a lot for you."

"I stepped in it. Literally."

He tightens his grip and pulls me closer. "Heard there was an incident in the kitchen earlier. If you need to talk, I'm here."

"Sorry about that. It is. A lot. To be here. With— But I don't want to ruin this week for you and Sienna."

"Trust me, you won't."

I wouldn't be so sure.

TUESDAY

CHAPTER 11

I've Seen You a Lot More Naked Than That!

I've been awake for hours.

Matty is passed out, flat on his stomach, one sock on, one off, snoring so loudly that even if I hadn't had the most awkwardly painful encounter with Ricky, I wouldn't be getting any sleep anyway.

As the golden sun rises, I make my way down the winding natural stone stairs carved into the rocky mountainside from the villa toward the sea to clear my mind. All I've done is replay the scene with Ricky, where I went wrong, what I could have said or done, going as far back as the breakup or further, questioning the entirety of our relationship, what was real and what wasn't.

I wish Matty was awake. He's good at centering me when I'm spiraling. I can't exactly go to Topher without him thinking I'm up to no good. *Which . . .*

I'm on my own.

Right now, it's me, the sea, and you, dear reader.

At the end of the path is not a beach, but a stone patio built seamlessly into the natural rocks lined with a few deep blue loungers. There's a rope around the perimeter, and clear No Jumping signs due to rocks in the water below. At the far end of the patio is a ladder that leads into the water. There's a rolled-up linen towel at the foot of the lounger closest to the sea, but it's far too early for anybody to be awake yet.

The sea is calm this early, but there's a salty mist in the air, and though the air is chilly, the sun has a prickly warmth that creates a beautiful dichotomy of sensations that lulls me into a false sense of security.

I close my eyes and see Ricky. But he's not my Ricky; he's a different version, one I don't have access to, and I'm reaching out my hands, but I can't grab hold, and suddenly it's like I'm outside my own body looking down, and holy shit this is a feeling I haven't felt since the breakup, and I was hardcore disassociating and *fuck, fuck, fuck*—

Bolting upright, I reach for my phone, but my hands are numb and I send it flying straight off the lounger and skidding across the patio toward the sea.

My heart stops.

In that moment, a head emerges from the ladder. With catlike reflexes, an arm reaches out and stops my skidding phone just before it slides off the stone and into the sea.

Too late for me, though, because I'm already tumbling to the ground, scrambling to chase after it.

"This is why I leave my phone in my room," my phone savior says.

When I register it's coming from Cam(!), I have to brace myself because my knees give out due to the sheer shock. Well, that and the confirmation that, yes, Cam does in fact have a total sleeper bod.

Cam continues his ascension from the sea, water dripping from his Olympic swimmer body complete with broad shoulders and slim waist, abs for days, and not a single ounce of fat. If I didn't hate him already, I would now. Cam bounds up the ladder toward me, all leggy strides the way tall guys do, grinning like a nice guy who's already won. His scruff is unkempt, but it doesn't hide a jawline that can cut glass. Big wet curls sit on top of his head, which I didn't notice yesterday because he was wearing a skater beanie.

He places my phone on the lounger next to me, then reaches out a hand to hoist me up. I look at him hesitantly. "I don't bite, promise." His palms are wet, and despite all the chiseled marble, his grip isn't that strong and I nearly bring him down. Once we're both on our feet, I take a step back, unsure what to do next.

"Also, sorry, didn't mean anything about the phone thing. I have a vacation rule where I like to unplug, you know? And Ricky isn't much of a phone guy, but I don't have to tell you that—" He winces. "But it's mostly because I have a history of losing things, and it's easier to find things that get lost when you're home than when you're in a foreign country, you know?" He chuckles, reaching behind his head to scratch his back, showcasing his armpit. "I'm rambling. I do that when I'm nervous."

"You're nervous?" I ask. "Why?"

"Aren't you?"

"I wouldn't say I'm nervous, more like caught off guard."

"That's fair. For what it's worth, it's nice to meet you. Officially. It was kind of awkward not really knowing what to say."

"It was awkward, right?" I ask. "I didn't know—"

"About me. I figured. Ricky told me you guys don't talk." Cam steps backward and turns around, bending over to grab his towel and his glasses. He presses them to the bridge of his nose. He dries his hair and drapes the towel around his shoulders as my anger builds.

Ricky told me you guys don't talk.

Ricky talks about me with Cam?

What does Cam know about me? What secrets of mine has Ricky spilled?

What version of me does Cam think he's meeting right now?

I want to shed my skin and get lost to the Tyrrhenian Sea.

Cam checks his Apple Watch. "It's almost time to head into town. I'm gonna go check on Ricky. We should all hang later."

Sure. Cue eye roll.

He holds out a hand for me, an official nice-to-meet-you gesture. I shake it because I don't want to come off petty. With a smile, he releases my hand and heads back up toward the main villa, leaving me more confused and lightheaded than I was when I ambled down here.

I reach for my phone, abuzz with notifications, but Cam's flip-flops echoing against the rocks inspire me to toss it aside, rip off my shirt, and jump into the sea, the burst of cold water the wake-up call I needed.

"Bon giorno, Vincenze. Come stai?" I wave to Vincenze in the villa's grand foyer.

"Va bene, Signore Lemon! Wait here for the carts to take you into town. Signora Sienna said to find your name." Vincenze points toward the glittery box of scrolls.

"Grazie!" I palm mine and Matty's, since he's in no condition to do anything but hug the cold walls of the villa, pressing his cheeks against the stone, and sip cold water from his water bottle.

After officially meeting Cam this morning, I ripped his ticket to the lemon grove to shreds and flushed it, leaving zero evidence.

Oops.

But you know what, reader? He's too perfect, and I don't like it.

Something feels off. My Spidey-sense is tingling.

I need to remove him from the equation. Get Ricky alone. Again. But this time, I wouldn't be going in blind. I need to go in a bit more armed. Do some reconnaissance. Find out some information on Cam, and then focus on repairing whatever broke between Ricky and me. Maybe getting some time with Ricky and the lemon farm might spark more meaningful connection, help me learn why he hates me so much, and we might actually have a chance.

Footsteps alert me to people coming. "Matty, look alive." As my spy on the inside, having spent more time with Cam than me last night at dinner, he's got more of an in, plus Matty has always been good at digging up information with a suave, spy-level eye for detail. Nobody suspects him due to his golden retriever himbo demure nature.

"Va funculo. My head." He grabs me by the back of the shirt and tugs. "I'm not doing so hot after last night. How do I look?"

I swirl around and give him the once-over: Four-inch inseam jean shorts for the thighs, tight sleeveless tank with bright neon nineties design for the arms. White pleather fanny pack. Scuff-free white sneakers.

"You look cute, all things considered."

He nods triumphantly. "Could be a hot dude at the tailor or the lemon thing." Matty fidgets with his fanny pack. Then he nudges me. "Cam, twelve o'clock."

Be cool. Unbothered. "Sup."

Sup? What even is that?

Cam's eyes widen, and he offers a cursory laugh. Avoiding his gaze, my eyes fall on his big ears, which stick out, so he wiggles them in a "hello."

I laugh; then my cheeks heat in embarrassment because I don't want to offend him. "Sorry, I—"

"I grew up with kids making fun of my ears. Called me Dumbo, if they were basic. I got Legolas once, that was creative. Once I realized I could wiggle them and make people laugh? It was over for the haters." Cam's voice sounds like his balls started dropping, then suddenly stopped, straddling the line between teenager and man. Actually, he sounds like the voice of Alberto in Disney/Pixar's *Luca*. I kind of want to make him say, "Silenzio, Bruno!"

Matty's staring at Cam, his charm working its magic on my eternally horny cousin. "He's good," Matty whispers.

Cam's in skinny jean shorts ripped at the hem just above his knees, black Chuck Taylors, and a black Beyoncé *Renaissance* concert tee with glittery embellishments. He adjusts his black-rimmed glasses.

Ricky appears behind Cam and hugs his waist. I reflexively turn away.

"My boys!" Topher shouts. "Let's go!"

Tyler and Trav pull up behind him and start shouting, "To-pher! To-pher!"

Benny and Ricky's dad follow.

"Straight men are exhausting," Benny says under his breath. "But love and light, I am bounty and beauty and am ready to receive everyone today!"

Trav grabs Benny in a headlock.

"Oh god, what's happening? I'm getting hate-crimed!" Benny shrieks.

"Field, you ready? You're the adult today," Topher shouts. His fine leather sandals that look like he's from ancient Egypt squeak against the marble floor.

"How'd that happen?" I ask, looking at Ricky's dad, the actual adult in the room, who laughs.

"Technically, Sienna just doesn't trust me," Topher says. "Or Trav or Tyler."

"Hey," Tyler and Trav say at once.

"You're proving her point," Benny squawks from inside Trav's headlock. Trav promptly lets him go, and Benny lets out an exhaustive breath. "That was deeply erotic *and* traumatizing."

"I need all hands on deck to keep us on task, men," Topher continues. "We gotta be at the tailor soon. Sienna will kill us if we're late and he can't get us done. Then we have the lemon farm for our private tour and lunch. They're sticklers for the personalized paper tickets with unique codes for this VIP thing. I plan to talk to them about optimizing and streamlining with LemonTech . . . ," he continues, but I stop listening, a knot forming as I look at Ricky and Cam, knowing Cam's ticket is in pieces floating in pipes below the ground right now.

"Got it! We're on a tight schedule. Let's get going, then." I turn and nearly bump into Ricky. "Mornayyy!" Air gets trapped in my throat. "Ha. *Tried* to say 'morning,' but the ole brain said, 'Make it *hey* instead.' " I'm the living representation of the sweating awkwardly emoji.

He laughs and cranes his neck, his Adam's apple and collarbone pronounced, and I want to trace them with my fingers. He brushes his hair back effortlessly, like a model mid-photoshoot. "Mornayyy."

What do I say now? "How'd you sleep?" Lame.

"Pretty good. Cam snores."

"Excuse me?" Cam drapes his arms around Ricky's shoulders like one of Nonna's winter capes. A waft of black licorice and incense emanates from him. "I'm constantly subjected to the symphonic range of your snoring, sir." He kisses Ricky on the side of his neck and looks up, as if he's making sure I caught it.

Ricky blushes, and Cam offers a smile that glibly says, *The boy is mine.*

May the best man win.

Tucked into a cobblestone side street down an alley, with windows and planters with hanging vines and colorful, blooming flowers bathed in warm sunlight, is a large, ornate wooden door with an understated but regal copper placard that reads, "Massimo Andreozzi." Topher was instructed to knock only once, and almost immediately the door opens and we're ushered inside. Within seconds, we're offered espresso with lemon rinds and almond biscotti. It's deceptively large inside, despite the narrow hallways, but it's still not large enough for eight grown men. Massimo's assistant, a tiny older woman with silver hair that spills in loose curls down her shoulders, is militant and directs each of us toward a small fitting room, but she must double us up. Topher gets his own while Tyler and Trav are in another, followed by Ricky and his father, me and Matty, and Benny is lucky enough to go solo.

"What about Cam?" Benny asks.

"I'm just along for the ride," Cam says. "Apparently."

"Sienna just booked the bridal party." Guilt pulls at the corners of Topher's lips. "Sorry, dude."

"A little harsh, bro, dontcha think?" Matty whispers to Topher.

Cam looks squarely at me. "It's totally fine. I'm happy to be here." He grabs Ricky's hand. "I can go shopping in the square."

"Cam can have my spot," I suggest.

"Fielder, you're my best man," Topher says, eyebrows arching in shock.

"It's totally okay," I say. "I can come back. I don't want Cam to feel left out."

A tall, slender man with starched caramel-colored chinos and a wrinkle-free linen shirt with rolled-up sleeves emerges in a doorway, arms crossed. He glares at Cam over the rims of his turquoise-and-gold thin-framed octagonal glasses. Clears his throat. Then starts rattling off something in rapid-fire Italian, throwing his hands in the air, gesturing toward each group and their fitting rooms. I catch some of the words, like "spicciare," as he rushes us inside.

"No," Massimo says. "No coming back. No more appointments this week!"

What a loud, angry man.

This is where I shine. Best man duties and all. "Mr. Andreozzi, look, this is my cousin's wedding, and we have one additional person," I say, cozying up next to him, laying it on thick, draping my arm around him. "Is there any way we can squeeze him in at all? I can be quick."

"It's not about quick," Massimo says. "It's not about quick. You cannot rush fashion." His thick brows furrow.

Topher comes up beside me and slyly slips what feels like a few hundred euros in my hands.

"I understand. It's a great imposition. And we really don't want to disrespect you and your art. We really do appreciate you being able to accommodate us," I say, pulling back and taking his free hand in both of mine, casually slipping the money inside, a trick we all learned as kids from Nonna at the local bingo hall. If you don't grow up learning how to bribe your way through gambling, are you really Italian? "If there's anything you can do, our family would be forever grateful to you. My cousin is getting married, you know. This doesn't happen all the time."

Massimo puts his hand in his pocket and, without so much as a second thought, says, "This is not a problem." He points to Cam. "You can wait in the lobby. We already have too many in the dressing rooms, yes?"

Ricky mouths a "thank you" to me before Matty and I are ushered into our fitting room. Matty closes the curtain quickly.

"Damn, that scored you some serious points," he says. "You should have seen Ricky's face. He was floored."

"Was he?"

"Cam too, honestly," Matty says. "Oof, this espresso is hitting the spot." He squeezes his eyelids tight. I grab a biscotti from a tray and walk it over to him, running it under his nose. Without opening his eyes, he snatches it and shoves it in his mouth. Big golden retriever energy. "Why'd you do it?"

"It was the right thing," I say.

He opens one eye and concedes. "Bet."

"And if Ricky and his dad and everyone else thinks it was an act of kindness, score one for me."

"You crafty sonovabitch. I have much to learn."

My pocket buzzes. "Topher wants me to come to his fitting room."

"Enjoy. I'll be here, alone," Matty says through gritted teeth.

Problem: Which fitting room is Topher's? By process of elimination, I follow Tyler and Trav's voices and move past theirs; then I hear Ricky's dad singing to himself in another. Then Massimo's voice booms, and I'm sure he's still working on Topher's garments, so I follow the sound of his voice.

"Bellissimo!" Massimo bursts out from a curtain and makes his way into another, his seamstress in tow, and I recognize one word from the stream of Italian emanating from his mouth: sposo. Groom. That must be Topher.

"Dude, what's up?" I toss back that same curtain, fully expecting Topher.

It's Ricky. Bare-chested, in nothing but tight boxer briefs and socks.

He looks up, very deer in headlights.

I grip the curtain, white-knuckled, unable to stop staring at him. His body, the body I once knew so well like a map of the world and I was Magellan, has changed so much. From working out or woodworking, his biceps have grown exponentially; his midsection is also broader, more defined.

Compose yourself, Fielder.

The freckles dancing across his large pecs used to remind me of the Big Dipper, and I trace them now in my mind. It's like finding my North Star again after living in the dark for a year.

A gold chain hangs around his neck with a circular pendant that looks almost like a ring, but I can't make it out because it's too dark. He moves so quickly to cover his junk that he inadvertently covers the pendant, too.

"Sorry—I didn't mean to—" I turn to leave.

"It's okay!" he calls out, moving again, but he nearly trips because his pants pool at his ankles. He laughs. "I mean, you've seen me a lot more naked than this."

Sure have.

I laugh nervously and say the honorable thing. "Was looking for Topher."

"Across the hall."

"Right." I don't know what to do now. There's so much tension between us, and it makes me want to cry or scream or create a diversion so I can duck out and run.

I turn to *walk* away, when Ricky says, "Hey, Fielder. Thanks. For Cam. That was . . . really very sweet. You didn't have to."

"Of course. My pleasure."

Why is this *so* awkward?

He nods and clears his throat. "What do you think about this look? Sienna picked it out for me for the ceremony, and I'm not sure about it."

"Why don't you ask Cam?"

"He took a walk into town to grab a water while he waits his turn, so—"

"You're stuck with me?"

"I wouldn't put it *that* way." He's wrestling to put on his clothes. "I always valued your opinion more than anyone's."

A burst of warmth blooms in my chest.

I turn back around, and the pants that were around his ankles are buttoned around his waist. His arms are loose at his sides.

Don't stare, Fielder. Keep it aboveboard.

My head is fuzzy as he smirks, puts his hands on his hips, his arms like arrows pointing toward—

My phone buzzes again, and it snaps me back. I try to speak, but my voice is suddenly gone. "What, uh, do you want me to see?"

"Ah." Ricky turns around to grab a shirt on a hanger, and there's his butt.

Good lord, help me. I'm weak.

"I love my sister, but I'm just not sure about these gold shirts. Sienna wanted me, you, and Matty to be distinctive, but." He shakes his head and sighs.

"Gold shirts?" I hadn't noticed anything in my own fitting room earlier.

Ricky's broad back distracts me, the way his muscles move as he fumbles with the hanger. The entire room could be covered in gold leaf, and I wouldn't notice.

Whipping the collarless Italian linen button-down around like a cape, he threads his arms through the sleeves, fluidly, effortlessly. He fluffs the front before buttoning it up. I study his reflection in the mirror in front of him. Furrowed brows. Thick thumbs fumble with small buttons. He looks up and into the mirror and runs his hands through his hair before turning back around and facing me.

He looks like a Roman god. "Thoughts?"

"Huh?"

"Gold shirt," he reminds me.

Right. "The shirt isn't gold, Ric. It's more of a muted soft yellow. Goes great with your skin tone." I move closer to study the stitching. It's a pearly stone color, flowers woven down the sides of the front like an Italian Mediterranean mosaic.

"Looks gold to me."

"This coming from the guy who only wears black or white tees from a Target five-pack. Or the occasional *Jurassic Park* hoodie."

"Don't hate on classics or reliables." Ricky's eyes glimmer. When Ricky's parents moved next door, the first time I met him, Ma had brought me over for a playdate and he was watching *Jurassic Park*. I was five, and I so clearly remember the scene when the T-Rex had broken free of the electrified fence and was terrorizing the two kids in the overturned jeep—pure nightmare fuel. I was terrified, but six-year-old Ricky grabbed my hand and said, "It's okay, it's not real, just cool." And even though I struggled to believe him in that moment, nothing bad happened to me. I quickly learned that that was who Ricky was—practical, grounded, caring. I also quickly learned just how obsessed he was with the entire *Jurassic Park/World* franchise. In another life without woodworking, he might be studying in college to become a paleontologist. Ricky was always so methodical and steady, and appreciated the world around him and how it was constructed, from fossils to trees to the materials he could uncover and use to make something beautiful. "Nothing wrong with simplicity," Ricky says. "This is just—"

"Not *you*," I finish his thought. "You look . . ." I exhale, pause, unsure what I'm *allowed* to say. I know what I *want* to say, but that feels too intimate, too unearned. At least right now. My voice shakes. "You don't like to stand out." My fingers trace the neckline. "But you look—*wow*." The word comes out as a whisper.

He laughs and shifts from leg to leg.

"Sorry." Not sure what I'm apologizing for, but it feels like the right move.

Then he says my name like a prayer, a confession, or a fellowship, a bridge forward. He opens his mouth to speak, but—

"Fielder, bro!" Topher's voice roars.

"I should go. Best man duties."

Ricky stands still. Stoic. Wood waiting to be carved.

Every part of me wants to stay with him, but I don't.

When I find Topher, he immediately commends me on handling Cam.

"I don't need any praise," I assure him. "Only peace. *For you.*"

"Good. Look, I know we haven't talked much about best man responsibilities, because there really aren't any besides you and Matty standing next to me, but there is one thing. First, I wanted to be sure you're cool with Ricky."

"We're cool." So cool I just saw him in his birthday suit, in fact! "Why?"

Topher leans against the wall and crosses his arms. "Sienna told me that Cam made a comment about you being cold to him this morning. Obviously this was before we left the villa, so maybe something happened?"

"Cold? Screw that guy. I look out for him and this is the thanks I get? Just because I don't hug the guy and say 'you won!' suddenly I'm cold?" Heat rises in my chest.

"Don't shoot the messenger, bro."

My teeth grind. "No shooting. I'm Peacemaker Fielder, right?" Deep breath.

"Right," Topher continues. "Cam told Sienna you're using the wedding and 'people' here to gain followers on Clock. I don't know what he meant by that."

"What?" I hiss. "You of *all* people know my entire life is on Clock." *What is Cam playing at?* "Sorry, I'm just"—deep breath—"sad."

"I know." Topher uncrosses his arms and motions for me to settle down. "I know. Believe me, Field, I get it. And so does Sienna. We obviously don't care if you're creating content in the villa. Go for it, bro. I just wanted you to know this is what's being said. But I have your back. Especially after what you just did for Cam. And it's okay to be sad."

I take another long, deep breath. "Thank you."

I don't want to bring Topher down, but there's so much wrapped around that word—"sad." I'm sad I can't hold Ricky, kiss him, talk to him about us, and ask him a thousand *whys*. I'm sad that we're in this place. But it's so much more than sad. It's devastation and confusion and disassociation because when I think about Ricky too much, it's like my soul separates from my body and I can't process anything or feel the ground beneath my feet. So I've hidden my heart away from any boy who's tried to get close to me, and buried my head in Clock content and pretending I'm perfectly well adjusted when I'm actually falling apart. I'm realizing now how hard it's been. Was Ricky right? Were we too intertwined—too connected to each other from such a young age that we didn't have time to figure ourselves out separately? My mouth goes dry as I replay the last year in my head—all the random guys, the endless food review videos. I've been going, going, going, all to prove something to Ricky but without ever stopping to take a breath *for myself.*

Who is Fielder Lemon?

Topher instinctively pulls me into a strong hug, and I sink into him, barely hugging him back, which makes him squeeze harder. "You're doing a great job."

Of what?

Add that to the list of questions I can't answer.

"Speaking of, after the rehearsal dinner Friday, I planned a surprise for Sienna. Chartered a moonlit boat ride to Capri afterward. Ricky will get her to the docks after dinner, but I need you to help me get the boat ready. Logistics and such. That means you and Ricky will have to work together. Or at *least* communicate."

No time to dwell on me—*thank god.* My back straightens and I'm back to daydreaming: Me and Ricky working alone on a romantic surprise late at night? Sneaking in moments together? I couldn't have asked for a better best man task.

Topher's wedding and happiness needs to be the most important factor in my actions. He deserves as much.

"You can count on me," I say resolutely.

CHAPTER 12

He's Kept You on a Pedestal

First act of Fielder Lemon, peacemaker extraordinaire: find Cam and try to bridge the gap, broker a deal, common ground and all that. After all, we must have something in common. My inner voice screams, *Yeah, Ricky, dumbass!* Which feels both too obvious and far too sacred, even though Ricky fell for both of us, so there's got to be something there worth getting to know, right?

That realization makes me feel ill.

Ignoring. Rising above. I'm suspending the urge to follow through with the original plan of lightly sabotaging their relationship!

Benny and Riccardo Sr. are outside Massimo Andreozzi's, leaning against the exterior of a stone building opposite in the alley.

"Was it just me or was Massimo daddy?" Benny asks.

"You need help, nephew," Riccardo Sr. says, which causes me to burst out laughing. He locks eyes with me, and before I realize what's happening, he's making his way toward me and holding out a hand for me. "I didn't get the chance to properly catch up. It's really nice to see you, Fielder." Suddenly, he pulls me into a man-safe hug, where we're still shaking hands, but his other is wrapped around me, patting my back. It's strangely relieving to be so close to him—especially since I haven't had this kind of contact with a father figure since my own passed away. I hadn't realized how much I missed this kind of affection. It makes me miss my dad. "We miss *you*, son, if you catch my drift."

A lump in my throat forms. "I miss you guys, too."

"One day, my son will wise up." Riccardo Sr. smacks my cheeks lightly. "Give him some time. DeLuca men always find their way home." His hands linger on my jaw, as if he's inspecting me for stock. Riccardo Sr. has always been a man of few words, like Ricky's nonno. For all the years I spent next door at the DeLucas, we're at the maximum of our usual word count.

"Yes, sir," I say. "I'm patient."

"Good. He loves you, you know. You never forget your first love. I should know. I married mine." He nods behind me as Ricky makes his way back toward the group.

"We ready to hit the Piazza del Duomo?" Topher asks. "Sienna is texting . . ."

"I can't find Cam," Ricky says. "I'm trying to call, but nothing."

Benny's antsy. "I'm hungry. All I want is the homemade pasta I was promised."

My stomach gurgles. "I can help. Sooner we find him, the sooner we meet the girls, the sooner we eat."

"Divide and conquer?" Tyler chimes in, hanging an arm on my shoulder and motioning for Benny and Matty to join us.

"Toph, you and Trav go meet the girls. The rest of us will go comb the town."

"We can all look as we walk," Topher says, checking the time on his phone. "As long as we make our way to the Duomo, we can divide and conquer."

"I'll stay here, just in case he comes back here," Ricky says, sounding more annoyed than concerned for the whereabouts of his boyfriend.

How often does this happen?

The group fans out on the way to the Duomo. We search shops and cafés, down narrow side streets, in between large tourist groups surrounding fruit stands—nothing.

No sign of Cam anywhere.

Matty is busy on his phone, sifting through messages from guys on a hookup app, and I'm looking over his shoulder trying to get in on the action, but he keeps shouldering me away.

As we're walking through the town, I move between Benny and Tyler to pick their brains about what they know about Cam.

"Honestly, I didn't know Ricky had a boyfriend until he brought him on the plane," Benny says. "It's not like he has social media, and we don't really talk, so he's not texting me all the gory details of his life. I found out at the same time as you."

Tyler says, "I thought it was interesting how last night Cam was going on about you and how he got the impression you were not really a nice person. But I wonder how much of that is coming from Ricky. And thinking you're a bit of a . . ." His voice trails off.

"A what?" I ask.

Benny looks at Tyler and shakes his head as if to silence Tyler.

"Now you have to say it," I demand.

Tyler braces for impact as he says, "A fame whore. His words, not mine!"

"Is that the worst he can do—hold up!"

I spot the back of a Beyoncé *Renaissance* tee, the glittery font sparkling in the sun's rays like a beacon. The thin-framed man turns his head, and Cam's black-framed glasses come into view. He's talking to some all-American beefcake in a backward baseball cap leaning against a stone wall. They're tucked away in the frame of an arching doorway, just out of sight to most, but now that I've seen them, I can't look away. From this far away, the guy could almost pass for Matty. Except Matty wouldn't be caught dead in American Eagle apparel; that embossed eagle logo is offensively large.

All-American Beefcake leans in and whispers something into Cam's ears.

Cam shows him something on his phone.

They share a stolen laugh, but quickly hide the phone screen from sight.

Grabbing hold of Benny and Tyler, I yank them down and we hide, careful not to let Cam see us.

All-American Beefcake checks the time on his watch, and I lip-read something that looks like, "I have to go."

Cam pouts, then checks the time on his phone and rolls his eyes. He turns his head in our direction, so we stay low and duck-waddle into a storefront full of white-painted terracotta pottery with bright blue-and-yellow brushstrokes. I hide behind a platter large and wide enough to cover my face.

We're close enough to hear Cam's voice. "Yeah, I gotta go, too. My phone is blowing up. My . . . *friend* is looking for me."

Friend?!

I'm simultaneously devastated for Ricky and angry enough to go full Coven Lemon on him. Not only is he cheating on Ricky, but he's also doing so as an all-expenses-paid guest at Ricky's sister's wedding. Ricky doesn't deserve this.

I'm in a blind rage, and all Topher's pleading leaves my head. As I dash out from behind the decorative platter shielding me from view and round the corner, I grab on to the fabric of his shirt.

Or, rather, I *think* it's his shirt.

"You mothafucka—" the New York in me jumps out.

"Excuse me?" a deep, southern voice says.

I wasn't paying attention, so in fact, it's not Cam at all. It's All-American Beefcake looking like all the hot, straight wrestlers I went to school with, and if I weren't so stressed I'd stop to ogle him.

"Sorry, I thought you were my friend." I gulp, wave, and duck out fast. I have zero desire to find out if he can use his formidable weight class against me.

Threading through bodies down the narrow streets, I move in the direction of the Duomo until I spot the glitter on Cam's back.

I struggle to keep track of him as the number of people on the streets grows by the second. Families milling in and out of souvenir shops, curious women in floppy hats perusing the windows of high-end jewelers, lines building in front of gelaterias.

Benny and Tyler bob and weave behind me, trying to keep up with me as we trail Cam's gazelle-like legs and large strides.

He's so carefree, swaying his hips like he didn't just cheat on

Ricky. Granted, I have no idea if physical cheating occurred, but just the fact that he was openly flirting and called Ricky a "friend" means he at least emotionally cheated.

Cam turns down the alley toward Massimo Andreozzi's.

We dash across the opening as fast as we can and start toward the Duomo.

"What happened?!" Benny shouts, sounding frazzled. "I haven't run that fast in ages. I need to get back to the gym."

Tyler eyes me curiously. "Do you think Cam really cheated on Ricky?"

The Piazza del Duomo is steps away. I make out the black-and-white-striped stone.

My hands are shaking. "I don't know what else it could be, but I'm not saying anything unless I know for sure—" Before I can finish, a Vespa nearly sideswipes me, skidding around me.

Tires screech.

Gasps from passersby.

The swift movement of the Vespa knocks me off-balance, and it swerves sharply as it grinds to a halt, the ass end of it bashing into me, sending me flying.

I crash-land hard on my ass.

An older woman screams.

The crowd parts, but like a wave, swells and returns once people realize I'm okay and not severely hurt. Bodies surround me quickly.

The driver rips off his orange helmet and starts furiously yelling at me in Italian. I hear the standard refrains: "Va funculo" and "disgraziato," but the rest is spat out so fast my head spins.

A young woman in Gucci sunglasses with black hair pulled back into a messy bun starts screaming in Italian at the Vespa driver, throwing her hands up at him until they're both air-fighting with their hands like some sort of magic duel.

An older man bends down and asks me in broken English if I can move.

The chaos of the scene around me cements me in place, and I can't answer. It's like I'm not in my own body, I'm somewhere else entirely, at home watching everything unfold on Nonna's TV screen.

Hands belonging to no one and everyone thrust a bottle of water in my face. The angst and expectation of it all causes anxiety to build in my chest.

Am I hurt?

Am I dead?

Or worse—am I bleeding? I don't do well with blood . . .

Everything is blurry, fuzzy. Benny, Tyler, random heads and faces . . .

The hot sun beating on my forehead weighs me down.

The Vespa crashing into me replays over and over, time slowing to a halt as I float above my body, above the entire scene. Suddenly, voices that sound like Ricky and Cam and Ma and Topher and . . . me . . . say, "Who is Fielder Lemon?" again and again.

My limbs are weightless, lifeless, and my chest rises and falls at a rapid rate.

All my thoughts and fears and pain—everything I've suppressed since Ricky dumped me— swirl around me and push me back down to the ground, hard.

I try to remember what to do when I have a panic attack, but I can't focus.

Suddenly, a hand on my shoulder and a familiar voice breathes life into me.

"Fielder, you're okay—" It's more of a statement than a question, more of a mantra of reassurance for the one delivering it.

Ricky. "I got you." Concern pools in his eyes. "Are you hurt?"

"What—" I can't say more. Words and meaning elude me.

"I saw the whole thing happen. I didn't realize it was you until I got closer." Ricky moves down my body, his hands inspecting every inch of my legs and arms before moving to my head. "No blood. Nothing looks broken." He grabs the water bottle from the stranger who kept wiggling it in front of my face expectantly and uncaps it for me. "Drink, you look pale."

"I'm fine." When I try to stand, my legs give out. "Actually, water sounds great."

He brings the bottle to my lips, places a hand on my lower back to steady me.

I can barely choke down a few baby sips.

Looking up, I focus on Ricky. The sweat on his brow. The concern etched into the lines next to his eyes. The way he folds his lips inward, and his teeth bite down in worry.

"When'd you get here?" I offer a smirk.

His lips unfurl and he lets out a *phew.* "You're okay."

I grab hold of him for support. "I'm more embarrassed than anything."

The owner of the Vespa tosses his hands in the air in my direction, a bit too violently for my liking, slams his helmet back onto his head, and revs his engine before taking off. Though he doesn't get far before people start yelling at him and tossing food in his direction.

"Nothing for you to be embarrassed about. He's the asshole." Ricky sneers in the Vespa's direction.

As my eyes steadily focus, Cam steps forward. Suddenly I'm hyper aware that Ricky is still holding tight to my sweaty hands.

"You okay, Fielder?" Cam crouches down beside me. He grabs hold of the other side of my body to steady me or make his presence known as I still cling to his boyfriend.

"So glad you're okay," Cam says. "I saw the whole thing; that driver was a lunatic. That was scary."

"Thanks . . ." I don't know what to say.

"Ric, your sister is looking for y—" Monroe says. "What the hell happened? Fielder, are you okay?"

Ricky looks to me for permission to leave.

"I'm okay, go." Though I don't want Ricky to leave.

Cam hoists me up.

"Thanks, I appreciate it."

"Least I can do after the tailor this morning." He opens his arms for a hug, which is weird as hell, especially since I might have just caught him cheating, but in the spirit of being peacemaker, I let it happen. Tyler and Benny look on confused as Cam whispers, "I can tell Ricky still keeps you on a pedestal, despite everything that's happened."

My heart thump-thump-thumps against my rib cage.

I pry myself out of his arms. "What—"

"I was there for him when you broke him," Cam says. I have no idea what he's talking about. Cam clearly has everything twisted. I wasn't the one who dumped Ricky and left without a trace. "And I was nervous coming here. I thought maybe you'd try to get back together with him or something, but after this morning . . . I had it wrong. He was right. You *are* a good guy."

So Ricky told him I broke him, yet he keeps me on a pedestal?

My head hurts.

It feels a bit like Cam is trying to get in good with me, and I wonder if it's because he saw me following him earlier.

I don't know what to believe or think.

Out of the corner of my eye, Monroe runs over to the Coven and the rest of the guys, including Matty, to relay what happened. Within an instant, they're all descending on us. At the same time, three golf carts with lemon-yellow bodies and bright green tops with "Avello Family Lemon Groves Tour" stamped on each side pull up in front of Piazza del Duomo, and anxiety builds in my chest.

"What the hell was all that?" Matty asks, as I recount everything that happened to him and Monroe, who sits next to Tyler. We're all sitting backward in the rear of the cart to the Avello Family Lemon Groves.

"What are you gonna do?" Monroe asks after I finish.

The Lemon Tour–branded golf carts carrying the entire Lemon wedding party and both of our families, including the screaming Coven who are so loud their voices carry up and through the thick mossy forests of the Valle dei Mulini, zip up the Via delle Cartiere, leaving the teeming swaths of tourists behind for quieter, narrow streets in the same direction as the villa. Ivy and roots cover short white stone buildings that almost look abandoned. The road is barely wide enough for any golf carts, let alone two, but I close my eyes and let the sun beat down on my face, and I focus on my breathing and taking in the crisp scent of citrus and salt in the air.

"Earth to Fielder." Monroe elbows me. "Where are you?"

I'm watching Ricky and Cam laugh together in the golf cart behind mine. "If what Cam said was right, that Ricky keeps me on a pedestal, is that why Cam would cheat? Assuming he is, which, I have to tell Ricky, right? And tell Sienna that I was cold and using the wedding for clicks and fame? Is he threatened by me somehow?"

"That does make sense, I think," Tyler says. "And I dunno, man. I wouldn't get involved in their relationship. That's playing with fire."

"You could come across as the jealous ex," Monroe says.

"You need proof that Cam is cheating," Matty says.

"I don't even know what I saw. It's all fuzzy now." I rub my temples, wondering if it would even matter. "Can two people still know each other after a long time apart?"

Monroe hums. We hit a bump in the rocky road, which aids her in swiveling her body toward me. "You'll always know a version of that person."

"I find it hard to believe that after knowing him for over twelve years, us being apart for a year means we're suddenly strangers."

"Can't both be true?"

This is too big of a conundrum for my brain to work through.

"Are you the same person you were when you were together?" she asks, and I shrug. "Do you think you are? Keep in mind, I met you two days ago, so you can tell me anything you want and I'll believe it."

"Sometimes. Ricky always had his woodworking dreams and a mentorship that took him to Seattle. Meanwhile I was all 'L-O-L, I'll become Clock famous.'" I make peace signs with both hands. "Sure, I actually managed to monetize my account and gain, like, a million followers since we were together, and I have this internship I'm gunning for, even though I haven't done a damn thing for it, but I still feel like I'm floundering. I'm a joke."

Matty smacks me. "You're not a joke. Don't say that about yourself. A couple years ago, you never would have done anything without Ricky. Now, you do everything on your own. You just don't see it because you've had no choice but to do everything on your own this past year."

"Sometimes we can't see our own growth," Monroe says.

The thing is, I'm not sure I have grown—I'm no closer to figuring out my life now than I was last year.

Each golf cart stops in front of a congested area full of parked Fiats and other short, stout cars, some with wooden flatbeds in the back for carrying fruits and other goods to market, made specifically for tight European streets.

"Is this where we die?" Monroe whispers.

"I'll protect you," Tyler says, hopping out.

"I'll protect myself, thankyouverymuch," Monroe says.

I high-five her. "Werk."

"I-I didn't mean—" Tyler stutters. "Sorry. My sister would punch me if she heard me. I was just—"

"Flirting," Monroe finishes with a lip cringe. "Do better." She winks, then links arms with me and pulls me toward a man who waits under a small faded wooden sign that reads Avello Family Lemon Groves Tour hanging from a trellis of vines and white flowers.

Ricky and Cam are off to the side, arm in arm, and my stomach sours.

Tucked in the middle of a valley, far away from the busy center of Amalfi and the crashing waves of the sea, tall lush green mountains envelop us on three sides, looming over us like we've entered an entirely new province. Next to the almost hidden entrance to the towering strata of luxurious groves that climb the foothills is an inconspicuous doorway that's currently closed with an aged metal sign that says Museo in gold script.

"Benvenuto!" A middle-aged man with olive skin dressed in a floral Hawaiian shirt and lemon-shaped sunglasses stands arms outstretched, beaming ear to ear. "Welcome to Avello Family Lemon Groves Tour! I'm Niccolò Avello, the owner of Avello Family Lemon Groves. I hear we have a special occasion today."

"We're getting married this week." Sienna rests her head on Topher's shoulder.

"Wonderful, moltissime felicitazioni!" Niccolò doesn't know us personally, but he seems genuinely happy for them.

"Grazie," Topher says, extending his hand.

"Va bene, va bene." Niccolò shakes it vigorously. "We are going to take you up into the mountains, through the groves, and end the tour today in our museo and limoncello factory before heading up to the outdoor kitchen for fresh homemade lemon pasta, va bene?"

"Amazing," Topher says. "Not sure Nonna can do all the stairs."

"Nonsense." Nonna pushes her way in between Topher and Sienna. In Italian, she says what I think is, "I let no man speak for me. I can walk."

Niccolò holds out his arm for her. "I'll escort this beautiful woman myself."

Okay, that's a baller move.

She makes sure to squeeze his bicep. For an older man, one certainly far too young for Nonna but who could easily be my father's age, Niccolò Avello is a chiseled statue of a man. The sun hasn't aged him the way I would think being out in the sun all day would. Time has carved him, but carefully. Etched in his dark skin are wisdom lines. His hands are massive, and I notice his skin is cracking and his fingernails are dirty, no doubt a byproduct of farming. He looks a lot like actor Jon Hamm, but with a choppy, unruly haircut that sticks up in odd places.

"Get it, Nonna!" Sienna yells.

Nonna turns and winks, then tells Sienna to mind her business. "You have your man; let an old lady live."

Niccolò laughs. "I like this one."

"You can keep her," Zia Gab yells. "Wait, no, I'm single. Take me!" She pushes Zia Rosa and Ma out of the way like we're at a cutthroat rose ceremony in *The Bachelor.*

"I propose with a lemon?" Niccolò bows.

Ma, Zia Gab, and Zia Rosa audibly swoon.

"But my wife might have words," Niccolò says. "We're going to have fun today! Andiamo! Before we head on up, I'll take the tickets, per favore."

One by one, we all rummage through our scrolls and hand over our personalized, embossed tickets to the Avello Family

Lemon Groves. Niccolò counts each ticket, then counts the number of heads, and cross-references the ones that are printed with each person's name and the list he was given.

Everyone hands theirs over, except Cam. Who scrambles through his collection of papers, rummaging through the pockets of his skinny jeans, bag, and, for good measure, searching the ground like a cartoon character in dramatic fashion as if it dropped.

"It's not here," Cam says. "I don't think I got one."

I swear, dear reader, everybody held their breath at once. Except Nonna, who sucked at the roof of her mouth and shook her head.

Topher steps in to bargain. "It's not a big deal, right? I can buy another for Cam."

Cam steps forward. "You know what, it's fine. I'm not feeling particularly welcome today. First the tailor, now this. If it's all right, I'd rather go back to the villa and relax by the pool. I'm not feeling so well after Fielder—"

Heads turn to look at me.

After a few awkward beats, he says, "The Vespa accident. Shook me up." I can't explain it, but I know he's alluding to me catching him potentially cheating on Ricky, and now his comment about Ricky keeping me on a pedestal and that I'm a great guy all feel icky as hell. "I'm exhausted and it's been a lot. I—don't feel welcome." Cam grabs Ricky's hand. "Babe?"

Nobody says anything or knows how to respond.

"I *need* you here," Sienna says to Ricky. "You can't leave."

"I have to stay." Ricky's voice is fragile.

Cam's nostrils flare, but he nods in agreement.

“Cam, you should stay, son,” Riccardo Sr. says, his voice stern.

Cam offers a smile. “I appreciate it, sir. But I’ll pass. You all have the *best* time.”

“We will. Take the villa’s cart back.” Riccardo Sr. nods toward the carts that Topher paid to have waiting for us later, not attempting to bargain. He turns his back immediately and says loud enough for everyone to hear, “I won’t let anyone ruin my baby girl’s day. Let’s get this show on the road, shall we? Andiamo.”

“That was weird,” Trav says, clutching Jenni Lee. I nearly forgot they were here. They’ve been sucking each other’s faces quietly in the background.

“Gays are so dramatic, *am I right*?” Jenni Lee says. “Like, right on cue!”

I turn to glare at her. *Did she really?*

Monroe leans in and whispers, “Problematic Jenni Lee strikes again.” She clears her throat. “Not cool, JL. Not cool.”

Jenni Lee waves Monroe away.

“Don’t feed the trolls,” Benny says. “Can we all *please* be done with the dramatics for today.” He rubs his belly. “I’m hangry. All the wedding hysterics and rom-com operationals have gotten to me. I’ve *had* it.”

“Andiamo,” Niccolò says, waving the Lemon-DeLuca clan into the groves.

CHAPTER 13

If You Love Someone, Say It Right Then, Out Loud

Though it feels delicate to do so, I hang back until it's just me and Ricky.

"He just—he loses his patience sometimes," Ricky says before I can say anything.

I'm surprised you deal with that.

He side-eyes me, and my cheeks heat.

"My lack of filter keeps getting me in trouble," I say.

"Some things never change," he says, and I wince. "Not that that's a bad thing; I always liked that, you know." He smiles, but it's strained. "Easy to know how you felt."

"Is that hard with Cam?" *Oof*, this *is weird*. Sweat snakes down my back, sending rippling waves of shivers down my body. I don't want to know these details about their relationship.

"He has a hard time expressing himself. He's not like us, coming from loud Italian families that pry into our business and want to know every detail of our lives, whether we wanna talk about them or not. He grew up as one of seven kids, with parents who didn't care if he ever came home. So he's quick to react when he feels left out. It's a trigger for him," Ricky says. "I feel bad. Sometimes he doesn't know how to act around people. Doesn't trust a lot, you know? I wish he didn't leave, or act like that. It's family. *You*," he stresses, "know how important family is to me. I can't just ditch."

"I'm sorry."

"It's okay, it's not your fault," he says, and I shrink down until I'm two inches tall. It *is* my fault. I'm the one who threw away Cam's ticket.

It's not lost on me how Ricky, always the quiet rock, the one who shies away from vulnerability unless pushed toward it, is opening up to me, especially after how tense everything has been between us since the PJ. Hell, since I got that postcard.

"Thanks for listening," he says.

"You don't have to thank me," I say.

He takes in a big breath.

"Least I can do," I say. "Maybe I won't be the monster in your head."

That slipped out, unplanned.

I look away because to see any confirmation in his eyes would break me.

But he intentionally steps back into my line of sight. "What?" His face has softened, his eyes swollen with concern. "I—"

"It's okay, I get it." Lie. If anything, he should be my monster; instead, I've been pining for him and weaving my entire world around him, even in his absence. If he knew that, he'd think I'm pathetic. I know I do. For all the work I've done to make it seem like I could be a better version of myself without Ricky, admitting it was all for him *to him* destroys the integrity of my entire plan. "Have you?" I whisper.

"Do you really want the answer?"

I shrug, then nod. "Rip the Band-Aid off."

"Quanto basta," he whispers and my breath catches.

A couple Januaries ago, I was out window-shopping at the bougie Westchester mall with Zia Gab, Zia Rosa, and Matty—one of our favorite pastimes, perusing stores we could never afford and pretending we would buy handfuls of items only to put them away decrying "practicality"—when Ricky called. The second I saw his name flash on my screen, I was flooded with unexpected dread. Intuition prickled my skin. He never called me when I was out with family—he knew it was sacred time.

When I picked up, he didn't say anything.

"Ricky? What's wrong? What happened?"

He was breathing heavy, and I knew instantly he'd been crying.

I ran through every scenario in my head. Fear wrapped my heart when Ricky hoarsely whispered one word: "Nonno."

I looked up at my zias and Matty, who had huddled around me in the middle of the busy mall, confusion brewing like a cauldron.

"I'll be right there." I knew he couldn't talk about it over the phone.

"Please."

"I'll stay on the phone."

He said nothing, but I heard his breathing steady as I told the Coven we had to go. I kept the phone pressed to my ear, listening for him the entire excruciatingly long drive from the mall to

Blossom Avenue in slushy snow. I didn't even wait for Zia Rosa to put the car in park in Nonna's driveway before I flung open the door and sprinted toward the DeLucas' house. Ma and Nonna were already at the kitchen table, Ma draping her arms around Ricky's mom, forehead to forehead. Ricky's father stared out the kitchen window, eyes red and blotchy, arms folded. He didn't turn when I opened the door.

Sienna had just gotten home from her apartment in New York City, her bags still in the kitchen, and she flung her arms around me. "I'm so happy you're here. He won't come out of his room."

"I'm so— I loved your nonno so much." I tripped over my words, remembering all the hollow condolences from strangers when Dad passed. None of them meant a thing to me, just served as a cold reminder of what I lost and left a bitterness in feeling obligated to respond.

She nodded. The DeLucas always held their emotions close to the chest, but I saw the pain in her glassy eyes.

"What happened?"

"H-heart attack," she choked out. She nodded toward the backyard, where Ricky's father's gaze was held. "In his workshop. Ricky found him."

My legs shook, and I nearly broke. I had to get to Ricky.

Ricky's door was open. He was at the edge of his bed, phone still in hand, resting lackadaisically at his side. When he looked up and saw me, his chest started to heave. He looked toward the door, then back to me, and I knew what it meant. I closed it. Instantly, he crumbled. The resolve he'd built dissolved, tears streaming steadily down his cheeks.

I held him tight. "I got you."

"I . . . n-never g-got to say g-goodbye." His sobs were deep and guttural, and I'd never seen him like this before. It took all of me to keep myself together. I needed to be his rock. "T-tell him I l-loved him."

"He knew," I said resolutely. "Without a doubt, he knew you loved him."

He burrowed deeper into me, and I held him tighter than ever before.

"I love you," he whispered, over and over, and although I'd said those words to and about him so many times in my life, I never felt them as strongly as I did that day. I wanted to protect him, shield him from the pain, let him know that no matter what happened, he *was* loved.

"Remember the story you used to tell me about your nonno? The first time you worked with him in his main woodshop, and you asked him a million questions, and you thought you were annoying him because you were so fascinated by what he could create with his hands and some tools." Growing up, Ricky would spend hours telling me about his nonno's work and techniques, and though I never cared about the actual woodworking elements, I was always nothing short of captivated by Ricky because his eyes sparkled when he would tell me what he learned. "You were so eager all you wanted was to do the work, and you asked him when, when, when, how, why, how much pressure is enough." I laughed because Ricky used to talk so much, way more than me, and the older he got, the quieter he became, but not with me. "And he always said—"

"Quanto basta," Ricky finished. How much is enough, is just

enough. It was an expression Nonno used for everything—woodworking, cooking, life—even when it didn't make much sense, it always made sense.

Hours passed. The sun set, and eventually his cries ebbed. When he eventually wanted to emerge and join his family, he stood next to his father and held back his tears. Through the wake and the funeral and the luncheon afterward, Ricky never shed another tear. He grabbed his father's hand and squeezed. Even when Ricky's father finally broke at their house after the last guests left post-funeral, allowing himself to cry, Ricky held his own inside. I never wanted to pry or push, but Ricky spent so much time in his nonno's workshop, working on his nonno's final project—the oak family tree—that I wondered if perhaps he was losing himself to his grief and the guilt he felt in not saying goodbye.

I wonder if now, like then, Ricky's working overtime to protect himself from feeling what he should be feeling. Then again, I don't know what he should be feeling anymore, but I wish I wasn't his monster.

"Can I change that?" I ask.

He shrugs and steps forward. "Anything's possible."

I take a deep breath and follow him into the Avello Family Lemon Groves under the vine-draped trellis.

The dirt pathway winds up from the road at a rather steep incline, and though I'm worried about Nonna ahead, it seems like she's holding her own. Granted, she's attached to Niccolò, but she's determined to see as much of her home country as possible, and I don't blame her.

I take out my phone and start recording new @LemonAt FirstSight content, and through the lens, it looks so much like a fairy-tale scene in a movie.

The farther we hike up and around the winding path that carves the mountain, the more the rest of Amalfi disappears, and we enter an enchanted grove of trees with branches dotted with tiny lemons and massive green leaves that stretch overhead creating a canopy, shading us from the beating sun overhead. Sturdy, handmade wooden trellises are constructed to hold the arms of the lemon trees, and their branches wind around their knotted spindles.

Sweet citrus bursts through the air, mixing with a hazy floral scent.

Niccolò stops after a bend leading to an overhang with classic Italian antique cars, a 1959 seafoam Autobianchi Bianchina next to a 1963 blood-orange Alfa Romeo Giulia TZ, beneath black-netted treetops. Don't think I'm some car gay—there's a plaque explaining each car. It's an oddity in the middle of a grove, but Ricky's dad and Topher both seem keenly interested. He brings Nonna to a small hand-carved wooden bench to rest for a few moments.

I prop my phone up on a nearby ledge of a stone wall to keep recording while I soak in everything I can.

"You might have noticed that, uh, these trees are still flowering, and these lemons here are small, too tiny to harvest yet. I know what you may be thinking, these are not strong Avello lemons, and you're right. They're"—he talks with his hands, motioning—"growers, not showers, ah?"

"Girl," Benny says, snapping his fingers.

Ma, Zia Gab, and Zia Rosa cackle so loudly Niccolò jumps.

Tyler jests, "I don't know what he means," which makes Monroe laugh heartily.

Niccolò reaches around his back to a pouch-like bag that looks like it's made of plant fibers slung around his shoulders and pulls out a normal-sized lemon, one that looks similar to what we have in America. "This is probably the size lemon you are used to." He turns to Nonna. "Cosa vorresti dire?"

"Sì, è guisto," she says.

"Va bene," Niccolò says. "But what about—" He goes back into his pouch and pulls out a bulbous lemon the size of my entire damn head! No joke. This is not hyperbole, people! It's basically a pumpkin or a cantaloupe. But a lemon! It's so large he palms it like a basketball. "This is the signature Amalfi lemon, which we grow here, and all across the Amalfi region. The typical product of this land is the Sfusato Amalfitano. It's longer in shape, bigger. Our lemon is different because of the rind, the peel. We"—he refers to the lemon as part of himself—"have a lot of essential oils. Very aromatic. If you want to make a fantastic limoncello or lemon cake or pastry, many master chefs prefer to use our lemons because of the essential oils."

"How does it get so big?" Ma asks.

"I'm resisting the urge to joke so hard right now," Matty says.

Zia Rosa smacks him upside the head.

"Ah, I'm glad you asked," Niccolò continues, and passes the massive lemon around the group, giving each person the opportunity to palm it and marvel at its gargantuan size. "Here, in Amalfi, we exist in what's called a microclimate nestled between the sea and the Monti Lattari—you may know, or not, but the soil here in Amalfi is rich in volcanic minerals. Potassium and magnesium. From two active volcanoes. Maybe you'll go or have been to Monte Vesuvio. Pompeii in Napoli? We plant the trees on vertical soils. The terraces you see here are fortified by stone walls built by hand by my great-great-great-great-great-great-grandfather—that's six generations of Avello! Over two hundred years—anyway, the way the terraces are built controls the flow of rain to help retain water for the groves. Cool breezes from the sea get trapped in the valley there, and with the coastal sunlight, it all creates an ideal ecosystem for our lemons, which you cannot get anywhere but Amalfi," he explains proudly. "My family have been pioneers of farming these lemons, and protecting them."

"Is that why we've never seen them in the States?" Zia Gab asks.

"And you never will. Not organically. Import, not really. The cost is—" Niccolò's eyes widen, and he makes an explosive gesture. "These lemons can only be grown here due to the region, soil, and climate," he says. "Even if you brought back seeds from the mother tree"—he walks over to one particular tree whose thin trunk's sprouted arms reach up and over our heads, threading into the wooden trellises over us like a vine—"like this one, which is about two hundred years old, most trees go through a juvenile growth period that could last ten years! At least, without any fruit."

When Ricky passes the lemon to me, his hand lingers on its skin and my fingers graze his, and an electric shock shoots between us. He looks up. His cheeks are red.

The shape of the lemon is wild! Knobby and strange, its soft yellow skin pebbly, and either end comes to what looks suspiciously like a nipple, especially given its swollen nature. Touching the rough-yet-smooth skin releases a lemony fragrance I've never smelled before—it's familiar, like slicing open lemons on a wooden cutting board at home with Nonna, but it's stronger, not pungent, almost . . . sweet. I want nothing more than to taste it, but that's just me. I've always had a palate for sour anything, but Ma used to yell at me for sucking the pulp out of fresh lemons, or segmenting them like oranges and eating each one with a strawberry half and a little sprinkle of coconut sugar.

"It doesn't even look real," Ricky says, barely loud enough for me to hear.

Niccolò doesn't miss a beat. "Oh, it's real!" He reaches into the breast pocket of his bright orange Hawaiian shirt and pulls out a knife as I hand back the lemon. "Grazie!"

Cupping the fruit in one hand he takes the knife, and, in one swift motion, slices it methodically through until it rests in two halves. He presents the inside. The fruit in the center is familiar, though the segments are semi-separated, and the pulp is a paler yellow and larger than anything I'm used to. Beyond that, there's about an inch of thick white flesh beneath the surface of the skin. My lips recoil with a sensory memory of eating too much white flesh off a lemon back home and the icky bitterness that filled my mouth.

In another swift cut, Niccolò slices through the bumpy skin, thick flesh, and fruit and says, "Here, when we eat, we eat *the whole thing*." AND POPS EVERYTHING INTO HIS MOUTH LIKE IT'S THE MOST DELICIOUS THING HE'S EVER HAD.

No flinching. No sour pucker.

Pure bliss!

Ma and Zia Rosa both gasp and clasp on to each other. "No," they say in unison.

Niccolò laughs. "Try it." He cuts another slice.

But nobody steps forward.

"The lucky guy." Niccolò gestures toward Topher. "Marriage is scarier than this."

Sienna side-eyes him. "You haven't seen me in the morning."

"Lies, you're breathtaking at all times!" Topher says. "I gotta get my main man Fielder over here to try this with me. He's the foodie of the fam."

Niccolò immediately cuts another piece and beckons me over.

"Field-er! Field-er!" Topher chants, and Tyler and Trav follow suit until every single person in our group is chanting my name.

Ricky leans in. "You've eaten worse." He places a hand on the small of my back. "I believe in you, Fielder Lemon."

"We don't eat the skin," Zia Rosa chimes in. "It's nasty."

"Rosa!" Zia Gab says.

"Is okay, is okay," Niccolò says, sensing the tension in the Coven. "Is organic. We don't waste any part; it is part of who we are. Here in Amalfi, we do not use fertilizers or pesticides like in the States. And absolutely *no* waxing." He scrunches his face in disgust, and I suddenly feel the shame of being American in my bones. "Everything organic!"

"Well, in that case, give me a piece!" Zia Gab steps forward.

"Molto bene!" Niccolò shouts. He hands perfect triangular slices to me, Topher, and Zia Gab.

"Salute!" Zia Gab exclaims and tosses it back like it's a shot glass. She scrunches her face in anticipation, but it immediately softens, and her eyes widen. "No, this is phenomenal; you have to try it right now! Hurry up, boys, before I snatch yours!"

Topher and I cheer.

It's soft and pillowy, and the flesh isn't bitter at all—it's sweet, paired with a slight acidity from the rind and a dash of sour from the pulp; it tastes like the best piece of candy I've ever eaten.

"It's perfectly balanced, holy balls!" I say.

"Fielder, mouth!" Ma yells.

"Sorry, but Ma, you gotta try this. Seriously, everyone has to try this! I want to eat this like a freaking hand fruit!"

"You can just bite right into it, like an apple." Niccolò grabs another lemon and chows down like it's his last meal.

"I need fifty of these!" I shout.

He hands me another slice and cuts pieces for everyone else.

"Candy." Monroe snaps her fingers like she's at a slam poetry event.

Matty spins on his tiptoes. "Insane."

Ricky smiles sheepishly and offers me more lemon, and everything melts away.

"You don't like it?"

"I love it," he says. "But you love it more. Have mine."

A breathlessness overtakes me, and though we're not alone, I feel like we are. Like this entire lemon grove is our sanctuary, it belongs only to us.

"Come," Niccolò commands. "We've barely gotten started! Now that we've all gotten a little of nature's zucchero."

Nonna gets up and starts to do a little two-step, and Niccolò follows suit, taking the lead, and together they waltz the group along the stone terraces and down the narrowing dirt path up the mountain. I grab my phone from its perch and follow.

Breathtaking views of green-and-black-netted crops quilted into the fabric of the surrounding forests enrapture me.

We stumble upon wooden wagons carrying handwoven baskets, and Niccolò tells us about the hard work of the harvest, how most of it is done by hand, and how his father, who is now too old to climb the wooden terraces to harvest, taught him the backbreaking work it takes to run the grove at a young age.

"It is harder and harder to find local work. Every year, we produce less and less because of the instability of the climate. A few years ago, a nearby crop was destroyed entirely by an uncontrollable fire. If it is a harsh, hot year with no rain, everything dries up, and all it takes is one spark." He explains how everything he uses is natural—there are no plastic ties for the branches of the lemon trees because they hand-split willow branches to tie them to the arms of the wooden arbors, the structures that allow the trees to grow and spread. The only manmade mechanism he uses is a pulley system that looks like a miniature gondola to help move crates of fruit from the peak down the mountain.

As we climb farther up, carefully traversing stone steps, Niccolò explains to us how tourism has kept Amalfi—and the crops it survives on—alive. "When we have a less than fruitful year, it's harder to pay workers, so they don't come back." The Avello family is the last surviving family of lemon farmers. Every other family has left the region, moved to Rome or Milan, started new businesses and livelihoods.

"What keeps you here?" Topher asks, threading his fingers in between Sienna's.

Niccolò leads us to a break in the terraces, and we can see the expanse of his grove, and the workers who climb tirelessly to harvest and reinforce the structures the Avello family have been using for centuries. Rolling hills blanketed in lemon trees. Patches of nets that protect the groves. Donkeys being led by farmers over a ridge through a patchy grove across from us. A glimmer of the Tyrrhenian Sea sparkles in the distance, a soft blue jewel set against tall mountains.

"This." Niccolò's voice catches as he shows us his bounty, his reason, his purpose.

"Two hundred years, my family, our history, this land. Mio primo amore. You never get over your first love, and I'll never stop fighting to save it." His fingers gently lift a small bulb on a nearby branch. "Funny what can grow from love."

I'm usually not an emotional wreck (lies), but something about the way Niccolò talks about his legacy and the deep ties his family has to this land makes me think about who I am as a Lemon, our family, and what I want my own legacy to be. Before today, I never would have thought about something like this, and maybe it's being here in Italy, our origin country, surrounded by the people I love most that has me in my feelings. An overwhelming wave of emotions crashes over me, floods me like a tsunami: What am I doing with my life? Where am I going? Does any of it matter? All the followers and content buzzing around me that consumes my daily thoughts, is it real?

Like Ricky wrote in his journal, I'm a seed from a mother tree that hasn't blossomed yet, stuck in a juvenile state, waiting to fruit.

"Lemons are the most versatile food source here in Amalfi—we use them for everything," Niccolò continues. "The lemon is the lifeblood of the local economy and ecosystem, and commerce throughout Italy, from seafood to desserts to limoncello to candles, oils, soaps, and anything you can think of. Here, nothing is wasted."

"I always told you, boys," Nonna says looking to me, Topher, and Matty. "La Famiglia Limone è forte!"

Matty flexes a bicep and Topher says, "Let's goooooo!" but I'm struggling.

Ricky places a hand delicately on my back, and together we walk to a secluded spot, tucked away from the prying eyes of the Coven and our families.

I take a deep breath and feel the air coat my lungs as we take in the stunning views.

"You okay?" he asks.

I clear my throat and shake off these feelings as best I can. "I could totally move here and work as a lemon farmer." I nod toward two workers clad in jeans in thick work boots in the blistering sun scaling the terraces and carrying baskets of the mutant lemons.

Ricky laughs heartily. "You have many strengths, Fielder Lemon, but manual labor? Not one."

"Burn, and touché, but also how dare you?" I laugh and shift my body until we're parallel leaning against the railing.

Neither of us move, not consciously anyway.

My mouth is dry, so I lick my lips, and his eyes travel down to watch me do so.

Following his lead, I study the balls of his cheeks, the scruff dotting his jawline, the way his plump lips part.

Our feet move us toward one another until I can feel his breath.

Though we aren't touching, it's as if his arms are wrapped around my back, putting just the right amount of pressure to lure me into his web.

Ricky's big, beautiful brown eyes with flecks of green like the sea in the sunlight plead. As I drink him in, his smell is intoxicating—cedar and oak, woodchips with a hint of his favorite Dove "clean comfort" deodorant.

One slight touch of his pinkie against mine on the railing and I shiver.

"I almost missed you two!" Niccolò exclaims, shattering our moment.

Ricky steps backward.

Niccolò's holding what looks like a regular-sized lemon, but it's rounder and has more of an orange hue. He holds his paring knife and quickly slices through its skin, juice bursting from its seams. "I was telling the group that we've also had some happy accidents. We also grow oranges here, and the way the trees are planted and the rich volcanic soil sometimes accidentally breed, how you say, hybrids?" He nods to Topher and Sienna, a Lemon and a DeLuca. "A marriage between the lemon and the orange, a dazzling pairing that creates a most intriguing flavor."

Ricky and I hold our cuts.

"Salute!" Ricky says and takes a bite.

"What does it taste like?" I ask him.

"Possibility."

Hundreds of lemons drip from the overhead terraces as we tour the rest of the groves, winding through endless trees and against stone walls. Lemons of all shapes and sizes and seasons. Some that will never reach full maturity in time and will have to be pruned, some that fell and rotted away, and some that look so ripe and juicy and full I resist the urge to pick them off their stems.

Tucked away behind trees are colonies of bees in wooden boxes full of juicy honeycombs from the citrus flowers. Niccolò explains how the bees are vital in their farming efforts, though, again, the constantly changing climates—colder, longer winters and hotter summers, extreme droughts followed by heavy rainfall in the autumn months—threatens them, too.

When we finally reach the outdoor kitchen near the end of the tour—a sprawling restaurant-esque area with a terracotta tile floor, hand-carved wooden tables and chairs from local wood that makes Ricky drool (and ask a billion questions about local artisan woodworkers), and more lemon trees filling up every available space—Niccolò tells us that the Avello family chefs (his mother and wife) are hard at work preparing traditional Campania dishes, handmade fettucine made from the Amalfi lemon, fresh-caught fish, lemon tiramisu, lemon wine, and of course limoncello in the state-of-the-art facility set into the rock on the far side of the patio.

I record everything, capturing the magic of the Avello farm as best I can.

Then, Niccolò clasps his hands together and exclaims, "My boy!"

We all turn to see one of the most gorgeous guys I've ever seen—he looks like a younger Niccolò, tall and tanned olive skin kissed by the gods. Face like the *David* carved by Michelangelo himself, with cheekbones for days and hazel eyes that sparkle in the sun. He smirks, and I hear Monroe gasp.

Tyler glances at her, clearly jealous.

"Sorry, but wow," Monroe says.

Even straight Tyler concedes. "Okay, fine. That's a good-looking dude."

I turn to Matty, but he's on the move.

Niccolò introduces everyone to his son, Nic Jr., as Matty pushes to the front of the line and holds his hand out.

The spark is instant. Even *I* feel it.

Their hands meet.

Nic Jr. blushes. "Buongiorno."

"Hi. Err, Buongiorno! I'm Matty," he stutters, nearly drooling. "You can call me Matty. Or, um, Matt-thew." His face scrunches in disgust. "Or whatever."

I smack my hand against my skull. Zero chill.

"Matty," Nic Jr. repeats with an Italian flare, his voice deep.

They gaze at each other for a bit too long, neither letting go. If I know Matty, he's so deep inside his head that he's imagining some movie dream sequence where they're dancing alone under the stars in a sweeping musical number.

Niccolò coughs, and his son drops Matty's hand, raising his own behind his head in a show of embarrassment, perhaps for being caught lingering too long on Matty. His muscles pop as he scratches the back of his neck; a tuft of hair peeks out from under his arm.

"If I wasn't getting married . . . ," Sienna says, breaking through the tension and moving forward to stick out her own hand.

"My son will help with the rest of the tour if he doesn't get distracted," Niccolò says. "Va bene?"

Nic Jr.'s gaze falls. "Si, va bene."

I slide up beside Matty. "You good?"

Starry-eyed and goofy, Matty turns slowly and says, "When did you get there?"

Before lunch, we end the tour in the Avello family museum full of rusted centuries-old farming equipment and black-and-white photos of the Avello family in their prized groves, followed by a quick look into the limoncello factory. Inside, a man in a chef's coat and hat bottles fresh limoncello and offers us sample tastings, which we'll have more of with lunch. There's a small shop full of all the products Niccolò mentioned earlier, oils and candles and soaps and crates of massive Amalfi lemons. I want to buy everything. But one item in particular sticks out to me: a journal made from lemon rind cured like leather. Ricky is palming it.

"That's really cool," I say. "Unique."

"I lost my journal. Last year, at—" He stops himself.

Do I tell him I found it? That I've read it every single day he's been gone, searching it with Matty for clues as to how to win him back? Sounds stalkerish, huh?

"I miss writing," he says.

"You haven't been writing?"

He shrugs. "Haven't been inspired. No muses like you."

"Not even Cam?"

"Oh, I, um—" He coughs. "Obviously Cam. I just meant—" He sputters out a laugh.

I take the book from him and go straight to the register. "Happy early birthday."

"My birthday isn't for another four months."

"Happy July, then." I smile as he takes hold of the journal. "Maybe you'll be inspired again."

"Why'd you do this for me?"

I say the only thing I can: "Possibility. You deserve to be inspired, Ric. Maybe this is the seed you need to plant."

His eyes narrow. "Yeah. Maybe."

Possibility.

Fast-forwarding through the footage shot at the villa after a transformational day, I see the story of the Avello Family Lemon Groves.

One simple fruit—the foundation for not only one of the most incredible meals of my entire life—the fresh pasta and the tiramisu, which was light as a feather and melt in my mouth orgasmic—is also the cornerstone of a whole culture.

It's impossible to shake the reality and trajectory of their livelihoods, the family history, so deeply impacted by global climate change as millions of tourists flock to the Amalfi Coast every single year to take Instagram-worthy shots of Positano and tour the grottos and chow down on the local catches, but how many of them give back? And I'm no better—my family isn't, anyway. We're doing the exact same thing (on Topher's dime, since none of us could even Google a trip like this if the entire bill wasn't being footed by my extremely generous cousin), so we're not absolved of this. In fact, now that we know, I feel like we have an obligation.

I have an *obligation*.

Maybe I've been thinking about this @FoodForChange contest all wrong. It's not about winning a mentorship—sure, that would really help jump-start me on some sort of path toward a concrete career—and it's sure as hell not about followers and likes. It's about at least trying to make a difference. I never thought of my platform as something worthy of a cause, of spreading awareness about something important—no, crucial! It was always about me. Doing what I wanted to do, building an audience around me, trying to find the spotlight to actually make sense of my life, gain purpose. Topher is a self-made millionaire at twenty-five. Matty always dreamed of going to college and being an "entrepreneur," whatever that means. Even Ricky's goal of being a woodworker like his father and nonno before him is within his grasp.

Me? Maybe I can use my following to spotlight the Avellos' lemon groves and the hardships they're facing, how they're losing farmers to cities due to a lack of crops, and that their entire way of life here in what outsiders consider to be "paradise" is dying.

I can't explain it, but I feel a kinship with the Avellos, with the land, my Italian roots burrowing deep into the volcanic soil and spreading, spreading, spreading.

For the first time in my life, there's a flame for something beyond Ricky and the artificiality of Clock. This goes beyond

Clock and even @FoodForChange. It's small. A spark, but that's all I need to start a fire.

With a renewed sense of purpose, I save all the footage I've filmed to my drafts and make this my goal, not just for the week or the contest, but also to explore more in depth beyond this week. According to Sienna's carefully laid out itinerary, tomorrow and Sunday are the only free days, so I'll go back both days and see if I can interview Niccolò.

Skipping up the steps of the villa toward the pool area, I spot Ricky on the lanai overlooking the pool and the sea, a short, thin cylindrical glass of bright yellow limoncello next to him. His strong hands furiously work a pencil. Every few minutes, the wood dangles between his fingers and he looks up and out at the blue water, crinkling his brow. Returning to the page in front of him, he writes.

My heart swells, then sputters out of sync because as close as he is, he feels completely out of reach. Tears swell as the realization settles I may have to love Ricky DeLuca from right here for the rest of my life.

As long as he's happy.

He doesn't see me as he gets back to work, furiously mapping out his emotions in words the way he used to in his former journal all those years we were together.

I wish I knew what he is thinking . . .

ACT II

RICKY DELUCA

"Quanto Basta"

As I overlook the Tyrrhenian Sea, salt and sunset warping the pages of my new journal, I replay the conversation with Fielder, where he asked if I've turned him into a monster in my head.

"Can I change that?" he asked. His voice was timid, but so raw, not like the shiny, filtered Fielder you see on @LemonAtFirstSight. It caught me off guard. I hadn't seen that version of him in a long time.

After Fielder stood up for Cam at the tailor, then seeing Fielder nearly get clipped by the Vespa, I don't know, maybe it made me soften up a bit.

My heart was beating so fast, almost as if Cam could hear me when I said, "Anything's possible."

Problem is, I meant it.

I spot Fielder by the pool staring at me, and my heart starts beating fast again, pounding against my rib cage the way it did all day with him at the Avello Family Lemon Groves—watching his face light up with every new fact Niccolò told us, seeing his eyes sparkle like fireworks on the Fourth of July when he tasted the pasta and chowed down on the lemons like apples, ripping at the flesh with his teeth, noting how the dimples in his cheeks creased, and I resisted the urge to press them like buttons the way I used to when we were together.

Fielder notices me looking, and I quickly turn away.

That's when I spot Cam walking into the pool area, towel draped across his bare shoulders. He waves half-heartedly to me. We haven't spoken since he left. When I got back to the room, he was asleep, and I didn't want to wake him, so I slipped out, and knowing him, he most likely won't bring it up if I don't, since he hates confrontation and prefers to move past all tough moments without so much as a conversation, another byproduct of his upbringing.

Cam walks over to Fielder to shake hands, and I sink into my seat.

Flipping the blank pages of the journal Fielder bought me at the Avellos' shop, I feel guilty because I told Fielder I'd stopped writing.

In Seattle, dorming at the woodshop, I wrote every night.

Mostly to Fielder, hoping that if I just got words down on the page, the loss and heartache would leave my bones.

Someone wraps their arms around my upper body and rests their chin on the top of my skull. Candied lilacs fill my nostrils as a manicured stiletto-nailed hand slaps the side of my face.

"Gorgeous view, huh?" Sienna slides next to me.

"Nothing like it."

She presses her cheek to mine. "Which one are we talking about? The sea, or the boys? If option B, please specify the boy."

"Not funny." I slide away.

"Oh, come on, I'm the bride, you have to amuse me." She offers a toothy grin, but I'm not smiling.

"I'm not that person, See."

"What person is that?" She leans forward, propping her chin up on her elbow.

"Never mind."

"Don't be so serious; I was only joking," she says. "I like Cam."

I glare at her.

"I do! He seems really nice. I just don't know him, not like I know Fielder. I grew up with Fielder. He's, like, basically family, you know? It's—different."

I grind my teeth.

"Sorry." She lays her head on my shoulder. "If I haven't yet, thanks for being here. Dealing with me."

"As bride-to-be, you've got me on a technicality. My loyalty as man of honor is to you in your time of need."

She laughs. "You've been around the Lemons too long. Dramatic much?"

"Speaking of, how's your new mother-in-law?"

She flaps her lips. "I love Topher's mom, but she's a bit of a—"

"Helicopter?"

"Right? I think she would build a house up Topher's ass if she could," Sienna says, looking around, making sure we're alone. "I love her, though. She's made sure the wedding planners have everything taken care of, that I'm good, Topher's good, Mom and Dad, too. She's been amazing with everyone. I'm just overwhelmed, and I can't help but think, if Nonno could see all this." Tears form in the corners of her eyes.

"He'd never shut up about it. He'd be happy to eat off a fruit stand on the side of the road. Or one of those sandwich stands."

"A little prosciutto and fresh mozz on ciabatta. Dash of balsamic."

"Fuhgettaboutit." I laugh despite myself.

"I haven't seen you smile in a long time." She dabs at her eyes with the sleeve of her oversized hoodie. "Not like you were today. All day. You're always so serious."

"Am not."

"Okay, Nonno."

"Scusi?"

"You're *so* Nonno. Very stern, focused, harder than you need to be. An old man in a nineteen-year-old's body."

Something Niccolò Avello said during the tour earlier today comes roaring back to me. Because his family has lived and worked on the groves for over two hundred years, he joked that his blood isn't blood, but juice from the lemon. Nonno used to say we had wood in our bones. I wonder if that's what hardened me?

"I miss him, too. I think about him all the time. But you need to loosen up a bit." Sienna shakes out her arms. "Ever since you moved to Seattle, every time I've seen you, it looks like you're just trying to get through the day."

I shrug. "Probably because I am."

Concern floods her face. "That's no way to live." She places a hand on my forearm.

I study her ginormous diamond engagement ring. "It's not that I dread *every* day."

"What *do* you dread?"

How do I answer this—put into words exactly what I dread when I myself don't even have the answer? My eyes search the grounds of the villa for something, anything, to distract me.

They fall on *him.*

Fielder.

In the courtyard by the pool, talking to Monroe and Tyler. He's laughing that full-chested belly laugh that infects everyone around him.

"You're smiling again," Sienna says. "Here I was worried you and Fielder would rip each other apart and ruin my wedding by falling into the cake or something."

"That only happens in cheesy Amazon Prime rom-coms."

"Who knew it'd actually be you two ripping each other's clothes off."

"I— What? We're not—"

She laughs. "Can I ask why you broke up with him? I still don't get it."

"We were on two different—"

"Paths," she finishes. "I know, I know. You've told me that a billion times. But from where I'm standing, your paths seem to be crossing at just the right place, and at just the right time."

"Dearly beloved, we're gathered here to celebrate the union of Topher Lemon and Sienna DeLuca," I say, stiffly mimicking a priest. "It's not exactly fate."

"How do you know? And why does it matter if it was or wasn't?" Sienna asks. "You're too practical for that anyway. You think it was fate that brought me and Topher together?"

"Actually, yeah, I do. You said you and Monroe were out in the city for her and her twin sister's birthday and ended up at some hidden speakeasy in the Village you needed a password for, which you didn't have, and as you were about to leave, the secret bookcase opened and who walked out?"

Sienna's grinning ear to ear. "I hadn't seen him in years, since we both left for college, and when I did again, it was like we were the only two people in the entire city."

I felt the same way earlier at the lemon groves with Fielder. When our pinkies touched like we were the only two people in Italy, and Amalfi belonged to us.

"As if the universe or the cosmos were reintroducing us." Her eyes are beaming and bright. I've never seen them sparkle like this. I didn't even know it was possible; I just thought looks like these were something authors wrote in books. "Our first date, we walked around the Lower East Side and got Artichoke Basille's pizza. Very low-key. Our second date, you know what he did? In his apartment, he re-created the time our moms set up a projector in the backyard and played Disney's *Tangled*. I don't know if you remember that; you must have been, like, six? But you and Fielder were there."

Of course I remember that. I didn't care much for fluffy Disney, preferring bloodier, more action-packed fare. But Fielder cried, and I couldn't stop looking at him.

"During the song 'I See the Light,' he found my hand and we held hands for the rest of the movie. It was really sweet. Topher and I were eleven? Babies!" She continues, telling me how she knew then he was the one. "He remembers the small things." She laughs as she reminisces how nothing happened when they were eleven, even though he asked Sienna out all through high school many, many times, but she didn't want a boyfriend yet.

"Back then, I had Nonno in my ear telling me to work hard and forget about boys. Which I'm grateful for because I ended up laser-focused on a career, and now I'm working with Monroe on building her fashion brand, with my marketing and merchandising expertise. I get crap a lot, especially from the Coven who 'joke' that I'm trying to fleece the golden child. Or that I'm the one who chose to get married in the most expensive place on earth." She shakes her head. "All Topher. I'm happy to go along with it, but I want a life with him, not just a wedding."

"You *love* love him," I say, almost as if reinforcing it for myself.

"I do. I wasn't ready for that in high school. But that's what I'm trying to tell you. I don't think it's fate that brings two people together; it's being *ready* for love, the kind of love that's earth-shattering and life-changing and time-consuming. The stuff hard wood is made from. Remember that old family tree Nonno was working on? I loved that thing so much. What I loved most was that it felt like he was immortalizing his love with Nonna, our family. Taking the seed it was grown from and carving our history into it, fortifying it into something that couldn't be broken."

I don't mention that wood can easily break, so I make vomit noises instead.

"I know, someone kill me." She reciprocates the vomit sound, and sticks out her tongue. "I sound like a Hallmark card."

"It's bad, See," I say. "But I get it. I *am really* happy for you."

"I'm happy for me, too."

I chuckle. "Just enough."

At the same time, we both say, "Quanto basta."

"Do you love him?"

"Fielder? What? I mean, no, why would you—"

"No, Cam?" she cuts me off. "Your boyfriend . . . ?"

"Oh, yeah. Um." I take a deep breath.

She rests her hand on my arm. "If you have to think about it . . ."

"I care about him. A lot. But I'm not there. He's a great guy, and it feels like something we're definitely working toward, you know." As I'm speaking, it sounds like I'm giving myself a pep talk before a big game, pumping up to make myself think I can do the impossible. The irony isn't lost on me, and it certainly isn't getting past Sienna because she's glaring at me with the most intense stare I've ever seen. "And he knows that. I've been very up front about where we stand. I'm—"

"How long have you guys been together?"

"On and off for, like, six months. Ish."

"I want you to be in *love* love," Sienna says. "You deserve that."

"You deserve what, babe?" Cam says, walking up beside Topher. A curious pair.

"The world." Sienna beams, seeing her fiancé. "The hottest man in Italy!"

"He certainly is!" Cam wraps his arms around my shoulders and kisses the top of my head.

Topher puffs his chest out in a show of masculinity. "Vincenze has our ride to Ravello leaving soon, babe," he says to Sienna. "You look gorgeous, as always."

"Hey, Sienna," Cam says. "Before you guys go, I already spoke to Topher, but wanted to tell you, too—I'm sorry about earlier. I know it wasn't your fault about the tickets to the lemon farm thing, and I didn't mean to cause a scene. I didn't mean to make it weird or—" His hands and voice are shaking. "I kind of felt left out, like I was being singled out or something. I talked to Fielder too, to get an insider's perspective. He's an actually good guy."

I can practically read Sienna's mind: *Don't sound so surprised!*

She nods slowly, eyes wide. "No need to apologize at all. It was clearly an oversight on my part. Do me a favor—check everything and make sure your personalized yacht pass is there before Thursday, just in case we have to call ahead. I double-checked everything, but mistakes happen, clearly."

"Clearly," Cam says, and I hold my breath.

Awkward.

Sienna clears her throat. "Cool, well." Wrapping me in her arms, careful not to smudge her makeup, she says, "Smell you kids later. I have a hot date."

Topher salutes us both.

Once gone, Cam wedges his legs next to mine. "How was the lemon thing?"

My lizard brain immediately goes to Fielder. "What lemon thing?"

"The farm?"

"Oh, it was nice. Fun."

"A man of many words, as per usual." He kisses my cheek.

"What did you mean by that, when you said Fielder's *actually* a good guy?"

Cam's brows crinkle. "Nothing." He lets out a breath. "You didn't really have many nice things to say about him when we started dating."

"I didn't?"

"You were heartbroken, babe. Don't you remember? Shut off from his life completely. How he was addicted to his phone, being so 'online,' which always bothered you, but couldn't be there for you when you needed him." He laughs. "You were pissed last night after talking to him, which you still didn't tell me what happened between the two of you, and the day before, too, leading up to the flight, you were anxious and moody *thinking* about seeing him. What happened today that changed all that?"

He's not wrong. I came here hell-bent on never speaking to Fielder again. I did not see a way forward with him. Not after Fielder's no-contact continued to wreck me in ways I never imagined possible.

But that's the thing about Fielder Lemon:

One look from him, and no matter the devastation, I'm hooked back in, despite not wanting to be.

"Just trying to keep the peace for my sister." I kiss Cam. "Thanks for apologizing. Means a lot. I know it wasn't easy."

He shrugs. "It's important to you. And I'm the right guy for you, right?"

"Why do you always ask me stuff like that?"

He kisses the tip of my nose. "Like what?"

"Like if you're the right guy for me?"

"Just making sure." Cam gnaws at his thumbnail, chewing on it. "I'm gonna go take a shower before dinner. Wanna come?"

"Mind if I write for a bit?"

"I didn't know you write. Where'd you get that?"

"I, uh, got it at the gift shop today."

Cam admires the journal. "Beautiful. I wish I knew Italian. Teach me one day?"

"Va bene," I say.

"What did you say?"

"Okay."

"Va bene," he repeats with a smile, and it makes my stomach cramp. After getting up, he bends down to kiss me, but before he leaves, he says, "Also, did Fielder say anything to you after I left the lemon farm?"

"About what?"

"Oh, nothing. Thought maybe he might have mentioned our, um, hug after the Vespa took him out. It was a real blended family moment." His voice goes up at the end, the way it does when he lies. I wonder what he's lying about.

Instead of doing the hard thing and digging, I finish what I started writing because for the first time in a while, I'm inspired. I'll figure the rest out tomorrow.

FROM THE NEW JOURNAL OF RICCARDO DELUCA

"QUANTO BASTA"

Nonno used to make fire
fuoco, zucchero, acqua, limoni
he taught me to measure twice, cut once, quanto basta
to be patient, learn his stories with ears and heart
zest 'til my hands ache—
sneak a bite of the rind, sweet white flesh, and pulp—

drop peels into a large glass jar
fan the flames for seven days
because fire requires time to spread, amore mio
and on the sixth day, boil acqua
add zucchero until it dissolves
for more hair on the chest, add more acqua
for a sweeter finish, add more zucchero
quanto basta
cool overnight, and in the morning
make a wish, quanto basta—
—che cosa vuoi?
When it's ready, serve chilled with the boy you love
at night under the stars by the Sea

I've sipped limoncello with Nonno,
I've had an Amalfi lemon,
I've been to the Sea,
but you—you're more elusive,
one none can equal,
the perfect amount
not too much
not too little

Un sogno, un giorno
quanto basta

RICKY DELUCA

"Measure Twice, Cut Once"

. . . One Year, One Month, One Week, and Two Days Earlier . . .

"I'm a coward," I said before the door to Sienna's car had clicked shut.

She idled in the driveway of Topher's Hamptons mansion, staring. "You're lucky I was still home at Mom and Dad's for the week." It was after my graduation. She hadn't gone back to the city yet. "You gonna tell me what's going on, or—" She stopped mid-sentence, reaching for my face. With her thumb, she wiped a steady stream of tears from my cheek I didn't realize were flowing. I couldn't feel anything I was so numb. "You're shaking, Ric. What the hell happened? Did Fielder do something to you? I'll murder—"

I shook my head. "No, he didn't do anything to me. *I* broke up with him, and I'll tell you everything, but I need you to drive before I change my mind and go back inside."

Like a dam breaking, I lost it. I hadn't cried that much since

Nonno passed away. I told Sienna everything, including how Fielder and I spent our last night in each other's arms, holding tight to each other like it was the last time we'd ever be together. When Fielder finally fell asleep and I knew I wouldn't, I slipped out and called Sienna. Packed my bags. I couldn't face him in the morning.

"You didn't even say goodbye to him?"

"How could I?"

"Ricky, I love you, but that's cruel." Looking in the rearview mirror, she slammed on the brakes and pulled over onto the narrow sandy shoulder.

"What are you doing?"

"Are you sure you want to do this? Because some things you can't come back from, and I don't want you to regret anything."

Dense fog drifted over dunes as Sienna's question swelled my brain, and though I already knew the answer—every bone in my body wanted to go back, take it back—I had made the right decision.

"Misurare due volte, tagliare una volta," I said, thinking about Nonno, steady at his workbench in the shed behind our house on Blossom Avenue. How, when he was alive he would instruct me to sit on my hands so that I wouldn't get myself into trouble. Twitching, itching to get dirty, to do what he did, sitting on them forced me to watch. To pay attention. To learn by example. He always took his time measuring, often going back two, three, four, five times, checking and triple-checking.

"Do it already!" I would say.

Laughing, he would shrug and "do it" as if on my command. His thick, callused hands moved effortlessly across wood grains.

"About time." My feet bounced back and forth in anxious anticipation.

"Anything worth doing is worth your patience," he said in his thick Italian accent. "What's hard won't be easy, and what's right is never wrong."

"Isn't that kind of an obvious riddle?"

"Obvious?" He didn't waver as he cut, but his eyebrow arched. "Seems that way, but what's hard and right doesn't come without careful consideration." He finished his cut, blew the sawdust in the opposite direction, and admired his work. Then he handed what he was working on to me.

I turned it over in my hand, and I had zero idea what it was—a spindle for a chair, or a table?—but I loved it.

He grabbed my face, cupping both cheeks with both of his hands so he knew I was paying attention. I looked down and studied a deep, healed cut framed by scar tissue that stretched from his pointer finger across the fleshy pad to his thumb. I'd heard the story countless times, how, when he was a young kid, he was so eager to do what his father did that he took a saw not knowing how to use it and nearly lopped off his thumb. He used a wiggly noodle to demonstrate how it dangled from the tendons. Luckily, he regained near full use of it and used the pain to make him stronger, more focused until he honed his skills and became one of the best woodworkers around.

"Misurare due volte, tagliare una volta," he said, then repeated for emphasis.

Measure twice, cut once.

He lightly smacked my face and sent me off to get him a glass of wine.

From Nonno, I learned to approach every cut, every decision from a place of information, logic, accuracy. It was paramount for a woodworker to not waste time and precious wood, and it became a mantra I used for everything: be prepared, thoughtful, and thorough before acting.

That was what I thought I was doing with Fielder Lemon.

When I got the letter that I was accepted as Christian Richards's apprentice at Sawdust Woodworkers in Seattle, Washington, my first thought was that Nonno would be so proud of me. If I couldn't learn directly under his tutelage, the way my father did, I would settle for the best-known craftsman in the States.

But my second thought, and nearly every thought that came after—Fielder. And my heart nearly stopped ticking.

What would happen to us? I went over it in my head a billion times: he was still in high school, had one more year to go, and it wouldn't be fair to him to keep him on a string. I would be busy learning on the other side of the country, and I wanted him to have a fun last year, to enjoy his senior year the way I did. I thought if we stayed together, neither of us would be present enough, not the way we needed to be. My mom echoed this when she said, "Most high school relationships don't work out," despite the fact that she met Dad in high school and started dating him shortly after, and Nonno married Nonna in Italy at seventeen. She told me she wished she had gotten to experience more of life before *settling.*

That word *settled* in my brain, burrowed its way in, and steeped like tea.

If I'd asked Fielder to wait for me, he would have. That was how much he loved me. And I loved him too, too much to let him put his life on hold for me, or to spend his entire senior year preparing for a move to Seattle when he needed to think about what he wanted to do with his life. I didn't want Fielder to delude himself into thinking being a Clock influencer could be a real career. He had to figure out what he really wanted, and he deserved that chance without me influencing him in any direction.

I agonized over what to do but couldn't shake that we were moving in two different directions physically—geographically—even though we weren't *emotionally*. As someone who deals in measurements, living across the country from Fielder and having to figure out how to make a relationship work while he was still in high school and I was pursuing a brand-new path on my own seemed impractical. And in woodworking, there is no place for impracticality. I needed space to take care of me, to find myself on my own. It would have been too hard to do that while Fielder still needed me, even though I needed him, too. That was what I told myself, as my body screamed for Fielder, and I knew I was making a horrible mistake giving up on the best person in my life.

Fielder did nothing but love me, and I couldn't love him hard enough to stay. I told him he needed to be more independent, that he never took care of me because he was so focused on his phone and building his Clock channel. But that was only partially true. Sure, he was on his phone too much, but he never stopped building me up and making time for me. I wanted him to do that for himself, too, the same way I wanted to see who I was without Fielder.

So I made him the wooden dream box and poured every ounce of love I had for him into carving its notches and assembling it, hoped that it would be enough for him to dream without me. Maybe in my absence, Fielder would learn what I had known my entire life: that he could thrive without me.

Maybe we would end up bringing each other down.

That was the seed of the story I started telling myself.

A text from Fielder came through as I mulled over Sienna's question:

You left without saying goodbye

No emojis, no questions, no pleas. The most un-Fielder-like text I'd ever received, and it made me nauseated.

I showed Sienna, and immediately, she said, "Oh my god, he's typing more!"

For thirty minutes, Fielder started and stopped typing.

Nothing ever came through.

"Are you gonna respond?" she asked. "You have read receipts on for each other."

I nodded. "I don't know what to say."

"What do you want to say?" she asked.

I love you

But my blue texts turned to green. Fielder had blocked me.

I didn't stop crying until I landed in Seattle three days later.

. . . *Two Months and Five Days Post-Breakup* . . .

Hey Fielder. Happy birthday! I hope you're celebrating at some cool new spot with the Coven. Usually we'd be getting ready for a new school year and going to the Blossom Avenue Italian Feast and stuffing our faces with zeppole and fried Oreos lol. Hopefully you and Matty continue the tradition. I just got back to the dorm from another grueling day at the shop. My hands are bleeding, but I love it. I'm still not sleeping well.

I wrote a new poem for you. It's called "you":

I made a list
of everything I love,
all I lost and missed out on.
It was only one word.

Happy birthday, Fielder ♥
Ricky

After I hit Send, I scrolled through three months' worth of green bubble texts to Fielder that I knew he would never read, and sent one more text for good measure. I could have tried some other way to get ahold of him, get a dummy phone and call or text, but it was more comforting to stay blocked than face the reality that he hated me and would tell me as much if I did reach him.

On the off chance that this slips through your phone's impeccable block feature, and you get the flood of messages I've been sending every single day since I left New York, I want to say it again: I'm sorry.

Tomorrow was a new day. Maybe then the skies would be blue.

... ***Six Months, Two Weeks, and Four Days Post-Breakup*** ...

"Are you afraid?" Christian Richards loomed over me, arms folded, studying my craftsmanship as I worked. He was a tall, slender man with a handlebar moustache like from an old Hollywood western. Standing at six-foot-seven, he towered over everyone in the class. He had long silver-blond hair pulled back into a ponytail.

"Sir?" I wasn't afraid of him, per se, but I wanted his respect, and it seemed like lately I couldn't do anything correctly. My work was suffering, and he was hypercritical of everything I was producing.

I lifted my safety goggles and rubbed my eyes. Something had felt off all day—my body wouldn't cooperate, and my head was back in New York. More than usual.

"You're working that wood like it's going to bite you. So timid. You are not in control." He crouched down. "You're distracted. You're not commanding the wood; the wood is commanding you."

He was talking at me, but nothing was sinking in. I wanted to scream. His words were far away, like I was underwater and he was yelling from above the surface.

A hand on my shoulder jolted me to attention. "Mind if I show you?" Christian and I traded places, and with a brilliant, fluid ease, his hands melded with the wood. "All it needs is your guidance, and it listens." He stood up and instructed me to do as he did.

The second I sat down, I noticed the date on the screen of my phone because Sienna texted. I wasn't paying attention, and the blade of the saw snagged my thumb, and I blacked out.

I woke up a second later in a pool of my own sweat, lavender smelling salts held under my nostrils, my head cradled in Christian's hand.

One of the other students handed me a cold bottle of water from a vending machine, and I could barely choke down a few sips.

"You might need stitches. Come on, I'll take you to the emergency room," Christian said. "Do you have somebody local you can call? Family? A friend?"

For months after I moved to Seattle, I had no friends. I largely kept to myself. After spending Thanksgiving at my parents' new place in South Carolina, Sienna convinced me to get on the apps. That was how I met Cam Wallace, a freshman studying computer science at the University of Washington. He messaged me instantly. He was the only guy around my age wearing a shirt *and* showing his face *and* willing to hold an actual conversation *without* it getting sexual once, so I agreed to meet him at a coffee shop. So we built a solid friendship, and he helped me get through my heartache in being without Fielder.

Cam was the only person I thought to call. There was no use calling Mom and Dad because they were in South Carolina, and I didn't want to bother Sienna and Topher in Los Angeles. There was nothing anyone could do for stitches. Besides, I was still reeling over the revelation that she was dating Fielder's cousin, a secret she told me I had to keep from our parents because neither her nor Topher wanted the families finding out. Not that I could blame them. I didn't want to know myself.

"Do you want to tell me what happened back there?" Christian asked, but as I waited with him for the doctor to see me, I had the overwhelming urge to call Fielder.

He was the only one I knew who would understand.

It was dark now, the harsh fluorescent lights contrasting the blackness outside. I scrolled through all the green bubble texts. I wasn't texting Fielder every day anymore. I gave up on that after I met and started hanging out with Cam because I started feeling less alone. I had sent my last text to Fielder on Christmas Day, nearly two and a half weeks ago. Fielder still had me blocked.

But I had Matty's number. I heard Nonno's voice: *Measure twice, cut once.*

"Do you mind if I make a call?" I asked Christian, who nodded and excused himself. I took a deep breath, closed my eyes, and pressed the call button.

It rang once, twice, three times.

"H-hello?" Matty's voice shook on the other end.

I nearly burst into tears. Not that Matty sounded at all like Fielder, but to be this close to him again felt like a fever dream. Maybe it was all the oxygen in the hospital. "Hey, Matty. It's—"

"I know. What's, um, up, Ma? I'm out with Fielder at the mall, remember?"

"Hey, Zia Rosa!" Fielder's voice came through like a burst of sunshine, and I couldn't speak. Then I heard him ask, "Everything okay?"

"Field, can you grab me a Mountain Dew? I can't hear. I'm just gonna go over here for a sec." Matty breathed into the receiver for a few paces. "What do you want, Ric?"

"I wanted to talk to Fielder."

"No. Absolutely not," Matty said. "He's finally happy and stable and doing well."

"Please—"

"Why?"

I couldn't answer. I needed to talk to Fielder because he would understand why I was so distracted today of all days. Because I needed him. He was my support system, the voice I wanted to hear at the end of a hard day, and the one mistake I wished I could unmake. The only regret I'd ever had.

My breathing rapidly increased as one thought crossed my mind: *I made a mistake.*

"Please ask him, Matty."

Matty didn't say anything.

"You there?"

"Hold on." Matty muttered a "fungool"—the bastardized version of "va funculo"—under his breath and muted me. A minute later, he came back. "He said, 'No thanks.' He's got to film some content for this new vegan health bar that opened in the mall." He lowered his voice. "I, um—sorry." *Click.*

If I were hooked up to IVs and machines, this would be the part of the movie where I'd probably crash, and all the nurses and doctors would rush in with carts and bloodstained gowns trying to save me.

But life wasn't a movie, and I didn't die, though it felt like an emotional death all over again.

As I was reeling, Cam rushed into the ER from the rain.

"Ricky! Are you okay?" His wet curls pressed to his forehead were endearing. He took my uninjured hand and held it as the doctor stitched my thumb. Lonely, I craved that kind of attention. "What happened?"

I didn't want to talk about it, but I knew I needed to. "Something was off. My body felt weird all day. All week, really. It's been this way for a couple years around this time. Then I saw the date, the anniversary of my nonno's death."

Cam nodded. "You've told me how much he meant to you."

"He was everything. I can't believe I didn't remember. Or put two and two together. My head just wasn't on right today." I nodded toward the bloody massacre in the doctor's hands. "Clearly, I miss him." The words jumbled in my mouth, and tears pooled at the edges of my eyes and spilled down my cheeks. I didn't know if I was talking about Nonno or Fielder at this point, but I missed them both, and in that moment, I hated them both for leaving me alone.

"And I stupidly thought, 'Hey, let me call my ex because he'd understand,' and turns out *that's* not the case at all. He'd rather post on Clock."

I had been wrong earlier. Breaking up with Fielder wasn't a mistake. He was too obsessed with his phone and that damn Clock App, spending more time cultivating his online persona than focusing on supporting me. He didn't care about me at all anymore. I was still stuck on him, but Fielder had clearly moved on.

It was time that I did the same.

Maybe now, I thought, *I can let him go and figure out who I am without Fielder Lemon.*

Later that night after being discharged from the hospital, we hung out in Cam's dorm room streaming the *Barbie* movie.

Cam moved closer and closer, and I let him.

The warmth of Cam's body felt . . . nice, safe, familiar, yet new and daunting all at once. His fingers threaded between mine, and his thumb stroked the top of my hand.

"Let me take care of you," he said.

"You're doing a great job," I whispered.

Cam's curly hair had dried and fell just above his eyes, which pierced mine as he stared so deeply at me. "Just wait until my world-famous head rub."

"What makes them world-famous?"

He shrugged. "You'll just have to see." Delicately, as if not to break me further, he slid behind me so that I rested my back to his chest. "Get comfy." He started massaging my scalp, and I closed my eyes in pure bliss. "Can I tell you something?"

I moaned.

"I like you," he confessed.

During "I'm Just Ken," as Ryan Gosling was belting, he leaned in and kissed me.

I kissed him back.

WEDNESDAY

RICKY DELUCA

"Scorza di Limone"

Amalfi's morning air is so cool and crisp it lures me from bed to the balcony.

Cam is already awake, shirtless, sipping a cappuccino and dunking a biscotti into the rich liquid.

A gauze of soft clouds encases the sky, but a warm yellow from the sun peeks through. A few anchored rowboats dance atop the waves as fishermen with beards and brown hats hope for a good catch.

I lean against the doorframe and take in the view.

"Morning, beautiful." Cam stands to hug me. His teal-and-gray-striped linen pajama pants flap in the breeze. "It's a literal dream, isn't it?"

"Sure is. What did you wanna do today? We have a free day. I was thinking we could go into town to meet local woodworkers—"

Cam rolls his eyes. "Sounds boring."

Startled by his admission, I say nothing. Am I too boring for him?

"JK, JK," Cam says. "Sounds like a blast." He avoids looking at me. Nonno always told me when people avoid direct eye contact, they're lying.

"Nah, it's fine," I say. "I do have some stuff to square with Sienna, and Topher asked me to help plan something for Sienna with Fielder, so maybe—"

"Can we have one day where we don't talk about Fielder?" He tips the rest of the cappuccino into his mouth in one swift gulp, and his nostrils flare.

"I thought you two were cool?" I ask.

"I'm fine, it's just a lot, being around him. All day, all night. Watching him laugh with your parents. They *love* him. I don't think your mom has said two words to me."

"She doesn't know you, Cam." I wince.

"I know you guys have history, but . . ." He takes a deep breath. "Whatever. I just don't trust him."

"You don't know him, Cam."

Nothing hammers my wood quite like someone going after someone I lo—

I catch myself.

Anyway. I can say whatever I want about Fielder, but if someone else says a word, it makes me want to take a sledgehammer to a cinder block. I grind my jaw and ask myself what Nonno would do. He'd center himself and *listen*.

"I know what you told me for months. How he spent so much time on his phone that he ignored you. How he blocked you so you couldn't even talk to him. *I* was there for you, remember? You don't have Clock or anything, so you wouldn't know, but he's using you for likes." He grabs his phone and taps the screen until he pulls up Fielder's channel, flashing me the screen. "Watch the last two. At least read the comments. Apparently, you two were a hot commodity once upon a time. You didn't tell me that."

"I don't need to. Whatever Fielder posts has nothing to do with me." I never cared about being on @LemonAtFirstSight, and I don't care now. It made Fielder happy, excited, and if the comments are blowing up from something involving me, let them. "The comment section is *not* real life, and I feel bad for the people who live there."

He scoffs.

"How deep of a dive did you do?" I ask.

"Deep enough to know his fans love Rickder-Fieldy content." His face scrunches, and his eyes go glassy. "The comment section noticed you in the background of his latest, and the way he edited it really makes it seem like he's hinting at something. I think he's using you being here to help boost his Clock videos." Cam's hands are shaking as he sets his phone down in front of me. "Guess they don't know Fielder wrecked you."

"I know you're looking out for me," I say, "but—"

"I don't want him using you."

"Don't you think I can decide that for myself?"

"You don't seem to have the best judgment," Cam says through gritted teeth.

"What's that supposed to mean?"

He crosses his arms. "I'm sick of feeling like I'm second to Fielder."

"When do I—"

"This whole week, I've heard stories from your family how you and Fielder used to be this iconic couple." Cam's pacing back and forth, and he looks like he's on the verge of tears. "I've seen it for myself on Clock, too. I get it, there's history." I grab his hands and lead him to the café table by the balcony railing where I sit him down. "I see how you've acted just leading up to coming here, knowing you'd be around Fielder. You were together for your entire lives basically. But we've been together for six months, and you won't even properly have a conversation where we define our relationship." His legs are shaking restlessly.

"What do you mean?"

"Like, are we actually boyfriends?"

"I call you my boyfriend," I say.

"That's not the same," Cam says. "And you know it. Every time I ask you if we can, like, define our relationship, you say, 'We're dating.'"

I nod. "We're dating, yeah."

My heart is beating out of my chest. I've avoided this for months because it's a scary conversation I've not been ready for. Defining our relationship with a label beyond "dating" terrifies me because it means having to open myself up to getting hurt again. Or worse, being the one who does the hurting. Maybe that makes me a coward.

Actually, I know it does.

"That really sucks, Ric." Cam buries his face in his hands. "I deserve more than that. I want you to *be* my *boyfriend*. Exclusively, in definition and promise."

"Cam . . ." I take his hands, pry them off his face so I can see him. But I can't do more.

His eyes are splotchy and red. "I want to occupy the same spot as Fielder in your mind. If I can't, let me go."

After a few minutes of silence, he says, "I think I'm going to go into town by myself. Maybe hit the public beach. You go to the woodshop. I think doing this separately today is a good idea. Gives us both time to think."

After a long hot shower, I emerge ready to take on the day, heading up to see Vincenze about getting into town by myself. Running my hands through my long hair, I shake out the remaining moisture like a dog when I run into Tyler, who asks what I'm doing today. When I tell him I'm heading into town and ask if he wants to join, he leans in close.

"Keep a secret?" Rocking back and forth excitedly on his heels, he looks like a giddy kid. "I got a date!"

My brows arch. "Monroe."

Color drains from his already pale face.

"Worst kept secret ever. You're all over her."

"Is it that obvious?"

"Only to people with eyes."

"Oh, okay." He scrunches his face. "Wait."

We both laugh.

"She's a goddess, dude," I say, having known Monroe since Sienna was a college freshman at FIT and Monroe was her roommate. "Smart as hell, probably more than all of us combined. *And* she's an *artist*. Like, a real visionary." Monroe has what it takes to become world-famous. Her designs are bonkers. Avant-garde. I admire her. Plus, she's always been a great, loyal friend to Sienna. When I came out to Sienna, they both invited me to the city and Monroe introduced me to her twin sister, Joey, and Joey's girlfriend, and her best friends Carey and Phoebe. Meeting so many LGBTQ+ people and seeing them thrive was something I'll never forget. I already had so much exposure, from Fielder and Benny, but it never gets old meeting new people who are authentically themselves. "Don't mess this up."

"Any advice?" he asks.

"For dating a girl?" My face scrunches. "Fresh out of tips. Though I did give pointers to some guys on the football team."

"You played football?"

"For five seconds." I air-measure myself against him. "Don't know if you can tell, but I was a bit of a runt." That gets a laugh. I learned a long time ago that short jokes got me far. "I got pummeled. Hated every game. I played tennis and swam. Varsity captain."

"Small but mighty," Tyler says.

"Small but mighty." I flex my biceps, and Tyler feels them.

"This feels very gay." Monroe appears from around a blind corner, Fielder in tow. She's wearing skintight black jeans with snakeskin boots and a vintage flowy, oversized resort-style button-down with a vibrant 1970s maximalist–pop art alligator print. Her bright pink lips and a slick cat eye complete the look. She contrasts Tyler in his baby-blue shorts that come just above his knee and a short-sleeve plain-as-hell Target button-down that's buttoned up too high. I reach over and swiftly unbutton a few until his collarbone and the upper part of his pecs show.

"Quick hands," Tyler says.

I crack my knuckles.

"Hey," Fielder says, and my mouth goes dry. "How'd you sleep?"

I shrug. "Meh. You?" I hate small talk. Fielder and I never had that. From the moment we met, we never ran out of things to talk about. Back then it was all about LEGO sets, *Adventure Time*, *Star Wars: The Clone Wars*, *Pokémon*, or, thanks to my dad, *Jurassic Park* (which scared the hell out of Fielder).

We teeter on the heels of everything unspoken between us until the silence becomes too much for Monroe.

"This is awkward," she says.

"We should, um, probably head out," Tyler says. "I asked Vincenze to get us a golf cart to go into town."

"What a knight in shining polyblend." She slaps his shoulder and Tyler blushes.

"Mind if I hitch a ride with you guys?" I ask. "I wanted to hit a woodshop or two Niccolò told me about yesterday."

Tyler looks to Fielder like I wasn't supposed to ask such a thing.

"No, sorry, no room at the inn," Monroe says. "But I think Fielder got a cart. Maybe you can ride with him?"

"You're going into town?" I ask him, my chest fluttering. Nerves or—

"I want to interview Niccolò Avello for my Clock channel. A three-part series I have in mind for . . . something." He squints as he does when he rambles and reveals more than he wants to.

"Mind if I . . . ?"

"Absolutely!" Fielder says excitedly. Then, switching to a breezy tone, he coos, "Or whatever. No big. I can spare a seat."

"Right," I say, looking between the three of them.

On the winding ride around the mountain and toward the center of Amalfi, Fielder and I don't say anything. Tyler and Monroe are huddled close together in the cart ahead of us, whispering like kids before a school dance.

Our driver pulls off and into the same area right out front of the entrance to the Avello Family Lemon Groves from yesterday and throws the cart into park. As the engine idles loudly, Fielder launches himself out and I follow suit.

Fielder looks at me quizzically.

"I figured you could use some company. You always loved going places for Clock with someone. Me, your mom, Nonna." I pause before adding, "Matty."

"I've gotten pretty good at going myself, believe it or not." He crosses his arms.

"Oh, sorry, I shouldn't have ass—"

"You know what they say about assuming," he says, and I know exactly where it's going: dad joke central. "You ass is for me."

"Still makes zero sense," I say.

"Which makes it hilarious! Remember when we said it in front of Nonna?"

"Yeah, she smacked you."

"Then laughed her ass off."

"Because she has the mouth and mind of a sailor." That's what

Nonno used to say about Fielder's nonna. Once, about five years ago, we tried to set them up on a date. Turned out, they hated each other romantically. Nonno was too soft for her, and she was too abrasive for him. They laughed about it and ragged on each other over mugs of Lipton tea and Stella D'oro breakfast biscuits every Sunday until he passed away.

"Love that woman." Fielder salutes the air. "Taught me everything I know."

He starts toward the entrance to the groves, and when I don't follow him, he stops and turns. "You coming?"

"I thought—"

He waves me on. "I'd love to spend the day with you. If you let me tag along to the woodshops with you."

Fielder always was enamored by everything that enamored me. "Deal."

More enthusiastic today than he was yesterday, Niccolò Avello is better than a trained actor: made to be on camera, bounding from lemon tree to lemon tree, talking about the hybrids and different varieties, giving viewers a rich history of Amalfi and his family. His blue eyes glimmer, and his crinkly, toothy smile is magnetic.

Fielder wastes no opportunity to ask him question after question about the land, rising sea levels, water scarcity, how tourism impacts the environment, and extreme temperature changes. He's filming everything with an expert eye, referring to a notepad full of ideas and research he must have spent all night gathering. Fielder is so professional, a far cry from the early days of @LemonAtFirstSight where he didn't know angles or consider lighting, and would aimlessly shoot.

Fielder frames Niccolò's face like a studied cameraman, capturing the best he has to give with great sound bites about everything from their hives of bees to how their season used to stretch to October but because of the drastic shift in climate now wraps up in late August.

The conversation is insightful, and the way Fielder elicits these responses from Niccolò is expert-level journalism. I can't help but look on in admiration, awe, and respect.

It's hotter than yesterday, and my pits are sweating through my shirt, making me thankful that Fielder is being careful not to get me in any shots; he has no qualms making it known that he's actively trying to avoid me, swerving animatedly out of my way.

"It's okay." I swipe the back of my hand across my brow. "I don't mind being in the background."

"The camera always loved you, Mr. Supermodel Hair and Jawline." He gnaws at his cuticles, a habit I thought he'd stopped years ago. I think about what Cam said earlier, how Fielder was using me for likes, but the way he's hesitating now makes me certain that he's not. "But maybe . . . for this, I don't need anyone but Niccolò."

"What *is* this for?" I ask.

"Not sure if you know what @FoodForChange is? It's a not-for-profit started by Michelin-star chef Mars Lyon, and their Clock channel is doing a contest to help raise awareness about sustainability in food production and consumption." Fielder's eyes light up in ways I've never seen before. "The prize is an internship at a new TV cooking competition series hosted by Chef Lyons called *Out of This World*, where budding chefs compete in weekly *Top Chef*–style challenges. It's a chance to work behind the scenes in promotion and marketing, making content for the show's social media accounts, *and* guest on the show as a special mini-challenge judge. If that sounds rehearsed, it's because I totally rehearsed it." He laughs, which elicits one from Niccolò, too.

My chest swells with pride. Fielder is going after something real, concrete. Something he's been afraid of—forging his own path out of fear that if he tried professional schooling, he'd fail out and disappoint everyone. He would tell me these fears late at night when we'd walk around Blossom Avenue. I never knew how to help him because school wasn't my thing, either. But I always had a direction: Nonno. Woodworking. Writing. *Creating.*

"You're a chef, then, yes? Didn't get a chance to cook with us yesterday," Niccolò says to Fielder.

"I don't cook, no, but I love filming." Fielder's eyes widen, and he looks to me for help. "I-I mean, I'd love to learn one day, but I'm more of a lover of food."

"What is cooking but making love to food?" Niccolò asks.

Fielder and I exchange a quick, heated glance.

"Let's learn, Field." I playfully knock sideways into him.

Niccolò grabs hold of Fielder and ushers him past a couple of overflowing baskets of lemons and into the restaurant-kitchen area where we ate yesterday. The bright lemons hanging from the pergolas like novelty Christmas bulbs are so enchanting I gasp. What takes my breath away are the hand-carved oak armchairs and tables. While everyone ate yesterday, I studied their construction, and it's exquisite. The craftsmanship is so earnest—no machines, no metals used, just a mass of beautiful imperfections from the splits to the cracks to the knots. It makes me excited to head into town later and explore the local woodshops.

"I have a tour, but you can find everything you need here," Niccolò says. "My lovely wife, Isabella, will guide you through the process of making homemade linguine. Anything you need. Please film as much as you like. As you said on the telephone earlier, any awareness you can bring to Avello Family Lemon Groves and the sustainability efforts is molto apprezzato!"

"Are you still okay if I come Sunday too, to interview you and do more research before I leave?" Fielder asks.

"Assolutamente, si, si."

"Grazie, so much grazie," Fielder says, and the Avellos laugh at his modest Italian. "I really appreciate everything!"

Niccolò bows and does a slow jog out and down the path to meet his next tour.

"Va bene, are we ready to make some pasta? Traditional pici . . ." Isabella is a bit less animated than her husband, but her warmth radiates out. "We're using zero-zero flour and semolina, and the Avello secret, scorza di limone." Zesting a giant Amalfi lemon into the mixture, she closes her eyes and inhales the bright, sweet, floral scent. With her hands, she creates a well in the center and adds egg yolks. With a fork, she breaks the eggs, then gradually draws flour from the edges of the well inside. "Va bene? You try."

Fielder looks like a child let loose in FAO Schwarz at Christmastime, pulling flour in and slowly mixing it until the dough gets firm and he switches to mixing with his hands. I record him, intent on sending him the footage. He narrates everything he's doing, and in a moment of pure pride, I hold the camera out in front of him and get in the shot, cheering him on like a coach.

"When the dough doesn't stick to your hands, you're done! Don't do too much," Isabella says. Once everything is incorporated and the dough has a slight yellow tint due to the zest, she kneads until it's smooth before wrapping it in plastic wrap. "Now, we wait and drink limoncello, and then we make the lemon sauce!"

"I've never had so much limoncello," Fielder says. "Thank god nobody cares about the drinking age. Salute!"

I catch him staring at his dough-covered hands.

"That was incredible," he says, eyes wide, like he just won the largest prize at the annual Blossom Avenue Italian Feast. "I've cooked with Nonna. Kind of. I watch professionals cook all the time. I know food. Ingredients. How to talk about food. But—but this? Getting to make pasta? It's stupid, I know. Shouldn't be a big deal; it's so small, and I'm not even doing it on my own, but—"

"I get it." I'm breathless *for* him. "How'd it make you feel? Being the one to *do* it."

"*Alive.* I get it now, in a way I didn't before."

Still brimming with energy, we walk (Fielder skips) to the far side of the open patio, and he says, "In another life, I totally lived here. Worked on this farm. Maybe my past self of something? That sounds ridiculous, I don't know. I feel a spiritual connection to this place. Like I belong here. Like it's mine. Even though before yesterday I didn't know anything about it. And yet!" He's speed-talking, and the light in his eyes is so bright I can't look away. "I've never felt more passionate about something. And I never thought I'd care so deeply about lemons."

I know the feeling.

I want to tell Fielder how happy it makes me to see him explore this. I can't, because if I do, I may uncork something I can't bottle again. Cam deserves better. *More.* Especially from me.

I glance at Fielder, who clearly hears it too as he turns his head toward a thick cluster of lemon trees. "Is that . . . ?"

"Whaaaaat! No way . . ." Fielder trails off as he spots Matty, sitting beneath a young budding tree, threading his hands with Nic Jr., the *very* hot son of Niccolò and Isabella Avello we met yesterday.

Matty leans in for a kiss, and Fielder gasps.

The boys perk up like scared bunnies and scuttle away through the bramble, leaving dust clouds in the wake.

We both collapse into each other and laugh until we can't breathe.

CHAPTER 14

If He Were Feeling What I'm Feeling He Would Know How It Feels!

Hi, reader! It's me again, Fielder Lemon! Did you miss me?

Let's check in with Operation: Ricky @ Second Glance, shall we?

- ~~*Lite Sabotage*~~
- ~~*Win over Ricky's family*~~
- ~~*Get Ricky alone to see if he still has feelings for me*~~
- *Remind Ricky what he's missing (I feel like we're here, yes?)*
- *Show him how much I've grown and changed (jury's out)*
- *Compare/Contrast: Pros of Fielder vs. Cons of Cam*
- *Figure out if Ricky actually loves Cam*
- *Isolate (then eliminate) Cam!*

I still feel a bit icky about that last one, but not terribly so because I still haven't figured out how to break it to Ricky that I think Cam might be hooking up with randoms on the side. I have no proof, though, other than what Tyler, Benny, and I saw.

Anyway, I'm not worrying about that right now because I'm having the single best day of the last thirteen months with Ricky, and I'm not getting my hopes up at all, but I'm saying nobody in the history of days has ever had a better day.

With the Matty of it all, it keeps getting better.

"Matty isn't answering his texts," I say.

"This is amazing," Ricky repeats, over and over again.

"Yes, except Matty didn't tell me he was going on a date! When I woke up this morning, Matty was already gone. Now I know it's because he was sneaking out to meet the lemon farmer's son! Which, hot. Kudos, Matty! But it's upsetting. Matty tells me everything!"

"Leave him alone," Ricky says. "He's *clearly* enjoying himself."

"But—"

"Are you worried he's going to somehow mess up your connection to Niccolò?"

I wasn't, but now that you mention it, yes! "Nooo."

He glares at me, knowingly.

"Matty can be messy . . ." I trail off.

"A Lemon, messy? Never." He rolls his neck and smirks, all suave, and it makes me swoon. Hard.

"Ignoring you."

"He's your best friend." Ricky's attributing the "best friend" label to someone other than himself hurts in a way I couldn't have expected. "I'm glad he was there for you this last year."

Well, someone had to bring up the elephant in the lemon groves.

I barter with myself about what to bring up. How much is too much? We have a lot to talk about, but it feels like we've finally started to reconnect, maybe even build something new, and I don't want anything to rock the boat. It's too delicate, so I say the most honest, true, and neutral statement possible: "I wouldn't have gotten through it without him."

Ricky's jaw pulsates as he looks away, off into the mountains.

"What's on your mind?" I ask, knowing the thoughtful look on his face, the one he has when he's writing a new poem and trying to turn a phrase or planning the blueprints of a new woodworking project and working through the schematics.

He lets out a heavy sigh and sips the fiery limoncello like freaking apple juice. I never liked the stuff, so I'm pretending to savor mine. "Nothing."

"Come on, I know you, Ric."

"Do you?"

It's a quick jab, but it hurts like a paper cut you don't see coming.

"I did, once," I say softly. "Until you left without saying goodbye. Then I wondered if I ever knew you."

He takes a step back, the color draining from his face. He turns from me, but instead of walking away, he takes a beat, a breath, and then starts talking. "I regretted leaving the second I walked out the door. I thought I was doing us both a favor—it doesn't matter now. But I-I regret it every day. When you didn't take my call, I knew I'd fucked up, but I thought maybe we could . . . I don't know. I'm not good at talking about all this stuff." His voice is shaking.

"Doing us both a favor? Your call? I never got a call."

He swiveled on his heels. "Yeah, I called you. Well, not you because you had me blocked. But Matty. Back in January."

"Uh, nope. You didn't. I *think* I would've remembered that. What happened? Piece it together because—"

Ricky grinds his teeth. "It was the anniversary of Nonno's death. I ended up in the ER after I cut myself in the workshop, and I wanted to talk to you because my head wasn't right. I didn't have anybody to call. I didn't wanna worry my parents or Sienna with something silly like stitches." He holds up his thumb, which I take in my hand. I run my index finger across a small scar down his pad. "I still had Matty's number, so I took a chance, and he was actually with you. At the mall. He said you were shooting content at some new vegan health bar place."

I vaguely remember that day, and Matty never mentioned Ricky calling, but . . . "Holy balls. He was acting *really* weird after he got a call from his mom. I kept asking him about it, but he was giving me attitude, so I left him alone. I figured he was pissy because he gets moody for no reason sometimes, especially with Zia Rosa, but what the actual fuck? That was you on the phone?" My legs feel wobbly. Come to think of it, that morning I got an alert on my phone that it was his nonno's death anniversary. I open my mouth to speak again, but nothing comes out.

"You really didn't know?"

"If I had known, I would have talked to you, no question." Anger builds in my chest, and I clench my fist. "I'm gonna *kill* Matty."

"It's not worth it."

"Isn't it?" Matty knew I spent every waking hour working

toward a plan to win Ricky back. That could have been an opportunity to do exactly that.

"Is it?" he asks calmly. "What would it have changed?"

We both chew on that question because the potential answers are too vast for either of us. My mind spins, *Avengers: Endgame*–style with reverse timeline scenarios of what could have happened if my dumbass cousin had just given me the phone.

Infinite possibilities, sure. But the only one that matters is this one. The real one.

Our eyes meet, and a single tear falls from his.

"What's wrong?" I ask.

"I hated you for that," he says.

I hated him, too. For breaking my heart and doing so without warning. For leaving like a coward. For making me feel like I wasn't good enough to keep. But I loved him at the same time. It's funny, the fragile line between love and hate—it's not really a line at all. Hate isn't the absence of love, nor is it the opposite of love. Hate is love with nowhere to go.

Being with him these last few days has made me remember the real Ricky, the quiet, fun, beautiful boy I fell in love with, not the Ricky who broke my heart and whom I became desperate to prove myself to in the wake of heartbreak. I spent the last year so hell-bent on my revenge bod and becoming a self-reliant Fielder because at the end Ricky made me feel like I was lost, floundering, and in need of being taken care of by him.

But maybe it wasn't that I needed to change myself so much as find myself. Maybe it was that Ricky just needed to be cared for, too.

"Can I have a . . . ?" he asks, holding his arms out.

I nod because *of course*! My body is screaming for his hugs.

All at once, I'm flooded with a sensation I haven't felt in so long I nearly cry.

Ricky wraps his strong arms around me, and I burrow my face into the crook of his neck, resting my cheek on his muscly shoulder. He pulls me so close, hugs me so tight, that our bodies fuse together. Cedar, oak, woodchips, Dove, citrus flowers.

And I exhale, expelling every ounce of nervous, frantic sadness that had been building and building and clogging me up.

Relief, safety, *home*.

If Mount Vesuvius erupted right now and blanketed the entire globe in layers of volcanic ash, it wouldn't matter because the combined power of the lemon trees and Ricky's arms would protect us.

Neither of us pull away. It's the kind of hug where both people are fully content to just *be*. Here. Now. In a space just for us. For as long as it takes.

He hums, and it reverberates through my chest.

Instinctively, we both loosen our grips at the same time.

Pull away, but only enough to look into each other's eyes.

The sun overhead peeks out from behind some clouds, and his face is illuminated golden from the lemon tree branches. His eyes are pools of honey. I want to get stuck in them.

"You know what Nonno said to me when I came out to him?" Ricky says, his voice a low, deep whisper. "He told me that when you love someone, say it out loud. Never let"—his breathing is ragged, labored—"those moments . . ." His chest heaves in and out.

Pass you by? I finish for him, recalling how it felt yesterday when we found ourselves in the exact same position, at the exact same lemon farm, except now it's just us, with nothing stopping us from righting all the wrongs of the past year.

Except, so much time has passed, and it's hitting me that as much as I want to kiss him and tell him that I love him, if I do, and it ends again, I don't think I'd survive a second massacre.

If he felt what I'm feeling, the way he changed me and left me to put myself back together without him, he would understand my hesitation.

All I've wanted all year is for Ricky to want me again. But now that he's here, inches away from me, I'm afraid. Do *I* really want *him*, after the way he hurt me, knowing he could do that to me again? Knowing that he probably will because when I'm with him, I feel like the Fielder he left alone on the beach.

Uncertain.

I step back, out of his arms.

He stares at me, brows furrowed, head tilting in confusion.

"There you boys are!" Isabella says. "Andiamo! It's time to finish the pici!"

RICKY DELUCA

"Master and Apprentice"

"You sure you boys don't need a ride back into town?" Isabella asks. "Niccolò is almost done with his tour. Or maybe my son? Ma non so dove sia." Brushing stray hairs away from her eyes, she turns every which way as if that will suddenly draw him out of hiding with Matty. "I find him—"

"No, no, it's okay," Fielder interrupts. "We can walk. A little exercise will help after all that pasta and pastry."

"Va bene!" She nods as if she agrees that we both need to work off our pasta bellies. She grabs my shoulders and presses her cheek to mine and makes a kissing noise vigorously. "Buona giornata!"

"I love her." Fielder nearly skips down the road toward town. "Her warmth radiates! Look!" He plays what he recorded of us making fresh lemon tiramisu and sweet honey lemon cake. Isabella's voiceover says, "Thank you for respecting the lemons. Many people come through here and think they can pick the lemons from our trees themselves. They damage the trees. My husband has worked for many years to get protection for the Amalfi lemon and preserve the coastline, and so many tourists don't understand the history and importance and how sometimes our ways of life feel so fragile. We work hard to preserve our history for future generations, like my son."

That's why Nonno taught my father, and then me, his craft. Why I work so hard to one day become the man Nonno taught me to be.

The last thing Isabella said reverberates: "Once you lose something forever, it's gone." So simple, yet frighteningly powerful. She held a Sfusato Amalfitano in her hand, and my own hands longed for the grip of Fielder Lemon's.

"So beautiful, huh? Anyway, sorry." Fielder slips his phone into his pocket. No editing software apps, no swiping or pinching or typing or squinting, spending hours editing content for his channel so intensely he would tune out the rest of the world in FTV: Fielder's Tunnel Vision. It's oddly unsettling.

"Why are you sorry? You don't wanna edit? You can."

"I'm working on being more present. Living in the moment. I'll edit the footage from today later." I surprise even myself with this. I'm not itching to be on my phone. At all. "Once we're back and we're . . ." He pauses.

Not together, I almost finish for him.

When I don't respond, he says, "No more FTV."

"Hmm." I study his face, the confidence in his voice. He seems calmer, and I want to peel back the layers of the last year, see what else I missed.

"It's a relatively new development," he says, turning to look at me. Though I don't turn to face him, I feel his stares. "Being here feels transformative . . . I honestly haven't felt the need to be on my phone as much since I've been here, the lemon groves notwithstanding. I'm living in the moment. Been doing a lot of that since the Great Commencement Massacre."

"The what?"

"Oh, that's what I call our, um—"

I laugh, maybe too hard. "Wow. Harsh, but . . . it's good."

"I thought so."

"I wish I could live in the moment."

He scoffs. "You're king of living in the moment. Remember when your parents took us upstate to Ithaca right before your senior year, and we were hiking in the gorges, and found that swimming hole?"

"We lost them we were so far ahead of them," I say.

"I was dying of heat, and you took off your shirt and jumped in, even though there were No Trespassing and Warning signs everywhere not to."

"My dad was so pissed," I say with a chuckle.

"You were like, 'Field, get off your phone,' and you pulled me in and—" He stops because he remembers what happened next. Though he was self-conscious of swimming without a shirt, I told him that we were the only two around, and that I loved his body. I wanted him to be as free as I felt in that moment, to see what I saw. As he peeled off his shirt and tried to cover his soft midsection, I pulled him into the water and ran my hands across his sides and told him how hot he looked. We swam across the pool and found an alcove and kissed for what felt like hours. It was only minutes, but it was heaven.

He clears his throat. "I still think about how we sat in that alcove on the rocks, kicking our feet in the water and played I Spy." We took turns describing every little detail of what surrounded us. "I felt like a kid. You were always good at that. Seizing the moment, making everything fun."

"I haven't felt like that in a while," I confess.

The closer we get to the center of town, the more crowded it becomes.

"What do you mean?" he asks.

How do I say the second I made the decision to break up with him was the second I stopped living in the moment? I let fear of holding Fielder (and myself) back, geographical distance, the improbability of high school love lasting worry me, until all I could think about was the future and how it might destroy us, this idea that I needed Fielder to have his entire life together, direction and all, that I needed him to know who he was going to be when I myself was afraid of the unknown.

I robbed us of the ability to see how it might play out in real time.

Proceeded with caution.

And look where it's gotten me.

What would Nonno think? Despite seeming like an old-school conservative Italian on the outside, he loved love, and believed in diving headfirst into the now. Taking risks. That's why he married Nonna and moved their entire lives to the States. Why he always said to say what I needed to say, and to never be afraid of love.

Maybe that's been what's held me back from Cam.

Fielder elbows me. Deep in thought, I hadn't been paying attention to where we were walking. Apparently, Fielder led me through the winding streets, carved a path for us between hordes of tourists, to the alley where Niccolò said I would find the best woodworker in Amalfi, Guiseppe Bernadi.

Fielder jiggles the door handle to no avail and curses. Locked. "They're closed. Sorry, Ric, I know how badly you wanted to come here." He peers through the window and shouts, "Hello! Buongiorno! Anybody . . . home?" His knocking grows frantic.

There's a small sign on the door above the handle: Guiseppe Bernadi è andato a Milano e tornerà ad Agosto. Vista guiseppe-bernadi.it per maggiori informazioni!

"Nobody's inside, but wow, you should see some of these pieces!" He moves out of the way so I can get a closer look.

But I'm watching him, the way his face is a mixture of concern for my happiness, but also excitement from wanting me to see the beautiful work inside. Though Fielder has always been slightly self-focused, it's never at my expense. When it's time for Fielder to enter *my* world, he's always first in line and ready to ride.

"I really am sorry, Ricky—"

"Stop apologizing." I point at the sign. "He's in Milan until August. So it wouldn't have mattered if we came here two days ago or three days from now."

"Does he know *the* Ricky DeLuca is in Amalfi for only a limited time? You should leave a card."

"Who uses business cards?"

"Touché." Fielder scratches his head. The blond radiates in

the sunlight. "Maybe there's another woodworker. Didn't Niccolò—"

"I checked last night online, and the other name he gave me doesn't have a public shop, so basically no info. I don't want to show up to some guy's house out of the blue, even if he's a friend of the Avellos'. That's stalker behavior."

Fielder laughs. "Well, guess it means these people are missing out on meeting the greatest craftsman of his generation. One day you'll have a shop here."

"You'll farm lemons, and I'll make custom pieces for tourists." I peer inside, and though there aren't many pieces, what I see is stunning—intricately carved chairs, tables, benches exactly like the ones at the Avello farm, a custom bar and an armoire, towering cabinets, and intricately carved grandfather clocks. Tools are scattered about the shop as if Guiseppe left in a hurry, and I wonder what took him to Milan. Perhaps a long-lost love, or an opportunity he couldn't pass up. Maybe both? "His work is beautiful."

My mind wanders to what a shop of my own would look like, what kind of pieces I would make—would I focus on custom furniture? Create my own line? Or I'll do what Dad does and be a contractor for engineers who want custom pieces, or do what Nonno did once he got too old to build his own designs and focus on fixing things for other people. According to Christian Richards, I'm a "visionary still discovering my point of view," very much an apprentice.

Fielder was always the dreamer; I was the practical one. In order to become a master craftsman, I'll have to figure out how to dream, and execute what I dream.

"What'll we call the shop?"

"The Woodworker and the Dreamer," he says, and my breath catches.

How does he know that title? My eyes narrow.

"I heard there's an old paper mill museum we could go to?" Fielder stammers, changing the subject and looking everywhere but at me. He starts walking ahead of me, leaving me behind. "Niccolò mentioned it yesterday. From the thirteenth century. Could be cool to see machinery and tools from back then. Tick all your boxes. Or we could go back to the villa and hang at the pool or sea. I haven't been down there yet." Fielder hates museums, but I don't want to go back to the villa yet.

I want to stay in the *here and now* with the dreamer.

Breathless, I run after him, not paying attention to what's in front of me and slam directly into him. "Let's do—oof!"

"Ricky, wait." Fielder's breathing heavy. He looks like he's seen a ghost.

"What?"

"I didn't want to say anything because it wasn't my place and I didn't know and and and, but—"

"Fielder, you're rambling again," I say, but he takes me by the hand and points down a nearby alley that funnels out to the beach. Framed by one terracotta building and one mosaic stone is Cam and some American Eagle Matty-looking guy, chest to chest, lips locked, Cam's messy curls between his fingers.

I clench Fielder's hand tight, then let go out of fear I might break his bones.

The audacity of Cam to demand I define our relationship, then do this? On a vacation paid for by my family, for my sister's wedding?

"You knew?" I ask Fielder.

"I saw Cam yesterday with that same dude, but it was right before that Vespa almost killed me, and I didn't actually see anything, so there wasn't proof, and I— Where are you going?" Fielder calls after me, but I'm already gone.

CHAPTER 15

Jell-O Can Never Be Crème Brûlée

"Ricky! I'm sorry, I didn't mean to piss you off, please! I should've told you!"

I really should've worked out this week more because running to catch up to Ricky and his muscular runner's legs when I was already breathless from the gag reveal of the century is really taking the wind out of my lungs!

The second Ricky reaches the end of a long row of stone buildings and into a more open clearing, he stops and lets out a breath.

I nearly keel over, hunching over on my knees, panting.

Then, in a twist I didn't see coming, he starts to laugh. It comes deep from the belly, like he's exorcising a demon, and once he's done, he's wiping tears from his cheeks.

"Did I miss something?"

He closes his eyes, clears his throat, and inhales. "I smell warm Nutella. Where is that coming from?" I follow his nose to a nearby pasticceria. "Do you mind if we get whatever that is, then maybe go to that museum you told me about and not talk about what we just saw?"

"If that's what you want."

"Thanks, Fielder." He opens his eyes, trying to hide the pain, but I know better.

"Can I ask one question?"

"One question."

"What do you want or need me to do right now?"

He smiles, his face softening. "This. And keep what we saw to yourself. I'm going to see if Cam tells me the truth himself. Give him a chance to be honest."

My face crinkles, brows furrow. "Then what?"

He narrows his eyes. "You don't approve."

"I—I don't have an opinion."

"I don't believe that for a minute." He smirks.

"You would give him a second chance?" I ask, wondering where my second chance was. Why didn't Ricky give me time before up and leaving?

"I don't know." He looks deep into my eyes, then down at the cobblestone streets. "But I know I want to spend today with you. Is that okay?"

For now.

Good lord, the Museo della Carta is the most boring thing I've ever done.

Not to sound like *that girl*, because old machines are cool and Ricky was a kid in a candy shop reading about all the techniques of making paper, and ancient trade routes from China, but I found myself wishing to be impaled on the rusty equipment.

Now we're back at the villa and he's somewhere with Cam pretending that he didn't just see him making out with a Matty look-alike in an alley by the beach! How tawdry and cheap! Ricky deserves better.

To be a fly on the wall.

What did I *think* was going to happen? That Topher and Sienna's wedding was the setting of some rom-com where I would win back the heart of the love of my life and send his twink boyfriend packing after a cute little group number where everyone in the bridal party including Nonna breaks out into song?

Sounds nice! Yet the closer I've gotten to Ricky over the last two days, the more my heart aches remembering the hurt he left behind. The more I want to kiss him under the stars, the more closure and insight I need about *how* and *why* we ended in the first place. Far too complicated.

I flop on my bed and press my eyes closed.

A good nap can cure all, including the twisty weirdness knotting up inside me.

Except I can't fall asleep.

So I try to edit the content I shot yesterday and today.

Except I can't focus.

And because my reptile brain is utterly broken and my coping mechanism for thinking too much over the last year has been sex, I'm suddenly picturing Ricky shirtless in teeny-tiny speedos at the pool, hard as a rock.

Matty isn't around.

The Coven is spending the day shopping and eating their way through Positano.

The villa was quiet when Ricky and I got back, and it's been days since I've gotten off, so there's a decent shot I can get off without worrying.

I sink deep into the bed, and the second I get to work, the door to my suite opens and I hear Matty's voice call out for me.

With superhuman strength, I pull a stop, drop, and roll and heave my naked body off my bed, crashing to the cold tile floor with a thud.

Matty scream-laughs from the belly as he catches the tail end (see what I did there?) of the show. "Sorry, Field!" His laughter grows into howls.

I bonk my forehead against the floor, thanking the gods I didn't break my dick before hoisting myself up and jumping out of my skin when I see Matty standing next to Nic Avello Jr., who stares me up and down with a smirk on his face.

"Ay, che vista! Bellissimo!" Nic says as Matty throws a pillow at me to cover up.

"I thought you left!" I shriek.

"Sorry, bro," Matty says through laughter. "I saw my mom coming down the stairs and had to get Nic inside."

"Why?" I focus intently on holding the pillow in place over my crotch.

"Because I couldn't let her see—"

"No, why is he here?" I nod to Nic. "Ciao, Nic. Come stai?"

"Bene, e tu?"

"Così così." I nod toward my crotch. "So you guys're, what, staying here tonight?"

Matty shrugs.

"Can you at least toss my shorts?"

Matty kicks them across the floor.

Carefully hoisting them on, I drop the pillow. "What am I supposed to do?"

Matty whispers something to Nic, who shrugs and kisses Matty's cheek. Matty blushes, then rushes over to me, hooks his arm around mine, drags me into the bathroom, and shuts the door. "Can you bunk with Benny?"

"Are you kidding?"

"Please! I really love this guy!"

"Love?"

Matty looks at me with the biggest puppy dog eyes. "Okay, not like *love* love, that was a strong word, but have you seen him? I—I *really* want him to be my first."

I rub the exhaustion—and blue ball haze—from my eyes. "Really?"

He nods. "We talked all last night and spent the day together today."

"Yeah, we saw you at the Avello farm."

His nostrils flare. "I knew it! I need more about you and Ricky STAT!"

"So much to catch you up on," I say. "We caught Cam cheating on Ricky."

Matty's eyes widen so large they look like they're about to fall out of his skull.

"I know, but tell me about Nic! How'd that even happen?"

He swoons and sighs, and the smile that stretches across his face can light even the darkest nights. "While you and Ricky were busy exchanging passionate looks and moments at the groves yesterday, I was off on my own, taking selfies against the lemons like a goober and not paying attention to anything when . . ." He recounts the rest of their fated meeting in Hallmark movie–level detail.

Making ridiculous faces, sticking his tongue out, Matty worked the camera doing one of those 360 videos of the grove and the valley and coastline, and as his body rotated and came back around to where he started, in the back of the frame, Nic Jr. was standing, arms folded, all devilish smiles, leaning against a guardrail.

Matty froze, unable to move. He wanted to "crawl up [his] own ass and disappear." But then Nic Jr. raised both arms, opened his hands, and pressed both to either side of his face, creating moose antlers. He stuck out his tongue for the camera and crossed his eyes. Matty caught it all on camera, and shows me the footage as proof.

"Love at first sight," I say.

"My knees got weak and my dick got hard," Matty confirms.

At once, Matty turned around to face Nic Jr., who did a twice-over at Matty's body. Then Nic Jr. held out his hand to Matty and said, "I'd like to show you something."

"Oh, spicy," I say. "I didn't even know you disappeared."

"Ricky Haze," Matty says. "I told my ma I was going off to explore on my own. I followed Nic up the mountain to an overlook." Matty describes the unobstructed panoramic near-360-degree view of the Amalfi valley, the way it felt like he was sitting on top of the world looking down, like a bird in flight. "And we just talked, for like an hour. And kept moving closer and closer."

"How'd he know you were interested?" I ask.

Matty glares at me. Blinks twice. "If my boner didn't give it away, my rainbow bracelet sure did." He lifts his wrist to the bracelet Zia Rosa gave him after he came out as a show of support and love.

"What'd you talk about?"

"He told me how isolated he felt here, and I told him I felt the same back home—excluding you, obviously. But, like, at school and stuff. We have a lot in common, and as he told me all about his life and what it was like to live here year-round, in such a small school, working on his family's farm, I don't know, I felt so connected to him. Like we understood each other."

"With all the backbreaking labor you do back home," I jest.

"Hey, I bench above my weight." He flexes for me.

"Did you do that for Nic?" I ask.

Matty raises an eyebrow. "Worked like a charm. He asked if he could feel my bicep, and one thing led to another, and he leaned in and kissed me and . . ." He sighs again.

"Good?"

"Best kisser ever. Very Fourth of July fireworks finale. And obviously I didn't want to stop. Neither did he. So we made plans to hang all day today. We tried not to be caught. Nic's parents are great, but, you know, not so many locals around here are. Nic doesn't want anyone to know he's gay."

Matty goes on to tell me about everything Nic shared with him, and how they bonded over their fear of being out. Matty feels comfortable with Nic because he gets it. I think every gay guy experiences that fear, even ones like me who come out before puberty, or are lucky enough to not have to come out. Between

Matty and Ricky and seeing stories from other teens on Clock in less accepting areas of the country or world, I know enough to know that's still not the case everywhere.

"I'm really happy for you. Both. That you guys found a safe space in each other."

"I've never been more ready to—" Eyes wide, he continues, voice lowered. "I'm . . . scared. Especially because Nic isn't a virgin. He's been with girls before."

"So it'd be both of your first times, then. With guys. You're on the same page. Don't focus on anything but each other. And don't do anything you're not ready for. You can say no or stop at any time—"

"No, I know." His fingers stretch anxiously, so I grab them. He's clammy, squirmy. "That's a good point. Thanks, Field."

"Breathe," I say calmly, and grab and massage his hands until they stop shaking.

He jumps up and down like a kid at recess. "This feels right. Whatever happens when we go home." Then, the big oaf pulls me into a bear hug and squeezes.

"I need to ask you something. About Ricky."

He releases me. "Oh boy." He takes a step back.

"Did he call you back in January?"

"I'm sorry, Field, I should've told you. I didn't want it to ruin your progress. You were doing so well without him. You were finally over him."

"I was never over him, Matty."

"You know what I mean. You were doing things on your own. You were happy again. You were entering this, like, new phase of Fielder Lemon, always going out. Filming content.

Working out. You were like this new and improved version. Everybody loved you; you were blossoming. I know you had this plan to win him back, I get it, I do, but I wanted to protect you. That's all."

Shaking my head, I say, "You didn't give me a chance to make that decision for myself, Matty."

"I know, I know. I am sorry. I should have."

"You should have." I give him the finger, then look at him square in the eyes. "But thank you. I think you were right. I don't think I would have been ready yet."

His pupils dilate. "Oh? Wasn't expecting that one."

I laugh. "I love you, brother."

"For what it's worth, Ricky looks at you like he's still in love with you."

"For what it's worth, Nic looks at you like he's about to be your first."

He jumps up and down again. "Thanks again. I'll let you know when he leaves so you can come back."

I don't plan on coming back. I want Matty to have the best night of his life, and I'm willing to sleep on the floor if it means he gets that.

"Oh! Did you bring condoms?" he asks.

"Black bag." I nod toward the Dopp kit on the counter near the sink. "I don't know if they'll fit, but have at 'em."

"They'll fit; I saw what you're working with. Maybe a bit tight," Matty jests.

I shake my head. "Just don't do anything on my bed."

"Aye, aye, captain!" Matty salutes me.

On my way out, I throw on a shirt and grab some PJs, my

toothbrush, and my phone charger, tossing it all into a cute crossbody I got for Christmas.

Wandering aimlessly, I wish I could go to Ma's suite for guidance and advice, but I can't; the Coven is far too smart, and they'll sniff out Matty's date on me, draw it out like a nurse draws blood. Maybe I can go to Topher's room, but I don't want Sienna to know what's going on in my head, and while I've historically relied on Topher's secrecy, I can't exactly tell him to keep it secret from his soon-to-be wife. Monroe and Tyler aren't back from what I'm sure must be an epic date, so Benny is my last option. But he's not in his room, so I try the pool.

"Ben— Ohhha—"

You know who looks eerily similar to Benny with his shirt off and sunglasses, lying on his stomach with his curly head turned to the side so I can't see his face?

Cam Wallace.

"Hey, Fielder!" Cam sits up and rolls over, his oily abs glistening. He swings his legs over the side so he's sitting upright and facing me head-on and pats the lounger next to him, beckoning me over.

Here we go.

There's a tray of leftover delizia al limone from dinner the other night on a side table next to him. Nothing like a sweet lemon cake with custard, a trademark Amalfi dessert, left out to melt in the hot afternoon sun, beads of sweat populating its surface.

"Moving out?" Cam nods to my crossbody bag.

"I, um . . ." I negotiate exactly what to tell him. I don't know Cam, so I can't trust him with Matty's business.

Cam's sunglasses fall to the bridge of his nose. "It's okay, I saw Matty bring that hottie back."

Still, I neither confirm nor deny.

"Can I talk to you?" he asks. "About Ricky?"

Oh, now this is a conversation I *really* want no part of. Have they spoken yet? Did Cam come clean about hooking up with a rando? I hold my breath.

"Ricky told me he spent the day with you."

"He did?" I don't know why I'm nervous. It's not like we did anything wrong.

"Can I— I know this is weird to come out and ask, but I have to know because he's acting so weird." Cam is trembling. "Did something happen between you guys?"

I exhale. "Between me and Ricky?"

"It's the only thing I can think of because ever since I got back, he won't look at me or talk to me, and all I keep thinking in my head is my boyfriend spent the last two days in the most romantic place on earth with his ex-boyfriend, and I know I fully freaked yesterday and bowed out of today and that's why Ricky ended up with you, but it's also, like, the pressure of seeing your two families together and knowing that I don't have the history with Ricky like you do. How can I compete, you know? So I . . ." He shrugs, stops himself just short of admitting a secret I know he's carrying, but he doesn't know I know.

Oh, the tangled webs of a cheater.

He looks at the sad, sad plate of delizia al limone. "It's like you're this lemon crème brûlée thing, and I have the depth of Jell-O." I don't bother correcting Cam's food metaphor—though sidenote, reader, it's a sponge, not a crème brûlée, but I digress. "I can't compete. I know you're in love with him." Hearing Cam say it out loud hits me like a Mack truck, somewhere between coming out of the closet and the teacher catching you pass a "will you go out with me, yes or no?" note to your crush in the middle of class that they proceed to read out loud. "You had your chance, and I can't lose him, Fielder. He's the best thing that ever happened to me." I so badly wish he looked like the cartoon villain version I have of him in my head, but instead he looks sad, desperate. As much as I want to hate Cam, I know how he feels.

I *am* Cam.

"Ricky deserves to be happy, whatever that looks like for him," I say softly.

For the first time since we broke up, I admit it's okay if Ricky and I are happy even *if* it means we don't end up together.

—I don't want that!—

Unlike Cam, I've realized I *can* live without Ricky, and that sends shock waves through my body; goose bumps spread down my arms.

I know I'll regret what I'm about to tell Cam, but I do it anyway. "Ricky responds to honesty, so if it makes a difference, just be honest with him." I'm not sure what else to say, so I let that linger in the air and hope it lands somewhere. "If it makes a difference, *nothing* happened between us."

As I walk away, I hear him exhale.

THURSDAY

RICKY DELUCA

"Seasick Hit Me Hard and Soft"

The lushness of Billie Eilish floods my ears as I sway in a hammock beneath an orange tree in the cool early morning breeze. I get lost in "BITTERSUITE," escape in her lyrics, in the transformation and evolution of the music from song to song, allowing the vibes to transport me somewhere far removed from Amalfi, where I don't have to think about Cam or Fielder or anything—

Tap-tap-tap.

Squinting one eye open, I see Cam standing over me, one hand now on my knee, smiling sheepishly. "I got you something for today." He hands me a bottle of Dramamine. "I know you get seasick. I figured you'd forget it, and I didn't want you to be green and hanging overboard all day today. I figured you'd want to be good for Sienna."

"That's really sweet. Thank you." I swing my legs over the side of the hammock.

He holds out his hands for me to use to steady myself as I get out.

"This makes me dread the yacht a little bit less. I'm not a boat person."

"Can we talk?" he asks, and suddenly he's breathing heavily and not looking directly at me. "I don't know how to say this, and if I look directly at you I'll never be able to say it, but I can't lie to you."

I feel the anger building. I already know what he's about to say, but I wonder if he'll have the nerve to actually say it out loud. Cam has the tendency to skirt around admitting when he's done something wrong. He's an "I'm sorry but" kind of guy, and I've always attributed it to his parents who don't care about him, but if he doesn't own up without a "but," there's no moving forward.

"I met up with someone yesterday. And kind of the day before. But nothing happened the day before. But something did happen yesterday."

I shove my hands with the Dramamine bottle in my pockets so he can't see them shake. "What happened?"

"We hooked up."

"Why?"

"Why?" he repeats.

"Why did you do it?"

Tears form in the corners of his eyes. "I don't know."

"That's not good enough!" I start to yell, but I don't want anyone to hear.

"You're right, you're totally, completely right. I'm a terrible person, I—"

"No, don't do that thing. Don't turn yourself into a martyr." I hold my hand out in front of him to stop him from talking. "I'm not everyone else in your life who is going to abandon you. I'm not that person. But I deserve a real explanation, I—"

“I wanted attention,” he says quickly. His eyes widen as if shocked he admitted it. “I was feeling so insecure about Fielder. It’s not an excuse at all, really, but I’ve been asking you for months to define our relationship, to be exclusive, to really commit to me because *I* love you, Ricky. And I told you I loved you. Remember that day, two months ago? We were hiking at Snow Lake, and we stopped to lay in the sun by the water for a while. You were holding my hand, and we were talking about everything and nothing, and you told me how comfortable you felt and that you hadn’t felt like this in a really long time, and I told you I hadn’t ever felt like this. You leaned up and looked me in the eyes and kissed me like I’d never been kissed before. And I told you I was so in love with you. We’d been together at that point for like four months, and maybe it was too soon, so I get that you couldn’t say it back, but now, after seeing you with Fielder, it all makes sense. So I freaked out and—I made a mistake.”

I remember that day at Snow Lake, how beautifully blue the sky was, the dichotomy between the snowcapped mountains and the blistering heat of the sun beating down on our bare chests. When Cam told me he loved me, it scared me. The last time I was in love, with Fielder, I hurt him and ran away. Was I ready to give in again? Are there other types of love? Because I did care about Cam, and I have grown to love him. Just in a different way.

Seeing his vulnerability and honesty now, I realize how my inactions have caused him pain. “I’m sorry, Cam. I never meant to hurt you.”

“And I never meant to hurt you, Ric. Really.” He takes both of my hands. “I do think that, if you gave us a chance, a real chance, you could be happy.”

"I really thought I had," I admit.

He nods. "I know you did. Do you think you could love me?"

His question, though not unfounded, catches me off guard. "I could, one day."

"Are you ready to give up on me?" His voice breaks, and I shake my head no.

In truth, I don't think I ever really gave Cam a fair chance, and I did really have fun with him. Being with him the last six months got me through a dark period. How can I walk away from that without giving it a shot?

"Do you love Fielder?"

I don't answer because I know saying it out loud would hurt him.

He lifts our still-joined hands. "You'll see—*this* is where you should be." He kisses both palms. "We should get ready, though. Today'll be great. Sailing along the coast, seeing the famed grottos!" Before he lets go of us, he says, "If you need space to figure things out with Fielder while we're here, you have it. No restrictions. It's the least I can do for you after what I did. But I'm not giving up, either. Game on."

What the hell just happened?!

The thing about Dramamine is that you need to take it at least a half hour before you get on a boat for it to have any impact; if you take it once you start to feel seasick, it won't work. I learned that at a young age when Dad saved all year to take us on a family cruise and I spent four out of the five days green in bed.

Cam did not expect to get seasick, so by the time the

superyacht pulled away from the docks at the Amalfi seaport, it was too late.

Now I'm in one of the small bedrooms below deck, rubbing his back as he moans. Despite the air-conditioning on full blast, the air is thick and smells like acrid vomit. I dip in and out of holding my breath.

"Oooh, bleeps, iown wan yew mids ow." His voice crescendos and crashes like the bow of the yacht.

"Scusi?" My hands rub his back in concentric circles.

He picks his head up, but it looks delicate, dangling like meat on a skewer. "You can go, please. I don't want you to miss out."

"No way, babe."

"I *want* you to go." His head crashes back down into the mattress. He pulls the comforter up between his legs and cuddles with a tiny corner of the fabric. "Ughhhh. One of us should have a good time. Plus, it's Sienna's big day. She needs you."

"Her big day is Saturday," I reassure. "I don't want you to be alone."

"I need sleep," he mumbles. "Can't help me sleep."

"I'll stay 'til you fall asleep; then I'll go. And if you need me, just text and I'll be back in a second. Deal?"

With a half-hearted thumbs-up, he moans and closes his eyes.

After a solid ten minutes of labored breathing and groans, he elicits the tiniest of snores, and I slowly start to slide off the bed. Before leaving, I crank up the air and turn on a fan for circulation.

Shutting the door behind me, I bump into Sienna. "Is he okay?"

I shake my head. "It's rotten in there. But hopefully."

"You're a better person than me." She stops to check her makeup in a hallway mirror. She looks Instagram-ready, glammed to within an inch of her life with a bridal-white, almost pearlescent one-piece bathing suit with massive cutouts on either side of her body to show off her curves. Her blond hair is curled and bounces as she fluffs it. "Ready to party? I need my brother up there! I've barely spent any time with you this week, and I hate it." She grabs my hand like we're kids again. "You've spent more time with your two boyfriends." She eyes me over her white-framed bug-eyed sunglasses with gold accents.

Emerging from the staterooms below deck to the main salon of the hundred-foot superyacht—which I didn't know was a term until we all arrived at the docks and were greeted by the captain, first mate, and ten-person crew—and out onto the sundeck, I take in the sheer magnitude of the vessel, and how stunning the mountains and coastline look from this angle. I didn't get a chance to appreciate it because when we all boarded the superyacht, Fielder avoided me and Cam, so I dwelled on that. I also noticed Matty brought the hot farmer's son, Nic Avello Jr., as his date.

The rich, cerulean sky is cloudless, contrasting the rugged mountains jutting up from the land, dotted with lush greenery set back against the rolling towns built into the rock. Amalfi is in our rear as we jet toward Praiano, which is a less assuming, more enchanting local town built into the cliffs.

We sail by Positano soon, the picturesque town associated with the glossy pictures on social media and videos on Clock with its layers of multicolored houses that rise up into the mountain.

Bright turquoise waters surround us. Smaller wooden boats and catamarans zip across the water along the coast. The hull of the boat cuts smoothly through the waves, creating a welcome breeze that's cool in the shade *and* sun. Synth-y music with sick 808 beats blasts through the speakers, and though it feels a lot like a fancy music video, I wish it were silent so I could lean over the edge and stare at the shoreline and think, dream.

No such luck, though.

Benny, clad in a matching white-and-blue terry cloth short and button-down set with a nautical neck scarf in a double wrap French knot, bounds toward us. Monroe and Jenni Lee flank him on either side. He hands us some sort of pink concoction.

"All my besties together!" Sienna squeals.

"Drink up," Benny encourages.

I stare at the glittery sugar swirling like a lava lamp. Whatever it is, I don't want it in my body. "I'm good."

Sienna laughs. "He's salty he's not with his boo."

"Which boo?" Benny tongues at his straw. He takes another sip.

Topher's mom, Gabriella, holding on to the sides of her floppy straw hat that's so big it needs its own carry-on for the plane ride home, bounds over. "What're we doing, kids? Shots?" She slides right into the mix quickly and grabs hold of Sienna as if they're girlfriends. "Guisy, Rosa, get your asses over here!"

"The Coven, yes!" Sienna shouts. "Shots for the Coven!"

Guisy pulls her gauzy black wrap over her shoulders. "I want to nap."

"Nap when you're dead," Gabriella snaps.

Guisy sticks out her tongue.

"I want a shot too!" Rosa yells, appearing from nowhere.

Guisy sidles up next to me. "Lookit my little Ricky, so grown up!" She squeezes my cheeks like she did when I was a young boy. "Get your mom over here." She winds up like an old wooden toy to shout, "Bianca! Bee! Come here, we're doing shots."

When my mom drinks, she's basically Regina George's mom from *Mean Girls*, the "cool mom." Mom throws her hands in the air and screams like she's in a sorority, and grabs Benny's mom, Zia Francesca, and pulls her over, too.

This whole scene is strange. I don't really drink, not like other guys my age. I like wine and limoncello, but it's more of a family tradition than to get drunk.

Sienna was right. I *am* Nonno.

"This is amazing," Monroe says.

"I want to yeet myself off the balcony," I whisper, slyly pouring the pink drink into the sea and pretending to throw it back.

Guisy turns to me. "I've missed having you around the house."

I nod and say, "Me too." Guisy was a second mom to me. Growing up next door and dating her son for my entire life will do that. Whenever the Lemons and DeLucas would get together, the story of how Bianca DeLuca met Guisy Lemon never failed to come up. Our family had just moved in next door. Fielder's mom and Nonna weren't home, and Fielder's dad was supposed to be watching Fielder, but Fielder was a handful, so his dad went next door and asked my mom—a stranger—to watch him to give him a break. When Guisy came home, she panicked, unable to find Fielder, when she heard his voice coming from the house next door. She didn't even get to the front door when my mom opened it and said, "I think I have something that belongs to you." They've been best friends ever since.

Guisy, Gab, Rosa, and Mom pound back shots like champs. Soon they're all cackling, cheering, and drinking Sienna and her friends under the table, who eventually migrate (with Gabriella in tow) to the sundeck on the bow of the yacht to take pictures.

"One thing I've wanted to say to you, Ricky," Guisy says, the way moms do when they're about to teach a lesson. "My son will never love anyone the way he loves you. I'm not one of those people who trusts love so easily, just ask Fielder's father's grave." She pauses, then bursts out laughing before doing the sign of the cross and begging Jesus to forgive her. "What I'm trying to say is, what you two had doesn't come around often."

"Oh, Madonna mia," Rosa exclaims, pulling her away from me. "He's moved on. He has a boyfriend. A whole new life." Rosa looks at me, eyes full of empathy. "I love my nephew more than anything, but you need to be happy, too. Fielder will thrive. Life always goes on; that's what makes it so beautiful."

Rosa and Guisy leave me to make their way toward the sundeck.

I'm alone, head spinning.

Listen to my head, or my heart?

How many times can I make the same measurements before I cut?

CHAPTER 16

Bite the Bullet, Tell Him You Love Him

Sienna forces Ricky to pose for pictures with her on the bow of the boat. Sienna is a natural model who knows her angles, and she uses every bit of the frame. It's obvious, even from my vantage point on the top sundeck of the superyacht. Ricky, on the other hand, is clunky and robotic, without any idea of just how much of a smokeshow he is. All the girls yell at him to take his shirt off, but he resists. He looks uncomfortable as he flexes for the camera.

"Damn, she's hot." Topher materializes beside me and leans over the railing. "I can't believe she said yes."

"Yeah, me neither."

He punches my shoulder. "Since we're alone, tomorrow night. Sienna's surprise. Let's go over the plan."

It sounds easy enough. All I have to do is sneak out of the rehearsal dinner without Sienna seeing (sure thing), somehow find my way to the docks of Positano alone and at night (. . . *right* . . .) and create a magical moonlit boat ride for Topher and Sienna to

Capri (no pressure) while I wait for Topher to show up. Topher will make sure Ricky brings Sienna once everything is set.

Okay, never mind, reader, it's not all that easy—in fact, it feels unnecessarily complicated and convoluted, but, hey, it'll give me more time with Ricky once they sail away.

"Sounds good," I say. "Whatever you need. She's lucky to have you, cous-bro."

"I'm the lucky one," he says. "To love a DeLuca is a privilege." I know what he means.

Maybe it's the sun and sea *and* being in such constant, close proximity to Ricky while realizing how much time has transpired *and* the fact that our entire family is in the same place at the same time *and* I'm next to my older cous-brother, something that doesn't happen often anymore, but I'm feeling overly sentimental.

"I'm happy you're happy. I've missed you, Toph."

"Me too, bro." He pauses, giving me a once-over. "You okay?"

I train my eyes away from Ricky and focus on the rows of houses and buildings that make up Positano as it slowly comes into view ahead of us. "I've been having a hard time. I don't really talk about it much because I feel like after last year, everyone got sick of hearing me cry, but I'm feeling lost, more than usual."

"Because of Ricky?"

"Being around him, but not being honest with him, telling him I love him—sorry, dude, I tried not to tell you, but I'm still so in love with him and I've kind of been scheming to win him back, which now feels futile because it's bringing so much to the surface instead because I'm realizing that though I love him more than anything, we need to also work through all the hurt and talk about everything, and it's suffocating me." The admission surprises me.

"What do you mean?"

"For most of my life, I made being Ricky's best friend my entire identity. Then I was his boyfriend. I used to dream about our wedding before I had my learner's permit. I grew up looking at my parents' relationship and how my dad treated my mom like garbage when I was little, but she took him back so many times, and when things finally got good, he got sick, and—" I take a deep breath and focus on a small fishing boat piled high with crab cages anchored offshore. "I never figured out who I was outside of Ricky."

"Fielder Lemon, born with sneakers on his feet," Topher says, echoing what Nonna used to say about me trying to be grown before I was ready. He drapes his arms around me and squeezes. "Give yourself more credit. Your Clock channel is—"

"It's hard being a hyperreal version of myself all the time online, especially now that Ma and Nonna rely on whatever money I make to help with the bills." It's not lost on me that I'm complaining about money while sailing around the Amalfi Coast on a superyacht, which compounds my guilt because life isn't bad, not by a long shot.

"Are you guys doing okay, financially?" Topher asks. "Have things been bad? My mom hasn't mentioned anything to me."

"Queen G basically works seven to seven, and between her paycheck, Nonna's Social Security, and @LemonAtFirstSight, we keep the lights on. And even though Ma needs my help, she's making me save as much of my money as I can, especially now, after graduation. But, like, a couple months ago, when we got that nasty storm, a tree fell on the house and Ma needed to replace the roof because insurance wouldn't cover it. That depleted her savings, and I had to cover her car payment. Sometimes, we have dollar ramen and PB and Js for a few weeks."

"Why didn't you come to me?" Topher asks. "I can help."

"It's embarrassing, Toph." I wipe a stray tear from my cheek. "Asking for help. Ma doesn't want to burden you. Or take advantage."

"Burden? Really? You're *family*," Topher says. "We were raised to help each other. I know what it's like to scrimp and save and barely get by. I worked my ass off to get out of that, but what's the point if I can't help my family? Why do you think I worked hard? For this? A superyacht? Sure, that's nice, but I wanted to help my family. So let me."

"I know, but—that also makes *me* feel like a failure," I admit.

He steps back. "What do you mean? You're still young!"

I empty my lungs with a force flap of my lips. "Sometimes it's hard to be your cousin. *Topher* is the smart one. *Topher* is the successful one. Matty is the funny, lovable one. I'm the lost one who spends too much time on his phone." Ma and Zia Rosa tell me and Matty all the time not to compare ourselves to Topher. His success is not our failure, but when your cousin is a tech start-up millionaire at twenty-five and you've decided not to go to college to instead make content eating and reviewing food, it's hard not to compare.

He takes his sunglasses off and stashes them in the breast pocket of his silk orange Gucci short-sleeve button-down. "Didn't know you felt this way."

Guilt arrests me. "I-I don't mean it in a bad way—"

He holds out a hand for me to stop. "I know, Field. I want my family to succeed. I want *you* to succeed. I don't want you to feel like I'm overshadowing your ability to become the best version of yourself. But can I let you in on a secret? You don't need to have everything figured out at eighteen. You may have been born wearing sneakers, but that's not a bad thing. You're searching for a comfortable place to stop running. One day you'll realize you're a great guy. Smart. Talented. Successful. All the things you think I am." He drapes his arm around me again, and I settle there. "I heard through the grapevine you've been researching Avello's lemon groves and how climate change impacts the ecosystem and their way of life here, for your channel. I think that's amazing." What he says next shocks me: "Believe me, I know with all the money I've made, I can and should be doing more. For people. For the planet. To make a difference. I want to. Maybe once you do enough research, you can pitch me something, and we can get some funding going. I'd love to help."

After going through and editing all my footage last night, I realized that people like Topher are part of the problem. Chartering private jets with the ease of ordering an Uber—using all that disgustingly wasteful fuel, which is infinitely more destructive than a standard airplane. I never thought much about my carbon footprint and the impact one person can have on the planet until meeting Niccolò Avello and connecting with the lemon groves in ways I never expected. It's hard to find time to look inward about something as global as climate change when every dollar I make goes to help Ma pay the mortgage and keep the hot water on, but that doesn't absolve me. I've made the decision to talk about that in a separate video since I already posted a Clock video on the PJ that's gained way too much attention. I can't ignore that, especially in the wake of the contest. Hopefully contextualizing why I was here in the first place will help my cause, though I suspect it will work against me. People in the comment section online don't care about nuance or intention or personal history. To my followers, and everyone else, I'm a privileged kid who comes from money, despite that being so far from the truth it makes me laugh. I acknowledge how I appear, though, and it's my responsibility to use my voice. Now that my eyes are open willfully, I can't close them. If I do, I'm ignoring everything I'm learning. But I don't want to bring down the mood today. I'm sure Topher would help, but there's no need to ruffle feathers while on a boat. Besides, contest or not, my passion for the Avello farm is stretching beyond the internship. I want to do all I can to raise awareness.

The captain's voice comes over the loudspeakers to direct our attention to the faraglioni, tall "stacks" of oceanic rocks eroded by waves off the island of Capri as part of the Campanian Archipelago. Rising up out of the sea, the rock formations tower over us, and for a moment I feel like I'm in an entirely different world, like an *Avatar* movie. It's as if they're floating, suspended in the sky, though they're grounded and surrounded by water. The ancient, almost mythical stature of the stacks makes me feel both small and alive, like I've discovered something that nobody else has and needs to be protected. The captain tells us their names are Stella, Mezzo, and Scopolo, and I nod in gracious *hello* to them as if they're gods.

"Tell me more about this scheme to win back Ricky?" Topher asks after the captain says he will anchor at one of the faraglioni after visiting the Blue Grotto to swim and eat. He moves in closer, hunching like a goblin.

My ears prickle.

"Dai!" he commands, and I tell him about Operation: Ricky @ Second Glance, and everything that has transpired, to which he says, "It's obvious to everyone at this point except you and Ricky, but Ricky is still very much in love with you."

A reel of us in the lemon groves—pinkies touching, bodies pressed together, the way I lost myself in his eyes and swore he did the same—plays in my head.

If it's that obvious, where does that leave us? Me? Cam?

If I take one step further, I risk getting my heart broken. Again. He's done it before, and he can do it again, by choosing Cam over me, or running away without warning.

Except it's different. Unlike last year, I'm not blind to our obstacles. And I can always be hurt. Anyone can. But Ricky is worth the risk. I'm stronger now. Fortified. I have my eyes open, and I know who I am. I'll survive.

But I have to try.

"Guys!" Matty bum-rushes us. "Did you hear what the captain said? See that mega yacht?" I follow his finger to a charcoal cruise ship. "That's Beyoncé and Jay-Z's! And Mariah Carey's Capri house is lit'rally right there! Wild! And some old actress named Sophia Loren maybe lives on the coast, too. Nonna nearly shat her pants."

I'm searching the bow for Ricky, but he's gone.

Matty's hands pound my chest like defibrillator paddles. "Did you hear me?"

"Where's Ricky?" I grab Matty by the shoulders, pleading.

Matty dips out from my grasp and says, "Hot tub with Nic Jr. and the other guys."

Quickly, my eyes a high-def spy lens, Ricky DeLuca comes into focus.

In one swift crossed-arm supermodel move, he tears his shirt off, baring his hairy chest. The sun catches the circular pendant and reflects back. A ring on a chain, the one I "made" him. He never took it off.

He turns and spots me, a warm, goofy smile spreading across his face.

"Go get him," Topher says.

"Finally," Matty says. "I'm sick of this story."

I'm gliding across the sundeck as the chorus to Harry Styles's "Golden" swells.

What do I do once I reach him—hop into the hot tub fully clothed, gently take his face in my hands, and tell him I love him before we have a movie kiss?

My heart is *thump-thump-thumping* so fast I'm lightheaded.

He stands, and beads of water drip down his sculpted torso.

Before I can reach him, the captain's booming voice patches through on the loudspeaker: "Benvenuti a Capri, wanderlusters! Welcome to the Blue Grotto!"

RICKY DELUCA

"Wanderlust"

The entrance to the Blue Grotto appears no bigger than a tiny mouth in the Capri coastline, a dark hole that, from the yacht, looks like it could barely fit a mouse. I lose Fielder to his nonna, who shuffles to the back of the boat along with everyone else to await instructions from the captain.

We keep exchanging prolonged, heated looks.

Turning the image of him striding toward me over and over again in my mind, I can't shake how mind-blowingly hot he looked with a sense of determination I haven't seen from him in so long.

Wonder fills his eyes.

The captain translates instructions from the tour guide, who has come aboard from a gozzo that tied up to us. "Some information and rules. You can only enter the grotto by rowboat. It's a natural cavern about twenty-five meters wide and sixty meters long, and the entrance is less than one meter high." He demonstrates the height with his hands. "We have a few rowboats waiting for you all, but these can only fit up to four, including your guide. When you enter, you must lie back flat in the boats in order to keep your head."

"Keep your head?!" Fielder's nonna says. "Sounds dangerous."

"I've done it before, it's perfectly safe," Dad leans in and says reassuringly. "With my father as a boy. It's something you'll never forget."

"Once inside," the captain says, "you'll be in for a couple of magical minutes."

"Can we swim inside?" Tyler asks.

"No. Swimming is not allowed. It's very dangerous," the captain says.

"I thought you said it's not dangerous," Nonna Lemon asks.

"I wanna swim!" Jenni Lee slurs.

The captain looks at her and says, "No to this one. Liability."

"I'll stay back with her," Trav says, disappointed. His fists clench in frustration.

"So, who's first up?" the captain asks. "Our tour guides have two boats that will circle back until everyone has a chance to go in."

"Topher, you should go in the first boat, since you so generously brought us all here," Gabriella says, quickly adding, "With Sienna. *Obviously.*" Then she leans into the captain and whispers so loudly we all hear her perfectly. "You said the boats fit up to four, including the tour guide. Maybe I can hop in their boat?"

"Gabriella!" Guisy shouts. "Absolutely not."

"I'm just saying, there's room!" Gabriella laughs it off, but we all know she's serious. If she could edge my sister out entirely, she would.

“Let the kids have the boat to themselves,” Rosa says. “The three of us can go together once they’re back.”

“Great idea.” Sienna’s voice is sharp. “The Blue Grotto awaits the magical stylings of the Coven.” She smiles sweetly, but her sass can slice glass.

Benny gasps. “Gooped and *also* gagged. I nominate Fielder and Ricky for the other boat. *Just* Fielder and Ricky. It’s time we cut to the chase and wrap up this storyline. Some of us have places to be.”

Monroe, Tyler, and Matty all whoop and holler.

I could kill Benny, and then thank him with a gift card to his favorite restaurant, LongHorn Steakhouse, to thank him for saying what everyone else is clearly thinking.

Everyone steps aside.

I feel a momentary pang of guilt for Cam, but he did say I was free to explore what I needed to with Fielder, so I take a deep breath and release it.

Fielder and I converge at the back of the superyacht.

The tour guide speaks very slowly in broken English. “Get comfortable together. It will be a bumpy ride in.”

Topher and Sienna move into their boat first, and he tosses up a “hang loose” hand signal and screams, “Let’s goooooooo!”

“You want me to go first, make sure it’s safe?” I ask Fielder, who nods rapidly. Once inside, I do a cursory inspection for show, making sure to balance myself so that he sees how steady it is. The small, white wooden rowboats have a deep V-hull built to cut through the waves smoothly. “Sturdy. Good craftsmanship.” I give Fielder a thumbs-up, then hold out a hand for him. “I got you.”

Once we're inside, our bodies are in such close proximity to each other we're basically cuddling on the floor of the boat. I should have put my shirt back on, but Fielder doesn't seem to mind, staring more at my skin than the rocky cliffs around the grotto.

The tour guide winks. "Lean-a back e enjoy!"

There are dozens of rowboats and gozzos wading in the sea outside the grotto's entrance. The closer we get, the rockier the waves are, and Fielder grasps for me.

"I got you," I whisper again.

His breath beats against me.

"How long-a you two, eh, being in love?" the tour guide asks.

Fielder looks to me, and I drown in his turquoise blue eyes. "Oh, um, we're—"

"Our entire lives," I answer, mouth dry, a bit breathless.

"Bellissimo!" He clasps his hands. "I sing a song just for you two inside." When we both look at him, wide-eyed, he says, "It's customary for, eh, sing." He motions in front of his chest, as if casting a spell.

"Grazie," I offer, and he nods in gratitude.

Fielder studies my face, his hand resting comfortably on my stomach.

"Ricky, before we do anything, we need to talk about . . ." His voice is a whisper so low it crashes with the waves against the rocks ahead. "Cam."

"I don't want to talk about Cam right now," I say.

Rowing closer to the mouth of the cave, the tour guide hooks the rowboat onto a pull chain. "Okay, ready? Stay low! Have-a you camera ready!"

But Fielder doesn't move.

"You're not going to record this? You record everything."

"I don't want to miss it," Fielder says. His heart beats so fast against his ribs it vibrates against my chest.

"You won't."

"Promise?"

"Always."

Sliding his phone out just as the rowboat bobs toward the opening, he fumbles with it, holds it out over us, and presses Record. He's not paying attention to the camera though, focusing entirely on me, us, and the grotto.

"Ready?" the tour guide asks. "Hold your breath, make a wish."

He counts to three, and a swell from the sea pushes us toward the mouth of the cave, which gulps us into the darkness.

I pull him close, and he grips the underside of my body.

He sucks in a breath, and I don't know how it happens, but one second I see a flash of the most brilliant blue emanating from under the water, illuminating the dark, dank walls of the cave in jewel tones, and the next second, I see Fielder's blue eyes level with mine. His lips so close I can taste them.

I hold my breath and close my eyes.

"You'll miss it," he says.

"Not this time."

I bridge the gap between us.

Almost.

Our lips hover over each other, the pull so strong they're made of magnets.

"Ricky, I lo—"

I kiss him before he can say it.

It's tender and soft, his lips fitting with mine so perfectly that I don't know how I lived without kissing him for so long.

It's like breath after being trapped underwater.

Every ounce of fear and trepidation and uncertainty that's been twisting me up every single day of this last year, wondering whether I made the right decision to leave Fielder, vanishes.

My lungs deflate into him, our bodies fusing.

He whimpers, a desperate sigh of relief and passion, and pulls me toward him with great force, and we devour each other.

I don't care about the grotto or the tour guide or the hunger of the sea; all I want is Fielder, so much so that I fight to hold back tears.

He releases my lips, and I search for his in the dark.

"Fielder?" I open my eyes.

He's staring at me, smiling like a goof. "Making sure you're real."

I grab his face and hold it gently in my hands. His eyes flutter as he leans his cheeks into the roughness of my palms.

"Piccioncini!" the tour guide exclaims.

"What'd he call us?" Fielder whispers.

"I think it means 'lovebirds,'" I say.

The tour guide nods, then says, "For you." He launches into a rousing edition of "Bella Notte," singing in an operatic voice so loud it echoes off the rock walls and rebounds. Though it feels strangely American singing an old Disney song, other tour guides on different boats don't hesitate to follow suit, and suddenly the cave is booming in song. It's like they're singing for us.

We hoist each other upright to get a better view, and the

bright blue glow radiating from below us is nothing short of magic.

A scene from a Disney movie brought to life.

Fit for a prince and his craftsman.

The gentle rocking of the boat lulls us deeper into our own fairy tale.

"This is incredible," Fielder says, panning the camera around the grotto, getting every angle, until he lands on me. "And so is *this*." He places a hand on my knee and squeezes as "Bella Notte" swells to a climax.

"I don't want to leave," I blurt after the song dies.

The hand holding Fielder's phone falls gently into his lap. "Ricky, I have to tell you something that I've been wanting to ever since we landed, and I'm afraid that I won't once we're out of this cave because life is messy and this is messy and I'm a freaking mess, but I have to say it. I love you, Ricky DeLuca."

Like a reflex, the phrase I always said in response to Fielder leaves my lips. "More than you know."

His upper lip twitches.

I lean forward and peck it softly.

When I pull back, his eyes are cloudy.

That's when it hits me. The last time he told me he loved me, I didn't say it back, and my stomach drops as the boat dips into the bowel of a wave surge. He moves beside me and rests his head on my shoulder, weaving his fingers in between mine.

I open my mouth, but the words never come out.

"It's time for us to be getting back," the tour guide says, paddling us back toward the mouth of the cave. Motioning with his hands, he instructs us to duck down.

We slide into the cavity of the rowboat together.

I hold tight to his hand, and he curls into me like a missing puzzle piece locking into place. I don't close my eyes, so his face is the first thing I see, bathed in the sunlight.

The ride back to the yacht is far too short, and I don't want this moment to end.

Before we sit up, he steals a quick kiss, and we breathe together, sinking into each other. *Deep inhale, long exhale.* "For the road."

"I—" There are a million things I want to say, but nothing comes out.

He sits up.

We move apart as we reach the yacht.

Fielder goes first, hoisting himself out of the rowboat and back into the yacht, suddenly surrounded by the entire bridal party asking how it was and what to expect.

Dad and Mom are eagerly waiting to ask me how it was when someone steps in front of them to greet me first.

"What'd I miss?" Cam asks.

◇**Story**

@LemonAtFirstSight ✔ 15min ago

Views: 1.3k

❤ 275

HOT MIC AUDIO TRANSCRIPT: . . . this is messy and I'm a freaking mess, but I have to say it. I love you, Ricky DeLuca.

12 COMMENTS

Grouchy.1505

RICKYxLEMON! I knew it!!

View 4 replies

Joey_Italiano

I'm gonna cry they are so adorable 🥺

Lemonstan007

i've been waiting for so long for this! they were always goals!!

amithedrama

Wow I heard Ricky was in a new relationship.

Guess not.

amithedrama

This is really disgusting behavior and rude to bf.

amithedrama

Fielder Lemon is a homewrecker

CHAPTER 17

The Misery! The Exquisite Tragedy! The Matty Lemon of It All!

Ricky kissed me.

And, dear reader, I told him I loved him. In one big messy word vomit, I did it.

And he said—well, he didn't exactly say it back, did he? But still!

Now we're separated by circumstance. *Again!*

While the parentals are journeying into the Blue Grotto—Ricky's mom, dad, and aunt in one boat, the Coven in the other—Topher and Sienna waste no time corralling the bridal party for group pictures.

Like a cancer cell that won't go away, Cam magically reappeared, a plot point of extreme inconvenience, and has ushered Ricky to the other side of the yacht, completely out of view, making me question my own reality, Ricky's phantom touch lingering on my bare skin like a soft breeze.

Matty leans in. "What happened in there?"

My ears perk. "Huh? Nothing."

"Lies," Matty says. "We just got out, and that place was the pinnacle of romantic." His arm wraps tightly around Nic's waist, the bare skin of their torsos fusing. "If Benny wasn't in our rowboat, we would have been naked."

I roll my eyes. "With the tour guide right there?"

Matty shrugs. "He looks like he'd enjoy the show."

Topher yells, "Let's gooooooo!"

"I'll have you know I make the best third," Benny says, before adding, "wheel."

Monroe covers Tyler's ears. "Fielder! Details! You and Ricky! Grotto!"

"Yeah, andiamo! You roped us into this on the PJ; you need to follow through and *not* be like every other gay man I've ever known and not disappoint me."

"I don't kiss and tell." I wink. "But I don't want everyone on the yacht to know, right now, because Ricky and Cam are still, whatever, and we haven't talked through our issues, really, so, but, yeah. We hardcore made out."

Matty slaps my shoulders hard, and Topher hollers like a frat boy.

"What're we screaming about over here?" Sienna's hands are perched on her hips. "As the bride, I demand to know any and every bit of juicy goss."

Matty grins nervously, and my cheeks grow hot. I freeze, but Matty swoops in to my rescue with a redirect nobody saw coming. "I lost my virginity last night!"

"That wasn't on my bingo card." Benny raises his cup. "But cheers to that!"

"Salute!" Nic Jr. doesn't miss a beat.

Tyler high-fives them both.

"Ew, you people really need a trigger warning," Jenni Lee says, her ignorance sucking out all the oxygen from the planet.

" 'You people'?" I cock my head.

Matty's cheeks go fire red, and his face falls to the floor in embarrassment.

"Relax, I'm an ally, a member of the LGBTQ+AI community," she says, suddenly sounding far too sober, and saying more than she has the entire trip. It's almost as if she was waiting for a spotlight.

"Did you just canonize artificial intelligence as gay?" Benny asks. "*A* doesn't stand for *ally*. Sorry, girl."

She looks unbothered, arms folded. "Isn't the point of your community to accept *everyone*? Hypocritical much? I have lots of gay friends. And a gay cousin. I think I'm—"

"Nope. That's not how it works. That's how we cannibalize our own," I say. "Why'd you say we need trigger warnings?"

"Everything is about sex with you people."

"Again with the 'you people.' " Heat builds in my chest. I don't want to blow up at Sienna's cousin, so I'm hoping she'll chime in and drag Jenni Lee before I do.

Instead, Sienna looks petrified.

Fine, I'll do it myself. "*You* keep othering *us*. There are a bunch of gay people here, and your ignorance and intolerance is showing. The bride's brother is gay. You're in a space that doesn't belong *solely* to you. Be normal and navigate it, don't be weird."

Ever the politician, she says, "You misunderstood. I was simply pointing out an observation. Guess what? I don't need to hear about *your* sex lives while at a *wedding*! Is nothing sacred?"

"Meanwhile, in straight religious wedding culture, 'wedding nights' and consummation is revered," Monroe says with an eye roll. "But go off."

Ignoring Monroe, Jenni Lee says, "I didn't consent to *that*." She waves between me, Matty, Benny, and Nic, as if we're taking turns blowing each other.

Monroe's eyes bug out. "Did you really just weaponize consent?" She crosses her arms and digs her nails into the skin on her forearm. "I want to skewer you over an open flame and serve you with a spicy dipping sauce."

"Relax, Roe," Jenni Lee says. "I'm just doing what you all do. Demonizing anyone who doesn't agree with you. I'm an advocate for *tradition*."

"You're a walking buzzword," I say. "And you make zero sense."

"You're a content creator, right?" Jenni Lee asks, but doesn't wait for an answer. "Kids watch your videos. They get exposed to nontraditional ideas. You get spicy online. You make sexual jokes sometimes, and all week, all I've heard you all talk about is sex, sex, sex. It's representative of a larger issue that needs to be addressed with gay media. What values do *you* uphold? I represent something more palatable."

Nic Jr. laughs. "I heard Americans are, how do you say, prudes, but—"

Matty turns to Nic. "Did I overstep?"

Nic Jr. shakes his head. "Amore mio, in Italian culture, we are open. Sex is something to celebrate. It's *passion*."

"But you're not queer!" Monroe says. "You don't represent anything for anyone here. You—"

Jenni Lee waves a hand in dismissal. "It's impossible to have a constructive conversation without being assaulted or contradicted. My opinion is valid, and I have a right to voice it."

"Matty said one thing that was pretty innocuous, and *you* imply you're 'assaulted' by that. That's not a conversation. That's an accusation." Monroe's voice trembles. "Beyond that, you're around a bunch of queer people and trying to play victim when you say offensive things about them. Sienna ignores it because you're family, but we all know your entire personality is going after gay people, and you think your law school education and mayor father protect you, but you're no better than a picture-less profile on social media who say whatever hateful shit they want yet hide behind anonymity. You have a history of saying you're queer so you can rail against LGBTQ+ content online from the 'inside,'" Monroe says, and Sienna's eyes widen, though Jenni Lee remains stoic.

"It's true," Sienna says. "I never said anything to you to keep the peace in the family, but it's offensive. Monroe showed me what you do online, how you constantly post about the need for laws that ban explicit gay content and propose censorship, yet you claim to be a member of the LGBTQ+ community. You use it as a shield—"

Jenni Lee interrupts her. "Don't police me."

"Are you queer?" I ask, knowing the answer.

Jenni Lee clenches her jaw. "It's gross that my own family is attacking me, but I'm not surprised. The bottom line is that *normal* people don't want to hear about *your* private activities, and I don't need your lifestyle shoved down my throat. Come on, Fielder just posted a Clock story making out with Ricky in the grotto for the entire world to see even though Ricky has a boyfriend and *I'm* on trial?"

As the blistering sun beats down on my skin, my blood runs cold.

"How about this: don't tune in, love," Benny quips. "We're people just *living*, not PornHub." He motions to me, Matty, and Nic. "All this ain't for you anyway." He makes another comment about how he's glad they're not blood related, but I'm not listening.

As Jenni Lee grabs Trav's hand and yanks him away, spilling his drink on himself, I fumble with my phone. My hands are numb and trembling. I nearly drop it when I see the light blue circle around my profile picture. I didn't even realize I was still recording! I run through everything in my mind—I thought I was pulling up the camera app, not Clock. But Clock is so second nature and I clearly wasn't thinking (I was busy quivering from being so close to Ricky while worrying about an ever-growing boner), and I just went to Clock instead. By mistake!

A few thousand views and almost ten comments in the last twenty minutes already. Stupid clumsy club thumbs and dizzy headiness from Ricky's beautiful, plump pillow lips! I blame him and the grotto.

Without hesitation, I delete it. No view count or "like" amount is worth losing the ground I've made with Ricky.

Matty leans in and whispers, "You okay?"

My mouth is dry; my heart races so fast my chest might explode.

There's no way Ricky saw, right?

"I dunno," I whisper.

Topher and Sienna argue. "I'm *not* cool with her talking like that. To our cousins, or anyone! I don't even want her here."

Sienna sits with her clear discomfort. "I know, I'm sorry. She's done after this week. But one thing I keep thinking about is why Jenni Lee does this. I mean, her mom is a romance author, and she has sex with Trav, so it's not like she's a nun."

"People tolerate gays existing as long as we're neutered. Whenever gay relationships come into conversation, the first thing associated with them is sex," I answer, and Monroe cedes the floor. "Historically, from gay liberation to the AIDS crisis to Folsom. Our sex is labeled degenerative behavior. And you'd be surprised how often it happens from *inside* the community, especially in our generation, from people who call themselves blanket 'queers' but don't stand up for *actual* LGBTQ+ issues. It, like, dilutes the power of individual identity, uses public outrage to distract, and then contributes to the very thing outsiders use to target us."

"And Jenni Lee uses that to her advantage, like a political tactic," Benny says.

I nod. "I see people like her all the time in the comments section. If I post anything overtly 'gay,' my views get suppressed. Real, authentic gay people and lives are targeted while more toned-down, sterile gays are supported because a neutered, sexless gay is more tolerable."

Benny adds, "A lot of terminally online people our age are offended by sex, not unlike her, which is wild because being open about sex has been key to my personal growth, and same for other gay guys I know, but c'est la vie."

"You can *not* want to talk about sex," Monroe says. "That's totally fine and justified. But to do what she does, wanting to ban or censor LGBTQ+ media, weaponizing consent *and* identity? No. I didn't want to make a big deal this week because she's your cousin, Sienna, but I couldn't not tell you after what she said to Fielder at the Lemon grove. She sucks."

Sienna soaks in our words. "I'm sorry, Fielder. I shouldn't have made excuses for her, or turned a blind eye. Ricky warned me, but I didn't— Whatever, that's no excuse."

"It's fine." I wonder what Ricky said. He never was her biggest fan, and he told me once that her father's politics scared him into staying in the closet longer than he would have, worried his parents held the same views. "You okay?" I ask Matty.

"This stuff triggers me," Matty admits quietly. "Kept me in the closet for years."

"Really?" Topher asks. "You never said anything."

Matty shrugs. "Hard to find a place without judgment these days. Everyone lives in the comment section."

He's not wrong. "I've seen this a lot on Clock. So many people our age sex shame. Nobody wants to feel uncomfortable by anything, ever. Everything is offensive to someone. And if it comes from someone with a pride flag in their profile, it adds more credibility to the shaming, which further weaponizes identity. Add to that how people outside the community view gayness, and it makes sense that seeing or knowing about gay sex is offensive." Their eyes are on me, and it feels important to speak up, something I'm discovering the importance of with every passing day here in Italy. "Everyone loves the gays. Especially soft cinnamon roll gays who just hold hands and do nothing else because that's what's acceptable. But when it comes to *actual* gay life and reality, most outsiders are offended we don't meet their expectations and weird fantasies. Makes me feel like the only palatable way to be gay is to put a rainbow emoji in my Clock bio but never talk about myself and how my gayness is intrinsically tied to sex. I don't wanna be shamed for it in the comment section. I'm not ashamed I've been having sex since I was fifteen, that it was with somebody I loved. And even if it wasn't, that's *my* journey."

I drape my arm around Matty's shoulder and pat his chest proudly. It wasn't that long ago he was hating himself and afraid to come out. All the nights Matty cried to me about his fears about being gay, how much he confided in me about sex, all the questions he asked me, and how he told me he felt safe knowing he had me to talk to and look up to. The entire reason Matty was afraid to come out was his own internalized homophobia that stemmed from feeling like even though *everyone* at school accepted and loved queer people, he saw how queer people online police LGBTQ+ identities, force closeted celebrities to come out to fit their narratives and expectations, talk about gay sex as jarring and offensive, assaulting and *gross* because they don't want to have it, so even seeing it in queer spaces and settings and content is "nonconsensual." It's the underlying reason why queer books all around the United States are being banned by conservatives, and why there are so many anti-LGBTQ+ laws bandied about: gayness, in totality, in its bravery is offensive. An "assault."

So I will never give space for people like Jenni Lee.

Zia Gabriella's voice booms through the tension as she wobbles toward us, her sea legs giving out underneath her. "That was BEAUTIFUL!"

Matty hums the Wicked Witch of the West theme song. "They're baaaaack!"

Topher nods. "I'm proud of you. You have grown. A lot, Field. Between this version, and everything with the lemon groves. You live out loud. You put your full self out there, and I love how passionate you've become. You're more than your channel. You're more than you give yourself credit for." He taps my shoulder before leaving Matty and me to go greet his mother.

In a quiet moment, I realize that he's right. I've done a pretty good job of growing on my own. Maybe I actually do have my life together?

Matty doesn't give me time to think, though, because the second Topher leaves, he says, "I have *so* much to tell you!"

"Spare no details."

Matty wastes no time, though his cheeks are bright red, from discomfort or the sun. As I could have predicted, it was awkward and intense and a bit fumbling at first—limbs akimbo, muscle strains, goofy faces, not knowing how fast or slow to go, a premature finish—but through sheer determination and a sweaty all-nighter, by morning, they'd developed a rhythm. "Overall, sex is phenomenal. Twenty out of ten would do it every day, all day."

"And how are you feeling about Nic?"

He shrugs. "He's great, but, you know, he lives here. I live in New York. We both know there's an expiration."

"You're okay with that?"

"I think so. I've obviously cleared it with Topher, but he's going to come to the wedding Saturday. Though not the rehearsal dinner tomorrow, which is fine. And then we have Sunday to say goodbye." Matty's lips tremble, and his eyes become glassy. He runs his hand through his copper hair. "Isn't that the gayest situationship of all time? Meet, have sex, fall in love, and end in four days' time."

"Maybe you'll follow each other on socials," I say. "Call it Insta-love."

"What a trope," he adds with a nervous laugh. "How utterly unrealistic."

Knowing he's not, I ask again, "Are you okay?"

"Ask me Monday?" His face falls, then rebounds with a patented Matty trademark smile. Ear to ear, dimples, balled cheeks, eyes blinking away tears he'd rather ignore.

I want to tell him to protect himself, his heart, to say everything he needs to say before it ends, but I know that's not entirely possible. The hardest part of falling is realizing that the fall means opening yourself up to the possibility of heartbreak. There's no protection for that, no magic formula, only trust you'll survive the crash.

The captain announces we've arrived at the faraglioni.

"Love you, Matty."

"Love you, too, Field." His lips twitch like they do when he's about to cry, but he bites it back. "Go find Ricky. Do what you came here to do." Despite what happened between us in the grotto, Ricky is still with Cam. Maybe we're finally in the same place, but at the right time? There are still so many obstacles to jump. That's the scary part about love. It's a leap *both* people must take. "Make your big speech about how much you love him and want him to choose you, and then kiss him under the Tuscan sun, call him by your name, or whatever." With a playful punch to my gut, he walks off toward the sounds of splashing and laughter.

Right on cue, Ricky emerges from the side of the boat. "There you are."

We're alone.

This time, I'm *done* fading to black.

At the same time, we both say, "We have to talk."

RICKY DELUCA

"Getting What You Deserve Is Unfair"

"I can't believe I missed the Blue Grotto." Cam is waiting for me the second Fielder and I return from the grotto, my T-shirt draped over his shoulder.

"On the bright side, you're no longer green." My peripheral follows Fielder, and my stomach twists in guilt.

Cam grips his abdomen. "I don't think I could have handled a teeny-tiny boat rocking back and forth in a cave." He burps and hands me my shirt. I pull it over my head. He continues, "How are you not dying? The rocking from those small boats would've taken me out."

"I took the Dramamine *before* we left the villa."

"Add that to my list of bad decisions," he jokes, but there's a pain behind his eyes. Am I on that list of bad decisions he's made—does he regret meeting me, becoming my friend, coming to the hospital that night when I needed someone, telling me he loved me at Snow Lake, coming to Italy?

"Wanna go for a walk?" I ask.

"If my sea legs don't give out." He wobbles a bit, grabbing hold of the nearest railing, but I reach for his arm.

"I got you." I thread my arm in his and steady him as we walk toward the bow of the yacht, ambling slowly, feeling the cool breeze.

"Thanks." He leans his head against mine for a brief second. "How was it?"

"I can't believe a place like that exists in real life. It was like a fantasy movie. It—"

"No," he stops me. "With Fielder."

"I, uh—"

"I have to imagine it was nice to be alone with him. Experience that with him. After everything you two have been through." There's no judgment in his voice, and I'm immediately brought back to the nights we spent in his dorm streaming movies before we started dating, the way he would listen to me and ask questions so intently. I never gave too much because I didn't know how, but he never stopped trying.

"You don't have to—" I say.

He stops walking and pivots to the side of the boat. It's private here; nobody can see us this high up. He leans over the edge, and I worry he's about to throw up, so I place a hand on the center of his back and lean into him, but he takes a deep breath and says, "I always wanted somebody to love me the way you and Fielder love each other." He turns toward me.

A single tear streams down his cheek.

"I really wanted that with you," he says. "You made me feel like I was a part of something really special. I liked how practical you were, and how much you love your family. I was so excited to come here and meet your family after hearing so much about them. I like how you came across as someone who knew exactly who you were—this guy who was a woodworker, deals in measurements and facts and had his head on straight, but honestly, Ricky, you always avoid having any sort of firm commitment conversation. You won't define me as your exclusive boyfriend, but we're in a relationship? You brought me to a family wedding in Italy, and I thought maybe you finally loved me the way I love you, but you're further away than ever. I just feel like I'm constantly swimming upstream and can't catch my breath. Meanwhile you're onshore with Fielder." He trembles and bites back his bottom lip. "I'm tired."

Maybe it's the way he sees right through me, or how vulnerable he's being right now, but just as I'm reconnecting with Fielder, I'm realizing I could be losing a potentially great future with Cam. Isn't that why I ended my relationship with Fielder in the first place, to find myself? To find out who I was without Fielder?

If I go backward now, will I know who I can become—*without* Fielder, *with* Cam?

All this time, I was afraid to truly commit to Cam out of fear I could never love him—or anybody—the way I loved Fielder. And maybe that's true. But I never allowed myself to try.

Taking my thumb, I wipe his cheek. "Cam."

I keep it there, holding his face.

He doesn't look up.

"Cam," I whisper. "Look at me."

He shakes his head. "I'm afraid."

"Of what?"

"What happens next."

My chest pangs and I sigh.

"Not of being alone," he says. "I've been alone my whole life." It makes me so despondent whenever Cam talks like this because he has six brothers and sisters, and when I think about growing up with Sienna in a small house with Mom, Dad, and Nonno, loneliness as a concept didn't exist. "I don't want to lose you."

"I don't discard people," I say.

"Promise?"

"Cam."

Breathless, he reaches out for me, and I move in closer, my hand still on his cheek.

He kisses me and the yacht disappears.

Just as quickly, he pulls away. "I need you to make a decision." He kisses my cheek softly and walks away.

I bury my face in my hands and slink down to the floor.

What do I do?

Who do I choose?

Which path is the right one?

It's like I'm right back where I was a year ago, unsure of everything, regret building in my chest; the pressure to be precise in my movements now makes my hands tremble.

The *clip-clop* of flip-flops jolts me upright.

Benny. He narrows his eyes at me. "You're playing with fire, you know."

"Huh?" I try to play dumb, but he's smart.

"You shouldn't be kissing your ex in a grotto and telling him you love him, then kissing your boyfriend," Benny says matter-of-factly. "Boy*friend*? Far be it from me to tell you how to live your life. I'm only an elder single fag. Get your house in order."

He taps me on the shoulder and continues walking on as the captain announces we've arrived at the faraglioni.

How does Benny know what happened between me and Fielder? Did Fielder run and tell everybody? I think maybe Cam's right. It's time I make a decision.

The second I emerge from the side of the boat, I see Fielder, talking to Matty.

I wait for Matty to leave before walking up to him.

At the same time, we both say, "We have to talk."

There's a fire in his eyes.

Fielder leads me downstairs into the main cabin, through a secluded hallway, and into the primary suite adorned with rose petals clearly for Sienna and Topher, untouched. I wonder if they knew it was here.

He moves in to kiss me, but I step back.

"Did you tell everybody about us in the grotto?" I ask.

His eyes widen as he licks his lips. "Define *everybody*?"

"Fuck, Fielder, really?!"

"I was telling Matty because I tell Matty everything. You know that, he's my best friend, and Benny was kind of there too, and Monroe and Tyler because, well, it's a long story that we can talk about once we talk about everything—"

My temples throb.

"So everybody knows?"

"Well, I mean, I didn't mean to post anything to Clock. I thought I just had my camera open. Reflex, I guess. My fat fingers must've accidentally uploaded to my story and—"

"Your *story*?"

"But it's deleted now!"

I'm seeing *red*. "That was a private, vulnerable moment. For us. This is exactly why we broke up, Field. You're always on your phone, missing life, and obsessing over dumb sh—"

"Dumb? We're dumb . . ." He takes a step back.

"No, that's not the point. I— That wasn't meant for the entire world to see. What did you think you were doing, capturing something viral? Hoping to get more likes or follows or comments? Looking for more validation? Real life isn't online, Fielder. Maybe Cam was right and you are using me for likes."

"Cam? What does Cam have to do with this?" Fielder's face cracks. He pauses, and tears fill his eyes. "I'm sorry, believe me when I say it was a mistake. I wasn't looking to record anything, and definitely not *us*. That was real. That meant everything to me."

I look away. "I don't know. I don't know what's real anymore."

He moves closer. "Ricky, please." His voice shakes. "I finally got you back. I can't lose you again."

I don't say anything.

"Did you mean all that stuff you said about me?"

My jaw clenches.

"You know what . . ." He's breathing heavy. "Fuck you, Ric." His chest is heaving in, out, in, out. "*You* left *me*. Like a coward. You don't get to turn me into your breakup monster because I went ahead and made something of myself. Yeah, maybe I spent a good deal of the last year pining after you and hoping I could win you back, and maybe that was misguided, but at least I was working on myself along the way." He turns his back on me. "I'm realizing now that I have actually changed. I don't post on Clock because I need validation; I do it because it gives me a sense of community and purpose, and I enjoy it—it's given me a way to express myself, especially when I didn't have direction, and now that I'm finding my voice and seeing where it can take me beyond the platform, raising awareness of environmental issues in food production and working in TV, but you know what? Maybe you don't deserve my time anymore. Maybe you don't know me at all if you think I could do something malicious like that. Maybe you never did." He reaches for the door handle.

"Fielder." I call out for him, anger building in my chest. "Wait."

I can't let him walk out.

"What?" The word slices through me like a knife.

"You can't leave like that." Hand on his shoulder, I spin him around.

His chest heaves, anger or passion, or both.

He pushes me away.

"I hate you," he says.

"That's fine," I say, and kiss him because I can't help myself; we're two magnets, and the universe is pulling us together, pushing us toward each other no matter the distance or obstacles thrown at us.

He's tearing at my shirt, ripping it over my head.

He stares at the ring around my neck.

"Tell me you don't love me," he says.

"I—" *Can't.*

He hooks a finger into the ring and pulls me forward. Then, slowly, tenderly, he kisses me, increasing in intensity. He moves from lips to cheek to earlobe.

My head knocks back against a window. My arms go limp, Eyes rolling from intense pleasure that sends shivers down my spine.

Unable to wait longer, he pushes me up against the wall, taking full control, which is so unlike anything Fielder that it sends me into overdrive. Sensory memories of Fielder's hands on my body, exploring me for the first time, flood me, but back then, it was never this intense, this fervent or urgent like both of us would cease to exist if we stopped. Usually, I was the one who took control, told him what to do and where to go, and he obeyed.

Now, I'm his, I'm his. "I'm yours."

Putty to shape or mold, do anything he wants.

Without warning, he pulls away. Locks the door. Eyes me with fervor, hunger.

My weak legs tremble, and I nearly crash to the floor.

Everything is so heady I barely register where I am when his hand grabs mine and he leads me to the bed and throws me onto it, messing up the rose petals.

He wedges himself between my legs, lifting the bottom half of my body and sliding our suits off. My legs wrap around him, and he hovers over me.

I stare deep into the lemon groves of his eyes.

I couldn't carve a statue as intricately beautiful or pen a poem as epic as Fielder Lemon. I take a moment to study him, commit his face to memory, the face I'd already memorized yet somehow see there's so much more to him than I knew.

Our lungs expand and contract together as our bodies rock with the waves.

Time slips through our entangled bodies, and I don't know

how long we're locked in this room, but I don't care. I won't go back to a life without Fielder Lemon.

Twisted in the sheets, I sit up, towering over him, my torso slick with beads of sweat. I brush my damp, shaggy hair out of my eyes.

He collapses on top of me, my body floating in another dimension.

Butterfly kisses on cheeks.

We rest in each other's arms. I allow him to hold me the way I used to hold him. The control over me he suddenly has is intoxicating and exciting.

I can't get enough.

We're awakened by the captain over the loudspeaker announcing our return to port in Amalfi. Fielder moves to check his phone, which somehow ended up on the floor. We missed the entire cruise along the coastline. The sun is low in the sky, casting a light orange glow across the sea, but I don't want this to end.

Not now.

Fielder sits on the edge of the bed, clutching the comforter to his chest.

"What's wrong?" I ask.

"It feels too delicate, like it's not real."

I gently rub his back. Tears fill his eyes.

"You don't believe me?" I ask.

"I want to. But I thought it was real before, when we were together, and now there's a you and Cam, so . . . I don't know. But I gotta be honest, Ric." He looks out of breath, like he just ran a marathon. "There's a lot you missed. A lot we *both* missed." His admission startles me. "We haven't talked about anything."

I grab his hand and squeeze it tight. I want to tell him I've regretted letting him go from the second I left.

He opens his mouth to talk, but stops himself, probably confused about how to act. Is he relieved, or angry at how I was able to walk away from him so quickly? I can still read his face, a gift and a horrible, flesh-eating, guilt-ridden curse.

I owe him an explanation. At the very least.

"Tonight," I say. "Back at the villa. We'll meet someplace neutral. The pool?" The first night at the villa floods me, standing there with Fielder under the stars surrounded by fireflies. It felt like meeting him all over again. "And talk about everything. Promise."

"No. Not tonight," he says. "I think after today, I need some time. We both do. You *clearly* have a decision to make."

"Tomorrow, then." I think of Topher's surprise planned for Sienna that Fielder and I are supposed to collaborate on. "After the rehearsal dinner. Promise. You deserve that much." *You both do,* I think to myself.

The weight of *tomorrow* presses against my rib cage.

CHAPTER 18

This Is What Comes from Telling the Truth

"I do not want to talk about Ricky DeLuca," I declare in our suite as I step into my shorts for dinner with the Coven. Tonight, we're breaking up into small family units, which, frankly, is needed after the emotional roller coaster of today. "This is a Ricky-free zone."

Matty stares me down. "All I've heard all year is *Ricky this, Ricky that*." He mimics me, walking around the room, stopping at the armchair by the window near my bed: "Ricky would love this chair." He moves toward the desk and inspects the top with his index finger. "Ricky makes tables." I nearly piss myself when he sashays to the armoire and drops it down low, pops his bussy, and pouts his lips as he whimpers, "Ricky carves a better dresser than the poor unfortunate soul who did this." He moves into a pseudo-Ursula accent from *The Little Mermaid*, but I don't care because I'm laughing so hard I nearly forget that Ricky has twenty-four hours to decide whether or not he's going to massacre my heart for a second time.

"Do a death drop next," I request as he crashes to the floor. "But point taken."

Matty hobbles toward me. "You're scared. You don't want to be hurt again. Devastated like you were a year ago, but that's not gonna happen. You're so much stronger now, even if you don't see it." He grabs hold of my hand. "You love him, but even if he doesn't choose you, you don't need him now like you needed him then. And I think you know that. Yeah, you'll be heartbroken, but it won't wreck you. You've proven that you're so much stronger than you give yourself credit for."

"You think?"

"Dude, look at you. A year ago, did you think you'd be able to be here?"

Reader, if you'd told me one year ago that Topher and Sienna would be getting married and that I'd have to stand across from Ricky, I probably would have been *more* delusional in my pursuit to win Ricky back (I know what you're thinking after roughly 300 pages of this, but I'm far more rational now).

"I'm not going to fight for someone who doesn't want to fight for me. If Ricky wants me, he can fight for me for once."

"That's the spirit!"

There's no way to protect my heart—getting back together is a leap of faith I'm not sure I can take now, and ending it feels like killing a part of myself. However, if and when we do talk, I *can* say everything I need to so I don't regret anything, and if it ends, it ends. And that, my friends, is growth.

Without warning, the door to our suite bursts open, and the Coven waltzes right in, not bothering to check if we're naked or on the toilet or showering. Typical.

"It's a pig sty in here," Ma says.

"Seriously, open a window," Zia Rosa adds.

"You let that nice boy from the lemon farm sleep here?" Zia Gab asks, and Zia Rosa whips her head around so fast you'd think she was possessed by a demon.

"What?" Zia Rosa yanks the pillow away from Matty's face. "He slept here? Did you kick Fielder out?"

"Ma, no, stop, relax!" Matty yells.

"You ready for dinner? That nice Chef Vittoria has our family meal ready by the pool for us. Topher is eating with the DeLucas, not that I'm mad or anything, but it'd be nice if he ate with us too, just saying," Zia Gab says, picking clothes up off the floor and gathering them in a heap on the desk. "There's laundry machines, you know. You're going to have to learn how to do your own laundry in college."

"I know how to do laundry!" Matty's armor is weakened. "Stop cleaning!"

"Where the hell am I sitting?" Nonna bellows from the doorway, her silhouette backlit like the badass Supreme she is. Shuffling quickly, she swats Matty off his own bed. "Shove over."

Matty mouths a "sorry" and says, "Thought you could use a Coven-tervention."

"Wow, you had sex and became funny. Welcome." I bow. "Your gay card should be here in five to seven business days."

Nonna smacks me upside the head. "Puttana!"

We all burst out in laughter. I've been so focused on Ricky this week I haven't spent any time with my family. I forgot how much I missed it, how much I needed them.

"Level with us," Ma commands.

With a deep breath, I plunge into the entire saga, from my super vague and not-at-all thought-out plan to win Ricky back to the Cam saga to the Clock App of it all, coming clean about the contest I hope to win but I'm even more grateful it gave me the oomph to research how climate change is impacting Amalfi and the lemon groves.

Ma reaches out her hand and takes mine. "You always thought you were running without direction; you made up this story for yourself that you were living a life backwards, but Fielder, you were living. That's the point, to live a full life. It's all I ever wanted for you." She brushes stray hair from her eyes.

"Doesn't matter how it happens, or how you do it," Zia Gab says, picking up the torch. "Most people just stay on autopilot, but you? You're figuring it all out in real time. It's beautiful and inspiring, Fielder! What you're building online, the passions you're pursuing, I'm so proud! Let me see this contest internship; maybe Topher can help."

I hand over my phone, scrolling first to @FoodForChange and pulling up the contest's bylaws. Zia Gab squints intently, reading all about Michelin-star chef Mars Lyon and their *Out of This World* TV series, how it promotes food sustainability. "I can't see a thing, this is so small; where are my glasses?"

"On the top of your head, Squinter!" Ma yells. "What's the point of wearing glasses if they're always on the top of your head, Madonna mia!"

"Shut up," Zia Gab says, pawing for her glasses. "Jeez, Fielder, this sounds exactly like the kind of stuff you're filming at the Avello Family Lemon Groves. I bet you're a shoo-in! What are you so worried about?"

"Sometimes I just feel so messy," I say. "Or, like, when I compare myself to Topher, I feel like I have zero direction. And being here this week, trying to win Ricky back and losing at that, it's another reminder I'm doing things all wrong."

"You're not messy," Matty adds. "Or backwards. Or wrong. You gotta cut that shit. Please, fam, tell him! 'Cause I'm getting tired!"

"Language," Zia Rosa says. "But he's right. I don't envy you. When we were growing up, we didn't have phones or laptops. It's no wonder you think you're living out of order: your generation is too exposed to '*everything, everywhere all at once*'—"

"Ay-yo!" Matty's obsessed with that movie and made me watch it a billion times. He was pissed I read the spoilers about the ending and twists and different multiverse storylines, but I needed to know how it would end before I committed.

Zia Rosa continues, "You're so exposed to everything that anything you compare yourself to is going to make you feel inadequate. We're not meant to be exposed to so much all the time."

"And don't compare yourself to Topher. He's twenty-five, you're eighteen in a couple weeks. You have a lot of life to live," Zia Gab says.

"You're doing just fine, baby," Ma says. "You're allowed to slow down and figure it out. Fall in love. Have your heart broken. Trust that it'll mend. It *has* already."

Nonna hums, and we all turn, knowing she's about to impart old-world wisdom.

Deep in thought, she rests her hands delicately in her lap.

"Is it a bad thing I fell in love with Ricky so young?" I ask her. "Should I leave him in the past and move on? Past him?"

"As old as I am," Nonna begins, "I know one thing. Love doesn't come along more than a couple times in your life. *If* you're lucky. What you and Ricky have? That's a genuine love that can't be touched, and it's one worth seeing through."

"Or at least hearing him out, whatever the outcome," Ma adds. "You might be surprised at what you learn about yourself."

"I'm afraid," I admit.

"We're all afraid," Zia Rosa says.

"You guys?" I ask, and exchange an incredulous stare with Matty.

"All the time," Ma says. "We're all single mothers here, either widowed or cheated on or deserted by men in a world that isn't kind to any of those circumstances. You don't think that does something to a woman? We got through it together. As a family. Mess with us, we bury you."

Nonna adds, "We're like the Mafia, without the death wish. Unless . . ."

Everyone goes silent.

At once, Zia Gab, Zia Rosa, and Ma all shout, "Ma!"

"They know what I mean," Nonna says, reaching her hand out for me. I kiss it.

"Anyway," Ma continues. "We keep going for you two, and Topher."

"Life is short," Zia Rosa says. "You never know what's going to happen next. That's a blessing and a curse. The beauty is you get to figure it out. Every step you take is a step forward. It's all how you look at it. Whatever you do, as long as it serves *you*, not anybody else, that's all that matters. What do the kids say? 'No regrets'?"

Matty rolls his eyes at his mom. "Main character energy!"

"Oh, what a unique saying," Zia Gab says unironically. "I love it! I have main character energy!" She waves her hand over her head like a spotlight.

"Sure do," Ma says. "We'll never hear the end of that one now."

Main character energy is considered a bad thing, but . . . why? Sure, I'm extra AF and act like the center of the universe, but it's always been because I never felt good enough or that my life made any sense. Parents never married, broke up, got back together, just in time for Dad to die. Knowing I was gay and in love with my best friend at such a young age but not understanding why or how to process that. Needing to know the ending of every story before it's even told. Deconstructing food on the plate to see how it's made. Knowing I can live with Ricky DeLuca, the one person I never thought I could live without.

Maybe *that's* main character energy, allowing myself space to be a whole entire person, fabulous flaws and all, without having to worry what people think? I can't please everyone, but this trip is showing me I can be both at the center of my own story and the driver, and that what I thought didn't make sense is simply part of life. It makes me, me.

That feels good.

Zia Gab hugs me from the side. "Don't be afraid to be your own main character. Your life is yours to live. Just remember, you're not alone."

Ma and Zia Rosa nod emphatically, both proudly smiling. It's saccharine and embarrassing and wonderful.

"And if anyone messes with you, I'll put the malocchio on

them." Nonna does the sign of the cross and recites her Roman Catholic incantation: "Nel nome del Padre, e del Figlio, e dello Spirito Santo, amen!"

Zia Gab laughs from her gut before saying, "Witchy!" She waves the rest of the Coven over, and one by one, they wrap their arms around me and squeeze.

"I want in!" Matty wedges himself in the middle of a Lemon sandwich.

Even if Ricky doesn't choose me, I'm going to be okay.

I'll be devastated, but I'll survive.

No, not survive. *Thrive.*

Main character energy and all that.

I'm a fucking Lemon.

(Who am I kidding. He better choose me!)

~~The Rehearsal Dinner~~

Ricky's Big Decision

FRIDAY

RICKY DELUCA

"A Trademark Move"

When I don't know what to do, I work with my hands.

Whittle, carve, shape, build, design plans, something, anything.

Except I have no tools or materials. I thought about sneaking into the utility shed on the side of Villa Limone Regale because there are some beautiful old furniture pieces, and if I found a hand sander, wood putty and a knife, and some varnish, I'd be able to—

Make a decision.

Benny eyes me like I'm something fragile, porcelain about to break. He's been doing that since last night when I showed up at his room, pillow and suitcase in hand. I thought it best to give Cam space. I want to be respectful to both him and Fielder and keep my distance. I've done enough damage.

I need a clear head, and I don't want to lead either on, or break either more than I have.

"You think an awful lot of yourself, cous," Benny says.

"Giving yourself an awful lot of credit, methinks. Come down off that high horse. Just a little bit."

I give him the finger and grunt, hoping he leaves me alone.

He rolls his eyes. "Don't get mad at me. I gave you a place to crash. You can go explain to Sienna why you're not bunking with your boyfriend. Or the love of your life."

"You don't have to be a dick."

"Don't I?" He runs curly hair pomade through his hair and primps in the mirror, crunching his locks. "Look, I might not be Cam's biggest fan, but I don't want to see the guy get hurt. And I don't want to see you hurt, either."

"I know what I'm doing."

"Do you?" Benny swivels around. "And I'm not trying to be a dick; I'm asking as your family because I care, and if you don't, if you need advice, I'm here."

I wave him on, bring it–style.

He snickers. "I know you like to go at things alone because Nonno taught you that men bottle up their emotions and express themselves through their hands by taking their anger out on wood, and men take care of other people before themselves and blah-blah-blah, but you gotta learn how to express yourself or else you're going to be running away for the rest of your life." He walks toward me. "Something Fielder's nonna said the other day struck me: that Fielder was born with sneakers on, that he's always running, but ever since I've known him, he's never run *away* from anything. He's always running toward something." He grabs my shoulders. "You're the one running, Ric. I know you *think* you made the hard choice to walk away from Fielder last year to find yourself, but you kind of ran away without giving yourself a chance to work through it. Forget about Fielder, and even Cam, because who you choose or end up with, it doesn't matter—despite everyone involved, including yours truly, loving a grand romantic gesture. What matters is you choosing yourself. So what decision is you choosing *you*?"

I have to sit down after that because the irony is, after all this time, all the heartache I've caused myself and Fielder and now Cam in my quest to find myself, I never actually listened to my heart, followed my gut, or chose myself. "Huh."

"I know, sometimes I surprise myself."

"Take me to church." I lift my hands in praise.

Hands on his hips, brows furrowed, he says, "What's wrong?"

"I don't want anyone to hate me."

"Girl. You're gay. Get used to it." He pops his tongue. "What's your plan? Because it sounds like you already know what you want to do."

He listens intently as I tell him everything I've never said out loud.

After, he nearly loses his footing. "Oof. I need a shot of tequila. And we need to enlist help. Let me think. In the meantime, you need to get ready. Sienna will claw your eyes out if we're late for this rehearsal and the first of her outfit changes."

Sienna brought three wedding dresses to Amalfi. One for the rehearsal and dinner, one for the ceremony tomorrow, and a third to change into during the reception. In case people forget she's the bride. Tonight's is a Marilyn Monroe–inspired halter dress modified to show off far more cleavage than the famed actress ever did. Her hair is tied up with a classic Hollywood flair.

One thing is clear: Sienna DeLuca is *the* main event. Despite their fight on the yacht yesterday, Monroe and Jenni Lee do their best to tend to Sienna like handmaidens while avoiding each other. Sienna is keeping peace with JL until the wedding is over; then, according to Topher, she'll be excised from the friend group. JL sees the writing on the wall because she's been nothing more than cordial to Sienna.

Their arbor, fashioned from two potted lemon trees whose branches have been woven together, sits in the center of the grassy courtyard overlooking the Tyrrhenian Sea. Small lemons drip down between lush green leaves. It looks painstakingly crafted, and it is in a sense because it's done in a way that protects the lemon trees, and I instantly dream up plans to make something similar out of wood and plaster and planters back in the woodshop in Seattle. Around the arbor in a semicircle are thirteen chairs. It's astounding, gorgeous golden sun, bright blue sky, and fluffy cumulous clouds floating in clumps.

At the end of the aisle, in some sick cosmic joke, Fielder and Cam somehow end up together side by side and, at the same time, turn to see me and wave.

"Oh, *this* is painful," Benny whispers, hooking his arm in mine and pulling me away. "Come, you're being imaginary called over here by nobody at all!"

"Thanks."

"Not a problem," he says.

It's a small wedding, so of course their procession down the aisle had to be confusing as hell. Here goes: (almost) everyone is part of the bridal party especially when Guisy, Rosa, and Fielder's nonna demand to be featured just as prominently as Gabriella since they all "had a hand in raising" one another's kids.

Topher's solution: Gabriella walks Topher down the aisle, followed by Nonna flanked on either side by Guisy and Rosa. Matty jokes about them looking like the Sanderson Sisters from *Hocus Pocus*, which makes them hiss and sneer.

Fielder laughs and my heart aches.

He tries not to look my way, but I can't stop staring at him, so gorgeous in a pale pink short-sleeve button-down and a cute white pleather fanny pack crossbody, hair messily combed to the side, his face full of patchy scruff because he never could grow facial hair the way I could.

After the Coven descend the aisle, Zia Francesca and Benny will walk, followed by Monroe and Tyler, Jenni Lee and Trav, Fielder and Matty, me and my mom, and finally Sienna and Dad. Sienna and Topher will stand beneath the arbor, with Matty and Fielder standing beside Topher, and me standing beside Sienna. Everyone else will be seated. We run through this twice. In the blazing sun.

I pick at the calluses on my fingers nervously to distract myself.

As the priest from the Duomo runs through the ceremony, I remember how, at ten years old, I used to dream about standing at the altar hand in hand with Fielder. The tension between us as we stand near each other is palpable. Some kids dream about becoming a space ranger or Batman. I dreamed of marrying my best friend, even if it would be years before I could say that out loud.

I grip tight to the ring around my neck.

Then there's Cam. We hop around each other like the floor is lava. Benny takes it upon himself to talk to Cam, to get to know him more, make him feel at ease, and his actions allow me to breathe. I really miss my family and it's small moments like this, actions from the heart, where I truly feel the distance of living on the West Coast.

I do my best to be present, to soak up family time and dote on Sienna, making sure she's drinking enough water between all the wine, that her hair looks perfect for the predinner family photoshoot. She deserves the best man of honor.

Like always, she somehow sees through my act.

"How're you doing?" Sienna places a hand on my leg above my knee to stop it from shaking restlessly.

"Nothing!"

"I said how, not what?"

"I should be asking you that," I say. "How are you feeling about tomorrow?"

"Never been more excited about anything." Sienna looks angelic. I truly have never seen her happier or more relaxed than when she's with Topher. Growing up, she was always playing mom, so concerned with being responsible and taking care of everybody that it's nice to see her not concerned with anything other than having fun this week. "You know what Mom said to me earlier? She said before I walk down the aisle tomorrow to be certain I want this. Messed up, huh?"

"Why would she say that? Not that I'm surprised because she always has opinions, but still, not cool."

"She's worried I'm giving up my dreams for Topher.

Following him around, moving where *he* wants to move. She thinks because he's got money, I'm surrendering to him and becoming a little housewife. Like her."

"But you're not." I wouldn't be her brother if I didn't double down to make sure.

She scoffs. "Of course not. Monroe and I are still going into business together, and I can do her fashion marketing and branding from anywhere. I'm not giving up anything. I'm only gaining. He supports me, and not, like, financially because I make my own money. Sure, I can't afford a villa in Italy or three wedding dresses or a superyacht, but without him, I would be able to live life exactly as I want to. He supports me emotionally. He's my biggest cheerleader. Mom doesn't get that. Dad is great and I love him, but he's very much the man of the house stereotype, and Mom had no life outside of taking care of us and him." She picks at her perfectly manicured cuticles. "I don't want her life, and she doesn't want me to have that life, either. And I don't. Topher adds to me, doesn't take, or expect anything."

"That's how it should be," I say, though it comes out more like a question.

"No, that's exactly how it should be." She kisses my cheek and excuses herself to go check her makeup before we leave for dinner.

As the sun starts to set, I hold my breath, and go up to Cam, and hand him a handwritten note and do the same to Fielder.

When Vincenze announces the arrival of the cars to take us to Positano, Topher pulls me aside. "Everything set for Sienna's surprise tonight?"

Truth is, I haven't spoken to Fielder about it in a couple days, but that shouldn't be a problem. Topher had everything taken care of, so Fielder and I working together was more of a cursory exercise anyway.

Matty wanders by curiously and offers a terse head nod.

"Yeah, no worries," I say. "Everything is under control."

My stomach is in knots.

"Sweet." He squeezes my shoulder and narrows his eyes. "Are *you* ready?"

CHAPTER 19

I Had the Strangest Dream

I play with the wooden ring Ricky gave me when he comes up to me at the rehearsal and hands me a poem from a piece of paper from the journal I bought him. It's rolled to look like a scroll.

Like, come on. First of all, how extra? (I love it.)

Second, he can't even let me have one night to myself, can he? It's not enough that he's been doggedly staring at both me and Cam, but now this?

"IF ONLY"

we could sail
to the middle
of the ocean
where horizon meets sky
wrap ourselves in stars
float forever in
infinite space

drift on waves and nebula
find a black hole
suspend time,
would forever be enough?

Tonight, meet me where the horizon meets the sky
tonight in Positano.

We used to stargaze together, getting lost in constellations. I was always in outer space, while he was firmly planted on the ground.

Everything the Coven and Matty said earlier clicks. It's taken thirteen months, but I'm finally ready to finish this, on my terms, not Ricky's. I'm choosing to be present with my family tonight rather than focus on Ricky. Yes, he's choosing the place—I'm guessing "where the horizon meets the sky tonight in Positano" is his poetic way of saying the place we're doing the surprise for Sienna because it's convenient. That's been the biggest lesson I've learned this week. I've lived my entire life for other people, but here in Italy, I'm finally focusing on discovering what I love.

And tonight, I want to have a good time with my family, so I roll it up and pop it into my pocket for safekeeping.

Then Cam pulls up a chair next to me. "I know what it's like," he says, and when I don't respond right away, he doesn't get the hint and continues, "To lose."

So much for peace.

"Lose? Dude, I'm done." I move to stand. "I tried. I thought you were cool, misunderstood, whatever. But, man, you're all over the place and messier than I am. I'm done playing these games. My life is not a game. Ricky's life isn't a game. Look around, Cam, this is my family. The Coven, the DeLucas. I haven't lost. I've won."

I can tell by the way the corners of his mouth twitch that he's trying to hold himself together—that I hit him where it hurts, family. But I don't care. His cheeks get red, his eyes glassy, and in one last-ditch effort to clearly best me, he blurts out, "What, am *I* the drama?"

That stops me dead in my tracks.

Am I the drama? "It's you. You're the one who's been commenting on all my Clock videos. For months. You tagged @FoodForChange, you've been commenting about me and Ricky, trolling me. Us. Why?"

"You had your chance. Ricky deserves better." He stands up and faces me, smooths out the wrinkles in his shirt. "I like you, Fielder. I think you're a great guy. But I love Ricky, and he deserves a chance at real happiness. If you're not willing to fight for him like I am, step aside."

He leaves me to sit in silence.

Winding down the narrow, treacherous streets of Positano, the car service Topher hired nearly clips three elderly women, a group of tourists in tacky Italian flag tees, and a man on a Vespa. I shouldn't have had so much champagne before this drive, but I needed something to take the edge off.

Ensconced high in the enclave of Positano, La Sponda is an elegant, chic fairy-tale dream inside Le Sirenuse, the most prestigious hotel on the Amalfi Coast. Pearl-white walls are decorated with arms of ivy growing upward toward the ceiling like fingers that stretch from arched picture windows and across walls, framing the white, beige, and pastel stacked houses and buildings of Positano. Emerald-green and gold tile floors, seafoam-green tablecloths, and grand chandeliers made to look like lemon trees with rounded glass globes lit with real candles make it feel like a high-fantasy film set come to life. It's old Hollywood glamour by way of the Italian renaissance.

My fingers fiddle with my phone, desperate to film this for @LemonAtFirstSight, but it's a Michelin-star restaurant, so I need to have *some* decorum.

Everyone is dressed in suits and designer dresses. Thankfully Topher had clothes for me and Matty because we would have been laughed out of a place like this in our Target polos. Still, I feel so grossly out of place, like I don't belong.

Matty's posture is stiff, and I'm sucking in my belly.

As we're led to a private room, I pray the Coven doesn't do or say something embarrassing, which of course is a fool's errand because Nonna immediately shouts, "I've never seen anything like this before, holy hell! Where the hell are we, the Taj Mahal?"

Facepalm. Topher should have known better than to try and tame the Lemons. We're loud enough that all of Amalfi could be in this restaurant and we'd still be the loudest in the room. We're very much a "two-for-one appetizers at Applebee's" kind of family.

Ricky and I are deliberately seated on opposite ends of the table. Benny seems to be enjoying connecting with Cam, as if they're old friends laughing and giggling.

I seethe with rage thinking of how Cam trolled me for months without Ricky knowing.

I won't let him ruin tonight.

Especially as the most stunning dishes I've ever seen are set in front of us. It's *Top Chef* come to life. Seared tuna with candied lemon that electrifies my taste buds, tomato gazpacho that simultaneously feels like being home during a snowy winter day with the brightness of running around Nonna's yard in the summer sun, Gragnano linguine with clams in a roasted zucchini pesto with scorza di limone that reminds me of a dish Nonna made when I was young, a pasta called "fagotelli" stuffed with beef with sauteed onions and fresh-shaved black truffle (the name alone makes me, Matty, and Benny howl with laughter—and, unironically, Jenni Lee scowls, finding our enjoyment "offensive" and "hypocritical"), and fresh-caught branzino that takes me back to the first time I had seafood in Maine with Dad.

I devour everything with a fervor. My palate lights up in ways I can't describe. I feel myself lift off the floor and soar into the space above our table.

Orgasmic. Wet dream material.

To share it with the people I love most in the world is what matters. That's what food does, it brings people together, and the laughter and conversation around the table is vibrant and infectious. I want to prepare dishes the way these chefs do, to make people *feel* with food.

Ricky savors every bite too, and I wish more than anything I was next to him, asking him what flavors he tastes, testing his palate, talking about what dishes we liked best. That was always my favorite part: *us*, our ability to talk about anything. *Possibility.*

What happened to that? Were we ever a possibility?

Monroe and Tyler snuggle up close, and it makes me smile seeing their possibility—how nearly a week ago, they didn't even know each other, and now they're blossoming into something real and beautiful. I want to know *their* story.

After dessert—an apricot tart with white chocolate mousse and almond gelato—Topher gives me the go-ahead.

The plan—as Topher, Ricky, and I had mapped it out days ago—is simple: slip out of the rehearsal dinner after dessert, grab the bags Topher packed for their night on Capri, head to the docks, meet some man called Giovanni who will supposedly have a gozzo outfitted with fairy lights and white rose petals. I'm to make sure everything is in place before Topher arrives. Shortly after he gets there, Ricky will bring Sienna, and boom. They'll head to Capri to the Gardens of Augustus, where Topher will surprise Sienna with a telescope he has set up staring directly at a star whose coordinates are perfectly visible from the gardens. The clincher—Topher named the star "Sienna" for her.

Standing up, I announce, "I'm going to the restroom!"

"Salud!" Nonna shouts back, raising a wineglass.

Probably not the stealthiest way to sneak out of La Sponda, but it works. I grab Topher's bags from the car like a pack mule and make my way to the piers to meet his event planner, who gives me said bag of rose petals and puts me to work, stringing up lights and laying out blankets.

We move lightning fast because time is of the essence!

I barely have time to ~~obsess~~ think about the fact that as soon as this is done, I'm going to have to face Ricky and his decision, and I wonder:

Which one of us will he talk to first?

Me, or Cam?

Between moonlight and cobblestone streets, set against fairy light lanterns and glittering black water, will this be our final massacre, or the greatest love story ever told?

RICKY DELUCA

"The Point of No Return"

Deep breath in, I center myself.

No time for fear. Not anymore. This is a point of no return, and I intend to tackle this head-on. I've done enough damage to Fielder and Cam, and I won't do more.

At the very least, I owe them both that.

When I step outside La Sponda, straighten the collar of my suit jacket, and see Cam underneath the lit restaurant sign in a delicate script hung on beautiful blush pink Italian tile that spills down to the ground, for the first time in a long time, the dense fog in my head clears.

"You knew where to meet me." I hold out my hand to him, and together we walk to the railing overlooking Positano. The cascading town built into mountains littered with lights looks like a world from a fantasy movie.

"Did you know La Sponda translates to 'The Shore' in Italian. Didn't take *The DaVinci Code* to crack your message." Cam recalls my message after the poem, mimicking my voice. "Meet me at the place they call The Shore overlooking the sea. Clever. And romantic." He threads and rethreads his fingers with mine, and I look down at our hands and smile.

The shoreline, with rippling gold-tipped waves falling in soft whooshes against the sand, comes into view. In the distance, on one of the docks, a gozzo is outfitted with lights.

Two shadowy figures wait, the captain and Fielder Lemon.

I hold my breath as I make my way onto the dock.

"Uh, surprise?" Fielder says, confused. "Where's Sienna? You were supposed to bring her. Did you forget your part of the plan? Topher is on his way literally right now; he's going to freak out . . ." His mouth is going a million miles an hour like Monroe, and I can't help but laugh because it's adorable. "Why are you laughing? This isn't funny, we had one job to do!" He starts pacing back and forth, and I have to stop him before he flings himself off the edge of the pier.

"They're not coming, Field."

He sucks in a breath. "What happened? Are they okay?"

I hold out my hand for him.

"I *was* afraid to love you," I admit to Cam. "I think I stopped myself." But I don't stop myself from looking into his eyes.

He kisses me, passionately, like he's never kissed me before.

"I don't understand," Fielder says, rubbing his temples. "I'm sweating like a stuffed pig." He slips his phone out of his pocket. "My battery is almost dead, and Topher isn't answering any of my texts. Why are you holding out your hand?"

"Do you trust me?"

Cam kisses me and I open my eyes; he curiously looks at me.

"Why did you stop yourself from loving me?" he asks. "Was it something I did?"

I shake my head. "It wasn't fair to you. I wasn't fair to you. I see that now." The corners of my eyes sting. "You made me feel like I wasn't alone, and I needed that."

"You do that for me, too," Cam says, then sits back and slowly lets go of my hand, our fingers coming undone. "You said 'made,' 'needed.' Past tense."

My heart sinks. "You're an amazing friend to me, Cam, and I want to have you in my life. I don't want that to end."

He pivots away from me, looking toward the water. "You think that's realistic?"

I go for his hand again and pull it into my chest. "I don't discard people."

"You did it to Fielder," Cam says, and that stings more than I was prepared for. "Sorry. I—"

"No, you're right. I deserve that."

His voice shakes, with sadness or anger I can't tell. "Why couldn't you love me?"

"I do, but I think what I've come to understand is that it's a different kind of love, more of a friend, which is why I want you in my life, and I know it's unfair to ask that of you, especially after bringing you here and putting you through this, and I get it if you hate me, but I don't want to keep putting you through this. It's not fair to you."

"No, it's not." He stands up, and I follow. Just when I think he's going to yell and scream or cause a scene, he bites back his lips, wipes tears from his eyes, and asks, "Can I have a hug?" His voice cracks.

Without hesitation, I wrap my arms around him. "Always."

"I love you, Ricky."

"I love you, too, Cam." Because friend-love is real and important, and it needs to be said and known. He needs to know I won't abandon him.

He holds me a little tighter as he cries into my shoulder.

"Thank you for an amazing six months," I say. "I'm not going anywhere."

He doesn't say anything back, and I don't expect him to.

CHAPTER 20

Shut Up and Kiss Me

Ricky holds his hand out to me, and my heart beats so fast I may pass out.

When I don't immediately take it—because why should I after everything he's put me through; boy owes me at least some sort of explanation!—he starts talking in Italian to the captain of the gozzo, asking for a few minutes alone. (God, that's hot.)

He turns back to me and takes a breath like the weight of the world is off his shoulders, and, well, isn't that presumptuous?

"I love you," Ricky finally says, and it tumbles out louder than even he anticipates, like a foghorn amplified across the water, and I wince. He starts laughing despite himself. "I love you." He sighs. "That feels good. I mean, obviously, I love you, I've loved you my whole life, I've said it a million times, but I haven't since before, you know, and I've wanted to so many times, but—"

"Now who's rambling?" I say, so calmly it clearly unnerves him.

"You're enjoying this."

“Yes.” I wave him on. “Continue.”

He chuckles. “You’re my safe place, Fielder Lemon. You never take from me, or expect anything. You only add to me. I’m not choosing you. I’m choosing myself. And choosing me means allowing myself to listen to what I really need. Be a little less practical. Listen to my heart. Take risks, like you do. To trust you, and us.”

It’s everything I ever wanted. Why isn’t it enough? “How do I know you won’t break my heart again?”

He shakes his head. “You don’t.” He holds his hand out again. “Just like I don’t know that this will work, but I know I love you and I can’t live without you.”

I sigh.

“What?” he asks.

“I used to think the same thing, that I couldn’t live without you,” I say. “But I realized I could.” I watch as his smile fades. “I mean, I don’t want to. But I know I can.”

This time I take his hands and hold tight to them.

He gets down on one knee.

“Ricky.” My eyes go wide. “What are you doing?”

The captain of the gozzo whistles through his fingers.

“Get. *Up!* I’m not marrying you.”

“Wait, what?” His hands drop. “No! I mean, what? I’m not, I mean, no—” He stammers. “I-I wasn’t asking you to marry me! I just thought it’d be romantic as hell to—” A laugh erupts from deep within him.

Dear reader, when I tell you my ass nearly fell out of my body.

We both keel over laughing.

When we catch our breath, Ricky says, “No, I was going to

officially ask you to be my boyfriend. I know we have a lot to talk about, though. And you deserve answers to every question you have."

"Go on." I wait. "Feel free to get back on one knee. For good measure."

He smirks. "I should have talked to you the billion times I had the chance to. I was thick. Thinking too much. It wasn't ever because I didn't love you or that you weren't enough. I felt like I was holding you back. I thought if we stayed together, you'd resent me, or I'd resent you, and maybe that would have happened, or it wouldn't have, but I was wrong because I never gave you the chance to talk it through with me. I was scared. Reconnecting with you this week has been like falling in love all over again, but different. I realized I needed to re-meet you, and it made me second-guess everything because how could someone as amazing as you love me after everything I put you through? What I'm trying to say is that I'm sorry, Fielder. I could spend my entire life trying to make it up to you, but it still wouldn't be enough. But I will try, if you'll allow me."

I crouch down to meet him. "It's been nice to re-meet you, Ricky DeLuca."

Every nerve ending in my body is alight as I move closer to his lips.

My chest flutters.

Breath is staggered.

Ricky bridges the gap between us—or, at least, attempts to because I stop him.

"I set up my own surprise, didn't I? Topher and Sienna aren't coming, are they?"

He shakes his head, telling me how he, Benny, and Matty(!) went to Topher this morning and they all plotted to make this happen, remembering how we used to love stargazing together, hoping this would replace our last night together, before the Great Commencement Massacre.

Dear reader, when I tell you I'm both gooped and gagged, tired and impressed, I start maniacally laughing, and he finally kisses me to shut me up.

Somebody had to.

CHAPTER 21

The World Is As It Should Be

Our gozzo drifts slowly out to the middle of the black sea; the fairy lights wrapped like it's Christmas illuminate the surface of the water. The steady sloshing of waves and the rhythmic rocking lulls me in a state of bliss I haven't felt in, well, ever.

Ricky and I are at the front of the boat, him lying back and me nestled safely in his arms beneath a blanket. His nose nuzzles my cheek. There's nothing in front of us but a few boats anchored and endless galaxies peppered with bright white stars.

We kick off our shoes, and his feet lightly push against mine.

Like the water, my mind is calm.

"What are you thinking about?" he asks, sounding suspiciously like me. I used to ask him all the time what was on his mind because I was uncomfortable not knowing.

"That I'm happy." It's the purest answer I have.

He hums. "Me too." He pulls me closer, kisses my ear, then neck. "I missed you every single day. I wanted to call you or text you. Fly home and apologize. Make sure you were okay." His voice breaks. "I texted you every single day those first few months." He hands me his phone, and I read through every single bittersweet message.

We were both in so much pain. Knowing he was hurting doesn't make mine heal faster or better, curiously. Hurt doesn't absolve hurt. It only grows until it's tended to, and even then, it takes time and forgiveness. Not of the other person, but of yourself.

That's why I can look at Ricky and see a future rather than our past. Because I release myself from the grief, everything I did to avoid dealing with it by thinking I would "win" him back, as if he were a prize.

I forgive myself.

I also forgive Ricky. Some people might not agree with that, but it doesn't matter. I know who he is, and I know who we are together.

I peer up at him, and he's staring at me, a goofy smile on his scruffy face. "What?"

"I used to know what you were thinking. Mostly because you said your thoughts out loud." He kisses my temple.

"Did not." I harrumph and cross my arms dramatically. "You don't know me."

"I'm glad I get the chance to re-meet you," he says.

The boat's engine dulls to a stop. We drift forward, and the captain disappears toward the back to give us privacy.

"Me too." I reposition myself so I can really see his face, study him like he's Michelangelo's *David* in the Galleria dell'Accademia, all chiseled chin and symmetrical face, save for one tiny freckle beneath his left eye like the North Star guiding me home.

The sky above reflects in his eyes, making them look like small galaxies.

I float toward them, get caught in his Milky Way.

We stay like this for a while, in each other's comfortable silence, gazing into each other's solar systems, orbiting the other like the sun and moon.

He plays with the wooden ring on my finger. "You kept it. All this time."

"I never took it off." My hand slips beneath his shirt, and he shudders.

His breath is shallow as he pulls a gold chain from around his neck. "Me neither."

My lips hover over his. I breathe out slowly, making him lurch forward to reach me, but I pull back, teasing him. He growls, so I do it again, tease him by getting close and pulling away.

When I finally give him what he wants, he kisses me with a hunger and fervor I match. It's been so long since Ricky and I have been together where neither of us have anything holding us back from each other, not unsaid words or fear of the unknown or anxiety over where we go from here. It's like we're shedding our skin, our former selves, the people we thought we were in favor of who we're becoming.

Under the blanket, I unbuckle his jeans and reach inside the elastic of his briefs.

He shudders as I move up and down. "Fielder, no."

I stop. Did I read him wrong?

"I want to," he continues. "So bad. But not here." He lowers his voice and speaks through clenched teeth. "We're not exactly alone . . ."

Points are made.

I kiss the balls of each cheek because how could I not? He's too adorably cute.

"Maybe it's time to head back," I shout, laughing.

Ricky pulls his phone from his pocket.

I kiss him again and he looks dazed. "That. I need more of that."

I slip out from under the blanket and move to the side of the gozzo, adjusting myself quickly, and Ricky follows suit. Except he's fumbling with his belt buckle and trying to hold his phone at once while the blanket snakes around his legs.

"Let me—" I reach for him.

"Va tutto bene?" the captain calls out.

Ricky jumps in fear, his legs tangled in the fabric, hand still on his junk.

He slams into the low railing behind him, causing him to flip over his head and flop backward into the black water.

CHAPTER 22

Life Goes On . . .

And that is how Ricky DeLuca dies.

CHAPTER 22.5

Lost in the Undertow

Kidding! That was mean.

But that is how Ricky DeLuca became a mermaid! Bet you didn't see that plot twist—this is now a full-blown fantasy! The plot of *Luca*!

Also kidding.

Ricky is neither dead nor a mermaid. Although to be honest, as I race to the side of the gozzo, screaming his name like an absolute raving banshee lunatic in a sheer state of panic, I do have fleeting thoughts of him drowning, spliced with scenes from *Titanic* of a frostbitten Jack clinging to that damn door as Rose just chilled (lol) there.

Normally, my brain would have led me down the road of, *Of course this would happen to me. Typical backward Fielder Lemon. Falls back in love with a dead guy. How Queen Guisy of me. Like mother like son and all that.*

Kudos to me for not going down *that* slippery slope.

I'm about to hurl myself off the side because this is actually how people end up on the news when he breaks through the surface, coughing and struggling with the blanket . . . *while laughing*!

Instantly, the captain dives in with a red lifesaver and swims it toward Ricky, who grabs hold. The caption dips below the surface and seemingly unravels the blanket from Ricky's feet so that together, they paddle toward the back of the boat, talking in Italian.

Ricky hoists himself up and back into the boat.

Bathed in moonlight, his shirt clings to his toned chest, and I nearly faint. (Sorry, I can't help it—if you could see Ricky right now, you'd swoon, too. Plus, there's something hot about skirting death and emerging triumphantly.)

The blanket lands on the floor with a loud *thwack*, spraying me with water.

"Oh, I'm sorry, princess, do you not want to get wet?" Ricky holds his hands out like the creature from the black lagoon, dripping and hungry, and he jolts forward to chase me.

"Madonna mia, non più!" the captain shouts sternly. "Please, be safe!"

"Mi dispiace," Ricky says before asking him in Italian to take us back to shore.

The captain nods, and I move out of Ricky's way, but he grabs me and wraps his wet arms around me and kisses my entire face like a dog.

"So, bad news," he says. "I lost my phone. Fell out of my hand when I hit the water. I asked the captain, and it's way too deep to dive down. It's too dark anyway."

He looks unfazed. Casual. As if he said he just ate a slice of pizza. No biggie.

My eyes go wide. "What are you gonna do?!"

"Get a new phone when we're back in the States."

"On Monday night?! Or TUESDAY!? That's forever."

He shrugs. "What does it matter? Life goes on, and I have everything I need here."

I check my pocket instinctually. My entire life is on my phone—

Wait. My breathing steadies. He's right. My entire life isn't on my phone. It's right here. I nuzzle into his slick, slimy neck, and I don't care that he's freezing or that the water is soaking through my shirt.

The slow glide back to Positano is awe-inducing. The soft glow of lights cast against buildings that climb up the mountain make the city look like a layered hive from a sci-fi film. There's nowhere on earth I'd rather be.

Okay, remember what I said a few lines ago? That my phone isn't my life?

Lies!

Because when we get back to shore and go to where Ricky says a car is supposed to be waiting for us, the spot is empty.

Not a problem, right? I can just call Topher—

Except *my* phone is dead and I don't have a charger.

It's late. No idea how late, but it must be after midnight.

The streets are empty.

We have no way of contacting anyone. Even if we somehow find a phone in a restaurant or by begging a fellow American tourist somewhere, I don't know anyone's number by heart.

Ricky's hands go clammy. He wriggles out from my grip,

shakes his wrists, and starts to pace. He's muttering to himself like his nonno used to, chest rising and falling rapidly in panic. Anytime something gets too complicated, and he doesn't have control, without a clear, concise plan, Ricky flounders. Seeing him like this is a reminder of how much I've changed because my instinct would be blaming the universe or panicking alongside him, essentially forcing Ricky to straighten his back and suppress his emotions in favor of protecting mine.

I place my hand on Ricky's back and force him to take a deep breath in, then out.

"Hey," I coo. "It's okay. We got this. We'll figure it out."

He stops marching. "You're not worried?"

I shake my head. "We're in Italy, and we have each other. Why worry?"

In the distance, past the beach, situated directly on the boardwalk is an old, dramatically lit building that has a turret with a dome towering over the others at shore level. A bustling restaurant on the ground floor and a few floors of balconies with what looks like tourists lounging and sipping wine.

Someone inside must have a charger, or a phone we could use. Not that I know how to dial internationally, or who to even dial.

My head spins.

Breathe, Fielder. You got this. What do straight footballers chant to pump themselves up? Big dick, full hole, can't lose? I feel better already.

Ricky follows my line of sight. "You thinking a room for the night?"

"That's not the worst idea. But we need to find a charger for my phone."

He grabs my hand.

With a fire warming our bellies, we start hand in hand toward the grand hotel, hopeful, knowing we have each other to get us out of this mess.

We deflate pretty fast when the receptionist says she doesn't have a phone charger, and according to her, any stores that carry chargers don't open until 10:00 a.m. tomorrow.

"We could comb the restaurant and hope someone has a ch—"

"Restaurant is closed," the receptionist cuts me off with her thick Italian accent, drumming her apple-red nails on the counter.

"But I saw people inside."

"Is closed." She looks high, half-closed eyes fluttering, hair frayed and mussed. Still, she's looking Ricky up and down, bending over the counter to see the puddle beneath his feet. To be fair, his vibe is very much "drowned rat."

Ricky shakes his head, a signal for me not to argue with her.

"How much is a room for the night?"

Without flinching, she says, "Two hundred fifty euro."

"That's a lot of money," I say, not having anticipated anything outside of the rehearsal dinner and helping Topher with his surprise for Sienna. I figured I'd be in bed crying over Ricky by now, not stranded with a boyfriend. Life is funny that way. I laugh to myself. "I don't have my wallet."

"I have mine." Ricky pulls out his wallet. "Dad gave me some euros, in case."

"Lifesaver!" I don't say that I'm also worried we won't make it back to the villa in time tomorrow for the wedding. According to Sienna's carefully planned itinerary, pictures start around 10:30 a.m., so already we're going to be late. How late depends on when we can find a store open with a charger and can charge enough to order an Uber.

That's Tomorrow Fielder's problem.

There's nothing more we can do. We have no choice.

Life handed us lemons, might as well take a damn bite.

The small room is a far cry from the luxuries of Topher's villa. Dirty, cracked tile floor. One old, chipped plaster dresser. Yellow cigarette-stained walls. One blue-framed painting of Positano. A desk so small it looks like it was made by Fisher-Price next to a skinny shelf that houses the board game Yahtzee from the 1970s and a vase of dead flowers.

A musty smell clings to everything and makes the air thick. I dash to the large picture window and throw it open, letting a gust of fresh air in.

But the pièce de résistance: one queen bed.

I laugh. "Only one bed, huh? What a cliché!"

"What are we gonna do?" Ricky raises his brows devilishly.

The door barely clicks shut, and I'm peeling his shirt off and tossing it to the floor. It lands with a shlocky *clap.*

"Wanna play Yahtzee?"

"Sexy Yahtzee?" He struggles to wriggle out of his jeans, his hairy thighs red from irritation. He moves quickly toward me, grabs the back of my head, and kisses me. He spins me around and throws me onto the bed, pinning me down.

The mattress is hard as marble, and the frame creaks, but it's perfect.

Our noses graze. He closes his eyes and purrs.

"We're really doing this, huh, you and me?"

"Wanna renege? Again? Already?" I joke.

He laughs and it's unencumbered. "Never."

Then he kisses me and kisses me and kisses me and kisses me until I'm drowning in him over and over again, lost in his undertow.

I close my eyes.

He arches his brows, then his back, as I slide down and take him into my mouth.

Our bodies wriggle into each other until we're face-to-face with entangled legs, our hands dancing fingertip to fingertip, intertwining and unwinding.

"I got you," he whispers as I sink deeper into the pillow. Then he surprises me, and maybe even himself, when he says, "I'm proud of you, Fielder. Seeing you prioritize your passions during this trip makes me more certain than ever that I am—have been, won't ever stop being—unequivocally in love with you. I let you get away once, but I won't ever let you go again."

His body is a wood-burning furnace, and he is my fire.

This time, *I* write a poem on his skin as he holds me.

One thing the room does not, in fact, have—an alarm clock.

When the sun streams in through the window, illuminating

our entangled bodies in the morning, I rocket launch out of bed.

The cobblestone streets are already bustling.

There's a tall clock in the square, and I squint to read the hands and Roman numerals: 10:15 a.m.

Shit.

"RICKY, GET UP, WE'RE LATE FOR THE WEDDING!"

Topher and Sienna's Wedding

SATURDAY

CHAPTER 23

Will Cinderella Dance Again?

Ricky's clothes are still damp, and he smells like mold, but we have negative minutes to spare. The receptionist from last night tells us to get up to Viale Pasitea to catch a bus to Amalfi, which might have been nice to know last night, but there's no time to get angry.

And certainly no time to find a charger and then wait for an Uber.

Ricky has twenty euros left, more than enough to get us back.

After checking out, we race up the narrow cobblestone streets, past art galleries and boutiques, cafés, and gelaterias, bobbing and weaving around bodies.

Positano is crowded and busy, plus the roads are narrow and hard to navigate, and we have no idea where we're going.

We run, with a prayer on our lips and a fire in our legs. We have to make it back to the villa. Topher and Sienna are counting on us.

People scream at us, throwing arms in the air as we race up streets, past vendors trying to sell carpet bags and pottery.

Hopping railings and bolting up steps, we push oblivious tourists out of the way, but we don't have time to spare to apologize. I'll repent at the Duomo later.

Bursting out onto Viale Pasitea, which is dirtier and full of locals in stained tees and tourists in straw hats and pastels, we nearly get clipped by a Vespa.

"Fielder!" Ricky points to the most hideous souvenir shop. Next door is the bus stop. In the distance, the roar and rumble of an engine.

In the bus's windshield in digital orange words—AMALFI.

Lungs on fire, we load onto the air-conditioned bus and flop onto the nearest seats.

"We did it," Ricky croaks. "We made it." His legs shake violently, so I place a hand on his thigh. "I hope Sienna is okay."

"I'm sure she is. Topher is probably chill as hell. It's the Coven we have to worry about."

"I should be there." He buries his face in his hands, and his feet squish, still wet from last night. "Help her get dressed. What if—"

"Cinderella *will* dance tonight."

"I don't even have my man of honor speech done," he confesses.

"We're supposed to have speeches?" I knock into him. "Kidding. Speak from the heart. She's your sister. You write poetry. Anything *you* say will have people in tears."

He hums and glances out the window as buildings and bodies flash past.

"What are *you* gonna say?"

"You'll see later, nosy." I kiss the tip of his nose. "Let's keep us a secret, though. Just for today. Not make anything about us."

"Everyone's gonna see us looking disheveled together." He slaps his damp thighs.

"Speaking of, you smell."

He lifts his arm, and a tuft of hair peeks out from his short-sleeve navy button-down. "Enjoy."

My hand is a spear diving straight in for the tickle.

He clamps down on my arm. "You're not getting this back."

"Fine by me." I hold tight to him, and he doesn't let go for the rest of the ride back to Amalfi, even as he does the sign of the cross.

RICKY DELUCA

"When Love Gives You Lemons"

Fielder walks down the aisle arm in arm with Matty, as a live band plays an instrumental of a song called "The Way You Look Tonight." It was Mom and Dad's wedding song, and Sienna's way to pay tribute to them during the ceremony.

I can't take my eyes off Fielder as Mom and I start our slow march toward the arbor. The linen shirt and slim slacks hemmed above the ankle, the brown Italian leather shoes, the blond hair golden in the sunlight. A veritable Prince Charming. The golden retriever boy of those cute romance books about closeted royalty. Except so much better because he's no fantasy. He's real.

"Don't cry," Mom whispers. "You'll make me cry and ruin my makeup."

"It's so beautiful, isn't it?" The blue sea and yellow sun with its golden rays as an epic backdrop, framed by lemon trees and a rustic Italian villa laced with ivy, surrounded by Sienna and Topher's closest friends and family. No stuffy suits. Just love. Though we've been here for nearly a week, it's striking me *now* that Sienna is getting married. My big sister. My best friend from birth.

"She deserves it." Mom squeezes my forearm. "So do you."

Mom's flowy seafoam-green dress is borderline stuffy Easter Sunday attire, but the way her hair falls gently around her shoulders and the natural makeup that draws out the wonder of her eyes, she looks beautiful, younger.

"So do *you*, Mom," I say as we stop before the arbor.

Hugging me, she whispers, "As long as my children are happy and loved, I'm happy and loved." She hugs Topher and takes her seat as her words pierce my heart. There's something so sad about that. I want her to be as happy as me and Sienna.

I shake Topher's hand, but he pulls me into a hug.

I've never seen Topher so happy—he can't stop smiling, and it's bigger and bolder and brighter and further reaching than the sun. He's swaying on his heels to the music.

Fielder's eyes are glassy as he nods to me. Matty elbows him and winks at me.

The music softens to a twinkling before the notes switch to a familiar song. "I See the Light" from *Tangled*. Opening note and Fielder completely loses it.

Before Sienna emerges with Dad, I take a moment to look around at all the others who love her, who are or have become part of our family this week. Monroe and Tyler holding hands next to Trav (who is not sitting next to Jenni Lee), Benny and his mom, Zia Fran, Mom, the Coven, and Nonna, who smiles sweetly at me, causing me to fight back unexpected tears thinking about Nonno and how much he would have loved to be here.

Sienna makes her entrance, looking ethereal in a simple

off-the-shoulder Greek goddess-inspired gown that trails behind her, and takes Topher's hands.

As they exchange vows and rings, the bond between them tightens. How they look at each other is so pure, something I've never seen before, and as the priest proclaims them husband and wife and everyone throws wheat, a Sicilian tradition Nonno passed down to Dad at his wedding, Nonno's words to me have never felt more prescient, and that's exactly how I start my man of honor speech.

"Nonno once told me, when you love someone, say it, out loud. Never let those moments pass you by. I had to learn that the hard way." I glance to Fielder and lose my breath. "But not you two." *Don't cry, Ricky!* I take a deep breath, steady myself. "Topher was doggedly persistent of my sister, and I give him credit. He knows a good thing when he sees it, and he wasn't prepared or willing to let her go, even when time and geography and life got in the way. He found his way to her, and her heart was open and ready. Nonno also used to say, 'Misurare due volte, tagliare una volta. Measure twice, cut once.' Some of us aren't as precise as Topher the first time, and have to cut a few times to find their Sienna, but once we do, trust me, it's worth it. Sienna, you've always been my protector and best friend, and you'll always be my big sister, but now my big sister has given me a big brother, and together, you've taught me it's okay to be vulnerable, to leap and take chances, but, most importantly, to *love*. And if there's one thing I know, it's that when love gives you Lemons, you've been handed real-world magic." I grab Sienna's hand, but it's Fielder I'm speaking to; I can't take my eyes off him. He's the only one I see. I pick up my champagne flute and lift it high in cheers.

"I know you said no gifts, but this is from me and Nonno. Cheers to you both."

I reach around my chair and pull out the oak family tree, Nonno's last project before he died, that I finished, adding the Lemon family into ours. Sienna's reaction is instant: tears stream down her cheeks, nearly ruining her makeup.

She wraps me in the tightest hug.

For a few moments, I sit alone with Sienna and Nonno in silence.

Everyone is crying and clapping, even as the band leader starts the music.

The Coven and Nonna beckon everyone to the dance floor. Everyone pairs up quickly: Topher and Sienna, Monroe and Tyler, Matty and his dashing Italian date, Nic Jr., Mom and Dad, Aunt Francesca and Vincenze (which is hilarious); Benny drags a lavender-clad Cam up to dance and elicits what looks like a smile from him; even Jenni Lee and Trav who haven't done anything but fight since the yacht day are getting down.

Then I look up and see him.

Fielder Lemon, and it's love at first sight all over again.

Is it possible to fall in love with the same person over and over again?

In one exquisite movement, he's off his chair, and I lose him behind servers and family. I'm on my feet, searching for him, needing to get to him.

Where is he?

The crowd parts and there he is, radiating charisma beside the lemon tree arbor.

His nose grazes mine. I wrap my arms around his waist, like

two lemon trees growing together, intertwined in each other's branches.

"What's next?" he asks as the music swells.

I spin him around on the dance floor and dip him backward.

Our lips meet.

Everyone cheers, and though it's not for us, it feels like it is.

EPILOGUE!

Or Prologue Depending on How You Look at Endings and Beginnings.

Precisely Four Months, Three Weeks, and Two Days Later

(But Who's Counting?)

@LemonAtFirstSight ✔ 8-1

Views: 3.3M

❤ 1.2M

CAPTION: Part 1 of 3. Support environmental conservation efforts in Amalfi, Italy, and help the Avello Family Lemon Groves using donation links in my bio #FoodForChange.

AUDIO TRANSCRIPT: Have you ever seen a lemon the size of a human head? Welcome to "Fielder Takes on Amalfi, Italy, and Learns Just How Much Impact Lemon Farming Has on Tourism and the Local Economy, and How Climate Change Has Rocked This Area," a three-parter you don't want to miss.

If you've been here for a while, you'll know I travel all over the US Northeast reviewing restaurants and eateries, holes-in-the-wall and undiscovered gems, but I recently got the opportunity to go to Italy. The Amalfi Coast, in the Campania region, just south of Naples, is renowned for its incredible seafood, hand-crafted pasta, and its use of the Sfusato Amalfitano, a lemon you can only get in this region, and let me tell you, it's so magical and delicious you can eat it like a hand fruit, giving new meaning to my classic expression "take a bite!"

Unfortunately, Amalfi and incredible farms like the Avello Family Lemon Groves have been severely impacted by global climate change—from temperature shifts to extreme weather, from rising sea levels to erosion to a lack of water and damage to the coastline. The change to the area's biodiversity has had an impact on their way of life, and a big part of that is in the growth of their world-famous lemons.

Over the course of this three-part series, we're going to do a deep dive into the history of the Avello family, with interviews from Niccolò Avello himself in Part 1. Did you know the Amalfi lemon is designated as an IGP—Indicazione Geografica Protetta—which means it's a unique crop that grows in only this region and is specific to the unique farming methods here. In other words, it's rare and distinct and unmatched. The Avello family is the founder of an association designated to the protection of the Amalfi lemon. We'll also explore just how unique their lemons are, and how their family and all farmers in the region are experiencing difficulties in adapting to how climate change is eroding their livelihoods, increasing stress on the already backbreaking work of manually harvesting the lemons and other fruit grown in the special volcanic soil of the mountains here.

In Part 2, we'll explore the Avello farm, its beauty and farming practices, and dive deep into the food of the region, showcasing the brilliant local chefs, from Isabella Avello to private chef Vittoria, and yours truly even gets his hands dirty making pasta.

In the final part, we will take a look at how to adopt and implement sustainable agriculture practices and conservation efforts, organic disinfestation in farming and how extreme weather patterns and changing temperatures present unique challenges, and why it's crucial we take a stand to protect this region at all costs.

Verdict? The Avello Family Lemon Groves in Amalfi, Italy, was not only a life-changing experience where I learned to let my guard down, trust myself, and the place where I fell in love again; it's a place where I learned the importance of conservation firsthand, from affected families who built the tourism we know today. It's an important ecosystem and economy suffering from the seemingly irreversible impacts of global climate change. As a citizen of the world, an Italian, and an "influencer," it's up to me to spread awareness, not just promote an unrealistic view of what many would consider paradise, because while it is a stunningly beautiful part of the world, it's also dying, and we need to be part of the remedy. It's the least I can do. To quote Isabella Avello, "Once you lose something forever, it's gone."

When life hands you Lemons, don't just take a bite; change the world.

3,169 COMMENTS

Lemonstan007

This series has been your best yet! You're an inspiration Fielder!

8-3

Joey_Italiano

thank you for raising awareness i had no idea this was happening. climate change is real wtf. donating now

8-4

Grouchy.1505

Haven't seen a Rickder update in months, are y'all still together?

12-3

VIEW 2 REPLIES

LemonAtFirstSight

Sorry I've been MIA, I'll post more content soon!

CraftsmanRickyDeLuca

Idk Lemon, are we? 😉

CHAPTER 24

The Blossom Avenue Snow Globe

Windows rolled up, volume turned all the way down, I wait for the ringing emanating from Ma's car speakers to finally stop as she drives slowly over patches of black ice and puddles of dirty, slushy snow lining Blossom Avenue.

Nearly every house on our block has at least one strand of multicolored Christmas lights strung on the gutters or wound around wrought iron porch gates. Too many have those inflatable characters like Mickey Mouse Santa Claus or Snowman Baby Yoda, which I find lazy. There used to be two houses with the best light displays on the block: big, chunky retro lights framing each window and both roofs, old-school animatronics robotically waving candles in every front-facing window.

Now, it's just one. The Lemon house with our washed-out Italian and Pride flags.

The other *used* to belong to the DeLucas. Before it sold last August, after the wedding. End of an era, if you ask me.

Our house might not win any prizes for light displays, but it's home.

Snowflakes gently flutter to the ground, making Blossom Avenue look like a giant suburban snow globe.

Ricky's voice patches through the speakers.

"Finally, what took you so long!" I shout.

"Hi, sweetie! Guisy here, you're on speaker!" Ma bellows. "How's Seattle?"

"Cold and rainy," Ricky says. "I'm guessing that means you landed?"

"Didn't you get my texts?" I ask. "I messaged you as soon as I landed! And again at baggage claim. And again while waiting for Ma."

"Sorry, I was finishing up a new project, and the woodshop is a—"

"Dead zone, I know," I finish.

"How was the flight from London?" he asks. For the past eight weeks, I've been interning at *Out of This World* as a marketing and PR assistant for Michelin-star chef Mars Lyon after I won the @FoodForChange contest. My account has grown tremendously, and all the new content has either been directly behind-the-scenes *Out of This World* food sustainability reporting or Avello Family Lemon Groves content that Nic Jr. has been sending me to keep raising awareness. It's been so rewarding switching gears, and though I miss going to restaurants and food trucks and trying new places and reviewing, I feel like I've found my calling. After the holidays, when I fly back to London for the final month of filming, I finally get to be on-air for the guest judge spot, which I'm super stoked about. It's exhausting with long filming hours, living on my own, having to learn on my own, and navigate this world, but I wouldn't trade the experience for anything.

Ricky and I have done our best to FaceTime when we can, but the time difference has been difficult. After spending a week together in Amalfi, I could only imagine how magical two months would have been with Ricky in London, exploring the English countryside, touring foggy castles, and eating fish-and-chips. All of which I had zero time for, but still. I am nothing if not a dreamer. That was enough to keep me going. Knowing that Ricky and I would be together again, somewhere, at some point, whenever and wherever that may be.

"*Long!* Being in the back of the plane next to a screaming kid and mom who scrolled Instagram the entire time gave me such a migraine. But it's *so* nice to be home. I miss you. I can't believe I'm not seeing you for Christmas!" Ricky flies from Seattle to South Carolina to his parents' new house tomorrow morning for Christmas. I wonder if Sienna and Topher are coming to town for the holidays, or if they'll end up going to South Carolina. Neither Ricky nor I know because Topher makes day-to-day decisions based on what direction the wind blows, so getting an answer from him over the last few weeks has been a futile effort.

"I know, but we'll be together for New Year's," he says, voice full of excitement.

"I can't wait!" I say, smiling ear to ear. "What time does your flight get in on the twenty-eighth? Noon, right?"

Ma pulls into the driveway, unbuckles her seat belt, and grabs her purse. "Merry Christmas, Ricky! I'm going inside. Wish you were freezing your ass off in New York with the rest of us!"

"Ha ha, me too! 'Bye, Queen G! Merry Christmas!"

Ma slams the door and walks to the side of the house. Nonna opens the door, and a beacon of light floods the driveway. Clad in her favorite Mrs. Claus apron, Nonna waves me over emphatically.

"Ricky, Nonna's making sauce!"

"FaceTime me and show me," Ricky says. "I miss that woman's sauce."

"Yes, please! I miss your face," I whine. I glance over to the old DeLuca house, which has one small light on in the living room, but a driveway full of strange new cars.

"Actually, go, enjoy the fam. Tell everyone I said hi."

"How dare you rush me off the phone!" I scoff.

He laughs and my heart beats faster. "Cam and Benny are about to pick me up anyway. A little Friendsmas dinner."

I roll my eyes. Thankfully we're not FaceTiming so Ricky can't see. I know what you're thinking, dear reader: How can Ricky be friends with Cam? How can Fielder "allow" this? What's going on here? Let's clear up a few things. I'm totally supportive of them being friends. Cam apologized to me for trolling my Clock channel, and I owned up to trying to break them up in Amalfi. Cam and I are never going to be besties, but we don't have to be. We're cool. Ricky and Cam find value in each other's friendship, and I love that for them. What matters is that I trust and love Ricky, and he needs Cam as a friend.

Also, yes, you did hear that correctly. Cam and Benny. Infer what you wish.

"That's nice. I'm glad he has you," I say. "Tell them I said hi."

"I hear the eye roll," he says. "I love you! Tell the Coven I love them, too."

"Love you too, Ricky DeLuca."

"Love *you* more *and* most, Fielder Lemon."

From outside the tangy smell of Nonna's sauce is immediate, luscious, and warm. The closer I get to the side door, the louder everything gets. Pots and pans banging and scream-talking and—

Matty!

In the window. Waving like the golden retriever he is. My heart races, and I nearly slingshot myself up the steps. He said he wouldn't be home from his first semester at Stony Brook until tomorrow!

Zia Rosa and Zia Gab sit at the kitchen table, laughing.

I race up the stairs. Topher and Sienna are stirring Nonna's saucepot, and behind them, Ricky's parents sip wine, his dad pouring a glass and handing it to Ma, who strains snow out of her hair.

Flinging open the door, Matty throws himself at me. "Thank god you're back. I have so much to tell you. So much has happened. I think I failed English, don't tell my ma. Oh, and the two guys I was dating kind of found out about each other, and . . ." His cheeks turn red. "*So* much to tell you."

He doesn't get the chance to say more because everyone else crowds me like I've been gone ten years.

"What are you all doing here?" I rip my jacket off and hug Topher and Sienna. "I didn't think—" All the emotions rush to the back of my throat, and I fight back tears.

Everyone hurls questions at me about London and the internship at once as if they all don't call me multiple times a week, and I can barely focus. Suddenly Nonna breaks through the noise and asks, "Pasta Dolce, be a good kid and go grab the Bluetooth speaker from your room. We need some music."

"More noise? Really, Nonna?"

She smacks me upside the head. "Did I stutter? Disgraziato!"

"All right, all right, Madonna mia!"

Sienna delicately clutches her belly. She gives me a knowing look as if I caught her doing something I'm not supposed to see, and her eyes plead.

My lips are sealed. Though, the Coven collectively is far more perceptive, so this should be an interesting Christmas.

Nonna shoos me down the hallway.

My bedroom door is cracked open, and the light is already on.

Nudging it open, the first thing I see is Ricky holding a small present.

"What—" I throw my bag to the floor and sprint into his arms, jumping on him and wrapping my legs around his waist.

Burying my face into the crook of his neck, I melt into him. "Nice cover."

"Yeah, I had to get off the phone before you came into the house." He nuzzles me back and squeezes tight. "You said you missed my face. How much?"

I pull back. "More than you know." I kiss every square inch of his beautiful face.

He's beaming, his dreamy brown eyes so full.

Sliding out of his arms and back to the floor, I hold my arms out. "Present?"

He laughs. "Some things never change. So, hear me out. I'd been racking my brain forever thinking of a way to come into my own as a woodworker. Find my voice. I still don't totally know what I want to focus on, but I'm leaning more toward custom art and more practice pieces whose intention is to make a difference." Between his fingers dangles a small wooden lemon carved from oak to resemble a Sfusato Amalfitano, the bulbous and beautiful Amalfi lemon. At its bottommost tip, it's painted yellow with flecks of metallic gold and sealed with epoxy, resembling the ceramics we saw everywhere in Italy. At the top is a thin white gold chain. He hands it to me.

On the left side is a small hinge, nearly invisible, and a latch on the other. I open it, and inside is a tiny packet of lemon tree seeds, and an excerpt of one of the poems I found in his journal, which he let me keep, repurposed:

"If love is a tree
Who planted its seed?"

It's a perfect reinvention and reinterpretation of us, his past turmoil and our ability to rebuild. All it took was for both of us to tend to each other, help each other grow.

"You inspired me with the whole @FoodForChange stuff," he says. "And I wanted to help. So I figured maybe we can sell these, with all different seeds since you can't grow a lemon tree in the Northeast, for example, and donate all the proceeds to the Avello farm, and others like it in Italy?" He's bouncing on his heels. "And—"

"I love that idea!"

"You do?" He's surprised, as if he thought he'd have to sell me.

"We're a team, I'm always behind you." My nose grazes his. "Except I *am* mad at you for not telling me you were coming home."

He pecks my lips, refusing my ire with his cuteness. "What fun would that have been? I missed you too much, Field. You didn't think I would spend one more Christmas without you, did you?"

"You played a good game."

He tips an invisible hat to me. "One last game."

I move to kiss him, but he jerks away.

"I've never done this before . . . kissed a *dude*." His voice is husky and low.

"Neither have I." My words are hazy, lost in a dream of a Christmas four years ago. "You wanna kiss a dude?"

He grabs a fistful of my shirt and pulls me into him.

I could stay lost in him forever.

If not for Matty, who knocks politely three times but doesn't wait for an answer and instead bolts to my bed and jumps on the mattress. "Okay, I know you guys haven't seen each other in months, but we're all starving and waiting for you to have your reunion to eat, but y'all could be in here fucking for hours and I'm not about that life." Before he can get in another word, Ma peeks her head in.

"I love having a full house again; it's been so quiet!"

"What am I, chopped liver?" Nonna asks.

"What are we doing in here?" Zia Gab pushes Ma out of the way. "I've been waiting to hear about Fielder's trip, and I'm not getting any younger!"

Zia Rosa trails behind and yells, "Gabriella, I was talking to you!" She sits right next to Matty, clearly without any intention of leaving quickly.

"Leave the piccioncini alone!" Topher calls out.

This noise and chaos is a comfort I'll take with me wherever I go.

Ricky slips his hand in mine.

We're home.

ACKNOWLEDGMENTS

***Dear reader*, if you made it this far with me,** you understand why it's important to have real gay and queer stories written by authentic LGBTQ+ authors. Young, messy gay guys deserve the hope that comes with falling *and staying* in love, and I wanted this book to be a celebration of the breadth of love: heartbreak, mending, friendship, fellowship, forgiveness, growing, and *loving* in a world that often doesn't showcase the complexities of capital G-A-Y love and sex because it's often filtered through straight and other indirect, inauthentic voices and lenses. Gay stories and experiences are inherently, fundamentally different from straight stories and experiences, and it's important to recognize that and celebrate it rather than trying to fit a mold.

It's my hope you had fun along the way. If you laughed, screamed, cried, threw the book across the room, hated or loved or felt an emotion of any kind, wanted to punch a character, and/or enjoyed the Salvatore-verse (lol) within *Lemon*, **this book was specifically *for* you**. (Let's normalize having a full range of messy emotions in books, please!) For all the faithful loyal Sallies (workshopping this name) who stood by me and championed Carey Parker + their friends (including Monroe!), Chase and Jack (and Benny!), and Olly and Alex and Tyler(!), **thank *you***! Their stories, along with Fielder's and Ricky's, are yours.

For my favorite person, Chris. Thank you for supporting me through the writing process of this book. You were by my side cheering me on from proposal to signing the book deal through the tumultuous drafting process during one of the most difficult times of my life, and its completion and publication. You've never wavered, bubs. You're my favorite. **"If love is a seed, who planted its seed?"** This book started as an idea after *Can't Take That Away* sold while on vacation in Amalfi, Italy, in June 2019. I had a transcendent, life-changing experience at a lemon grove. What I learned and experienced stayed with me, a germ of an idea, a love story I didn't know what to do with for years until one day, Fielder Lemon, a dreamer who lived his life in reverse—fell in love with his best friend as a kid and seemingly had his life all figured out just to have his heart broken and path shattered all before high school graduation—and Ricky DeLuca, a practical woodworker, popped into my head and wouldn't leave me alone. **This book finally came together because I was happy enough to write it, thanks to you, Chris. You nurtured that seed and allowed it to grow and flourish. I love you, Bubs!**

For my big fat loud Italian family, especially the Witches who support me through everything and always have my back—**Mom, Missy, Sandy**: it took a village to raise me, and I love you all immensely! I wrote this in large part because I miss having you all living close by, and this was a way to keep you near. Uncle

Chris, Uncle Bobby, Adriana, Christopher, Cassie, baby Cash, and Grams (miss you, G-Money), Giselle, Steve, Carole, Mary (Ma!), Mark, Ruthann, baby George, my nephew Huddy Buddy, niece and goddaughter Harper, Kevin, Patti, and Mike—I love you all so much. Family is my heart and soul, and the heart and soul of this book. I would not have survived the last few years without **my sisters Marissa and Nikki.** Y'all are my Day Ones, my *family*-family, my ride-or-dies, the sisters I go to for everything, comfort and support, help, to have fun, or reminisce. You hold my fondest memories, my deepest, darkest secrets sacred, and you protect them. I love you both more than you'll ever know. **To friends who are like family**, Melissa, Nic DiDomizio, Sam, Jenna, Liz: it's important to hold tight to those who matter, even if you don't see each other all the time. I'm grateful. Thanks for allowing me space.

For the fellowship of authors and those friendships that lift me, thank you for continually showing up: Matthew Hubbard (I would not have gotten through this book or the last couple years without you, friend!), Jason June (the biggest ray of sunshine I know—so much love for you always), Kelis Rowe (TRULY the most talented author and most beautiful soul), Jess Verdi, Abdi Nazemian, Anthony Nerada, Erik J. Brown, Amy Ewing, Bill Konigsberg, David Levithan, Sher Lee, and every other writer friend I've made over the last five years! The fellowship (and getting to learn from you all) has been my favorite part of this experience.

Finally, for everyone who helped make *Lemon* a reality and my career as an author a dream achieved: Eternal gratitude to my incredible **agent Jess Regel** for believing in Fielder Lemon and dropping everything to read early drafts and give feedback and get on calls to strategize. Hats off for dealing with me. You're the best, always! For my **editor Camille Kellogg**, you believed in this book from the jump, but it was in working with you through revisions that allowed me to see its fullest potential. You came in, clocked my shortcomings, and pushed me to make it the best it could be, and *PRAISE BE* because I'm so deeply in love with how it turned out, so thank you! **Ricardo Bessa** for the most beautiful cover I've ever seen, realizing my vision in expert detail and making me cry gay tears. I'm fully convinced it belongs in the Louvre! I hope my words live up to your beautiful art! To the entire **editorial and marketing teams**, from copyeditors to proofreaders, publicity to marketers to everyone in between at Bloomsbury who are so crucial to the process of bringing a book to life and getting onto store shelves. **You make dreams come true**. People don't realize what it takes to get a book traditionally published, how many people are behind this process, how long it takes, how much time and effort and talent it takes, so please, when you turn the page, read the credits and give everyone their flowers, because I sure as hell do. **Thank you, thank you, thank you! You've made my dreams come true.**

And to *My Best Friend's Wedding*, the movie that had a chokehold on me as a young closeted gay kid with a romantic heart. It has, in my opinion, the most perfect bittersweet ending. It healed me and gave me hope and made me laugh. So for all the gays out there still waiting for love: Don't give up. Love with your entire heart. You're the star of your own movie, however cute or raunchy or romantic or messy it is!